T0354910

THE IMMIGRANT

A Collection of 120 Short Stories

By

Max H. Lombardi

Trafford
PUBLISHING

Order this book online at www.trafford.com/08-0902
or email orders@trafford.com

Most Trafford titles are also available at major online book retailers.

Illustrated by: The Author
Edited by: Martin Sabarsky

Note for Librarians: A cataloguing record for this book is available from Library and Archives Canada at www.collectionscanada.ca/amicus/index-e.html

Printed in Victoria, BC, Canada.

ISBN: 978-1-4251-8297-7 (sc)

ISBN: 978-1-4269-2029-5 (dj)

ISBN: 9781425182991 (e-book)

We at Trafford believe that it is the responsibility of us all, as both individuals and corporations, to make choices that are environmentally and socially sound. You, in turn, are supporting this responsible conduct each time you purchase a Trafford book, or make use of our publishing services. To find out how you are helping, please visit www.trafford.com/responsiblepublishing.html

Our mission is to efficiently provide the world's finest, most comprehensive book publishing service, enabling every author to experience success. To find out how to publish your book, your way, and have it available worldwide, visit us online at www.trafford.com/10510

www.trafford.com

North America & international
toll-free: 1 888 232 4444 (USA & Canada)
phone: 250 383 6864 ♦ fax: 250 383 6804
email: info@trafford.com

The United Kingdom & Europe
phone: +44 (0)1865 487 395 ♦ local rate: 0845 230 9601
facsimile: +44 (0)1865 481 507 ♦ email: info.uk@trafford.com

10 9 8 7 6 5 4 3

To Martin, Maria, Alexandra,

And Sophia Sabarsky

With my Everlasting

Gratitude and Love

Table of Contents

Chapter 3: Adventures in College

Chapter 4: The Second Coming

Chapter 5: Cornell University

Chapter 10: A Time to Remember

Chapter 11. Protecting and Defending My Health

Chapter 12: The Interview

PROLOGUE

Marco Antonino Donnatti awoke at 2:15 a.m. in his apartment of Venice, California. It took him some ten minutes to realize where he was and what he wanted to do. Lately, everyday had been the same. Waking up in the wee hours of the morning, getting up and working on his word processor, putting in writing his ideas to improve the manuscript of his new textbook, the second edition of *Radiation Safety in Nuclear Medicine*. He had been working on it since December and hoped to have it completed by the dateline given by the publisher–April 30. Now, he was approaching the end. It was a good book he thought. It should be very helpful to the new students of Nuclear Medicine Technology. He also thought that because it was a highly technical book, sales would be very limited. Only a very selected class of students would be interested in the book. But he did not care. The book was not written for profit but to help undergraduates understand the complexities of the nuclear medicine field. For many years he had loved teaching the safe handling of radioisotopes to chemists, biologists, and medical personnel first in Oak Ridge, TN, and later in Tampa, FL. He appreciated the opportunity he had of putting his ideas and experience in this second edition of the book. And the book was an expression of that experience of four decades. Teaching is a form of love he thought. Teaching is hard work. It takes many hours of preparation for each class, for each demonstration, for each hands-on laboratory exercise. That was the best way to teach a science subject he thought: with hands-on lab exercises. In two years of intense training his students graduated with an A.S. degree, then they passed their nuclear medicine technology boards, and went to work as physicians' assistants in hospitals and clinics. Their success had been his success.

Marco then reflected on how his own life had evolved over the years as a high school student, as a college student, as a soccer player, and as a college instructor in Lima, Peru, many years earlier. He then thought about how he had earned a Rockefeller Foundation fellowship to do advanced studies in Radiation Biology in the United States and earned a Master of Science degree and how he had returned to Lima to work hard for the National University of San Marcos, the oldest in the Americas. He also thought about how a few years later he had become an immigrant in the U.S., about his work as a scientist at Oak Ridge, TN, and as a college professor in Tampa, FL. He had been very fortunate for having had some opportunities offered to him and for having acted positively on them. He thought that after forty-one years of work at one hundred miles per hour, his retirement would have killed him if it was not for the project of writing of the first edition of his textbook in 1999. Retirement is not for the coward or the insecure he thought. It takes hard work and determination to stay physically and mentally active.

His thoughts then took him to his five years at Treasure Island, FL, immediately after his retirement in 1997, his one year at Clearwater Beach, and his moving to California in 2003. He had had a good, positive, and rewarding life. Perhaps he should put those thoughts on paper, he thought. He then turned on the lamp by his bedside and scribbled some notes on a sheet of paper. At 4:30 a.m. he was ready to sleep some more. He turned the lamp off and covered himself with the sheet and blanket. He woke up one hour later just in time to catch the early news on TV. He had a 15-inch LCD TV set with a pair of ear phones. That way he could watch and listen without disturbing the neighbors. The news told stories about the war in Iraq, the weather, the local traffic, the crossing of the border by illegal immigrants bringing illegal drugs. He thought that he had been fortunate for having received a job offer from Oak Ridge, TN, and for having obtained his green card in Lima before coming to the U.S. Later that morning he was working on his word processor writing something about his reflections of earlier that morning. Then the bell rang. Someone was at the door. He opened it. In front of him was a young woman, about 28 or 30 years old. She identified herself as Judy Hartfeldt, a reporter from the News Herald, the local newspaper. She showed her photo I.D. card. The dialogue went like this:

Reporter Judy Hartfeldt: Are you Marco Donnatti? I am on assignment. May I come in?

Marco Donnatti: Yes, I am. Yes, you may. Please excuse the chaos, I was not expecting anyone. Please sit down.

Judy: This will not take very long, I promise.

Marco: All right, what can I do for you?

Judy: Sometime ago, you submitted a poem to my newspaper about September 11, 2001. My editor told me that the poem was good, but also very strong and divisive. For that reason, the editors decided not to publish it.

Marco: That was a long time ago. I wrote it while at the stage of anger. When I did not receive an answer, I figured that the poem was not politically correct. I respected the wise decision of your editors.

Judy: But that is not why I am here. I am here to set up some appointments at my office to interview you. We understand that you are an immigrant in this country. That you have worked as a scientist in Oak Ridge, TN, and as a college professor in Tampa, FL. My newspaper would like to know if you have an immigrant's successful story to tell. You could come to my downtown office once a week for a two-hour session in which I will ask you some questions and record your answers. Later, my editors will decide which parts are of best interest for printing in the paper as an immigrant's interview. This process may take several sessions. Agreed?

Marco: Yes, of course. I am at your orders. Here is my card. Just call me about the date and time of the first session.

———◦◌◦———

This book tells the story of Marco Donnatti, an immigrant from Peru, South America, who was offered a job in the U.S. in 1963. That was an offer he could not refuse and, by his own measure, after four decades of hard work, had resulted in a feeling of accomplishment and success. The recollections of this immigrant are presented in the form of 120 short stories that tell his adventures before becoming an immigrant and after arriving in the U.S., his struggles while learning the sophistication of the English language and his adaptation to the culture of his adopted country. The excerpts of poems inserted in some stories are from the author's book of poetry "Reflections," published by Watermark Press of Owings Mills, MD, in the year of 2000. The illustrations preceeding each chapter and the book cover are the author's original drawings.

This is a book of fiction. The names, places, and times mentioned in the stories are fictitious. Any resemblance with real persons, places, or dates are merely coincidental. My gratitude goes to my personal editor Martin Sabarsky for reading and correcting the original manuscript . Also, I would like to express my gratitude to my family for their patience and constant encouragement, support, and advice during the preparation of the manuscript. My appreciation goes also to Trafford Publishing for their excellent job in making this book a reality.

The Author

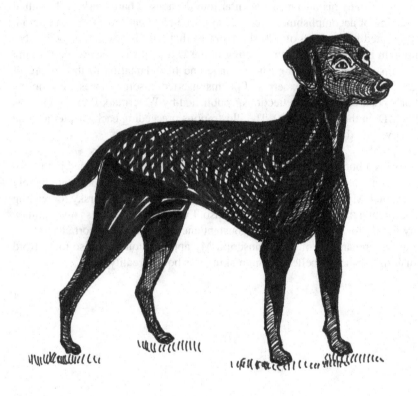

"Tarzan" the Donnatti brothers' pet in 1937 (Story 3)

CHAPTER 1

THE EARLY YEARS

Reporter Judy Hartfeldt: Your last name, Donnatti, is Italian, isn't it? Why not Spanish?

Marco: Well, that was my grandfather's fault. He was an Italian immigrant from Milano who went to Peru about the year of 1900. Someone had lied to him. He had been told that, to get rich, he had to go to Peru where the streets were paved with gold and silver. Obviously, he had been misinformed. All the riches of Peru had been taken by the Spaniards during the three centuries of conquest and colonization. Peru was then a poor, developing country.

Judy: Tell me about your youth.

Marco: It has been so long! I can only tell you some short stories. They should give you an appreciation of the times.

1. Spaghetti and Wine on Sundays

My father, Massimo Davide Donnatti, was born in Cajamarca in the northern region of Peru. In 1928 he had become a young officer in the police force and had been transferred to Lima, the capital of the country. While working in Lima, he attended night school and earned a diploma in accounting. My mother, Maria Vitalia Soriano, was born in Lima and attended primary and secondary schools there. With a superb soprano voice, she aspired to become an opera singer. But things were not to happen as she wished them. They married in 1929, and soon the children came, two years apart. By 1940, the family was complete: Daniel, age 10, was the oldest and born in Lima. Then came the twins Marco and Giovanni, age 8, born in Huanuco. Then was our sister Rachel, age 6, and brother Pietro, age 4, both born in Tacna. Last came Gina, "the baby," only six months old and born in Mollendo a small port and summer resort in the southern coast of Peru. With six children to care for, my mother's dream of becoming an opera singer gradually faded in time. She only sang for us, at times, and we loved it.

At meal times, the five older children sat at a low, side table. We defended our territory on the table with conviction. "Mi qualda" ("my area") we called it in baby talk. I remember very well that from a very young age our mother prepared spaghetti for lunch on Sundays. That's how we knew it was Sunday. The spaghetti sauce sometimes contained beef and tomato sauce, sometimes chicken and mayonnaise sauce, other times garlic and olive oil. To go with the pasta we always had bread, grated cheese and a glass of half-and-half red wine and water. That is how we learned to like wine. Of course, that was well before it was discovered that wine, in moderation, was good for the cardiovascular system. In retrospect, I guess, we were ahead of the times! At the time of this story, Daniel was in the third grade of primary school. The twins were in second grade, and Rachel was in first grade. Pietro and the baby were not ready for school yet. In Peru, boys and girls go to separate schools. That, I believe helped the learning process a lot. No distractions. On Sundays, all of us went for walks on a park or took a bus to the countryside, where we would walk, play, and eat something before returning home. Those family outings were pleasant and memorable.

2. The Swinging Whip

In 1940, we lived in Mollendo, a port and summer resort with beautiful beaches, in southern Peru. Our father worked at the police station situated on the main square, and we had been fortunate to rent a three-bedroom apartment nearby on Comercio street, the town's main street. We attended public school number 487, some ten blocks north on Comercio street. Every day, we walked to school. The principal was Mr. Paredes, a gentleman well known for the strict discipline he demanded of all— students and teachers alike. That was great in a school of boys at the critical age of character formation and learning.

We had one recess period in the morning and another in the afternoon. During classes, while the teachers were busy with the students in their classrooms, and during recesses, Mr. Paredes patrolled the hallways and patios with his hands hidden behind his back. But all of us knew that he carried wrapped around his right hand a short, thick, black leather whip. He would swing that whip like lightning, right and left, when he discovered mischievous behavior by "his boys." One day, on the back of the main patio, some boys were playing a game with crystal marbles which they, in turn, propelled with their fingers to place them in holes they had carved on the dirt ground. Mr. Paredes was very proud of his perfectly flat dirt patio. He hated any imperfection. He hated the small holes carved by marble players. He had a grounds keeper who constantly was watering and leveling the ground of his patio. Giovanni and I were watching the game of marbles when, suddenly, Mr. Paredes showed up swinging his whip. The boys scattered fast and disappeared in the crowd. Giovanni and I were frozen; sitting by the wall. We did not dare to move. Mr. Paredes looked at us and quickly realized that we were not playing. We were only watching the game. He then yelled: "go to your classroom, now!" Next, the bell rang, and recess was over. In those days, teachers could whip misbehaving students. Nobody thought anything wrong with it.

3. A Dog Named "Tarzan"

One Friday evening, my father came home from work bringing us a present. A black male puppy dog. We were marveled by him. It was instant love. We fussed over him. We took turns to feed him and to clean after him. The pup had been given to my father by one of his co-workers who could not take care of him. Thus, he offered him to my father, who gladly accepted him. We were glad too. That was the best present we could ever have, we thought. We named him "Tarzan." We thought the pup would grow to be a strong, fast, and fearless animal–a hero, just like the Tarzan of the movies.

Indeed, Tarzan grew quickly. In one year he had reached the weight of 35 pounds. We knew then that he would be a medium-size dog. And he was fast, strong and fearless, just as we had predicted before. In those days, city rules had not yet required dogs to be on a leash when walking outdoors. Thus, Tarzan was allowed to rum free on the streets. At first, he walked with us everywhere. By age two, though, he used to leave and disappear for hours at a time, we never knew where. However, he was punctual for meals. We were glad to see him. We would talk to him, asked him about his escapades, and imagine the exploring adventures he might have encountered during those escapades. One holiday, we spotted Tarzan some 200 yards away in the middle of a group of people and other dogs. I remember hollering his name: "Tarzaaan, Tarzaaan!" Like magic, he lifted his head and ears and ran fast toward us, arriving in a few seconds. We thought he was the fastest dog in the world, and we loved him very much.

One sad day, we had our hearts broken. Tarzan came home that afternoon stumbling, falling, and trying to stand and walk again. There was foam in his mouth, his eyes were glassy and vague, there was perspiration all over his body. We gathered around him. Daniel ran to the police station to get father. Our father came with Corporal Arce, the station's male nurse, who immediately told us that Tarzan had been poisoned and that he would try to induce vomiting. He asked for a quart of soap water, which my mother quickly prepared. Then the nurse introduced a rubber tube into Tarzan's stomach, attached a funnel to the tube and poured some soap solution through the funnel. Tarzan remained immobile. His glassy eyes became clearer and clearer.

Corporal Arce then told us that it had been too late, that Tarzan was dead. We, leaning against the walls, could not contain the tears. Then my father asked the Corporal quietly to pick up Tarzan and take him to bury in the back yard of the station, where there was some suitable space. He then came to us an hugged us while softly telling us that Tarzan was a hero, because he had been so brave and loyal that he did not want to die on the street. He had come home to die in the arms of those he loved. Then he added, "May God forgive those who did this to him." A few days later we visited the place where Tarzan had been buried at the foot of an apple tree at the back of the police station yard. We said a quiet prayer in his name. That way we said good-bye to our dearest friend and we promised never to forget him. That was the first time in which we, the children, learned about the death of someone in the family.

4. The Sewing Machine

Giovanni and I were about six when the accident occurred. One afternoon, we were playing in a room that my mother used as storage. On top of some crates and boxes, at about four feet from the floor, was my mother's hand-driven sewing machine in its beautiful wooden case. On the side of the case, the word "Singer" was stamped in golden letters. We were playing cowboys. Thus, I climbed to the top of the machine and rode it as if it were a horse hollering "Go now Silver!" imitating what we had seen in the Lone Ranger movies. I did not realize then that the motion and vibration made the machine slide and suddenly fall with me to the floor. I was lucky that I did not get hurt badly. Some abrasions and contusions perhaps, but the machine was undoubtedly broken. The noise brought my father running to the storage room. Realizing what had happened, He took off his thick leather belt to whip me for what I had done. At that moment, my mother jumped in between and covered me with her body saying, "It was an accident, just an accident." Without a word, my father walked away. I was crying and saying, "I am sorry, I am sorry." Later that evening, at the dinner table, my father spoke. He said that it had been an accident, but that accidents could be prevented if we used judgment and common sense. That repairing the machine would probably be very expensive and that we did not have the money to have it fixed right away. That our mother needed the machine to make our clothes and to mend them. He then asked us if we had understood. We nodded. He then ordered, "Let's eat." That was a lesson we never forgot. Accidents happen because of ignorance, carelessness, or negligence.

5. Paper and Pencil!

In 1939, the port and summer resort of Mollendo was still a small town perched on the hills overlooking the Pacific Ocean. During the summer, many tourists came to enjoy the beautiful beaches. Life was peaceful, quiet, and playful. My father was a dedicated worker, punctual, strict, and respected officer. He was respected by his superiors as well as those working under him. We, the three boys in the family, also respected and obeyed him without question. All he had to do was holler once to have us jump to our feet and act on his commands. But that was the way to keep discipline and educate three very active and mischievous boys. My father was also an accountant and loved to study geometry and calculus. Consequently, he wanted the boys to learn basic math quickly. He started with arithmetic. Every day, when he arrived from work at about 5 p.m., the very instant he walked in the door, he would yell, "Paper and pencil!" Like lightning, we would come out of our hideouts in the back yard, secure a sheet of paper and a pencil and report to him at the table in the dining room. He would then dictate an addition, a subtraction, a multiplication, and a division problem. We had to do them in less than two minutes, and correctly. We did well most of the time. When we made an error, he would yell and point at what we had done wrong. When one of us did all operations correctly, he would shake our hand and congratulate us. That was the proudest moment of our short lives. We did not realize then how useful those exercises were going to be when we attended the latter years of primary school. Those exercises set us on a pattern of success in high school and even in college. Only many years later we were able to gratefully recognize their value.

6. Concussion and Peaches

In 1941, my father was preparing for his promotion exams in the police force. In addition to the exams to test his knowledge of police procedures, he had to demonstrate minimum levels of physical and athletic aptitude. He studied his books in the wee hours of the morning and at about 5 a.m. he would wake us up— the three boys—to accompany him to the beach, where we timed his 100-meter runs. For the high jump, we–the twins—held a taught string just on top of our heads some twelve feet apart. Sometimes he went alone. One of those days when he went alone to practice his running, he did not return for showering and breakfast at the usual time. At about 8:30 a.m., a police officer came to our home to tell us that our father had suffered an accident on the beach and that he had been taken to the hospital. My mother dropped everything she was doing, asked Mrs. Adelina, a neighbor who also was a godmother to my sister Rachel, to watch us, and rushed to the hospital. My father, we were told, was unconscious, suffering from "cerebral congestion" and they were applying ice bags to his head to minimize swelling of the brain. In those days there was very little they could do. Apparently, he had suffered a fall during a sprint.

Several days passed, and my father remained in critical condition. My mother never left his bedside. One afternoon, Mrs. Adelina brought a basket of peaches for us and left it on the dining room table. I took some without permission and ran to the bedroom where I ate them quickly. A few minutes later, I returned for more. I must have eaten ten or twelve. That night I felt very sick. I had a high fever and what, in those days, was called "intestinal fever." The fact was, that most likely, I had a salmonellosis infection due to eating the peaches without washing them. The doctor came and prescribed some medication in the form of some red syrup and ordered me to remain in bed. In a couple of days, my temperature was normal and I felt better. I was on the way to recovery. And so it happened that while my father was fighting for his life in the hospital, I was paying for my mischievous behavior, sick in bed, at home.

After four days in bed, the doctor told me that I could get up and walk around. Behind our house on Blondell street there was a long ravine that led to the railroad station some five hundred yards away. Next to the house there was a granite rock with a smooth surface. Wearing one of my father's jackets, like a coat, I walked to the back of the house and sat on the ground with my back to the rock to watch the coming and going of the trains from Arequipa. It was a sunny, lukewarm spring day, and the sky was blue. I thought about my father in the hospital. I wondered when he was going to come home. Suddenly, someone walked slowly, quietly, and sat next to me by the rock. It was my father. We hugged each other and then remained in silence for a long time. He spoke first. He said that there was always a next year, that next year he will try again to pass those exams. Later, we were told that my father had awakened from his coma the previous night and that he was hungry and anxious to get home. The doctors discharged him in the morning with the recommendation that he seek medical treatment in Lima. At the time we, the children, did not comprehend the magnitude of his accident, but we were glad he was home and that we were a family again.

7. Lima, the Capital

Later that year, my father requested his transfer to Lima upon medical recommendation. The transfer was granted by the proper authorities. He traveled to Lima by airplane. Besides his medical appointments, he worked at the first precinct police station of Callao street, and started to look for an apartment for us to rent. In the month of October, 1941, the rest of the family traveled on the steamship "Mantaro" from Mollendo to the port of Callao, fourteen kilometers west of Lima. The trip took three days. I remember that, on the ship, we took turns watching our sister Gina, only one year old, and already walking. We did not want her to fall onto some lower deck or, God forbid, into the sea. We, the boys, went everywhere on the ship. We were very much impressed with the elegance of the ballroom, with its golden candelabra, red carpets, and furniture. We went there to play quietly every time we had a chance. When we arrived in the port of Callao, father, aunt Bianca, my mother's sister, and her husband, uncle Pablo, were at the terminal to see us. We were pleased to see the grand city. My father had rented a small apartment on La Milla street, near his work, and across the street from boys' public school 434.

The next day, my mother took us three boys to the school, where they were already aware of our arrival because my father had applied for a transfer through the Department of Education. The principal of school 434 was a little reluctant to accept Daniel in the 4th grade and the twins in the 3rd grade because we came from a "provincial school" where the level of education was thought to be not as advanced as in the capital. In his office he suddenly pointed at me and asked "72 divided by 8"? I looked at him and replied "nine!" He then said "OK, you all are admitted." We then understood how useful our father's "paper and pencil" sessions had been. All of us boys quickly jumped to the top of our classes. It turned out that our teachers in Mollendo had been as good or better than those in the capital. The principal was proud to have us in his school. We were on cloud nine!

8. Christmas, 1941

The 7th of December, the Japanese had attacked Pearl Harbor. The war of the Pacific had begun. We, Peruvian children, did not grasp the meaning of all this, but like our father, we felt that all the Americas should remain together in the conflict. Soon we were going to feel the effects of the war in the form of scarcities. Scarcity of charcoal and kerosene, scarcity of sugar, scarcity of rice, scarcity of cooking oil, scarcity of meats. Despite government price controls, the price of foods, clothing and medications soared beyond the reach of our family income. We, the boys, had to get up at four in the morning to go and stand in line to buy one kilo of rice, or one kilo of sugar, or a bottle of cooking oil. My father's salary remained low and with no hope for increases.

Suddenly, one day, Christmas came. That morning, we the children, found in our shoes ten cents each. That was our Christmas. No toys, no tree, no decorations, nothing. We were sad because in previous times we had received some toys, brought to us by Papa Noel (Santa Claus). We understood that, because of the war, we had to prepare for harder times yet to come. One thing though, our parents made sure that we would never stop attending school.

A neighbor and friend of my mother's taught her to make lamp shades from crepe paper and wire using the sewing machine. She made some in various colors and sent us to sell them door to door for one sol and fifty cents each. She told us that we could reduce the price to one sol and twenty cents if the customer asked for a discount. We walked in three different directions. After three hours or so, two shades had been sold and one was not. That night my mother took the money, went to the store and bought bread and cheese. That, and a cup of tea was our supper.

According to his work schedule, my father had to patrol the streets of our district on a bicycle at night. His rotation sometimes ended at 12:00 a.m., midnight. He would then come home to rest. Sometimes he would wake everybody up. He would then stop a taxi and take all of us to Chinatown, where he knew the owner of a Chinese restaurant. We would eat to our hearts' content. We would then take a taxi and return home to sleep tight. We have a warm recollection of those times.

9. On the Move Again

In 1942, the Department of Education had increased the length of primary school from five to six years with the provision that the most advanced students could be promoted from the fourth grade to the sixth. The less advanced would be promoted to fifth grade. Giovanni and I were promoted to the sixth grade. That change coincided with my father's transfer to the second precinct police station on Italia square in the east part of town. We moved also to be near his work and requested a transfer to public school 967. Our brother Daniel was admitted to the "Alfonso Ugarte" high school situated next to the University Park. Our new home was situated some ten blocks from school 967 and twenty blocks from Alfonso Ugarte high school. Giovanni and I walked to and from school. My brother Daniel took the city bus. In those days the one-way bus fare for students cost only 5 cents.

About that time, the Department of Health sponsored a program by which needy students would receive a midday meal in a popular restaurant near by. Giovanni and I qualified and thus were granted free lunches. Every school day, Monday through Saturday, an older lady of the school administration would show up after the morning classes, and standing on the patio stairs a little higher than our heads, she would call the names of the students and pass out the lunch cards. With those cards, we walked to the popular restaurant, some eight blocks away, where an employee would take the cards as we came in. We took a tray and followed the line where other employees served the meals cafeteria style. We then went to the marble tables that could accommodate ten students each. After lunch, we walked back to the school for the afternoon classes.

Our sixth grade teacher was Mr. Cordoba. He was a tall and heavy set man about thirty-five years old. He always spoke in a loud voice, and he yelled at the boys if he had to. He was a good teacher. He was fascinated with Darwin's theory of evolution of the species by natural selection. Many times he would interrupt himself and suddenly change the class subject. He would start talking about the Neanderthals and the Cro-Magnons. Personally, we thought he was one of them!

Once a week Mr. Cordoba organized a math contest by which he would dictate a sheet worth of four long arithmetic operations— addition, subtraction, multiplication, and division. Sound familiar? He was good at them himself. He would do those sheets in about 60 seconds and demanded that his boys do the same. Some of us, the fastest, could do them in about two minutes. He would then have the students exchange sheets and grade each other. He would then collect the sheets and shake the hand of those who had no mistakes and call one by one the names of the students who had errors on their sheets. He would ask the student to show up the palm of his hand. With a wooden board he would then hit it hard. Once for each wrong operation with a maximum of four hits. In those days nobody thought anything of it. It was a common believe that "knowledge enters with blows." Of course, today's psychologists would disagree, but what do they know?

10. The First of May

The first of May was Labor Day, a national holiday in Peru. In the mid-forties, that was the day when laborers, blue collar workers, organized demonstrations against the government in protest of unjust policies and low salaries. They also organized peaceful demonstrations and parades with bands of music and fireworks. In the afternoons, people ate spicy food at street vendors (lamb, beef, chicken, or fish) and drank beer or "chicha fuerte," a strong native beverage made from corn. In the evening, people ate "anticuchos" (charcoal-grilled beef heart pieces on a stick topped with hot pepper sauce) and more beer, of course. Others preferred something sweet, like "picarones" (fried soft doughnuts) covered in brown sugar syrup. To compensate for, or to attenuate, the unrest of protesters, the government made sure that there was some car race scheduled for the first of May and that the most popular radio stations broadcasted the race with minute-to-minute reports. The newspapers gave, morning and evening, tabulated race standings, their timings, and described the perils of drivers, co-drivers, and their machines. The government made sure that the Peruvian idols of automobile racing, like Arnaldo Alvarado, Chachi Dibos, and others, participated in full force. And it worked. That day, the old and the new generation of blue collar workers were concentrated on the race, glued to their radios all day with no time for demonstrations of any kind. Car races drew a huge audience. More than soccer games, more than the October bullfights, more than the processions of the Purple Christ.

The race that I remember most was the international Buenos Aires-Caracas, organized by the International Automobile Association, and in which about 140 automobile drivers from all countries in South America participated. Among them, Juan Manuel Fangio, the famous Argentinian driver, who had won some races in Europe. The race lasted ten days in stages of about 12 hours per day over dirt and gravel roads, across plains, mountains, canyons, and deserts. The race was a terrible test for drivers and machines. During the nights, while drivers and co-drivers rested, the machines were reconditioned for the enduring next day's stage. Peruvians had their hearts and hopes in Arnaldo Alvardo, a native of Nazca, who knew the Nazca-Lima stretch of the road so well that he could drive it blindfolded, they said. That stretch consisted of a dirt gravel road across Peruvian mountains. It then connected with the well-paved panamerican highway that lead to Lima across the deserts.

The day of the race's arrival in Lima, my brothers and I decided to go very early to the desert of Lurin, a few miles South of Lima, through which the panamerican road led to the capital. We wanted to watch the competitors rushing on the well-paved road to the city. We took a bus to Chorrillos, and from there we walked about 5 miles to the desert. Other young people had had the same idea. We saw them in droves walking toward the sand dunes of Lurin. Hundreds, perhaps two thousand people, were sitting on the dunes by the highway, with their radios on full volume, awaiting the competitors. At about 11:30 a.m. through the loud radios we heard: "Coche a la vista" (car in sight), and then: " It's a brick color car, with the lights on, it is number 47, it's the car of Arnaldo Alvaraaaado!!!" He passed at full speed with his arm high out of the car's window, saluting the people on those sand dunes. Our hearts pounded hard with pride. Arnaldo Alvarado had started the stage in 28th position, yet he was first approaching Lima and the winner of that stage. Like us, millions of Peruvians followed the race through the radio transmissions. They were proud too, to see our hero win the southern Peruvian stage ahead of Fangio and other very famous car racers.

To close, I must tell you that, due to accidents, machine failures, and other events, many racers were forced to quit the race to Caracas. Among them Fangio and Arnaldo Alvarado. The winner was an Argentinian newcomer, I believe his name was Marimon. Those were exciting, unforgettable times.

Reporter Judy Hartfeldt: Well, that is enough for today. Shall we meet again on Thursday at 9:00 a.m. for the second session?
Marco Donnatti: Yes, by all means. What will the topic be?
Reporter: Think hard. I would like you to tell me about your high school years.
Marco: I will think hard. Thank you.
Reporter: You are welcome. Good-bye.
Marco: Good-bye Judy.

Soccer became the favotite sport of the Donnatti brothers (Story 14)

CHAPTER 2

THE HIGH SCHOOL YEARS

Reporter Judy Hartfeldt: Good morning. This is our second session. What do you have for me today, your high school times?

Marco Donnatti: I would prefer that you ask me some questions.

Reporter: OK, I will. Let's start at the beginning. When did you start your high school education?

Marco: That was in 1944. Some stories may illustrate our condition at the time.

Reporter: Go ahead. I am recording.

11. The Book on Natural History

My twin brother, Giovanni, and I were admitted to Alfonso Ugarte high school in April of 1944. We were 12 years old and registered in the first year. In those days, high school education was five years long. Each semester lasted four-and-a-half months. The first semester lasted from April to July and the second, from August to December, with a two-week recess between them. Summer vacation was three months long, from December to the end of March. We followed the steps of our older brother, Daniel, who was then in the second year. By then, the three of us walked to and from school every day, some twenty blocks each way. There was a lunch and nap break from 12:00 noon to 3:00 p.m. each day. On Saturdays, there was only a morning session. We lived then in an apartment building of La Victoria, a populous district situated in the eastern part of the city. That year, the war in Europe and the Pacific was particularly horrible, with innumerable casualties on all sides. In Lima, the scarcity of basic necessities continued to be severe.

On our birthday, my father gave Giovanni and me five soles each, as a present, and said: "Buy yourselves something useful." In those days, five soles was a great gift, specially in a low-income family. The following weekend, I walked to the flea market on Aviation avenue, where many hundreds of vendors offered all kinds of merchandise on carts and on the sidewalk. I wanted to find something useful and lasting. I stopped by a vendor displaying many used books. One of those attracted my attention. It was a small, but thick one, hard-bound, with a green cover. The title, stamped in white letters, read: "Natural History." I asked the vendor if I could see it. He nodded. I opened the book. It was published in Paris in 1907, a relic by 1944, but in Spanish, on good quality paper, and described both the plant and animal kingdoms with brief texts and the most beautiful illustrations in the form of black and white drawings. I asked for the price. The vendor sized me up and said "eight soles." I said "Too much" and walked away. Immediately he called me: "Wait, wait, I let you have it for six soles." I said "Five." He agreed, and I walked on with the book happy for having successfully completed a difficult transaction.

During the following year or so, I read the book, from cover to cover, three or four times. Today, it would be like watching a black and white movie classic several times. I did not know it then, but that book of natural history was going to change my life.

12. Gunpowder, Homemade

That year, like every year, summer vacation started around December 20, just before the Christmas and New Year holidays. People crowded the businesses and streets downtown. Everyone was preparing for shopping and the parties of the end of the year despite the horrible war going on in Europe and in the Pacific. It was a tradition that on those nights, at midnight on December 24 and December 31, people would ignite all the fireworks in their possession, on the streets in hallways, on the beaches, everywhere. On those occasions, if you climbed a tall building, you could see the innumerable flashes of light and feel the city vibrate under your feet with the millions of firecracker explosions. Some people could afford to shoot rocket firecrackers that exploded high in the sky with a shower of colorful lights. The spectacle lasted some twenty minutes. Then gradually it would die down. At about 1 a.m. you could still hear sporadic shots.

One day, just before the holidays, my brother Daniel came up with the idea that we could make our own firecrackers. All we needed was to make gunpowder with a recipe he had obtained somewhere. He said that we needed perchlorate, charcoal powder, and brick powder in equal amounts. He said that we had to purchase half a kilogram of perchlorate in a store that sells fertilizers around the Lima central market. Then he flashed a fiver and asked me to go and purchase the stuff. He then asked Giovanni to get a small red brick from a construction site and grind it to powder. He asked also one of boys who used to play with us to get some charcoal and grind it to powder. It took the whole morning to complete the tasks. Perchorate, I believe, was potassium perchlorate in the form of white crystal aggregates. When I came home with the stuff, Daniel asked me to grind it also. When all the ingredients were ready, we gathered in the hall at the entrance of our apartment building. We made a circle around Daniel. He then said that we would mix a small amount first, to test the formula. He carefully measured one teaspoon of each substance on a sheet of paper and mixed them with the spoon. It took several minutes. The mixture had the appearance of a dark grey powder. He then poured the mixture on a tile of the floor, in the middle of the hall. All of us were, still around in a circle, looking with great expectation. He then lit a match and carefully brought it over to the small pile of mixture.

When the match made contact, a huge yellow flame arose to about three feet and sparks sputtered in all directions with a hissing sound. Two of the sparks hit me on the face and a bluish-white smoke spread all around us. Instantly, we jumped backwards to get away from damnation. When the smoke dissipated, we saw Daniel sitting with his back to the wall with a big grin on his face. "It worked, he said." The rest of us were stunned. We did not speak. The burn had melted part of the tile on the floor. A black depression, a small crater, was left in the middle. Then Daniel slowly picked up the rest of the three powders and packaged them for safe keeping. But we all knew we had a weapon in our hands and wondered what was in the Daniel's mind. When I got home, I looked in the mirror. I had two small burns on my face. I did not know it then, but they were third degree burns that would leave permanent scars.

During summer vacation, we used to practice soccer on the streets. Usually some of us would provide, or borrowed, a medium size rubber ball. We practiced for hours in front of the entrance of our apartment building which served as a goal. Someone acted as a goalkeeper, another as winger, whose charge was to center the ball high, and the others tried to score by heading the ball into the goal. Sometimes, when we had too many boys, we went to the next block of our street to play a game. There was not much traffic in that street in those days. The two best players would first flip a coin to decide who would choose first. They then would choose teammates by calling alternatively the names of those present. Clearly, the best players were chosen first, it was a fair way to obtain two well balanced teams. Sometimes we bet 50 cents or even one sol per player. We would then play to reach 3 or 6 goals. The players of the winning team doubled their money. But, most of the time, we played for pleasure, not for money.

On that block there was only one two-story building. It was a factory of metal cabinets for offices. Sometimes we lost the rubber ball over the ten-feet wall of the building entrance. We would then knock on the door to apologize and beg for the ball to be returned to us. But the man, the custodian of the property, always refused to return the ball. That way, we lost several balls that summer. In retaliation, we had broken two second floor windows using slingshots. I do not know whose idea it was that we could scare the custodian by setting up a gunpowder flame in front of the entrance of the factory. We doubled the amount of mixture this time. It was about 6:30 p.m. when we lit the powder and ran away. The flame rose to about six feet and sputtered sparks as before. From the distance away, we watched the custodian come out and see the results of the high flame. Except for a dark spot on the sidewalk, there was no damage of any kind. But then he noticed us some 50 yards away and came to ask questions. He recognize us as "those soccer players" and grabbed Giovanni's arm and shouted "Police, police." Immediately, I gave a hard push to the man freeing Giovanni. When the man tried to catch me, I ran fast back towards the field behind the factory with the man in pursuit. I was only two yards ahead. I turned around the building into an open field. I quickly climbed a small hill in front of me. The man had not seen the hill. He fell flat on his stomach on the slope. I got away and went home. We did not hear anything about the incident in the days that followed. We did not play on that street ever again.

13. The Coca Cola® Sign

Our apartment building had a flat concrete roof. We and our friends, used to climb on it to play, read, rest, etc. when the weather was good. One day, out of the blue, we found a huge Coca Cola® sign, rectangular, about ten by fifteen feet in size, and made of a wooden frame and plywood. The sign was installed on the corner of our roof, in vertical position, facing the 28th of July avenue. The sign was supported by a number of two-by-four pieces of timber. The sign had a picture of Coca Cola® bottle over a red background and in white letters read "Tome Coca Cola®" ("Drink Coca Cola®"). None of the boys in the neighborhood had seen when the sign was installed. The sign did not bother us at all. In fact, we were proud that the Coca Cola company had chosen our building for advertising their product.

In those days we, the Donnatti brothers, played soccer on a dirt field two blocks away from of our apartment building. We had started to play soccer late. Most children started playing at 3 or 4 years of age. We started at 12 and fourteen. We played during vacation, every day, morning and afternoon, until we practically dropped from exhaustion. We used to place two rocks some five yards apart at each end of the field to mark the goals. Every day, we chose teams in the usual manner, and we played to our hearts' content. We usually played from about 9 a.m. to 12 noon. Then we took a break for lunch and returned to the field at about 3 p.m. and played until it was dark, or about 6 p.m.

But we had a problem. Every time someone shot the ball above the rocks marking the goals, an argument would ensue. The shooter's team would claim a goal and the defending team would claim a wide shot. My brother Daniel, the leader, the guy with the ideas, offered a solution. We needed real goals, made of wood, and he knew where to get it. We would take a couple of pieces of timber from the Coca Cola sign. "Nobody will miss them" he said with authority in his tone. One afternoon we met on the roof and proceeded to loosen two long pieces of timber that we thought were superfluous to the contraption. We then cut the pieces to size and kept them until the next day. The next morning, we carried them to the field where we nailed the parts together to form the goals. We dug holes in the ground at both ends of the field and planted the goals. We used rocks and dirt to secure the posts in place. We were proud of our accomplishment. And we played a game just to test the new goals. And we played and played.

But we had another problem. After the game we had to remove the goals and carry them to safe storage. That was too much work for exhausted players. Daniel had another solution. He said that nobody would want to steal the goals, because the pieces were too short for construction purposes, and besides the wood was too dirty with dust and sweat. He recommended that we leave the goals planted on the field and that surely we would find them just fine the next day. That was the solution we all wanted to hear. None of us wanted to carry the goals home. We did not have a place to store them anyway. Thus, we went home. It was dark when we showed up for supper. Mother yelled at us, "Get clean, now."

The next day we went early to the field with our hearts pumping hard with anxiety and hope. When we got there, there were no goals on the field. Someone had stolen them during the night! We were very disappointed, of course, considering all the work we had done to make them and install them. Someone in our group reminded us of a well-known Spanish saying: "whoever steals from a thief earns 100 years of forgiveness." About two weeks later, we noticed that the Coca Cola sign had disappeared. We climbed to the roof to see what had happened. The sign had fallen flat on the roof. Apparently, the wind had brought it down, because of the weakened support. It had not flown away as we first thought. We had more wood now, we thought. But nobody wanted to try that project again. One month later, the sign disappeared. Someone had come and removed it from our roof. Nobody had seen when that had happened.

14. Nil to Nil

The Donnatti brothers learned the art of soccer quickly. Soon, they became some of the best players in the neighborhood. Some of the adults in our apartment building took interest and guided the boys in organizing a club to pursue the practice of our favorite sport. We called it the "Students Football Club." This came just at the right time, because boys entering adolescence are bound to get into all kinds of trouble. The club, in its first session, elected by acclamation Mr. Jorge Torres, President, a gentleman neighbor, the one who brought about the idea of a club. Other reputable persons were elected secretary and treasurer. The new president in an emotional gesture offered to donate new uniforms, blue shirts, white shorts, and white socks. He also donated and a new soccer ball. Raul Alarcon, an older boy who did not play, but always attended the soccer practices, volunteered to be custodian of the soccer ball and to act as the coach. Each player was responsible for maintaining his uniform clean and mended at all times. My brother Daniel was elected team captain. He was fifteen at the time and the fastest player in the team. He played in the position of center forward. Years later, I would write:

> I asked Raul, our coach pretend,
> Why should "skinny," my brother Daniel,
> Always be captain of our team?
> 'Cause he is the fastest? 'Cause he's fifteen?

We quickly learned that playing on the street or on a dirt field was very different from playing on a real field with grass and real goals. For one thing, both were much larger! You had to have stamina. You had to have strategy depending on the kind of adversary we were playing against. You had to have dominion of the ball, in other words, skillful control of the ball. Our club president had said one time that "those things would come with time and practice." We quickly subscribed to the administration of the three soccer fields on the property of Barbones, a military base on the East of Lima. The administrator was a young man whose name nobody could remember. He was known by everybody as "Cholo." He was in charge of the scheduling of games, charging for the rent of the fields by the hour, and of rewarding the winners with a small "silver cup." Of course, it wasn't silver. Most likely was some cheap alloy that looked like silver. I played fullback in the defense, and Giovanni played in the middle line helping both, the defense as well as the attack. Daniel played center forward. That first year we won most of our games. Daniel was unstoppable with his speed. He scored many goals. We rarely lost a game. We thought we were great!

One winter morning, we arrived at the field at 8:30 a.m. for a 9-10 a.m. game. We found "Cholo" setting up the goals of the fields. Other groups of players were already changing for their games on three different fields. We asked Cholo, "Who are we playing today?" He said, "A visiting team from Huarochiri," and he laughed. We thought that he was kidding us, because Huarochiri is a province in the sierras northeast of Lima, most likely, legitimate native Peruvians. Cholo then asked for the money to cover the rental of the field and the trophy. Our coach Raul had collected the money and handed it to him. Soon, when we lined up for the start of the game and we had the opposing team in front of us, we realized that Cholo had not been kidding at all. Our adversary was indeed a team of sierra natives wearing bright yellow uniforms. We thought that the game was going to be a "walk in the park" for us. With Cholo acting as referee, the game began. We were much more skillful and quickly gained control of the field and the game. We pushed them into their own eighteen yards and shot to the adversary's goal many times. Their goalkeeper was good. He deflected some shots. Some shots went wide, some were deflected. Later, I would remember the occasion this way:

> The Huarochirians, blocked every shot,
> Their bodies, faces, got in the way,
> Some shots went wide, some were deflected,
> Inconsequential, those corner kicks...

One hour later, the game had ended and the score was nil to nil. We could not believe it! We were exhausted and wet in perspiration with nothing to show for our efforts. Despite the obvious superiority of our team, we had not been able to score even one goal. According to the rules, the two captains would join the referee to flip a coin for the cup. Cholo suggested: "Give them the cup." We did not respond at first. We were still in shock. A few seconds later though, I repeated: "Let's give them the darn cup." That was followed by a chorus of "Yes, yes, give them the cup." Cholo walked slowly to the equally exhausted yellow team and gave their captain the cup saying " The blue team congratulates you and have asked me to give you the cup because you deserve it." We heard the cheers. Seemed far away. The yellow warriors, ran down the field, carrying the cup, holding it high.

15. The Gypsies

One grey morning, in the cold and misty winter of Lima, the boys in our neighborhood noticed some tents on our old soccer field. They had been installed overnight! There were three large tents, about 12 by 8 feet of base area and had pyramidal roofs about 4-6 feet tall. People said that they were Hungarian gypsies and that they would not stay there very long because they were nomads. From the distance we observed that there were some gypsy women and children living there. Later, we learned that the men in the clan went to work in the huge wholesale and retail market east of Aviation avenue. The rumor was that the male gypsies were expert pickpockets. The gypsy women, some of the prettiest women I had ever seen, with blue eyes, golden hair, and fair complexion, took care of the children in the mornings and later in the afternoon they went to offer their services as palm readers. People said that the gypsies could tell the future, but that their beauty was ephemeral, by age thirty-six they were wrinkled and looked much older. But what was most amazing was that those Hungarian gypsies spoke Spanish!

The following weekend, our neighborhood boys decided to play a practice soccer game with a rubber ball, like in the old days, on the paved street across 28 of July avenue. From there, we could see the gypsy tents clearly. We were preparing to choose teams when we noticed a bunch of gypsy boys, six to be exact, coming toward us. They were taller and older than us, about 15-17 years old. We were about 13-15. They challenged us to a soccer match to three goals and with a bet of two soles per player. We did not have the money. We could collect only fifty cents per player. But Mr. Carrion, a neighbor who was passing by and had watched the challenge, told us that he would cover the bet for us. Twelve soles per team! We had never played for so much money. We were nervous. He would also hold the money from both teams and deliver it to the winner at the end of the game. And so, we lined up the teams, six players per team, to start the game on the cement-paved street. The team who scored three goals first would take the money.

We were confident that we had excellent skills and that we could run circles around the older gypsies. But we were in for a surprise. They did play well, European style! They pushed us, pulled us from the shirts, hit us with their shoulders, tripped us, purposely stepped on our feet, used their elbows at every encounter, etc. We protested fouls, but nobody would listen. The game continued at full speed. We shot to the gypsy goalkeeper twice in the first few minutes, but the gypsy knew his business. He stopped the shots with class and style. We were surprised by this kind of playing. The gypsies imposed their stature and their weight on us. In about twenty minutes, they had scored two goals. We were doomed, we thought. We were very close to losing the game, in our field, and losing the money. We were frustrated and worried that we would disappoint Mr. Carrion, who had placed his confidence in us. After half an hour, we agreed with the gypsies to take a five-minute break.

During the break, we talked about how we could turn things around, I offered the idea that we play faster and shoot at one touch. All agreed that it was worth trying. Mr. Carrion was a true gentleman. He said, "Don't worry about the money, just play your darn best, but give them hell!" The second half of the game began. We moved the ball skillfully and faster. The gypsies were disconcerted for the first few minutes. Suddenly, I received a pass from behind, rotated half a turn and shot hard, one touch. The gypsy goalkeeper touched the ball, but could not stop it. We scored a goal! Mr. Carrion, watching on the side, jumped up and down celebrating the goal. The score was now 2-1 in favor of the gypsies. Next, a quick combination led to a pass to our left winger, Ricardo, who shot hard, low, and across. Goal!!! We had tied the game! The gypsies held a quick and secret meeting. We watched and waited to restart the game. Suddenly, the gypsies decided to quit and asked for their money. Since the game was tied at two goals, and we had not specified any conditions before the game, we had to accept and let them go. We then sat on the curb to comment on the incidents of the game against such an unusual adversary. Mr. Carrion was proud of us. We were happy with our performance. We were also wet with sweat! A few weeks later, the tents disappeared overnight! The nomads had left. The pretty fortune tellers were no more.

16. The Bullies

Federico Chang was a third-year student in our "Alfonso Ugarte" high school. He was about 15 years old and of Asian descent. He bragged about his expertise in martial arts and demonstrated his skills at any occasion. For some reason, he decided to pick on me. Well, I was in the second year of high school and only thirteen. He was in the third year, taller and stronger than me besides being an expert on wrestling. During the morning and afternoon recesses, he would look for me to practice his art. He would twist my arm and demonstrate the Nelson hold and or the double Nelson strangulation hold. At first, I played along with his demonstrations. But when, one day, he tightened the hold, I protested and he let me go. After that incident, I would hide so that he could not use me as a dummy for his demonstrations.

One day, I was distracted, and he found me and took both my wrists and twisted them outward. I pulled him toward me and hit him with my head on his stomach. He fell backwards, his eyes turned white, and he remained unconscious, I was told later, for two minutes. I had run to hide in my classroom before the discipline inspectors arrived. When Federico came to, he was taken to the school's nursing station, where the nurse gave him some stimulant to drink and send him to his classroom. After recess, my classmates returned and classes resumed. Nobody mentioned the incident, no investigation followed. The bully never again picked on me. I figured that I must have hit him in the liver-gallbladder area. A perfect K.O. He needed that badly.

Come to think about it, there was another incident, much earlier, in our neighborhood. Rojas was a young man about eighteen, a truck worker, one of those who loaded and unloaded trucks. He was also into wrestling and picked on me for his practice. One evening, it was already getting dark on the street where we lived. He suddenly grabbed me from behind in a strangulation hold and began to tighten his hold. With my left hand I held his arm in front of my throat and with the other hand I reached into my trousers' right pocket, looking for anything that I could use as a weapon. Luckily, I found a small, rectangular piece of metal that I had found earlier behind a construction site. Some metallic refuse, I thought. Because it was a shiny piece of metal, I had picked it up and put it in my pocket. With the corner of that piece of metal, I scratched his arm, the one around my neck, as hard as I could. I made a line about six inches long. I saw the blood run along his arm when he let me go. I ran home as fast as I could. Because the piece of metal had no sharp edges, I figured the cut was superficial. He never complained. He could have been charged with a worse case of abuse. He never again tried his wrestling techniques on me. Come to think about it, we did not see him again in our neighborhood.

17. High School Courses

In those days, high school consisted of five years, divided into two semesters each. Each semester was divided into two quarters. We took 13 courses each year and one exam per course per quarter plus one final exam in each course. The total was 65 exams per year. Very few courses had a good textbook. I remember that zoology, in the second year, had a text written by the teacher himself, Mr. Alberto Carpio. That was a great help, because, in class, we could listen to him and later study his book. Unfortunately, none of the other courses had a text. Thus, we had to take notes fast while the teacher spoke to the class. Taking notes and trying not to miss something important was hard to do. Some students, like Giovanni and me, developed a kind of shorthand that was extremely useful when taking notes and, later, studying for exams. Some students could not take notes as fast. They depended on studying with someone who did or simply flunked the tests. We, the Donnatti brothers, were very fortunate. We did well all through high school and even earned some awards.

We must recognize though, that we were fortunate because the teachers were specialists. They held college degrees in the subjects they taught. They had a well planned curriculum and followed it closely so that nothing was left behind or forgotten. Our school, the Colegio Nacional Alfonso Ugarte, had about 1,500 students in the day cycle and another 1,500 in the nocturnal cycle. The management of orderly operations and discipline was in the hands of "inspectors"— persons with education degrees. They had responsibility for keeping accurate records of attendance and for lining up the students before entering at 8:00 a.m. and at 3:00 p.m. And also after leaving the classrooms at 12:00 noon and at 5:00 p.m. in the afternoon. Each inspector took care of three sections of about 50 students each. Teachers came punctually to their classes without having to worry about discipline. They could concentrate on their teaching. In retrospect, I can appreciate how well the organization worked. We were proud of our school. We demonstrated that pride when we competed in pre-military parades on the 27th of July and later in athletic competitions against other high schools, like Colegio Guadalupe. Colegio Labarthe, and Colegio Militar Leoncio Prado.

We recall now those wonderful days of our youth in which we learned a lot of subjects which, at the time, we had no idea they were important. We warmly remember some teachers and some subjects that quickly became our favorites. In general, we liked the sciences; for example, Professor Palma, who taught botany, with his wonderful drawings on the blackboard. Professor Carpio, of zoology, with his intimidating approach to make the students give a maximum effort. Professor Vera, of algebra, with his step by step approach to teaching the solving of equations. Professor Delgado, a doctor, who taught human anatomy and physiology. He used to bring a basket of human bones to the classroom. With that, and his drawings on the board, he kept us fascinated on the topic. Professor Butron, in charge of the laboratories of physics and chemistry, with his stern voice and pop-quizzes, scared us to death. Too bad that, in the whole year, he only conducted two lab demonstrations. Professor Ortega, who taught us about second degree equations, arithmetic and geometric progressions, polynomials, and the Pascal triangle. We were fascinated. Professor Cantor and his patience when teaching organic chemistry and the physics of electromagnetism. We shall always remember him. We remember our teacher of universal history, Mr. Alvarez, who believed that "While there were two men on the earth, there would be wars." We enjoyed the kind approach of our teacher of psychology and the logics of our teacher of logic. We enjoyed also physical education, taught by professors Montovani and Barrios, in which we learned proper techniques of running, jumping, and participating in field games. Occasionally we would go to the stadium of La Victoria to do our thing in athletics. Also, the courses on technical initiation, where we learned to work with paper, cardboard, plywood, wood, plastic, glass, clay, sheet metal, and paint. Regretfully, I have forgotten the teachers' names.

And then, there were the subjects that we hated, indeed. We did not see or understand the reasons why we had to learn them. We were too young at the time, I guess. One of those courses was the pre-military course. My father had told us once that he did not want us to pursue a career in the military. He said that in the military, a superior officer had the right to yell at us and offend us verbally, just because he outranked us, even though he was an ignorant and stupid jerk. We never forgot that advice. The course was usually taught by an army officer. We learned about the combat group and its components, their roles, and their weapons. We learned about the Mauser rifle, its parts and function. Once a year, we went to the shooting range to practice with live ammunition. Of course, we did not understand then, that the best way to avoid the horrors of war was to be prepared for it and that those courses were really preparing us to prevent another war. Another course that we hated was religion, usually taught by a priest. The Catholic religion was supported by our government. That is why we had to learn about catechism, biblical stories, and the parables of Jesus. We had to have one hour a week of class on religion. We barely fulfilled the requirements of those courses and passed them with minimum marks. Thank goodness! One year, during a religious week, Padre Menen, a Franciscan monk, came to our school to preach. In all there were one thousand five hundred students, standing in formation on the school patio, in the sun and having to listen to his preaching. He told us of his past as a movie actor and singer, and of his past life as a sinner. And of his repentance, his becoming a monk, and his service to the grace of God. We were bored to tears. That Friday, all students were expected to make confession, and on Saturday, there was a mass and communion. A team of priests came to the school to hear confessions and to give penitence and absolutions. My brother Daniel looked for us—Giovanni and me—that Friday at about midmorning, during recess, and asked us to follow him. We went to the main office facing Abancay avenue, and looked around to be sure that nobody was there. We then simply walked out of the building and went home. That is how we avoided confession. The next day, after attendance was taken, we went to the auditorium and escaped through a window to a side street. Other students followed us too. Nobody missed us. Even though the Peruvian constitution guarantees the freedom of religion, that week we saw some sacraments imposed on a trapped audience of 1,500 high school students.

We were sort of indifferent to a third category of course subjects. One of those was literature, where we had to learn the biographies of ancient writers and their works. Santillana, Lope de Vega, Cervantes, Becquer, and others. We understood that there were some masterpieces worth studying, but why so many? For example, Don Quijote de la Mancha, of Cervantes, and Rimas, of Gustavo Becquer, yes, but why so many others? Another course that held little interest to us was English. We did not see, at that time, how important English was going to become in culture, in economics, and in science and technology. So, we did poorly in those courses also. However, we remember with affection at least one of the teachers of literature. Professor Sarmiento was a picturesque character. He had memorized the classics of the literature, and he would enter the classroom reciting in loud voice: "Volveran las oscuras golondrinas a tu balcon sus nidos a colgar..." ("The dark nightingales shall return to hang their nests on your balcony...") from a poem by Gustavo Becquer. The class, at that point, applauded, yelled "bravo," whistled, shouted: "bravo, loco!" ("bravo, nut!"). Professor Sarmiento would then call the inspector and put the whole class under one-hour detention that day. Detention was from 5 to 6 p.m. in which our inspector would have to remain supervising us during one hour of silent study. The following week, the scene would repeat itself: "Mosa tan fermosa, non vi en la frontera, como una vaquera, de La Finojosa,..." (" A beautiful maiden, I saw on the frontier, she took care of cattle, (from La Finojosa..."), from a poem by Santillana. The yelling followed and, of course, the one-hour detention of the whole class that afternoon.

With 1,500 students, it was difficult to know everyone at the school. However, we did recognize some of the most outstanding students: Ernesto Lopez, of our very own class, who always got the highest marks in every course; Americo Ferrari, the poet of the school, who wrote poems for every occasion; Carlos Zapata, the sprinter who gave us many victories in the 100-meter sprints during the intercollegial olympic games; and Manuel Vargas, a first division soccer player who played for Alianza Lima and for our Colegio Alfonso Ugarte.

In December of 1948, we were in the postwar period. Brother Daniel had been admitted to the University of San Marcos and had completed his first year of pre-medical school. Giovanni and I had successfully finished high school and looked forward to entering the University too. Giovanni had won an efficiency award, and I had earned a diploma for good behavior. I also won first prize in a contest of posters for the intramural athletic games. My poster was a drawing in India ink of boxer Antonio Frontado standing on guard. He was, at the time, the South American champion of the middle weights. The prize was twenty-five soles. Not too bad for a class of 240 graduates.

18. Admission Exams

As soon as we finished high school, in December of 1948, Giovanni and I began to study hard for admission to the University of San Marcos. We wished to pursue, like our brother Daniel, a career in medicine. We purchased the developed curriculum for admissions, which had some 1,200 pages and covered the whole spectrum of subjects to be included in the admission exams. Most of the time we studied separately. Occasionally, we had a brainstorming session to discuss difficult topics and to clarify our understanding. This cramming of topics and courses went on seven days a week, at least 12 hours a day, from December to March. No Christmas, no New Year holidays for us. We wanted to succeed so badly. We took breaks only to perform some of our other obligations to the family. For example, the three older boys took turns to make breakfast for the clan, usually a big pot of oat meal with evaporated milk, sugar, chocolate, and cinnamon. We took turns to go to the bakery to purchase the warm bread rolls for breakfast. We took turns to accompany Mother to the market to do the shopping. We took turns to assist Mother with preparing lunch. We took turns to clean the apartment. We took care of our own clothing, mending, washing, and ironing. We did not have a washing machine at the time, so we had to wash our trousers, shirts and underwear, in a circular zinc tub with soap, a brush, and a scrubbing board. Later, we did get a washing machine with two rollers that squeezed most of the water out of the clothes after washing. We did not have a dryer. We hanged the clothes on a line outdoors. We did not know it then, but what we learned then was going to be extremely useful later, when my mother had to go to work to support the family.

The admission exams were in March. We knew that about ten thousand students would apply for admission to the National University of San Marcos, because it was essentially free. And only about 10-15% would gain admission to the twelve colleges of the university, but we were sure of our aptitude and preparation. On the day of our written exam, Giovanni and I were confident that we were going to do well. After all, we had done it through five years of high school. And we had studied hard to cover the whole curriculum for admissions. I recall finishing my answers about ten minutes before the two-hour limit. I was pleased with my answers. I turned to look at Giovanni, sitting on a back row, and saw him writing in a frenzy. I knew that he was also doing well. We expected our names on the list of those passing the exams. Ten days later, the rolls came out. Giovanni had passed. My name was not on any of the lists! And according to the rules, the Admission Committee's decisions were unappealable.

I came home heartbroken. I did not understand how it was possible. I had been pleased with my exam. I knew that I had done well and yet, success was not to happen to me. I hated to have to tell Father and Mother that I had failed. Our father and mother took things in a stride. They said that "There is always a next year. Next year you'll pass." I remembered then that my father had said the same thing after recovering from his accident while preparing for his exams eight years earlier (Story 6). I promised them that the next year I would pass. In April, Giovanni began attending premedical school. My mother started a retail business whereby she would purchase foodstuffs wholesale and sell them to the public at retail prices. I went with her daily to help her with the heavy lifting, the carrying, and the watching of the merchandise. She worked hard and was successful.

Soon the family was in a better situation, and all six children could continue their education.

19. Tragedy

In May of 1949, my father fell ill and had to stay in bed for a few days. He had weakness, insensitivity, and partial paralysis of both legs. He was referred to the military hospital, where doctors examined him and prescribed some medications for sciatica—a condition affecting the sciatic nerves and the lower spinal cord. They also ordered the application of diathermy to his lumbar region—that is, heat using infrared lamps. He followed the treatment as scheduled. Twice a week he would take a taxi to the hospital, where he would receive the heat treatments to the lower spine. With him went my sister Gina, nine years old, who also needed heat applications to her chest for her asthma. Both then returned home in a taxi to rest and recover. My mother and I went to work early every morning and returned by mid-afternoon. The rest of the clan went to their respective school assignments and returned later in the afternoon. Mother prepared dinner and so, the family had a reunion every evening at about 6 p.m. We then read, listened to the radio, or simply went out to meet friends. Sometimes, some of us went to one of the neighborhood theaters to watch an old movie. We never thought that tragedy was just around the corner.

One cold morning in June, my father went to the hospital with my sister Gina, as usual. At about 11 a.m. a policeman came to our apartment and gave the news to Giovanni that our father had fainted, fallen, and died at the hospital. My brother went quickly to my mother's place of work, and she took a taxi to the hospital to get my sister Gina. That morning my brothers and I met on the roof of our apartment building and cried together over the loss of our beloved father. At that moment we decided that we, the three older brothers, would go to work and postpone our education for a year or two. Because the doctors did not agree on the cause of death, they requested permission to do an autopsy. No details were given, but the autopsy revealed a massive stroke. In retrospect, it seems that the stroke was most likely due to rupture of an aneurysm or a hemangioma caused by the trauma my father suffered eight years earlier. Tragic that the doctors, knowing the history, did not look for a vascular lesion in the brain and decided to treat the lower spine instead. For heaven's sake, my father was only 40 years old!

My mother was well mannered, polite, and educated. But when we told her that we wanted to find jobs and help support the family, she hit the ceiling, "No way!" she yelled and with a very firm and a stern voice told us that we were to work only during vacations and that during the academic periods we would stick to the books and do well. No arguments accepted. She decided instead that she was going to work harder to help the family succeed. She was a saint. Of course, that year, I continued to assist her with her work while I prepared to retake the admissions exams the following year. We, the three brothers, did work during summer vacations. One year we purchased construction materials and delivered them to construction sites on a rented truck. Bricks from the factory, gravel from the quarry, sand from the Rimac river, and cement from the factory. Since we did the loading and unloading of the truck ourselves, it was very hard work. Another year, Daniel worked in a cotton thread factory. He was proud to tell us that he had learned to operate a huge machine all by himself. Giovanni worked in a chocolate factory. Lucky him. We loved the "samples" he brought occasionally. One Summer, in partnership with two other boys, I worked carrying sand, cement, and water from the street to the third floor of a girls' school. We had to do it at night, because the bricklayers needed those materials in the morning. The school was adding a third floor to the building. Another summer I worked painting houses in a residential district of Lima. Whatever money we made, we gave part to Mother and used the rest to purchase our own clothes, books, notebooks, etc. that we needed for our studies.

My father's funeral was memorable. A company of police officers stood at attention on the street in front of our apartment building while a cornet player played "silence." Many dignitaries of the government and police force, family, and friends attended the services at the "Presbitero Maestro" cemetery of Lima. We shall always remember our father. He taught us order, discipline, dedication to the job at hand, respect for others, but above all, basic mathematics. He also taught me how to develop photographs and to make enlargements. I have enjoyed that hobby all my life. Of course, nowadays, I use a digital camera, a computer, and an inkjet printer.

20. Admission Exams II

The year of 1949 was one of work and study for me. Since I had not been admitted to the university the previous year, I had time to help mother in her work, to do chores at home, to study in preparation for another round of the admission exams, and to practice my favorite sport, soccer. I was seventeen. That year we heard the rumor that admissions to the university were being sold in the black market, secretly, underground. We also heard that, to enter the university, you needed to have "yardage"—political influence. That you had to have a recommendation from someone with political power, someone "connected" to the admissions committee. That the exams was a mere formality. That the committee decided who was admitted and who was not. And only ten to fifteen percent of those who applied were given a slot in the great Universidad Nacional Mayor de San Marcos, for a price.

We did not give any credit to those rumors. I reassured my mother that I would be better prepared this time and that I could not possibly fail. Secretly though, I was afraid that my place could be given to someone politically connected or to someone with a thousand American dollars to spare. I did not have any other recourse. I came from a poor family. In addition to studying the whole curriculum, I also enrolled in a free Academy consisting of high-ranking volunteer students of engineering, medicine, chemistry, etc. who were willing to teach for free, to review most subjects for classes of about twenty students. Classes were held in the evenings, from 6 to 9 p.m. in a building situated on Azangaro street near downtown. Courses lasted from October of 1949 to February of 1950. I concentrated on the subjects of mathematics, anatomy/physiology, and physics/chemistry. I vividly recall Mr. Tello, a fourth-year student of engineering, who reviewed mathematics. His approach was to dictate problems to the class and then give two or three minutes to solve them. If nobody solved the problem, he would explain how to propose the equation and solve it to arrive at the correct answer. Then he would prove the validity of the answer.

I made a discovery during those classes. I discovered that I could solve most of the problems mentally, without writing an equation. When Mr. Tello finished the dictation of the problem, I would exclaim: "piece of cake!" and proceed to write the answer on my notebook. I would then hand it to Mr. Tello, who would nod and smile. Another problem, another handing of the answer to our instructor, another smile. It became a pattern. Of course, Mr. Tello would wait for the other students to finish and show their answers too after two or three minutes. One day he dictated a problem that I could not solve mentally. I grabbed my notebook and started scribbling hurriedly to arrive to an equation. At that moment, a girl in back of the classroom, asked in a loud voice: "Where is the piece of cake?" I turned to look at her and smiled. She smiled back. Then I realized the problem was incomplete, that it could have multiple answers. I told Mr. Tello that, and he told the class that he had mistakenly left out a piece of data. He then said that I should study engineering. I thanked him for his good wishes, and I told him my mind was set on studying Veterinary Medicine.

One day shortly before the month of March, when I would retake admission exams, my mother surprised me by saying the we had an appointment with Dr. Pablo Olaechea and that I needed to dress up a little. I put on my navy blue suit, white shirt and tie. We took a taxi to Miraflores. On the way she explained that she had investigated the admissions process and that, although she was sure I was well prepared, that it did not hurt to meet and talk to Dr. Olaechea. He was a well known lawyer and a professor at the school of law in the university. My mother, through an acquaintance, had obtained an appointment to talk with him that afternoon. Dr. Olaechea was very nice, kind, and polite. A true and distinguished gentleman. I assured him that I would not disappoint him, that I was well prepared, etc. He said that he gladly would recommend me to the admissions committee. We came out of his office partly in shock, partly happy that we had some hope of entering the darn old university!

So, it came to pass that, one day in late March, after my written exam, my name appeared on one of the lists of applicants admitted to the school of pre-veterinary sciences. I had chosen Veterinary Medicine because it was a five-year career, much shorter than the nine years of Medicine. Since I had lost already one year, I thought it was a reasonable choice. I did not know, at the time, that later I was going to lose two more years: one for falling in love with a lovely girl, and another due to illness. But that is another story.

Reporter Judy Hartfeldt: Those stories were very special. Next time I'd like to know about your college years. Good-bye now.
Marco Donnatti: Good-bye Miss Hartfeldt and thank you.

Fresh water planarians, flat worms from Agua Dulce Beach in Lima (Story 21)

CHAPTER 3

ADVENTURES IN COLLEGE

Marco Donnatti: Good morning Miss Hartfeldt, how are you?
Reporter Judy Hartfeldt: Well, thank you, and you?
Marco: No complaints so far.
Judy: You were going to tell me about your times in college. Let's begin.

21. Pre-Veterinary Science

On the first day of classes, I learned that there were about 30 students in my class. They had come to Lima from all regions of the country and, somehow, like me, had managed to gain admission to the pre-veterinary sciences class. Our curriculum consisted of comparative anatomy/embryology, physical chemistry, zoology, mathematics, and believe it or not, Spanish and English. With the solid base I brought to the class, it was relatively easy for me to obtain high grades and to jump to the first place in the class ranking. Some courses were difficult. For example, comparative anatomy began with the embryology of fishes, amphibia, birds, and mammals, including humans. All new to me. But we did have a good text by our professor, Torres Vidal. That helped a lot.

Another difficult course was zoology, because it covered the whole animal kingdom, including so many microscopic creatures with which we were not familiar. The course included two 4-hour laboratory sessions each week. But we did have a good textbook. Professor Melendez taught that course at the Museum of Natural History on Arenales avenue. He had two female biologists to assist him with the labs. In the labs, we dissected toads and earthworms, examined specimens under the microscope, protozoa, insects, arachnids, etc., made drawings, assembled the bleached bones of a small vertebrate, etc. Professor Melendez loved to give occasional oral pop-quizzes at the beginning of some classes. We never knew when he was going to call someone to the front of the class and ask him questions about any previous materials in the course. We felt that he enjoyed embarrassing students in front of the whole class. Of course, we studied a lot for those classes. One day, it was my turn. Professor Melendez called me to the front and asked me about flagellates, their classification, and examples. I was prepared for his quizzes and responded well. He smiled for the first time since the course had begun. He then asked me if I had a question for him. I asked him if there was any explanation for the fact that snakes have one lung much larger than the other. He kept silence for a whole minute and then he admitted that he had not encountered that fact in his studies and that he had no explanation for it. He asked me to sit down and proceeded with his class. When the class was over, we walked out slowly toward the exit from the museum. My classmates surrounded me and congratulated me: "Bravo Marco, you stuffed him with his own medicine," said one, "You rubbed his nose in his own mess" said another. Professor Melendez did not give any more pop-quizzes that semester. I had read about the snakes' lungs in that old "Natural History" book which I bought at the flea market several years earlier (Story 11). One day, Professor Melendez announced an optional "field trip." He asked that those students who wished to collect planarians—fresh water flat worms with very primitive eyes. Planarians could sense the light and react to it, but they could not form images. Dr. Melendez said that we could meet him at the Parque Confraternidad de Barranco the following Saturday at 8:00 a.m. We were to bring an empty glass jar with a lid. Most of us went that morning and waited. At 8:15 a.m., Professor Melendez arrived in his automobile, parked near-by, and joined us. Looking at his watch he said, "let's go, 15 minutes is enough time to wait," and he smiled for the second time in the semester. We walked with him down the road of Quebrada de Armendaris (Armendaris Canyon) all the way down to Agua Dulce (Sweet Water) Beach. There, at the foot of the vertical hill-side was a fresh water stream. The water fell from the hill at various points and ran parallel to the highway. Professor Melendez lifted a stone in the stream and showed us some dark brown globular organisms attached to the surface of the rock. "Planarians," he said, and carefully collected them and placed them in one of the jars with some fresh water in it. We all proceeded to do the same. Upon exposure to the light and possibly sensing motion, the flat worms curled up into a ball some three millimeters in diameter (Fig. 3). Then Dr. Melendez said good-bye and walked up the canyon to his car. Some students went with him. Others like me, remained for a while collecting planarians by the beach. I took my jar with some twenty planarians home to show Mother and my brothers and sisters. Mother yelled at me: "Take those worms out of the house immediately!" I argued "But they are harmless!" I managed to hide the jar in the house and changed the water every day. I fed them tiny bits of cooked meat. The bits floated on the surface of the water. Somehow, the planarians sensed the meat and immediately crawled from the bottom of the jar to the side walls and, believe it or not, under the surface tension film of the water surface, to get to the meat. They then curled around the meat and began to digest and absorb the nutrients. I had never seen anything like it! One day I found that a new, small, red planarian had appeared overnight in the jar. They were obviously reproducing themselves! And, best of all, I had right in front of my eyes, a genetic mutation, a red planarian. I decided to transfer that red planarian to another jar. Thus, carefully, I did the transfer and proceeded to feed her. A few days later there were six red planarians in the jar. That was a true mutation because it had persisted for two generations. I decided to take them to Professor Melendez and show him my findings. But that was not to be. That afternoon when I came home, I found the jars clean and drying on a kitchen towel. My mother had found the worms, dumped them in the sink, and washed the jars. I was very sad, but I did not say a word. Not a word.

Another incident occurred one evening at the beginning of a mathematics class. Professor Barringher came in to the classroom , walked through the aisle, and stopped in front of me. He then placed a piece of chalk in my hand and asked me: "The diagonal of a square is ten meters, what is the length of its side?" I stood up and walked slowly to the blackboard and wrote on it: "7.1 meters." He was surprised. He said, "That's right! How did you do it?" I explained that I had squared the diagonal, divided by 2, and taken the square root of that, which is about 7.1 m. He went on to explain to the class that the solution involved the Pythagorean theorem. He then proceeded with the topic of his class: polynomials. And I said to myself, "A piece of cake." Of course, a more accurate answer to the problem would have been 7.07 meters. Once again, my father's "paper and pencil (Story 5)," and Mr. Cordoba's exercises (Story 9) had begun to pay off.

22. The Math Tutor

In the summer of 1951, through one of our neighbors, my mother learned that a family in the district of Jesus Maria needed a tutor to review mathematics with two of their daughters, who were preparing for admission exams into the Maria Parado de Bellido high school. That school was one of the best high schools in metropolitan Lima. Somehow I had been recommended for that job. Thus, I took the bus and went to visit Mr. and Mrs. Linares, the parents of the two girls, who were concerned that their daughters were good in all subjects except in math. They wanted to correct that. We agreed to have two 2-hour sessions per week, in the afternoons from two to four p.m., for 6 weeks. A total of 24 hours of tutoring, from the first week in February to mid-March. Admission exams were in the third week of March. I had never done a tutoring job before, but I was confident that I could teach basic math to anyone. The first three months of the year are the summer months, when students are usually on vacation.

Tutoring classes began. The two students were Graciela, age 14, and Margarita, age 13. We sat around the table in their dinning room. The girls showed up with one thick notebook each and several sharp pencils. In each class, I would begin by demonstrating some exercises I had brought along with me and show how to solve them, step by step. Then I would give the girls a sequence of similar exercises to do within two or three minutes. They were intelligent. They learned quickly and had very few errors. When they made a mistake, I showed them what they had done wrong. I also showed them how to avoid errors in the first place and how to check their answers quickly before turning them in. That way, we reviewed basic arithmetic operations, rule of three, percentage problems, powers, square roots, and progressions. Some afternoons, after class, Mrs. Linares suggested that, being so hot, we, the two girls and I, could go to the municipal swimming pool to swim and cool off. On those days, I brought my swimming trunks and a towel with me. We walked to the swimming pool building, which was only three blocks away from their house. Those days were the happiest of my life. I think I was in love with Margarita. She was a stunning beauty. Always silent, smiling, pretending not to notice my admiration. Graciela, on the other hand, was cheerful, always laughing, telling stories, smiling. That summer I discovered puppy love. I had fallen in a whirlpool and there was no way out. But that was not meant to be. We really rotated, translated, and precessed on different orbits. Although I met secretly, with the girls on two or three occasions, the fury cooled off, and everything stopped. It was painful for me, even now when I remember that summer of 51. Years later, I would write:

> And your elusive and playful eyes
> Stopped my heart, they took my breath,
> Even the planets stopped to watch,
> The constellations stood still...
>
> With furtive glances and with smiles,
> We couldn't help it, much less resist it,
> An endless fall, we were in love,
> That warm and tender, that Summer still...

Tutoring ended as scheduled. Mr. Linares paid me for my services, and we all waited for the results of the admission exams. A week later, I called Mr. Linares. He was delighted. "It worked," he said, "They both passed with high marks, thank you." I was delighted too. For several days, I walked around with a grin on my face.

23. A Course on Spanish

One of the courses in pre-veterinary college was Spanish. That course was part of the curriculum to make sure that all students were able to communicate, both verbally and in writing, in correct Spanish. A noble cause, certainly, especially, where so many students came from the interior of the country and their Spanish was not necessarily the best. I was fortunate in that I grew up in Lima and in a family that cared very much about how we spoke. In any case, we had to take that Spanish course and pass it if we were to advance to the four years of veterinary college. Professor Fernando Lopez was in charge of teaching it. He was a short and chubby character who spoke Castilian Spanish at any occasion, just to show off. Castilian sounded affected, effeminate, to us. Our group of 30 pre-veterinary students had been lumped with one of the small groups of pre-medicine students for a total of some 70 students. We received those classes at the "Annex" of Padre Geronimo street, some six blocks from the School of Sciences at University Park. The classroom was like an amphitheater, with rows and columns of desks going up the room steps. Each desk accommodated two students. Classes were from four to five p.m. twice a week.

For some reason, Professor Lopez considered the pre-veterinary students the noisiest, the least disciplined, the worst in grades, etc. It is possible that we inherited that reputation from previous classes of pre-veterinary students. Right at the beginning of the course, Professor Lopez issued an ominous threat: "None of the pre-veterinary students shall pass this course." The pre-medical students exploded in laughter and hollered with expressions of delight and pleasure. Professor Lopez looked at the audience with a smirk. We, the pre-veterinary students, smiled like

idiots in front of the laughing pre-med students. We were in shock at having heard
a professor of the great University of San Marcos threaten us in such manner and
get away with it. He then outlined the course: 70% of the final grade came from
the final orthography exam (Spanish spelling), 20% from the theory of Spanish
pronunciation, and 10% from the recitation of a poem in front of the class. We had
a text for each of the first two parts. But there was a catch—"Anyone who failed
the orthography test would fail the course automatically." The pre-med students
were not laughing now. The pre-veterinary students were.

In every class, Professor Lopez would dictate 50 words from the orthography textbook, only once and within two seconds of the next word. On a sheet of
paper the students scribbled quickly the words, and, at the end, the students grad-
ed themselves. Those drills were for the purpose of preparing the students for the
final exam. I joined forces with a classmate, Miguel Tebes, who lived near me and
had purchased the orthography book. We practiced for hours, in his room of plaza
Buenos Aires, mostly at night. In every class, Professor Lopez would call some
five or six students to recite a memorized poem of their choice in front of the class.
I remember what happened to a pre-med student. He recited a very long poem and
poorly. He mispronounced some words and phrases, made overly long pauses,
etc. Professor Lopez had listened patiently, and, at the end, he harshly criticized
the provincial accent of the student and made fun of it. He then gave the grade, in
a loud voice, for everyone to hear,"Ocho" he said (eight, on the basis of twenty),
a flunking mark. The whole class exploded in noisy delight at the misery of the
student. I thought "that is ridiculous! Why to choose such a long poem?" I chose
to memorize "La Leyenda de Coquena," a sonnet, of only 12 lines. When my turn
came, Professor Lopez, knowing that I was a pre-veterinary student, smirked at
me before I even began. I did recite the poem clearly, without mistakes, and taking good care to reflect the correct punctuation. It was a perfect performance.
The whole class waited in expectant silence. Professor Lopez looked at me with
the same smirk and said: "Diez" (Ten, a flunking mark). The pre-med audience
exploded in noisy delight; another pre-veterinary student had bitten the dust. My
classmates were really scared then. They thought, "If Marco cannot pass with a
perfect performance, what will become of us?"

The day of the final exam came. I had studied the orthography book really
hard and was confident that I could get a high mark on the final drill, perhaps even
49/50 if not a perfect score. But I had not studied the anatomy and physiology of
pronunciation. I sat in a desk half-way up the steps on the left side of the classroom. Some students begged me before the exam, "please help us." I promised
to do so, if I could. Most of the pre-veterinary students sat near and around me.
Professor Lopez indicated that upon finishing the dictation all students should
stand and pass their drill sheets to the right, where he would collect them. Anyone
who did not do that would get a zero in orthography. The drill began. Professor
Lopez dictated: "catalizador, censura, cohabitar, halogeno, heterogeneo..." (cata-
lyst, censure, cohabitate, halogen, heterogeneous...). I wrote each word quickly,
and, at the same time, I whispered, respectively: "z, c-s, h, h-accent, h-g-accent..."
Those were the clues to correct spelling of each word. The pre-med students im-

mediately adjusted their ears to my wavelength. Somehow, the rumor of whispering reached Professor Lopez down there, at the stage. He immediately and very quietly climbed the room steps in hopes of catching the whisperer. Of course, I stopped when he got close. He continued to dictate. Some whispering began in front of the classroom. He then went back to the front and stood there till the end. The whispering resumed again in the steps.

When all the sheets had been picked up, Professor Lopez passed a blank sheet of paper to each student and wrote on the board two questions, one for column 1, and a different one for column 2. Those were the positions in each desk, left and right, respectively. My question (column 1) was, "Describe the anatomy and physiology for the pronunciation of the letter G." I did not have a clue. I had spent all my time studying spelling because it represented 70% of the grade. I figured passing spelling with a high mark should be sufficient to pass the course. All I knew about the pronunciation of letter G was that there were two main sounds, the hard sound like in gato (cat), and a soft sound like in gelatina (gelatin). But how the anatomical structures of the mouth and throat produce those sounds, not a clue. I just sat there calculating that, if I did well in the orthographic drill, I could pass the course. I also remembered very well the ominous threat that Professor Lopez had made at the beginning of the course, and that he gave me a failing mark on my perfect recitation of a sonnet. I was sitting on the left of the room next to a window. Then, I noticed a shadow outside, in the corridor, and below the window. A young fellow who kneeled under the window outside had a book. The premedical student in front of me, in column 1 also, threw a crumpled piece of paper out of the window. Only then I noticed that the window was open. The one outside picked up the paper and read the question. He then opened the book and began to whisper the answers to his pal inside. Ingenious, I thought. I caught his wavelength and filled the page with all the intricacies of the G pronunciation. The exams were collected and I went home hoping for the best. A week later, the grades were posted. Only two pre-veterinary students had passed the course. I had passed with a 75% grade, and one of my classmates, named Moreno, with a grade of 55%, the minimum passing grade. Twenty-eight pre-veterinary students had flunked! Many of them flunked during the time that I stopped whispering. About my passing the course with a good mark, I was delighted for two reasons, first, because Professor Lopez knew his math. He had allocated proper percentages to my grade, and, second, because he had not acted on his ominous threat of flunking all pre-veterinary students.

24. The Apprentice

Even though I had completed the pre-veterinary course with excellent grades, I decided to work the following year. I told my mother that I wanted to earn enough money to support myself and to help her with the household expenses too. She tried to dissuade me, but I was firm and 18 years old. She let me look for a job. With the recommendation of a former friend of my father, I started to work in a diesel engines repair shop on Argentina avenue. That shop specialized in the repair and maintenance of Caterpillar tractors. Thus, from April, 1951, to March 1952, I worked in that shop. I started as an apprentice, washing bolts and nuts for 12 soles a day. Each work week consisted of five and a half days. That meant 66 soles, weekly. I gave about half of my salary to Mother for house expenses and used the rest to purchase my own clothes, books, and entertainment: movies, soccer games, dating, etc. I was punctual at work and learned quickly. Soon I was assigned to the injectors and fuel pumps repair section under the direction of Mr. Reiter, an experienced mechanic. He taught me to clean injectors and pump boxes as well as to calibrate the sequence of fuel injectors according to data in a manual. Soon I became an expert on that job to the point that Mr. Reiter would let me do all the work and he just read the newspaper. Of course, he signed the reports that went along with each repair job so that the office would charge the labor hours to each client.

One morning, an older man and his son, about my age, visited the huge shop and stopped at various working stations. When they got to my station, I was testing and calibrating some fuel pumps. I made the special "T- wrench" spin to remove the nuts that held a pump in place onto the testing machine. Then, I replaced the next pump, adjusted the fuel output, and proceeded to the next pump, always spinning the T-wrench very quickly. The gentleman, in the meantime, when he thought I was not watching, would gently hit his son with his elbow or kick him softly on his shoe. Like saying to him, "Watch how a young man is supposed to work" A few minutes later, they said, "Thank you," and walked to another station. One afternoon, Mr. Reiter had an accident in the shop. He injured his right hand on a grinding wheel. He was taken to an emergency post and later was hospitalized in the American Clinic of Miraflores. The shop manager asked me if I could do the job while Mr. Reiter recovered. I said yes. He smiled and went to his office. A few days later, one of the mechanics had trouble starting the engine of a huge Caterpillar leveling machine. He told the manager that he suspected the fuel injector pump, which had been calibrated by our shop previously. The manager ordered the removal of the pump box and wrote a work order to me to check and/or recalibrate the pumps. I asked the mechanic what the serial number of the pump box was. He replied "9K." I had never seen that serial number before, so I commented that "9K does not exist." He then countered with: "Then I am stupid jerk." I smiled and went to the catalog that listed all fuel pump boxes and, sure enough, on the last page, there was a "9K." I told the mechanic that I had found it and that, simply, I had not done one before. I proceeded to work while he watched. That box had been calibrated by Mr. Reiter a few weeks earlier, and possibly he had used the wrong serial number to do so. When I finished the work, I turned over the box to the mechanic who immediately proceeded to install it on the leveling machine way out there on the yard. I followed him to see the testing of my work. The manager was there too. The engine started on the first attempt! Blue smoke came out of the exhaust. I was pleased. The mechanic came and shook my hand. The manager walked to his office without saying a word. Later, he called me to the office and told me that he was raising my salary from 12 soles to 14 soles per day. I thanked him and went back to my work station. I realized then that blue collar work was not for me and that I had to return to school and do well. I promised myself that.

25. Return to College

   After the awakening of 1951, I returned to college in April of 1952. I registered in the first year of Veterinary Medicine, one of the 12 colleges comprising the University of San Marcos. The college was located in Las Palmas, a district about one mile southeast of Barranco, which, in turn, was about 20 miles south of Lima. I had saved some money from my work the previous year. My mother had also saved too all the money I gave her during the year. She gave me the money I needed for registration, books, lab coats, bus fairs, dissecting instruments, thermometers, a stethoscope, etc. Everything was going as planned and well. It took about 45 minutes to go from my home to Barranco by city bus and, from there, a few minutes to Las Palmas on the Veterinary College bus. Every morning, I would get ready, have breakfast, and walked to the bus stop on Antonio Bazo street, at 7:00 a.m. At about 7:45 a.m., I would arrive at Barranco and walk three blocks to the main park, where I waited for the second bus. The school bus would then take all the waiting students to the College in time for the 8:00 a.m. classes. When I had to review material for an exam, I would get up earlier and arrive at Barranco at about 6:30 a.m. I would then go over all materials, in a last minute review, for the exam. It was a good tactic. I always got high marks on my exams. Remembering those days, later I would write:

                  Early morning, misty and cold,
                  Ride the bus, across town,
                  To the College, math exam,
                  Polynomials, trigs, and logs...
                  Thousand mornings, to Barranco,
                  Shiny street, briskly walk,
                  Two blocks straight, one right down,
                  To the park, City Hall...

                  Still early, precious silence,
                  Some sparrows are cavorting
                  By the fountain, where she waits,
                  Every morning, faithfully...

                  Marble statue, gentle beauty,
                  Magic, music, harmony,
                  From a bench, at a distance,
                  Contemplation, fascination, secret love...

                  Noisy students are arriving,
                  No more magic, no more silence,

Till tomorrow, dearest friend,
Polynomials, trigs, and logs...

That year we took courses like equine anatomy, animal husbandry, biochemistry, medical botany, genetics, histology, and a special pre-military cavalry course. Anatomy, biochemistry and histology had parallel laboratory courses. From the beginning, I liked the courses and specially the labs. At the same time, I enjoyed playing futsal (salon soccer) on a basketball court on the back of the yard behind the main building. Between classes and after classes we played soccer. We would then shower and go home. On Saturdays, we played after classes until 1:30 p.m. and, after showering, we would go to a restaurant on the Panamerican Highway to eat fried or grilled calamari and to have beers. Those were the best times, I thought. We organized the College soccer team that would participate in the inter-collegial tournaments. Some of my teammates, at that time, were Osorio, Ruiz, Cortez, Rivera, Sanchez, Sotelo, Tudela, Arteta, Quinones, Olmedo, Dominguez, Toledo, Duarte, Tevez, Vargas, Murillo, and Robles. We did very well in those tournaments despite the fact that ours was a small school of only about 150 students.

In December, the school year was over and I had passed all courses with excellent grades. My mother was pleased. That was the summer in which I worked as a house painter in the district of Magdalena. I also assisted my boss, Mr. Duarte, a construction contractor, with his accounting and payroll sheets. He worked on several construction sites under contract. He did not know math at all. I discovered soon that one of his close friends had systematically stolen 28 thousand soles from him. I showed the documents, the amounts, and the dates to Mr. Duarte and encouraged him to confront his friend. A few days later, the friend's wife, a handsome lady, very well dressed, came to the property, where, at the time, I was painting the railing on a balcony. While I worked, she introduced herself and asked me some questions like, "How long have you known Mr. Duarte?," "What are you studying in college?," "Would you like to work for me and my husband?." I answered politely to all her questions and said that my goal was to graduate as a DVM in three years and that I was only working during the summer to save some money for the next year. She seemed pleased and said good-bye. Later, when Mr. Duarte came, he informed me that his friend had admitted the discrepancy in the balance of his account, which according to him was due to an oversight, and promise to pay the difference. Mr. Duarte then said that I was not going to paint houses any more. I was going to keep his books and accompany him on Saturdays to get the money from the bank and assist him with the payroll at three construction sites. That very Saturday we withdrew 53,000 soles from the bank. He asked me to carry the briefcase containing the cash. I had never been responsible for so much money. We went in a taxi to the construction sites, where Mr. Duarte paid his employees. At each site, he had a foreman keeping records of hours worked by each worker. I quickly checked the math of hours times rates to arrive at the amounts to be paid each employee. We then went to have some lunch. After that, Mr. Duarte payed me for my services as an accountant and dismissed me. He had to go to purchase some construction materials. My love for mathematics had began to pay. I thanked then the memory of my father who, in life, had tried so hard to teach us basic math.

26. The Second Year

Classes began just fine at our college that year of 1953. I enjoyed the classes, the labs, and the soccer games. Life was wonderful in those days. In the second year, we took courses that were going to be the foundation of our professional careers. Animal physiology, general pathology, microbiology/immunology, and parasitology were the core courses. Each of them had four hours of laboratory work per week. It was hard work, but we were learning a lot and fast. We also took some complementary courses like special animal husbandry and principles of pharmacy. Aside from our intense academic activities, there were some memorable events that happened that year.

The first day of classes, Fernandez, one of my classmates, had brought to the school two yard-long live snakes from Ayacucho, a province in the sierras of Peru. He offered them to me if I wanted to keep them in a large glass jar covered with metallic screen. I asked him, "Are they poisonous?" He replied, "No, they are harmless." "What do you feed them?" I asked. He said, "Milk in a little dish." "How do you clean the jar?" He replied, "Transfer the snakes to a cardboard box once a week, wash and dry the jar and then return the creatures to the jar." I thought that was simple enough. I could take the snakes home, watch them for awhile to study their behavior, and later, when I got tired of them, I could give them to someone else. The creatures were beautiful. One was pitch black with a white diamond design all along its body. The other was gold with a diamond design in white color. I was very pleased with my acquisition. At home, my brothers and sisters were curious and asked many questions, which I answered like an expert. My mother, though, yelled at me and asked me to get those creatures out of the house immediately. I explained that the snakes were well secured, that they were harmless, and that I would assume full responsibility for them. Nothing doing said she. Tomorrow you will take them to wherever you got them from, period. No arguments.

The next day, I did not have an early class. Everybody in the house had gone to work or to their own schools. I went to get the snakes to take them to my college where I could return them to Fernandez. But there was a problem. The black snake was missing! I carefully examined the screen on top of the jar and found a small crack through which it had escaped. I had to find it right away. I looked everywhere without success. I began to worry. I took the jar to the roof of our building and secured the screen to prevent the escape of the gold snake. Later that day, I went to my class and when I returned home, I resumed the task of looking for the missing snake. At home, nobody asked anything. I guess they assumed that I had returned the snakes to their proper owner. But every time I had a chance, I continued to look for the black snake feverishly. Several days passed. I was worried that the snake could bite one of my brothers or sisters in the middle of the night. I thought also that perhaps the snake had escaped out of the house and that it was no longer with us. Then where? A neighbor's house? I continued to go and return from my classes as usual. One day, about a week after the disappearance, I came home early and I found our kitten, only six months old, wrestling with the black snake on the sofa in the living room. Immediately, I got a cardboard box, captured the snake, and placed it in the box. I placed the gold snake also in the box and secured the top. Immediately I took the bus to Barranco. My worries were over. I had been in a state of terror and suspense for one week. I never told the story to a soul till now. I thought to myself, "Thank heaven, for little kittens!"

Another incident occurred on the futsal court. Dr. Galvez, instructor of the pathology lab, had given us an assignment. We were to prepare blood smears from five animal species on microscope slides. He had given us the clean slides and recommended that we go to farms and take a drop of blood from chickens, goats, cows, rabbits, pigs, turkeys, cats, or dogs. On the surface the task seemed simple. But obtaining the blood and a permission from the owners to do the bleeding by puncturing an ear or a wing is not so easy. A few weeks later, the instructor reduced his request to two smears instead of five. Most of us had at least one smear by then. Most had a smear from a cat or a dog. Some students had acted in groups: one dog, seventeen smears. But the second smear was hard to get. One day, while playing soccer, one of the players got a nosebleed. Immediately, someone, perhaps it was me, yelled, "Pig's blood," and we ran to get the slides and proceeded to make the smears right there by the side of the field. One "pig," twelve smears. Then someone asked, "What if Dr. Galvez discovers it is not pig's blood?" I answered, "There is not a way to tell by microscopy, go ahead." And that was how we completed the assignment.

27. The Exterminator

In the Lima of 1952, we did not have companies like Orkin or exterminators that come once or twice a year to homes to fumigate and take care of insect pests. In those days, the families themselves purchased petroleum or kerosene to mop the floors with, once or twice a year, to control fleas, roaches, and other pests. That year, on a Saturday afternoon, a friend and a teammate on the neighborhood soccer team, Luis Otero, invited me to visit his place of work on Avenida Argentina, near the Caterpillar shop where I had worked the previous year. We took the bus to his place of work. He was proud to show me the main office and told me that he was now assistant manager of this branch of the company, Massey Harris, an importer of tractors for use in agriculture as well as an importer of crop pesticides. He then walked with me through a huge pavilion where there were thousands of bags containing toxaphene, one of the crop pesticides that is spread from small airplanes on cotton and corn fields. The floor area of that pavilion was about that of two football fields. Some workers, wearing dust masks, were loading a truck with those bags of toxaphene. I asked Luis if that pesticide could be used on any kind of insects. He replied, "Certainly." Then I asked him if I could take a sample and try it on some roaches I had noticed in my kitchen. He said, "Sure, here, take some." He handed me an envelope. I took about 4 ounces from an open bag. Then

I remarked that the workers were wearing dust masks. I asked Luis about us wearing a mask. He said, "If you are going to work many hours in this pavilion, you should." After that, we returned home. That evening, I spread some toxaphene powder under the stove in kitchen and some under my bed to possibly prevent a flea infestation. I had noticed that our kitten had some fleas. Two days later, I found several roaches and one mouse dead under the stove. The dead mouse had a drop of coagulated blood on his nose. I disposed of them.

The following week, I was playing soccer on the court with other students. Suddenly I felt something in my throat. I went to the side of the court and spat. For an instant, I saw that it was a small blood clot. Nobody noticed it. As a precaution, I slowed down my rhythm of play. Later, in the bathroom, I spat another blood clot. At the time I did not relate that to the aspiration of toxaphene. Inasmuch as the episode did not repeat, I threw it completely out of my mind. A month later, the students in my class were given an appointment for a full physical and medical exam that included a chest radiograph, as well as blood and urine lab work. Two weeks later, I was given an appointment to see Dr. Pando, a radiologist at the university's medical department. I took the bus in Barranco toward the university park. I arrived at about 12:55 p.m. My appointment was at 1 p.m. I had barely 15 minutes to turn around and return in time for my afternoon classes at 2 p.m. I went to radiology and saw Dr. Pando talking to another doctor inside the radiology lab. I interrupted, "Good afternoon, doctor, I have an appointment..." Dr. Pando asked me to wait outside. I sat on a bench and waited. Ten minutes later, I decided that I could not wait any longer, so I left toward the exit. As I walked down the hall, Dr. Pando came walking fast behind me and took my arm. "Why are you leaving?" he asked me. I said, "It is obvious that you are too busy to see me. I was going to call later, for another appointment. I need to leave right now in order to arrive on time to my 2:00 p.m. class in Las Palmas." At that point, I swiftly got loose from his grip on my arm and walked away. He let me go. I did get to my class on time. Two days later, one of the college secretaries brought me a note from Dr. Pando asking me to report to the office of Dr. Rodolfo Mayer, whose address was on Avenida Larco, Miraflores.

28. Psychological Evaluation

Dr. Mayer's office was very elegant. Beautiful leather furniture. Carpets, glass art pieces on wooden stands on the office corners. Paintings on the walls. A beautiful receptionist asked me to sit and wait. A few minutes later, Dr. Mayer came in and sat in front of me. He was a distinguished gentleman of fair complexion and dark brown hair. He was about 45 years old. He asked me a number of questions. Why I had chosen a career in veterinary medicine, what was my daily schedule, did I enjoy my classes, what sports did I practice, was I good at them, did I work on vacations, did I have girlfriends, what subjects did I like the most, had I read any books aside from those in my chosen profession, what was my relationship with other students, with other members of my family, etc. I responded to all his question categorically. He then stood up and told me that I could leave and go home and that he would write a good report to Dr. Pando. I asked him if he was going to examine me or take another radiograph. He laughed and said that he was not that kind of a doctor. It was then that I realized that he had examined me for a mental condition. That had been a psychological evaluation. Undoubtedly, Dr. Pando had ordered the evaluation because of my reaction when I came to his office and would not wait more than ten minutes. Soon after, I met again with Dr. Pando, who explained to me that I had tuberculosis (TB) and that I needed to be admitted to the hospital for proper treatment. He also mentioned that he had received a report of my evaluation from Dr. Mayer indicating that I was psychologically normal and of superior intelligence. I came out of his office devastated. All my dreams had been shattered in the last two weeks. I did not relate the diagnosis to my inhaling of toxaphene then. In the meantime, Dr. Pando had learned that I had an older brother studying medicine. He got in touch with my brother Daniel and told him that he had already made all the arrangements necessary for my admission to hospital "2 de Mayo," an institution for male patients, and that I had to report to admissions the following Monday at 8:00 a.m. Later, my brother said that he would accompany me to admissions. I thanked him. At that point, I stopped attending classes and dribbling the soccer ball. Later, I would recall:

Some years later, Marcus had found,
An explanation, for his nightmare,
Before his illness, suffered exposure,
To deadly poison, called toxaphene...

29. The Hospital

My admission to hospital "2 de Mayo," Saint Rose's ward, went well. I was assigned to bed 19 on the second floor. The ward had a capacity of 96 beds, 48 upstairs and 48 downstairs. Across the gardens, there was another building also for TB patients. That was Saint Camilo's ward, which had a capacity for another 48 patients. Criminals and other delinquents, who were ill, were brought to St. Camilo under heavy guard.

At St. Rose's, I was informed of the daily routine and of the need to obey all the rules. The manager of the ward was Sister Cecilia, a flying nun; male nurses were Mr. Robles and Mr. Denegri. Physicians in charge were Dr. Perez, a radiologist, and Dr. Villalta, a surgeon. When, upon admission, the doctors saw me, Dr. Villalta commented "This one does not look like a TB patient, he looks like an athlete." "Yes," replied Dr. Perez, but look at this, and he placed my chest radiograph on the viewing box and pointed at some spots. The schedule at St. Rose's was like this: breakfast was at 7:00 a.m. That was followed by one hour of rest on cots on the balcony. Doctors' visits were 9:00 to 10:30 a.m. Lunch was at 11:00 a.m., followed by rest in bed. At 3:00 p.m., patients could get up and play checkers in the dining room, rest on the balcony, or receive visitors in the gardens that surrounded the building. On Sundays, for those who had no visitors, Sister Cecilia turned on the 13-inch black and white TV set mounted high on a wall in the dining room. We could watch some soccer games live from the national stadium. Supper was at 5:00 p.m. At mealtimes, Sister Cecilia led the praying while all stood around the marble tables. At 6:00 p.m., all went to bed. At about 7 p.m., Sister Cecilia would walk the ward's two floors jingling her keys to warn patients of her coming and making sure that all were quiet in bed. At that time, the lights were turned off. A night watchman slept on a cot by the entrance on the second floor. He could be awakened by any patient to report an emergency. Many patients were in very poor condition and could not follow the schedule. They stayed in bed most of the time. Some died during the night. In the morning, they were carried to the hospital morgue on a stretcher covered with a white sheet. When a patient died, the bed was disinfected and quickly readied for a new customer. At that time, Lima was second to only Manila in world tuberculosis incidence. It was a privilege to be admitted to the hospital. There were many thousands outside, in the large city, walking the streets, hoping and waiting for a bed. My memory of those days went like this:

> A city park, one block around,
> A water fountain, geraniums' scent,
> A hero's bust, sidewalks and lawns,
> Children pass by, in uniform...

> Men's hospital for indigents,
> Government run, an iron fence,
> The bed is free, x-rays are not,
> Connections needed, for admission...

Sister Cecilia favored patients who attended mass services at the Chapel on Sundays and those who went to confession on Saturdays and had communion on Sundays. She would pay for the monthly radiographs of those patients at 24 soles each. I was not one of the favorites. Fortunately, my brother Daniel came up with the money for the radiographs every month.

Our building was a solid two-story one made of concrete and steel with strong railings on the balconies. The floors were made of high-quality tiles. Some employees kept those floors clean and shining all the time. The partitions on the floors were solid walls covered with white ceramic tiles, also kept perfectly clean. One day, while we rested on our cots on the balcony, an employee who was constantly mopping the floors, was verbally offended by patient 13, who was resting some six cots from mine. I did not hear the what patient 13 had said. The employee went toward patient 13, grabbed him by the pyjama jacket and dragged him to the floor. He then kicked him on the face and went away. The next day, patient 13 had his face black and blue. The employee came to me and asked me to testify in his favor. He asked me to say that patient 13 had attacked him first. I told him that I would not lie for him. He left. Later that morning, Sister Cecilia came to talk to me. She said that the employee had named me as his witness. I said that I did not know anything about the conflict. That I only saw the employee go to patient 13 and attacked him while he rested on his cot. I saw the employee kick patient 13 on the face. Sister Cecilia left. The employee was fired from his job.

Doctors decided when some patients were to be subjected to thoracoplasty, a surgical procedure in which segments of three of four ribs were removed in the front to open a window into the thoracic cavity while the patient was connected to a pump that forced air into his lungs rhythmically. The surgeons would then either removed the affected area of the lung or compress it with a number of sterilized ping pong balls. It was a mutilating experience. I saw patients recover very slowly and remained crippled for life. One day, about one hour after one of those operations, the patient expired. From the balcony, accidentally, I saw Dr. Villalta in the garden, leaning against the wall and crying like a child upon receiving the news. Years later, I would write the following:

> Five in the morn, call of the doves,
> Some flying nuns, jingling key chains,
> Hundreds of workers, come to their jobs,
> To care for patients, hear their pains...
>
> Outside the walls, many outpatients,
> Stand in line and wait with patience,
> To see a student, pay fifty cents,
> They wait and wait, and wait in silence...

On my second day at the hospital, doctors prescribed injections of streptomycin. The first injection was given to me at about 10 a.m. That night, I had a bad reaction to the streptomycin. At about midnight, I awoke with very high fever and was delirious. I thought I was seeing an animal moving under my bed cover. Then, I lost consciousness. Later, when I woke up again, I was in the bathroom drinking cold water from the faucet. I do not recall having gotten up and having walked to the bathroom some 40 yards away. I went back to my bed. One hour later, I woke up with a hemoptysis–the spitting blood from my lungs. I turned over onto my stomach and took a spitting cup from my night table and let the blood collect in it. In that position, the blood does not block the glottis and you do not drown in your own blood. Then, I heard someone yell: "Huayco!" (Avalanche!). That was a slang term for hemoptysis. Several patients had gotten up and had come to watch me. It was then that my rebellious spirit took over. I thought, "These guys have come over to see me die. To see a show for free. Well, I will not die. I will run out of blood first!" In about two minutes, the blood stopped and, slowly, I leaned backwards and rested. The audience went away disappointed. Nobody said anything in the morning. Apparently, the toxaphene inhalation had caused severe lesions in my lungs. Lesions that resembled TB lesions. But I did not know that then.

The subsequent injections of streptomycin did not cause a reaction. Go figure! From there on, my recovery was quick, I thought, but the monthly radiographs did not show healing. For me, that was a disappointment. Later, the doctors tried pneumothorax on me. That procedure consists of injecting sterile air into the pleural cavity of the affected lung. The bubble of air compresses the affected part and favors fibrosis, the healing of the TB lesions. That procedure caused a reaction in me. A pocket of fluid appeared between the apical lobe and the middle lobe of my right lung. Doctors then used a needle to extract the fluid. It was a yellowish, clear fluid. The fluid was sent to a mycrobiology lab to search for the TB germs, *Mycobacterium tuberculosis*. The lab result was negative. No TB germs. A week later, the pocket of fluid had appeared again. That was frustrating for me and for the doctors. Another puncture, another sample, again negative to TB germs. Finally, one day, the doctors decided to order a new drug named Neoteben, from Germany. The drug arrived a month later. Then, doctors removed the fluid and through the same needle injected the German drug. Success! The fluid never reappeared again. Then the doctors sent a sample of my sputum to a lab for inoculation in guinea pigs. That was the ultimate test to find the *Mycobacterium tuberculosis*. Four weeks later, the result came: Negative. No TB germs present in my sputum.

30. Thoracoplasty

Because the radiographs continued to be positive, the doctors decided to operate on me. When Dr. Villalta told me about the surgery, I responded that I was grateful for everything they had done for me, but that I was going to be buried with all my ribs intact. No operations on me. And I challenged them to dismiss me from the hospital. Then, Dr. Perez called my brother Daniel and asked him to convince me that the operation was absolutely necessary. The "Semigods" had spoken! My brother Daniel came and talked to me for over one hour one evening before the lights went out. I was unrelenting. I told him that I was ready to go and live in the streets if they dismissed me from the hospital because of my refusal of surgery. He conveyed my stubbornness to Drs. Perez and Villalta.

A couple of days later, Dr. Perez ordered a tomogram of my right apical lobe. That was a radiographic procedure that took sectional radiographs of the lung so that they could see the lung in three dimensions. Two days later, my brother Daniel came and took me in a taxi to the air force hospital where they had a tomographic machine. I remember that the technologist who positioned me under the tomograph, a good looking red hair woman, about thirty years old, smelled like a heavy smoker. So much for attractiveness, I thought. After the procedure, Daniel invited me to have something to eat. We stopped near the national stadium and entered a small restaurant on 28 of July Avenue. The music being played on the speakers was "Blue Tango." I never forgot that. When the doctors displayed the tomogram films on the viewing box, they could not see a lesion. The apical lobe looked perfectly clean. It was a miracle, they said. And they had planned to do a thoracoplasty on me! I am sure they wondered how right I had been when I had refused the surgery. The next morning, they told me that I was cured and that I was being discharged from the hospital that very day after fifteen months of seclusion. The nightmare was over. I took my few belongings in a handbag and took a taxi home. I knocked on the door. Daniel opened the door. I told him: I am cured. They discharged me this noon. We hugged and then sat down to talk about the tomography and the guinea pig test. Both negative. Remembering this events, years later, I would write:

> When he refused thoracoplasty,
> Doctors prescribed tomography,

Could not believe it! Was negative!

One of the few, Marcus will live...

Over the years, the mystery of my positive monthly radiographs made me think a lot. They reminded me of the movie "The China Syndrome." In the movie, some radiographs were copied over and over to make the nuclear power plant look safe. Now, for the kicker. Were my monthly radiographs copied to show no improvement and thus force the doctors to operate on me? Otherwise, how could we explain the negative tomograph?

There are some anecdotes dealing with the patients I met at the hospital. Some memorable personalities. For example, "Violin" was a young fellow, about seventeen, who had a bed on the first floor. He was called "Violin" because he was so thin. He was in poor condition and remained curled in bed most of the time. But sometimes he felt good, got up, and walked the ward aisles slowly, smiling, making jokes, and greeting everybody. I admired his spirit at a time when he and everybody else knew that he was dying. He had been declared terminally ill, incurable. One night he passed away. We all said a prayer for "Violin" that night. Among the patients, the rumor was that Violin was given the "orange injection" during the night and fell asleep forever. One patient swore that he had seen the night watchman, who was a male nurse, give the orange shot to other terminal patients who had died overnight. I prefer not to believe in rumors. But if that was true, those were cases of active euthanasia.

Another patient was an elderly man. He had gray hair, was short and thin and walked slowly, almost dragging his feet. He loved to tell stories. He would come and tell us that he had seen a suspicious man in the garden and that he had followed him at a distance just to see what that fellow was up to. He would then tell us that he had lost the suspicious fellow in the crowd of the chapel. From there on we called the old man "el detective" (the sleuth). He could make a mystery out of nothing. He was always following suspects and telling us about it.

One night, patient 26 woke me up at about 2 a.m. He told me that patient 25, a truck driver, was dying, choking because he could not breath. He asked me to go to see him. I went and realized the man was completely asleep and choking. I tried to wake him up without success. He was drowning in his own bronchial secretion. I asked two fellows to turn him over onto his stomach and to hold him with his head down below the side of the bed. Then, with my fingers, I pulled as much mucus as I could from his mouth. Then I climbed over his back and applied pressure on his ribs to expel more mucus and to clear his trachea and glottis. The man began to breathe while still asleep. We left him in his bed. Apparently, the crisis had passed. A few minutes later, Sister Cecilia came with a priest, who administered the man his last rites. Later, at about 4 a.m., patient 26 came again to tell me that patient 25 was again in crisis. I went and repeated the procedure of clearing his airways. He recovered. In the morning, he woke up and went to breakfast. He was told of what had happened during the night. He said that he did not remember a thing. That afternoon he came to my area to thank me for saving his life twice. As it turned out, the man had been very upset about having to cough so much during the night and bothering other patients. Because of that, he had taken a high dose of sleeping pills. He had passed out and could not wake up to clear his airways by coughing and expectoration.

When Sister Cecilia was told of my rescuing operations during the night, she was not pleased. After all, she had gone to a lot of trouble to have the man receive his last rites. Besides, they needed the bed for a new customer. During the following days, the truck driver came to the side of my bed, every afternoon, to tell me stories about driving his truck up the sierras carrying heavy cargo, over gravel roads, crossing bridges over rivers and canyons, along deep cliffs, etc. I listened with interest. But one day he went away. I never saw him again. He was perhaps released or something. That happened quite often in those days. People came and went quietly, with no explanation.

One warm afternoon I was walking by the garden behind our building. There were decorative plants with colorful flowers. One of the plants caught my attention. I had seen that plant before. Then I remembered, it was in my old book on "Natural History," the one I bought in a flea market many years earlier (Story 11). I did not have the book anymore, but I remembered the picture of the poppy flower plant with its characteristic bulbs. I knew that the bulbs popped, one at a time, and a flower opened up instantly each time. Carefully, I cut four bulbs with a foot long stem each. I brought them to my place and put them in a flower vase with water on my night table. Then I sat on my bed and waited for any to pop up. After about thirty minutes, I got tired and quit. It was time for supper anyway. When I returned, one bulb had popped! A beautiful purple flower occupied its place. I watched for a long time waiting to catch another one to pop. No dice. I decided to read for a while. That evening, at 7:00 p.m., the lights were turned off. Next morning, one flower, three bulbs. After breakfast, I came to my station, a red flower had popped out of its bulb in my absence. Then, I decided, "What will be, will be." If I am lucky, I will catch the popping of one of the two bulbs left. If not, that is OK too. In the following days the other two bulbs popped always in my absence. A bluish flower and a red flower had appeared in their places. Perhaps the flowers were too shy to show themselves at the moment of birth.

Sister Cecilia had a favorite patient named Roberto. He was a fifteen year old who came from a prominent family and suffered from scoliosis, a lateral deformation of the spine. One afternoon, Sister Cecilia brought a large box to the dining room during play time and gave it to Roberto for his use. I could read on the box in big letters the word "Meccano." I then realized that it was one of those sets of metallic parts that you can use to build things. I had never had a chance to play with one of those in my whole life. I decided then to help Roberto with his meccano playing. I took over, really. Using the manual, soon we had assembled a model of the Eiffel Tower with an elevator even. Sister Cecilia was pleased because nobody had been able to use the set before. We placed the tower on my window sill. During the morning visit, Drs. Perez and Villalta admired the contraption. The next day, we decided to disassemble the tower and assemble the Golden Gate bridge. It came out great. And it fit perfectly on my window sill. The doctors were pleased. One day Roberto decided to return the set to Sister Cecilia, and that was it. We never saw the set again.

Pablo Esquivel was a 17-year-old boy who became my friend. He was patient 30. His bed was on the other side of the partition from mine. He was always asking me to tell him stories of my soccer games, and I usually obliged. Every evening, a young man would walk the aisles of our building announcing in loud voice "La Cronica," the fifty-cents evening paper. Pablo always bought the paper to read in bed before the lights went out. He would then toss it over the partition for me to read. It never failed, on the page before last, along with the announcements of movies and movie theaters, usually a large photo of a movie actress in a bathing suit appeared on the right side. Pablo was an artist. He would carefully use a pencil and an eraser to remove the bathing suit. That way, I saw Marilyn Monroe in the raw a few times.

Reporter Judy Hartfeldt: "You really had some endearing stories to tell."
Marco Donnatti: "There are more to come. Stay tunned to this channel."
Judy: "I will. In our next session, I would like to hear about your adventures in college soccer and about your graduation from college."
Marco: "Certainly. I will put something together. Arrivederci"
Judy: "Arrive... Whatever!"

Macchu Picchu, the unforgettable Lost City of the Incas (Story 33)

CHAPTER 4

THE SECOND COMING

Reporter Judy Hartfeldt: After your nightmare as a student, you had some difficult decisions to make, I am sure.
Marco Donnatti: Yes. But my experiences of 1951, 1953 and 1954, had clearly demonstrated that I had to return to college and to do the last three years
uninterruptedly.
Judy: OK, tell me what happened.

---

31. Repeating the Second Year

Because of my illness, the years of 1953 and 1954 were lost to me. When I returned, I asked Dr. Canepa, secretary of the college, what I needed to do to be rein-
stated. He told me that, because my attendance in the second year had been better
than 70%, I could request to take the second-year exams, pass them, and advance
to the third year. I replied that I was not prepared to take the exams, and, rather
than do poorly, I preferred to repeat the second year and take advantage of the updated second year curriculum that was starting that very year of 1955. As a matter
of fact, that year Dr. Velarde was teaching a new course in Animal Physiology. He
had just returned from Cornell University, where he had trained under the famous
mammalian physiologist Dr. Dukes. Similarly, Dr. Morales had returned from
Cornell also and was starting a new course in Microbiology and Immunology.
Further, Dr. Diaz had returned from advanced training in Parasitology in Sao
Paulo, Brazil, and was starting a new course also. I figured that taking advantage
of those three new courses would make me a better professional.

And so, the new second year began. It was relatively easy for me to study and
to get high marks right from the beginning. After all, I was repeating the second
year. I knew that later in the year things were not going to be so easy, but by then,
I would have had a good momentum, and my success would be guaranteed. I
greatly enjoyed our four-hour animal physiology lab sessions under the direction
of Dr. Velarde. In those sessions, we worked in groups of six students with specific responsibilities. We performed experimental surgery on anesthetized dogs.
We used a solution of pentobarbital sodium, intravenously, as anesthetic. We also
cannulated the carotid artery to record the changes in arterial pressure on smoked

drums that rotated at a constant speed. That way, we did two or three lab experiments on each animal system: the heart and the circulatory system, the respiratory, the digestive, and the urinary systems. I discovered then that I had "the touch" needed for animal surgery. My group of students always finished first the whole lab protocol. For that reason, the other students called us "the Russians." In those days, physiologists in Russia had reported outstanding animal experiments which had appeared in the newspapers. We also enjoyed the lab sessions in bacteriology under Dr. Portello. It was fun to learn to prepare culture media, use the autoclave as a means of sterilization, planting and replanting of bacteria on petri dishes, staining bacteria with various types of stains, culturing viruses in chicken embryos, and doing serological studies, antigen-antibody reactions. Dr. Diaz taught us the new methods of diagnosis for internal and external parasites along with their life cycles. I shall never forget that year. Really, it changed our lives.

Coming to the end of the year, Dr. Inclan, Professor of Animal Anatomy, told us that on the final exams he was going to test us on the book Anatomy of the Horse by Sisson–specifically the chapters on the digestive, urinary, and endocrine systems. I went to the library to borrow a copy of Sisson's book. The librarian, Mr. Solorzano, told me that all 17 copies of the book had been loaned to other students already. My classmates had beaten me to them. He suggested that I join one of them to study. I was not sure that would work because my style of studying was different, I thought. He then told me that he had a copy of the book, but in English. I said: "OK, I'll take it. At least I can look at the pictures." When I got home with the book, I began to look at pictures and tried to read the captions. To my surprise, I could read them and understand them. Then I proceeded to read the chapter on the digestive system and to translate some of it. Slowly, I began to make progress. Unwittingly, I had discovered that I could read technical English. But progress was too slow. The exam was only nine days away. I called on one of my classmates who, I knew, had a book from the library. I asked him if he could lend me the book for a couple of days. He said, "No way. I need it badly. My first exam was not very good. I need to raise my average if I can." Then he added, "I let you have it tonight, but you have to bring it to me tomorrow by 8:00 a.m. I said, "I will, thank you." I took the book and went to see my brother Daniel. I explained the situation. He said that when he studied Human Anatomy for an exam, he and his classmates had used an stimulant called amphetamine to stay awake all night and cram for the exam. He then pulled one tablet of amphetamine from a little box in his desk and gave it to me. He said that he would not give me more because he did not want to risk an overdose. I thought, that was very smart. I went to study and swallow the tablet with some water. It was like magic, 11 p.m., 12 midnight, 1 a.m., etc., no somnolence at all. I did prepare outlines of all key sections of the chapters required and returned the book at 8:00 a.m. When I recovered from the effects of the tablet, I rested well and began to review the summaries I had prepared from the book. Quickly, I went through all the chapters. The next day I did it again. Soon I realized that I knew all the material very well, and the exam was still five days away. Thus one afternoon I took a break; I went to play soccer at a park of the neighborhood of El Porvenir (the future). I was playing with fury and sweating hard when I heard my name called. Three of my classmates were walking by and decided to stop when they saw me among the players. One of them, told me, "And this is how you study for the anatomy exam?" I responded that I already knew the material. They laughed. They did not believe me. But, on the other hand, I knew that they could not understand how it was possible that I could get high grades playing soccer in the park.

The day of the exam came. Dr. Inclan gave us twenty printed questions on a sheet of paper and some blank sheets to answer them. Three days later the grades were posted. I had 19 correct answers out of 20, or 95%, the highest mark in the class!

32. The Farm at La Raya

Our college, working under contract with the Peruvian government, Department of Agriculture and Livestock, had began to study the anatomy and physiology, as well as illnesses of, the Peruvian camelids (llamas, alpacas, vicunas, and guanacos). The work was conducted by professors of our college during the summer months of vacation. That year two groups were planning to go to La Raya, a government farm for alpacas situated at about 15,300 feet of altitude at the border between the departments of Cuzco and Puno. That is about 3 times the altitude of Denver! The first group, under the direction of Dr. Velarde, was planning to study some blood chemistry of alpacas: the plasma proteins and the chloride concentration in the blood, among others. The second group, directed by Dr. Morales, was going to study the bacteriology of infections in adult alpacas and the causes of death by overnight pneumonia in tuis (too'is, baby alpacas). Dr, Velarde invited me to join the expedition as an assistant, all expenses paid. I accepted immediately. Each professor had a team of four students. The third year students were working on their thesis research. In January 1956, during summer vacation, the members of the expedition prepared and packed all that was needed (instruments, glassware, chemical reagents) to install two laboratories high in the mountains. One to do blood chemistry and another to do microbiology. Early in January, we traveled from Lima to Cuzco (11,400 feet) by plane and from there to La Raya by train. Agronomist Mr. Olave, director of the farm, was at the station to see us arrive and to take us to the farm on a pick up truck. At the farm, there were also some agronomy students learning the husbandry and administration of alpaca farms. From the farm, we could not help but admire the impressive Auzangate peak (20, 930 feet), whose top was covered by ice that never melted.

Upon arrival, we all began to feel the effects of hypoxia, the thin air, at the high altitude. The palm of my hands looked like a checker board with clear and blue patches. My breathing was shallow and fast. I felt dizzy, as if I was going to faint. Mr. Olave ordered some coca tea from the kitchen which we took as a stimulant, and then he sent us to bed. It was about 4 p.m. The student beds were in a pavilion at about 70 yards from the main house. I took a good nap. At 6:00 p.m. we were awakened and asked to come to the house for dinner. During dinner, plans for the work were discussed. The following morning we began to unpack the crates and to install the laboratories. Adaptation to the high altitude takes time. During the first week, I had a nose bleed every morning. I kept it to myself and said nothing. Each time, I managed to stop the bleeding and continued my work. We went every morning to the fields to take blood samples, from the jugular vein of various groups of alpacas. Some samples were taken with anticoagulant to obtain plasma by centrifugation, and others without it to obtain serum. We returned to the labs at about 10 a.m. Then the analytical procedures began and continued all day and into the night.

Gradually, I began to feel better adapted. On a Sunday, ten days after our arrival, I played soccer at 15,300 feet. But I could only run one minute and rest five, and then repeat the cycle. But I did managed to score three goals. Later that summer, on a Sunday night, after dinner, the leaders, Mr. Olave, Dr, Velarde, and Dr. Morales, had the brilliant idea of preparing a cocktail and playing drinking games. Dr. Morales went to his lab and brought a gallon of alcohol. Mr. Olave provided the concentrated coffee and the orange peals. They mixed about half a gallon of alcohol with some dark coffee in a deep laboratory tray. Then, they added the orange peals and lit a match to the potion. Mr. Olave, blew the flames quickly and declared the liquor ready. He then designated himself to be the judge who penalized those who committed errors during the "Seven's Game." The game consisted in going around the table calling the ordinary numbers 1, 2, 3, etc., For number 7, multiples of 7, and numbers ending in 7, the player had to clap instead of calling the name, and then the direction was reversed. Any one that delayed the rhythm or made a mistake would have to take a penalty: to drink a shot of the potion! Let the games begin, said the director of the farm. Drs. Morales and Velarde grinned. There were about 15 people around the table. My good friend Lucho Pando, a senior student, excused himself from the game and went to get his first aid kit. "Someone may need it," he said. The game began, and soon some had to take penalties. I concentrated my attention and did not make mistakes. After one hour, two players had been pulled from the table, sick. Lucho Pando gave them a shot of coramine, a cardiotonic, and took them to bed. Mr. Olave, called everybody's attention to the fact that "Marco has not missed even once, and therefore, upon consensus of the crowd, he must take a penalty," he said, and placed a shot of the coffee-alcohol potion in front of me. I drank it. Everybody yelled and applauded. The game continued. Another hour passed. Two more students were removed from the table, got their shot of coramine from Lucho Pando and were taken to bed. Again, Mr. Olave stopped the game and asked that I take another penalty for "not missing during the second hour." I did. By then it was about 11 p.m. The game broke up, but drinking and chatting in loud voices continued in small groups. I believe, I took two more shots of the potion. At about midnight, everybody decided to go to bed. I remember feeling drunk. I walked out of the house. The outside lights had been turned on so that the survivors could find the pavilion and their beds. It was raining cats and dogs, but I did not care. I walked through the water puddles, splashing water and mud with my shoes. I arrived at the pavilion. My bed was the last one at the end. I sat on the bed and tried to undress myself. I could not do it. My head was pounding hard with the rhythm of my pulse. I laid on the bed for a while. My head kept pounding, pounding, hard. I could not stand it any more. I wanted to put an end to that pounding. Then, I remembered that in the pavilion, on one of the window sills there was a Mauser rifle. I wanted to shoot myself in the head and end the pounding. I tried to get up. I do not remember anymore. I had passed out. It was Sunday midnight in the high sierras of Peru.

I woke up Tuesday afternoon at about 4 p.m. In front of me was my friend Lucho Pando. He smiled and said, "Welcome back." I told him that I was hungry. He said, "Stay put. I just saw two ducks on the lacune outside, I'll be right back." A few minutes later, I heard two shots, in a sequence. Lucho then walked into the room and showed me the ducks. He said, "I'll have them prepared for dinner," and left. Later, I was told that Monday morning everybody had been looking for me around the farm fields. That my bed looked like I had not slept in it. That later, about noon, someone happened to look behind the bed and found me lying between the bed and the wall. I was alive, unconscious, and burning with fever. The diagnosis was acute pneumonia. Lucho had then given me coramine and antibiotic shots every four hours since. That I had been unconscious all day Monday and most of Tuesday. Tuesday evening I went to dinner with the rest of the players of the game. Everybody was cordial and amiable. The roasted duck was great. "Thanks Lucho," I said. My recovery had begun. The next day, it was time to pack for the return to Lima. In retrospect, I think the leaders of the expedition had exercised very poor judgement when they decided to play that drinking game. I am sure that they were praying that I would not die. The consequences could have been catastrophic for their careers. Lucho Pando saved my life that Monday with his kit of medications and antibiotics. Secretly though, I promised myself never to have more than two drinks at any future social event no matter how hard the peer pressure might be. I would honor that promise for the rest of my life. Nobody would ever see me drunk.

33. Macchu Picchu and Yucay

On the way back from our expedition to La Raya, Dr. Velarde and team took some days off in Cuzco. Dr. Velarde hired a truck with a driver to take us to Macchu Picchu and later to Yucay, where he was planning to visit some relatives. We arrived at the famous great ruins, made of solid granite on top of a mountain that looks like a truncated cone. The cone is connected by a saddle ridge to a taller cone: Huayna Picchu (Fig. 4). We toured the temples, terraces, passageways, innumerable stairs, trapezoidal gates and windows and, of course, "Intiwatana," the Inca sundial. We marveled at the location and type of construction of perfectly fitted boulders and stones. The cliffs on all sides of the cone and the river Urubamba circling the base of the cone. I was enchanted. It was my first visit to Macchu Picchu. I did not know it then, but I was going to return to it three times with other members of my family during my long life. I am pleased I did. We then continued our travel, on the truck, toward Yucay, passing through the town of Quillabamba. We arrived at that town a little late, at about 6:30 p.m. It was already dark, and the straight streets and perfect squared blocks of Quillabamba were already illuminated by artificial lights. Dr. Velarde decided that we should stay there that night and continue the trip in the morning. Our group of students found a small restaurant where we could eat some sandwiches and drink sodas. When we came out of the restaurant, it was raining very hard. We asked about possible lodging. There were only two small hotels and two small inns in town, but they were totally occupied. In the rain, we went to the church and knocked hard. A voice of a man answered from inside, "Who are you? What do you want?" I responded, "We are university students from Lima, there are no rooms available in town, we would like to have a place out of the rain to rest on the floor." Then the person on the other side of the door yelled, "Go somewhere else, this is the house of God." So much for "giving shelter to pilgrims," I thought.

The rain had slowed down somewhat. We were very tired. Finally, four of us students, decided to sit in front of any house entrance. I lay down on the stepping stone at the door of a house, with my legs folded. I covered my eyes and tried to sleep. I did sleep, but only a half hour. I woke up with the rain falling hard on my face. Then I saw a bus parked across the street. I called my classmates, sitting on the three of four doors nearby, and told them: "Let's go to sleep in that bus." We went and managed to open the door and lay down on the seats. Two hours later, the bus driver came and threw us out. By then, it was about 4:30 a.m. It had stopped raining. We went to a water fountain, situated in the middle of the main street, and washed ourselves. It had been a terrible night. We then looked for a place to have some coffee and some bread rolls with butter. At about 7:30 a.m., our truck driver came and the whole group started the ride to Yucay. We arrived at about 10:30 a.m. We got off at the main square and noticed some signs announcing a soccer game. I did not pay much attention. Dr. Velarde told us that we were visiting his uncle Mr. Rocaforte, mayor of Yucay. The town was situated next to many Inca terraces that were still being used to grow crops. The crops that I had a chance to taste were the large grain white corn and the most delicious peaches. While walking the town, I ran across Rivera, a student from our college in Lima who played soccer too. He was going to play for Cienciano, a well known first-division team from Cuzco, and invited me to join them. I accepted the invitation. At that moment, I did not realize that Cienciano was playing Yucay, the team of our host, Mayor Rocaforte. Later, I felt bad about having accepted an invitation to play against Yucay. At about 1:00 p.m., the Mayor, his family, Dr. Velarde, and the students walked to the stadium of Yucay. The stadium was a soccer field with some ten yards of grass all around for people to sit and watch the game. Around the grass, there was an adobe fence open at the corners. There were no gates. We just walked in and took our places on the grass. I went to where the Cienciano players were changing. Rivera told me that his team was complete and that they did not need me anymore. I felt better because I did not want to play against Yucay, the team of our host.

I was sitting watching the teams line up, when Dr. Velarde told Mayor Rocaforte in loud voice, so I could hear, "If Cienciano does not want Marco, then he should play for us." I did not expect that. I tried to make an excuse, "I am recovering from pneumonia." I said. But the crowd insisted. Thus, I went to the Yucay players and asked if anyone could loan me his shoes, shorts, and socks. They let me try some shoes. None fitted. They were too small. Then came a tall native player. His shoes fitted me just fine. I got ready and then the Mayor gave the signal for the game to begin. There were some four hundred people around the field, mostly locals, watching and cheering the local team. I decided that, for safety, I should play as a full back, my preferred position. I talked to the other defenders and told them that we were going to hustle the Cienciano players before they got the ball, we were not going to wait for them to come to us. I noticed that a tall and athletic man, whom I had seen in a police uniform earlier, was now lined up for our team as center forward. The game began. Cienciano players were very fast. They came toward us with triangulation passes and shot to our goal and missed. The ball went over the bar. I heard a booo! from the crowd. After that though, I settled down and pushed one of my defenders toward the attacker bringing the ball. The adversary dribbled my defender and I was just behind to take the ball away. It worked every time. Right and left. Balls that came high I rejected with my head every time. Whenever I took the ball I made a long pass to the policeman. In two touches, he would score a goal. He had a deadly rocket shot. He scored four goals that way. At times, I heard the people shouting my name: "Donnatti, Donnatti, Donnatti." Something to remember. The game ended 5-1. That was the first time ever that Yucay had beaten Cienciano. While I was changing, the policeman came to talk to me. He said, "I am glad you were on our side." "Same here," I replied. We shook hands and said good-bye. Mayor Rocaforte, Dr. Velarde, and the family were pleased. We walked to the house. I showered and went to dinner. They had arranged a special place for me at the table. Then they brought me a plate with yellow rice and two sides of roasted guinea pigs on top of it. That was a delicacy in Yucay, Cuzco, and anywhere in the South sierras of Peru. I did not know it then, but I was considered a hero in Yucay that day. I had never eaten guinea pig meat before. But when I tried it, the meat was delicious and tender. It was a banquet! Mayor Rocaforte went arround the table serving wine. I thanked him for his hospitality and the special consideration he had dispensed me during our visit. The next day, we departed on our trip toward Cuzco and the flight to Lima.

34. The Junior Year

My third (junior) year began in April of 1956. That month, I received a letter from the Department of War in which the general director informed me that, because I had obtained the highest marks in the two first years of pre-military courses, I had won the diploma and silver medal, first cycle, assigned to our college. I was invited to visit their offices on Alfonso Ugarte Avenue to claim my award. I did. The medal was in the form of a silver radiant sun and was decorated with a purple ribbon. That year we took a number of courses that were key to our professional training. Among them, clinical diagnoses, pharmacology and therapeutics, large animal surgery, small animal surgery, special pathology, animal reproduction, and veterinary hygiene. And we continued our series of pre-military cavalry courses: one hour of theory per week and some field trips to a cavalry base in Magdalena.

Surgery courses were mostly demonstrations of operations on horses by cavalry surgeons at the veterinary hospital near our college in Las Palmas. Small animal surgical operations were demonstrated by professors at our college small animal clinic or by Dr. Rondinel, our college professor of small animal surgery. That year, Dr. Velarde had requested that I assist him as an instructor in the animal physiology labs for the new second-year students. I would get a special dispensation from other classes on Tuesday and Thursday mornings to do that job. My performance would be *ad honorem*, since there was no budget for it. Because I did hoped to join the faculty of Dr. Velarde's department later, I had accepted. Thus, while I was a junior student, I was teaching and grading second year students reports on animal physiology labs. Of course, my second-year students did not like it one bit. They tried to get even with me on the futsal practices. But I was too fast for them. They could not catch me!

Sometime that year, I suffered from sialorrhea, a condition where there is excessive secretion of saliva. This condition is due to an imbalance in the autonomic nervous system, the one that regulates involuntary functions. I consulted with my brother Daniel, who at the time was in the sixth year of medical school. He gave me a small box with some tiny pills. "Atropine," he said. "Take one whenever you have the excessive secretion." I was familiar with atropine because we had used in animal physiology as a blocker of the parasympathetic system. I took the pills with me to my classes. One morning, while in a class of special pathology with Dr. De la Torre, the saliva began to flow. During the ten-minute break, I went to the bathroom and swallowed a pill with some water. I returned to the classroom. The excessive secretion had stopped. Professor De la Torre resumed his class. I was taking notes fast. Suddenly, I lost consciousness, but I did not fall or anything. I just came to a couple of minutes later and noticed that I had written a whole paragraph, but I did not remember having listened to any of it. I then became aware of my surroundings. I was still sitting on my bench. The professor was there, lecturing. All my classmates were there, also taking notes. Nobody had noticed my passing out. I resumed my note-taking when it happened again! I lost consciousness! This time for several minutes. But I continued to perform my duties of quietly taking notes. Then, I came to again. I was glad that nobody noticed. I had fallen asleep while continuing to write in my notebook, automatically, like a robot! I decided then that I would not take those pills during classes. Fortunately, the sialorrhea did not happen again; I was cured with only one pill. I had discovered then that I was extremely sensitive to medications and that the side effects of medications can be dangerous. Perhaps that was why I had passed out with only four drinks of coffee-alcohol in La Raya, the previous summer.

One Saturday afternoon, I was standing on a street corner of my neighborhood chatting with some friends on our soccer team. In the group, was also my brother, Giovanni. Suddenly, we heard a crash of broken glass. We looked into the cafe-bar at the corner and saw a man standing by the near table. The man turned around, raised his arm, and a stream of blood hit the mirrors behind the cafe's counter some twelve feet away. Then, the man dropped to the floor. My brother ran toward the man while yelling at me, "Come with me," and then, "A handkerchief, please!" Someone handed him a handkerchief. Giovanni tied it around the man's arm, just above the elbow, making a tourniquet. He then asked me to pull hard from one end of the handkerchief while he pulled the other. The blood stopped. The man got up and wanted to fight with another man at the table. By then a policeman had arrived. He took the man to the nearest emergency post in a taxi. We were told later that the man had argued bitterly with a friend at the table where they were drinking beers. That the man had stood up and, to make a point, had punched the table. Instead, he had hit a glass. My brother explained that the broken glass had severed the palmar arterial arch in the man's hand. That was why the blood pressure had reached the mirrors twelve feet away. He also explained how you must apply the tourniquet above the elbow, to stop the bleeding. That was a great lesson for me. A lesson that I never forgot, and it had happened right in the trenches, right in the battlefields of the large and populous city of Lima!

By December that year, all exams were over. I had successfully completed all exams and maintained my high grades. Another expedition to La Raya was being planned. I was invited again to join the team lead by Dr. Velarde. Only this time I would be collecting valuable data on alpacas for my very own bachelor's degree thesis! That was an opportunity I must take, I thought. Thus, in January of 1957, before my senior year, we were on the move again to the high altitudes of the Andes mountains. This time again, we were taking a lot equipment and chemical reagents to reassemble the laboratories of physiology and microbiology at La Raya and to continue the work on alpacas. Under the direction of Dr. Velarde, my objectives this time were to determine the concentration of inorganic calcium and phosphorus in the blood serum of alpacas of various ages, in adult males and females, and to explore the role of the parathyroid glands in the calcium-phosphate balance. It was hard work. Most of the time, I had to work after dinner to complete the analyses on the samples taken each day. By mid-March, I had three notebooks of data, and it was time to return to Lima. The expedition had been a success.

35. The Senior Year

During the first semester that year, we took courses like infectious diseases, medical pathology, diseases of poultry, obstetrics of cattle, meat inspection, foods analyses, and public health. We also took the fourth course in pre-military cavalry. That year, I continued to serve as physiology lab instructor, *ad honorem*, as approved by the college council. In the second semester, from August to December, we took ambulatory clinics, which consisted of seven three-week rotations through farms dedicated to various types of operations. In groups of three students, selected by the students themselves, the rotations included two farms dedicated to dairy cattle (Maranga, Lima, and Punchauca on the road to Canta), one dedicated to sheep (Pachacayo, Junin), the small animal clinic at our college, one poultry farm in Lima, one porcine farm (Trujillo, La Libertad), and the cavalry equine hospital (Las Palmas, Lima). In our class, the three soccer players who played for the college team formed a group: Portillo, Osorio, and I (Donnatti) became partners in crime because when the inter-collegial soccer tournament came in September and October, we would be called to play from wherever our rotation was, and, not only would this give us a break, but also dispensation from clinical sessions, and paid travel expenses. It was a good partnership. Suffice it to say that we were successful at all three levels: academically, in our clinical practice, and on the soccer field. Our college, competing with 11 other colleges, had ended in second place. We were vice-champions that year. We lost only the final game against the school of economics. They had three professional players on their team and were champions. Anyway, we got silver medals and a trophy. Quite an accomplishment for a school of only 150 students.

One morning that year, I was walking home and passing by the stadium of La Victoria, my district, where I saw a game being played. I entered and watched the game for a while. It was a game of the tournament my college was in. The college of chemistry was playing against the college of dentistry. Then, I noticed that the goalkeeper of chemistry was a very tall, heavy set, blond fellow, very unusual in Lima. He looked Swedish. He was very athletic, about six feet, 6 inches tall, and weighed some 180 pounds. He bounced laterally, like a cat. Fantastic reflexes. He would catch any high or low ball with conviction. I wondered who could possibly score a goal against such superman. It never crossed my mind that one week later, I was going to score a goal against the "Swedish." In those days our tournament college representative, a volunteer student, attended the meetings at the athletic department in the old house of San Marcos. The meetings were held at odd hours, usually at night. So, I don't blame him for not telling us in advance when, or against who, we were playing next. We learned that at the last minute, usually. We should have had a printed schedule. But somehow we did not. That was the way things were done in those days. The day we were playing against chemistry came. It was also at the same stadium of La Victoria. When I arrived at the field, there were already several players changing into their gear. Alberto Salas, a very dynamic junior student, was acting coach. The first thing he told me was, "Today you are going to play as left winger." I was shocked. I usually played defense or in the middle line, but forward? And on the left side? Oh, well, I decided. He's the coach, I'll do what I can. I saw that on the opposite side of the field, the "Swedish" was warming up. We lined up to start the game. The referee and the assistants were professionals from the Peruvian Federation of Soccer, contracted by the university. I was very fast in those days. The chemistry player who was to mark me was a Japanese-Peruvian player, very fast also. On three occasions we run parallel to each other, and I could not beat him to the ball. The first half of the game ended nil to nil.

During the break, I talked to Robles, our key player in the center field. I told him that all I needed was a two-yard advantage over my marker. To do that, I have to surprise him, I said, you have to pass me the ball without even looking at me. Just shoot toward the little flag on the corner of the field. The instant that you take the ball, I will start running before you kick the ball, leaving the Japanese behind. I will get to the ball first and center it to the 18-yard line. You will then run to head the ball against the ground and toward the goal. He said that it was a good idea. He then said, "We'll try it." The second half began. When Robles took the ball in the middle of the field, I ran like hell toward the corner flag. My marker wondered why. Just in case, he ran behind me. I got to the ball first and centered the ball with my left foot. Only the grass on that part of the field was overgrown and mushy. I did not quite catch the ball at its center. The ball did not go to the 18-yard line. Instead, it went toward the penalty spot and then bent toward the goal. The "Swedish" ran backwards, but he never got there. Making a weird curve, the ball entered the goal next to the far post! An incredible goal. With the momentum I was carrying, I slid over the line at the end of the field. A group of veterinary students were watching the game on that side. They raised me high in the air. Then they placed me on the ground patting me on the back. I looked at Robles. He was applauding me. It was a lucky shot. The best goals are many times sheer luck.

36. Senior Year Adventures

Another day, I was at home, studying. Someone knocked on my door. It was Jorge Garten, a classmate of my brother Giovanni in the college of medicine. He said that his dog was acting strangely and asked me if I could come to see him. I got my bag of tools and medications and said, "Let's go, now." He lived about ten blocks away. So, we walked. On the way, he told me that the dog had been brought from Tingo Maria a week earlier and that he was very friendly, obedient, and ate his meals regularly. I asked about his breed and his weight. Jorge did not know about the breed or weight, but described the dog as a big light brown male one. When we got to the house, the dog was hiding behind a sofa in the living room. He was a mongrel weighing about 75 pounds, a big one. Jorge's mother explained that the dog had been hiding there since the day before and had not come out for meals or anything, even after being called many times and enticed with cooked meat. I told them that, considering that the dog had come from the jungle, there were two possibilities: the dog was having an attack of encephalitis due to rabies or the dog was suffering from some kind of poisoning. And I added, "Rabies is common in the Amazonia region of the country." Then, I asked if the children had been playing with the dog. The lady answered, "Yes, these three little girls, ages three, four, and five." I explained that I was going to try to give him an intravenous injection of glucose to help him in case we were dealing with a case of poisoning. I loaded my syringe with 20cc of solution. I asked Jorge to move the sofa away from the wall a little so that I could reach the dog. When I approached the animal, he snapped at me. I moved away just in time. Then I knew the an I.V. injection was not possible. I asked Jorge to move the sofa back to where it was before. That would secure the dog in place. I also asked to place a pillow above his head in case he tried to snap again. I proceeded to disinfect an area of the skin with alcohol and proceeded to inject the solution under his skin. Then I told the family that we needed to secure the dog overnight because he could have a violent attack of encephalitis later and bite anyone in sight. Jorge brought a heavy rope and we tied one end to the dog's heavy collar. We then slowly but firmly pulled the dog out from behind the sofa and took him to a huge backyard that was used by a mechanic to do his work repairing trucks. Way in the back we found a rusted heavy rear truck axle that nobody used. We tied the other end of the rope to the axle making sure that the dog could not break loose from it. We then brought food and water to the dog and left. I promised to return the next day in the afternoon after my classes.

The next day, I went to Jorge's house. The lady opened the door. She was very much alarmed. She said that the dog had an attack that morning hauling and jumping with fury, just as I had said it could happen. She said that the dog had dropped and lay flat on the ground. Jorge thought the dog was dead because it was not breathing. I went to see the dog. The animal was not breathing. I checked his eyes. The typical mydriasis was present. With my stethoscope, I verified that there was not a heart beat. That confirmed his death. I told the family the we needed to take the dog to the Hygiene Institute for an examination of its brain for rabies. Jorge said that we could take him in the trunk of his car. I asked Jorge to cover the trunk with newspapers. I phoned the institute and explained the situation to the veterinarian on duty. He said, "Bring him immediately." I also told the family that if the test at the institute were positive for rabies, the three little girls would have to be vaccinated. They understood. We took the dog. I knew the veterinarian who received us. He was Dr. Solano. He had been a guest lecturer in our college the year before. He was very kind. He said that the microscopic examination of the brain could reveal the characteristic lesions of rabies encephalitis. He also said that he would phone me at the college. He did three days later. He said simply, "Marco? The dog's brain was positive for rabies." I immediately, phoned Jorge, "The test was positive for rabies. Please contact your family doctor and ask that he make arrangements with the Department of Public Health for the vaccination of the three little girls." He said he would do that right away. Some years later, on one of my visits to Lima, I had a chance encounter with Dr. Jorge Garten, and I asked him about the little girls. He told me that the three little girls were now some beautiful ladies 17, 18, and 19 years old. "Bless their hearts," I said.

On the college anniversary, it was a tradition that the senior students organize the celebration program and serve lunch for some three hundred people. Quite a task. In addition to all the students and professors, guests were expected from the Department of Agriculture, from all clinical sites, from the Agrarian University, and the "girls" from the College of Pharmacy. Thus, our class of 24 prospective graduates was divided into 6 "committees." The dean of our college and all professors contributed about one hundred soles each toward expenses. Professors' families were also invited. One committee was responsible for printing announcements inviting the usual guests, preparing and mounting the decorations, and of securing the beer, sodas, or "chicha morada," a sweet drink made from Peruvian purple corn. Another committee was in charge of securing and preparing the roasted lambs with the assistance of the Cavalry Veterinary Hospital near our college in Las Palmas. Another committee was in charge of cooking potatoes, sweet potatoes and ears of corn. My committee was responsible for preparing a cebiche, a typical dish from Lima using bonito fish, for three hundred people. Almost nothing! The party was to start at noon on a Saturday. By then, all committees would have to have completed their tasks. At that time, or soon after, the guests would arrive. Also, a futsal game between our college and the Agrarian University was to start at noon. The band of the Republican Guard would play Peruvian music: marineras, tonderos, and Peruvian waltzes all along. At one p.m. lunch would be served. My committee got up early that morning and went with a pickup truck to the central market where we purchased one dozen fresh bonitos, four hundred lemons, two kilograms of ground yellow hot peppers, ten kilograms of onions, one kilogram of ground salt, lots of parsley, and hot red peppers. We converted the laboratory of anatomy into a processing plant for the fish. We got all members of the committee and some volunteers involved in the cutting of the fish meat into small pieces about half-inch cubed. We placed all cut meat into some deep enamel trays with lemon juice and let it rest for one hour. Then we added salt and the ground yellow hot peppers and mixed well. In the meantime, the red hot peppers and the onions were being cut to size. At twelve noon we began serving. On small plates, we placed a portion of the fish cooked in lemon juice and seasoned with salt and yellow peppers. On top we decorated with fine cuttings of red pepper, onions, and parsley. The committee in charge of potatoes, etc. brought their products. They cut them in small portions. Each plate then received two side pieces of potato, sweet potato, or corn.

While plates were being served, a game of futsal was being played. Free from my cebiche committee, I was captain of the futsal team. The Agrarian University had a much better team than ours. That was a mismatch. On the bleachers, there were some professors, the dean's office secretaries, and some students. In the heat of the game, jumping for the ball with an adversary, I would place my elbows in front to cope with the imminent collision. The player of agronomy would fall down. I had four such collisions with them. Every time the adversary fell. I remained standing. I was told later, that one of the secretaries on the bleachers, had commented, "Everytime that Donnatti crashes against one of agronomy, the agronomist falls." At that point, a student on the back of the bleachers responded, "Donnatti neuters them in the air." We lost the game 5-1, but we did have fun, just before lunch. At one o'clock the line of guests began to pass the line of tables, and a plate of cebiche was given to each. Down the line they received another plate with a portion of roasted lamb, and further, they received beer, sodas, or purple corn drink. It was delightful. A crowd of our faculty, our distinguished guests, students and their families having a wonderful lunch while music filled the grounds with the best of their repertoire. An unforgettable day.

37. Clinical Rotations

The three members of my clinics group, Portillo, Osorio, and I, had a lot of fun during the clinical practice under very skillful and experienced veterinarians. At the farm in Punchauca, North of Lima, on the road to Canta, we shared a large room as a bedroom. One night, at about 4 a.m., we heard a strong voice and a hard knock on the door: "Jalar ternero, ahora mismo." ("Pulling a calf, right now") We jumped off the cots and dressed up as quickly as we could. We got out in two minutes. The farm worker took us to a stall where a cow was having a difficult delivery of her calf. Dr. Arce, our clinical Professor, asked us, in turns, to feel the calf's shoulder presentation. He then said that he would apply the two-force technique to correct the position and facilitate delivery. He then proceeded to demonstrate the technique. At some point, the two front legs of the calf showed up. He then aligned the head of the calf and asked me to pull from the legs. In a few seconds we had a healthy baby calf on the yard. Dr. Arce then said, "Wash up and go to bed."

Dr. Arce had received a number of capsules of frozen semen of a special breed of cattle from Canada. In his laboratory he had defrosted and diluted some semen and had brought it in a thermos to the field where we were waiting, at 1:00 p.m., one afternoon. He said, "We have nine or ten heifers to be artificially inseminated today. I need a volunteer to assist me with the insemination. We, the students, looked at each other. My classmates pointed at me and smiled. They volunteered me. Dr. Arce said to me, "OK, put these gloves on. Now listen, you are going to fix the uterus with your left hand by rectal palpation. I am going to prepare the pipette with the diluted semen and hand it to your right hand. You will introduce the pipette into the vagina and place it into the cervical ostium. Once you are sure you are in the ostium, you will tell me and I will shoot, OK?" I nodded. The farm foreman had a notebook in his hands. He identified the heifer to be inseminated and we proceeded as instructed. With my left hand I felt the uterus, then I sled my hand toward the cervix. I said, "I have the cervix." Dr. Arce handed me the loaded pipette. I introduced it carefully into the vagina and felt it with my left hand. I placed it into the ostium. "Pipette in ostium," I said. Dr. Arce pushed the plunger of the syringe connected to the other end of the pipette. Then Dr. Arce said, "Pull the pipette out." He received it and placed into a bucket with disinfectant solution. Then, he said, "Let's go to the next one." That way we did ten heifers that afternoon. I was appreciative for the opportunity given to me of participating in such special practice of the profession. About 8 weeks later, while on other rotation, we received word from Dr. Arce saying that " Marco, of the ten heifers we inseminated that day, we had 9 confirmed pregnancies. I could not have done better myself." My classmates congratulated me for having "fathered" 9 calves. That night, I paid for a round of beers!

In Pachacayo, department of Junin, in the central sierras, we had practice with sheep. That farm raised sheep for mutton and lamb meat. At a young age, male lambs are castrated to suppress the production of testosterone, a catabolic hormone. After recovery from castration, the lambs gain weight quickly, due to the predominant anabolic functions. We usually got up at 5:30 a.m., had breakfast at 6:00 a.m., and were at work by 6:30. During castration session, a number of farm workers caught the male lambs and held them for us, exposing their abdomens, one at a time. The veterinarian in charge, some technicians, and we, the students, wearing a special apron with wide pockets, pulled a special rubber band from a pocket, placed it on a special instrument that stretches the band wide open, then, we held the scrotum of the lamb with the left hand and placed the rubber band tight around both testicles. Then, the lamb was released. It was sad and funny at the same time. Sad because the poor animal was in pain. And funny, because they ran and jumped alternatively after the operation. We were told that the lambs calmed down in a few minutes because they lost sensation in that region, that they remained depressed for a day or so, but that they recovered quickly after that. We did over 2,000 lambs that morning.

38. My Thesis Research

During my senior year, I managed to work on the data collected in La Raya the previous summer. I had tabulated the data for blood inorganic calcium and phosphorus of alpacas divided in groups: adults males, adult females, young animals at various ages, from birth to one year of age; and a group of three animals which had been parathyroidectomized. Now, I needed to do the statistical study of the various groups. Most important were the mean values, the standard deviations, and the probable errors. After that, I was in a good position to make comparisons with the values reported in the literature for other species and my own alpaca groups. And to do that, I needed to do some library research. Finally, by September, I had just about everything in place and began to write and type my thesis. In those days, it was customary to type on special stencils that later could be used to print multiple copies. The college required eight copies. I printed ten, just in case. I also drew some histograms and curves with India ink and had them photographed to obtain multiple copies. Once the text and illustrations were ready, I assembled the ten copies and took them to a professional binder and printer to put them together and to print the blue cover in gold letters. The final product was good. I presented the eight copies required to the secretary of the college with my application for the designation of an examining committee and, later, an appointment to defend my thesis.

About two weeks later, I was in front of the three professors of my thesis committee. They were; Dr. Velarde, my thesis sponsor, Dr. Saenz, professor of genetics and animal reproduction, and Dr. Rondinel, professor of small animal medicine. They asked me several questions about why I had chosen the subject of blood chemistry, what methods were chosen to do the analyses and, finally, what were the most important findings. I responded to all questions well. Regarding the findings, I told them that the study was unique in that nobody had measured those blood components previously, that the minor differences between males and females was inconsequential, but the differences found in the youngest animals was highly significant. Further, I told them that the work brought an important question as to why the animals in which we removed the parathyroid glands, did not show the expected hypocalcemic tetany. And I offered some possible answers. Perhaps there were some aberrant parathyroid glands that were not extirpated, or perhaps other organs played a more important role in the calcium-phosphorus balance in alpacas. Then, the president of the committee, Dr. Saenz, asked me to leave the room and to wait outside. I excused myself and went outside. In a few minutes, I was called in. Dr. Saenz congratulated me for the good work I had done in my thesis. He said, "You are now a bachelor in veterinary medicine (BVM). We will communicate this to the proper authorities." I was pleased that I had fulfilled one more requirement in my race to a professional career.

39. DVM Examinations

The appointments for my five doctor's degree (DVM) examinations were made in February of 1958. The appointments were two or three days apart. I reported to those appointments as well prepared as I could. My first exam was on small animal clinics. I reported to the clinic wearing my white lab coat and gear. Dr. Ronquillo was my examiner. He asked me to examine a small dog with an eczema on the dorsal region of his body. After a quick external examination of the patient, I took his temperature and proceeded to examine the lesions on the skin. At that point, Dr. Ronquillo asked me, "Well, what do you think?" I said that we needed a to do a scraping of the lesions for microscopic examination to rule out a parasitic condition. I also added that another possible condition was an allergy. In such case, a palliative treatment with cortisone ointment would be recommended until the cause could be identified. "Anything else?", Dr. Ronquillo asked me. I responded that, if an allergy was confirmed, we needed to question the dog's owner in regard to possible causes of the allergy. Dr. Ronquillo then said, "Fine. That is all," and he dismissed me. I learned later the he had given me a grade of 18 or 90%. I was very much pleased.

My next appointment was with Dr. Ramirez, professor of small animal surgery. I reported to his laboratory in full gear. A technician had anesthetized a dog and prepared all necessary instrumentation for surgery. Professor Ramirez asked me to perform a resection of the cecum. Wearing latex gloves, I proceeded to disinfect the lower right quadrant of the abdomen. Then I made a 3-inch incision on the skin, which was then extended to the interior planes, muscles layers and peritoneum. At this point Dr. Ramirez excused himself to make an urgent phone call and left promising to return soon. Then, I proceeded to search for the cecum, which could be easily recognized by the ileocecal artery that runs along its peritoneal folding. But I just could not find it. I began to perspire profusely. The technician smiled and dried my forehead with a towel. I thanked him and continued the search. It took me some ten minutes to finally find it. The ileocecal artery was right there pulsating in front of me. I isolated the cecum. Dr. Ramirez walked in. He saw the cecum and said, "That's enough for now," and then, addressing the technician, he added, "You close the incision." I collected my gear and thanked professor Ramirez. I learned later that he had given me a grade of 15 or 75%, a good grade.

My next appointment was with Dr. Alvarez at the Maranga dairy cattle farm. I reported to the appointment in full gear, including boots. He asked me to examine a cow. I proceeded with the external exam. I noticed the depressive state of the animal. She also seemed to have a fever. I took her temperature. It was high. I examined the udder and found it swollen, warm, and sensitive to my touching. I collected some milk into a glass jar. The milk looked thick and creamy. The genitals seemed normal. Finally, Dr. Alvarez asked for my opinion so far. I said that a presumptive diagnosis would be acute mastitis, which could be confirmed by a bacteriological culture. He said, "Yes, that is the most probable diagnosis. What do we do now?" I responded that, because of the fever, a treatment with antibiotics would be appropriate. The first shot could be given immediately. He then gave me a tray with a vial containing the antibiotic, a syringe and some needles. He then asked me to load the syringe and to give the cow an intramuscular injection. I then proceeded to disinfect the hip area of the skin, to prepare and load the syringe, and to give the injection. Dr. Alvarez was pleased. He said that I had performed well. I learned later that he had given me a grade of 16 or 80%. I was pleased.

The next appointment was with Dr. Salinas at the military hospital of Las Palmas. As usual, I reported to my appointment in full gear. Dr. Saenz told me that they did not have surgery scheduled that day and that he would give me an oral exam instead. We went to his office. He asked me to describe the most common anesthetics, for local interventions and for general anesthesia. I did proceed to describe the most common local anesthetic, procain hydrochloride, also known by its commercial name, novocain, used for regional surgery. Then, I indicated chloral hydrate, used as general anesthetic in large animal practice. Next, I mentioned ethyl ether, administered by inhalation for general anesthesia in small animal practice and in laboratory animals. I mentioned pentobarbital sodium, also known as nembutal, administered intravenously as a general anesthetic in small animal surgery and in laboratory animals. I also mentioned meperidine, also known as demerol, a pre-anesthetic, and pentothal, a short duration a general anesthetic. Dr. Salinas then said: "Very well. That is all for now. Thank you."I thanked Dr. Salinas for his attention and said good-bye. Later I learned that he had given me a grade of 15 or 75%. Not bad.

My last appointment was with Dr. Arce at Punchauca. This exam was on cattle obstetrics. I was ready. Dr. Arce, looking at his notebook, asked me to diagnose a cow for pregnancy. The foreman verified the identity of the cow by reading the number on the aluminum earring of the animal. I proceeded to do the rectal palpation of the uterus. Earlier in my clinical training, I had learned that by holding the uterine wall between my fingers and letting it slide away I could feel two membranes in a pregnant cow, and only one in a non-pregnant one. "Pregnant," I said. Dr. Arce checked his book, but said nothing. We walked few steps and Dr. Arce said, "This one, go ahead." I disinfected my hands and arms. I proceeded to do the palpation of the uterus as before. "Not pregnant," I said. Dr. Arce checked his book again, but said nothing. We continued like that, examining other cows, apparently at random. When we had done six tests, Dr. Arce said, "OK, I am convinced. You have diagnosed correctly four pregnant an two non-pregnant cows. Congratulations!" Later I was pleased to learn that he had given me the maximum grade: 20 or 100%. Bless his noble heart. Sometime in March, Dr. Cardoso, the interim dean, in a simple ceremony in the Dean's office, gave me and my classmate Altamirano, the oath of honor of the profession. We had earned the DVM degree. With that, we were ready to take on the world, we thought.

40. Instructor of Biochemistry

By the end of my senior year, I had three job offers. The Department of Agriculture had offered me a position as regional vaccinations program director. My responsibilities were to provide and supervise vaccination programs in coordination with the farmers in the region. That job involved a lot of traveling. They would provide me with travel expenses, a new pickup truck well equipped, and a driver assistant. The second offer came from the cavalry division of the army. Because I had completed the four courses of pre-military instruction successfully, I would be admitted to the armed forces with the rank of captain. My responsibilities would be to join the team veterinarians at the animal hospital of San Martin military base in the Magdalena district of Lima. The third job offer came from Dr. Rangel, dean of our college.

On a Saturday morning at about 11:30 a.m., the dean of our college, Dr. Mario Rangel Tagle, sent for me. The messenger found me, where else, on the soccer field! Said he: "Marco, Dr. Rangel needs you right away." I stopped playing and went to wash up to make myself presentable. I changed into street clothes in five minutes. When I got to the dean's office, the secretary, Miss. Lorena, smiled and told me, "Just walk in, Dr. Rangel is waiting for you." "Please excuse me, Mr. Dean," I said, I was practicing some soccer. He said, "Never mind that, I wanted to catch you before you left. I know that you have been working as instructor of animal physiology, *ad honorem*, for the past two years. I know also that you hoped to join Dr. Velarde's department as an instructor. But what a person wants is not necessarily what our college needs. Institutions are more important than persons. We need you in the Department of Biochemistry and Animal Nutrition. Dr. Batista, the principal professor in that department, has had health problems this year, so we had to use substitute instructors. That is not how we want to run the department. We need you to be the full-time faculty in that department. I know also that you have other options open to you that could pay you better than the college, but I am in a position to make you a promise: Within two years, we will send you to the United States for special training under the sponsorship of the Rockefeller Foundation. If you need time to think about this offer, please let me know next week." I was very much surprised. I said then, "Dr. Rangel, I am honored and grateful. I trust your understanding of what is best for our college. I accept your offer right now. Thank you very much." Dr. Rangel, smiled and we shook hands. I walked out of the office. Miss Lorena, smiled and winked at me. I smiled too. Apparently, she knew all about it.

In January of 1958, after the holidays, I went to the college one day to arrange the appointments for the DVM degree exams. Walking by the main hall of the building, I stopped in front of the bulletin board. In the glass encased board, I saw a letter to the dean of the college. It was from the Department of War. It notified the dean about the pre-military instruction award. The notification named me as the winner of the diploma and gold medal for having obtained the highest marks during the second cycle, the third and fourth years, of pre-military courses. It gave directions as to when to report to their office on Alfonso Ugarte avenue to claim the award. The next day, I went the office and received the diploma and the medal. The medal was a golden radiant sun with a red and white ribbon, the colors of the Peruvian flag. I was greatly honored by receiving that award.

Officially, my new job of instructor of biochemistry and animal nutrition began in April of 1958. But in February and March, in agreement with Dr. Batista, principal professor, I started to reorganize the series of laboratory sessions to be taught to the new freshmen students in April. Most of the work was done during the year along with the lab sessions. In those days the labs consisted of tests done on "unknown" solutions, urine, or blood serum, all in test tubes. Reagents were delivered into the test tubes by droppers or pipettes. With the assistance of a lab technician, named David Calle, we prepared and tested a large number of reagent solutions. Then, they were dispensed into six sets of small bottles and droppers for six expected groups of students. All containers were properly labeled. All lab protocols were rewritten in accord with the new set up. By the end of the year, the protocols were then bound into a manual. A number of copies were printed and bound by our college printing shop. The students could purchase the manuals at cost price at the beginning of the course. The lab course lasted two semesters, and included tests for the detection and quantitation of sugars in urine and blood serum, tests for acetone and starch, tests for fatty acids and fats, tests for bilirubin, tests for amino acids, and detection of sugars and amino acids by paper chromatography. Another important event occurred that year; the University of San Marcos approved and funded the construction of a new building for the College of Veterinary Medicine in the new district of Monterrico, east of Lima and close to the new hippodrome. The following year, Dr. Batista asked me to take an additional responsibility: teaching the theory of some chapters of the course of biochemistry as well as those of the course of animal nutrition taught to third-year students. Needless to say, I was extremely busy.

—◦⊚◦—

Reporter Judy Hartfeldt: So, you ended in a different department from the one you expected to work at. True?

Marco Donnatti: Yes, definitely. I had to study a lot that year. I had to review both biochemistry as well as animal nutrition. Gradually, I took responsibility for teaching both subjects. Fortunately things went well.

Judy: Our next appointment will be Thursday morning, as usual, in my office, OK?

Marco: Agreed. Good-bye.

—◦⊚◦—

Alpacas, one of the four species of Peruvian Camelides (Story 38)

CHAPTER 5

CORNELL UNIVERSITY

Reporter Judy Hartfeldt: You worked as instructor of biochemistry and animal nutrition for two years. And took responsibility for both the theory classes and the laboratory sessions. Is that correct?

Marco Donnatti: Yes. Thanks to my determination, both subjects were successfully completed during the years of 1958 and 1959.

Judy: Did the university give you any recognition?

Marco: No. Not right away. But that is coming in the stories that follow.

Judy: Fine. I am recording. Please tell me.

---

41. Sorcerers' Town

During the year of 1959, Dean Rangel had returned from his long trip to Europe. He was a consultant with the Food and Agriculture Organization (FAO), a subdivision of the United Nations. Dr. Rangel had arranged interviews for me with Drs. Kelly and Robertson, representatives of the Rockefeller Foundation. In July of that year, Dr. Kelly visited our college. He was fluent in Spanish. We had a brief conversation. He insisted that I improve my English as soon as possible. Of course, I told him that I was attending evening classes at the Peruvian-American Cultural Institute, three times per week. He was pleased. Dr. Rangel was also key in initiating a college council resolution to promote me from instructor to assistant professor by December of 1959. That year, our college moved from Las Palmas to a new building in Monterrico.

But let's go back a little. Sometime in October of 1958, during those months of intense work as an instructor, I did manage to practice soccer, my favorite sport. I discovered that going out in the field and playing hard and fast removed the stresses of work. In those days, I called it "sweating it out." In other words, it relieved me from the stress. I did not know it then, but I was going to use that approach to handle stresses for many years to come. Early one Sunday morning I was reading the newspaper at the desk in our apartment when a knock in the door interrupted my reading. I opened the door and met my friend Emilio Prado. We played soccer together in our neighborhood team. He said that a team from the wholesale market of Aviation Avenue needed reinforcements for two games to be played that afternoon in the town of Coayllo, some 35 miles south of Lima. Both games were in response to a challenge received by Mr. Jorge Cano, a notable business man who was also the President of the Wholesale Market Association. The association had a team, but Mr. Cano was not confident they could win a game against the best Coayllo Team. He decided to have their team play a "second division" game at 1:00 p.m. and to bring a complete new team, made of reinforcements, to play the "first division" game at 3:00 p.m. I told Emilio that since I did not have anything urgent that day, a trip to the countryside would be great. He also told me that he had recruited Jorge Castro, Jose Porteno, and Manuel Cortejo from our team and others from the neighborhood of Mazanilla. The meeting site for the trip was the first block at Aviation avenue. Departure time was at 11:00 a.m. Mr. Cano had chartered a bus to take all players and officials of the association to Coayllo. The trip lasted about one hour. We first rode the well-paved Panamerican highway south of Lima for about 30 miles and then we turned east on a dusty gravel road to reach Coayllo. During the trip, Emilio surprised me with the story that Coayllo was a "Sorcerers' Town," that many people from metropolitan Lima went to that town to consult about their most personal problems and to seek help, that the sorcerers charged hefty sums for their services, that they truly had special powers, and that they could undo curses made by other evil sorcerers. It was a fascinating story, I thought. But I did not believe in witchcraft or sorcery and I told Emilio so. But he insisted in that it was true. Then I asked Emilio that if what he said was true, why were we going to play a soccer game against players that may have such powers. "What if they put a curse on us before the game and our legs go num or something?" He smiled and coming closer to me he whispered: "I have brought a special remedy to counter any maleficence. Remind me to give you some before the game."

We arrived at Coayllo at about noon. Lunch time. Jose Porteno and I went to a small restaurant on the main street of town and ordered some sandwiches and sodas. Over lunch, we discussed quietly Emilio's version about the reputation of the town. Jose did not believe in sorcery either, but "Just in case, we should take the remedy," he said. The first game began on time, at 1:00 p.m., on the dirt field of town. Under careful examination, the field was more like a bowl. The areas near the corners were elevated slightly. We, the reinforcements, watched the Association's team be slaughtered by the second division local team by the score of 5-1. Some members of the Association lost money on bets with local persons. While watching the game I noticed that the local team had a very skillful and fast left winger. He was unstoppable. Also, that an equally skillful middle line player would pass the ball to the winger with a fast rolling ball. At first, the ball appeared about to leave the field, but it would not. It would slow down as it approached the corner flag. The association defender player would not pursue the winger who would then reach the ball and enter the area and shoot to the goal. In fact, they repeated that play many times. The local left winger scored all five goals that way.

All reinforcement players were changing for the 3:00 p.m. first division game. I knew only those of our team. There were some five or six players whom I did not know. Destiny had brought us together to this town and at this time to play for unknown sponsors and against a team of sorcerers. Someone asked the players about what positions we normally played. Surprise! There seven full-back players, including myself. At that point, we set up the team with three full-backs in the defense. I was placed to mark the left winger, although we did not expect the same player of the first game. Emilio was to mark the right winger. Three full-backs were placed in the middle line, and Manuel Cortejo, also a full-back, was asked to play center forward. Our Jorge Castro was the goalkeeper. Jose Porteno was placed also in the forward line. We certainly had a very strong defensive team. Just before the game was to start, Emilio came to me and gave me a small head of garlic. "Male Garlic," he said quietly. "Put it in your short's pocket." I did. That was the countermeasure against witchcraft. The association's business men and local businessmen made huge bets several hundred soles each. A local man was selected to referee the game. The game began. I stayed close to the opposing left winger. I placed myself always between the ball and him. That way I could intercept any pass to him. When the ball came high towards the corner of the field, I rushed and got there first. I practically annulled completely the left wing of the opposing team. Cortejo scored a goal. We were ahead by one goal at the end of the first half of the game.

During the ten minute recess, some local men and women came toward us to treat us with shot glasses of "Pisco,"the famous Peruvian liquor made of grapes' distillate. We politely refused asking the hosts to postpone the celebration until after the game. The teams lined up for the second half. I noticed a change in the local team. The left winger was now the same player who had scored 5 goals in the first game. I had a big responsibility now. But the "male garlic" must have worked. I managed to annul him too. Those passes toward the flag with on the elevated terrain did not work this time. Cortejo scored a second goal and we won the game 2-0. Mr. Cano and other officers of the association were delighted and grateful. They made good money on bets too. The trip back to Lima was pleasant. We arrived home at about 7:00 p.m. It was already dark outside.

42. The Fellowship

In October of 1959, I had another interview with a representative of the Rockefeller Foundation. This time, Dr. Robertson visited our college. He was pleased with my progress in English and promised to recommend my appointment for a fellowship. Dr. Rangel had written a number of letters to obtain my admission to the Radiation Biology department of the Veterinary College at Cornell University. He was most interested in my training in radioisotope work in veterinary medicine. He told me that his recommendations and arrangements were based on my record of high grades in physics, chemistry, and mathematics throughout my college education. "If anyone can do it, it is you," he said to me. I responded that "I loved the sciences and that I would do my very best to deserve his recommendations." My trip to the U.S. was scheduled for January 4, 1960. I had obtained a student visa for a one-year stay in the U.S. In preparation for the trip, I purchased a new suit, some shirts, ties, etc. in downtown Lima. By

September, I had completed all 12 grades of English courses at the Peruvian-American Cultural Institute. So, I decided to take short courses in English for doctors, English grammar, and scientific English, also offered at the same institution. Despite all that, I was soon going to discover that my English was far too limited for my own needs. That was because English is so rich in idiomatic phrases I had never heard before.

All arrangements for my travel contacts, etc. had been made by Dr. Rangel, dean of our college. With the assistance of Dr. Bustillos, professor of clinical laboratories, I had made contact with Mr. John Wolfe, a gentleman who rented rooms to students in his house on Stewart Avenue in Ithaca, New York. Mr. Wolfe had reserved a room for me and promised to meet me at the greyhound bus station when I arrived from New York City. Thus, I flew from Lima to Panama City, and from there to New York City. As our plane approached the airport, I was fascinated with the view of the island of Manhattan from the air. And there they were: the Statue of Liberty on Liberty Island and Ellis Island, the symbols of hope for so many immigrants from around the world. I did not know it then, but I was going to become an immigrant myself four years later. As instructed, at the airport I took the shuttle into town and stopped at the Abbey Hotel where I had a single room reservation. From there, it was a short walk to Rockefeller Plaza and the offices of the Rockefeller Foundation, where I had an appointment the very next morning. The next morning, I walked to the plaza, entered the main building, and took the elevator to the 21st floor. Dr. Mettler, a distinguished older gentleman, was expecting me. We chatted for a while. He told me that I was free that afternoon and asked me what I wanted to do. I immediately told him, "I would like to go to the Bronx Zoo." He then asked his secretary to write out instructions as to how to get there. He then told me that, at the zoo, I should always stay close to groups of people, never alone in one of those zoo alleys. I thanked Dr. Mettler and his secretary, and left. My instructions indicated that I was to take the subway train to the Bronx, getting off at the stop for 168th street. As we traveled, I watched through the window, the street stop numbers as they went by. Suddenly the train stopped at 184th street. I do not know how, but I had passed my stop. I got off and climbed the stairs to the city surface. I was in the middle of a black neighborhood. Some men were kneeling in a circle at about 50 yards, perhaps gambling with dice. They elbowed each other and pointed at me. But my instinct told me that to them, in my grey suit, white shirt and tie, I looked like a lost pigeon. Lost, yes, but I also came from Mazanilla, a no-good neighborhood in Lima. I could smell danger. I looked straight at the men to let them know that I was alert. Then, I raised my arm and stopped a taxi. I told the driver, "Take me to the Bronx Zoo." He took me around and around to inflate the meter, but I did not care. He dropped me off right at the entrance. I enjoyed the animal displays, but specially the huge polar bears. I'll never forget one of the bears standing on his rear legs and reaching with his paws the top of a 12-feet iron fence. He looked about two stories high. The next morning, I took the Greyhound Bus to Ithaca, NY. Mr. Wolfe was at the station to receive me and to take me to his house. I got worried on the way because I could hardly understand a word or two of his lively conversation. But when we got to

Steward Avenue and met Mrs. Wolfe, I felt a little better because I could understand her much better. Mrs. Wolfe told me a week later, "Don't listen to him, he has a speech impediment." And I was trying to learn English from him! But even then, whenever I went to a store or to the dry cleaners, I had to think of what I was going to say in advance. Many times, I did not understand the reply and was too embarrassed to ask people to repeat it or to talk slowly. My tribulations with the English languge had just begun.

43. Graduate School

On my first morning at Ithaca, I got ready at 7 a.m. and walked, with the snow up to my knees, to the College of Veterinary Medicine, about a mile north of Stewart Avenue. It took me a long time, but I got there. At about 8 a.m., I went to the office of Dr. Carter, director of the Department of Radiation Biology. Dr. Carter was well known in scientific circles for his work on mineral metabolism. At the entrance, I introduced myself to a young lady, a secretary, I thought. She announced me to Dr. Carter in the next office. I was invited to enter. I greeted Dr. Carter. We shook hands. He knew that I had come highly recommended for a postgraduate position in his department. He smiled, almost mumbling, he said, "Ah, yes, yes, and, suddenly, he wrote: "10^6" on a piece of paper and asked me, "What is that?" I responded, "One million." He said, "You will be OK." He then asked me to attend the classes of the International Course on Radioisotopes, which was starting that very morning at 8:30 a.m. The course was attended by some 48 scientists from all over the world. Dr. Carter asked his secretary to show me to my office, which I was to share with one of the course attendees, Dr. Sherghi, a chemist from Poland. Dr. Sherghi and I soon became good friends. We did the course assignments together. I learned a lot from him. He could handle logarithms like a pro. Soon I was doing it too. After classes, I walked to the campus store and bought a heavy coat, a hat, and a pair of winter gloves. Sub-zero temperatures were common in winter in upstate New York.

A few days later, I went to the graduate school building, where I asked a lady about the procedure to apply for admission into a M.S. (Master of Science) degree program. She gave me some blank forms and asked me to fill them out and sign them. She then told me that I would be notified in a few days. Two days later, Dr. Carter called me to his office. He told me that he would recommend me to the Rockefeller Foundation for the M.S. program. I thanked him. He also said that the program requires a committee and some course work. He asked me what courses I was willing to take. I said that, since I taught biochemistry and animal nutrition in Peru, I wished to take those courses. I also wished to audit the classes of famous Dr. Dukes, in animal physiology. He approved. He added that, as Director of Radiation Biology, he would be an automatic member of my committee and I needed to chose another. I asked him to recommend someone. He said that Dr. Lester, Director of Animal Nutrition, could be the other logical member. He asked me to talk to Dr. Lester. I went to see Dr. Lester that afternoon. Dr. Lester was very congenial. He accepted my request to become a committee member. I informed

Dr. Carter the next day. I attended Dr. Lester's classes. He spoke clearly, pronouncing every syllable very carefully. I understood him very well. So did other
foreign students. We appreciated his classes very much. The other teacher in Dr.
Lester's department was Dr. Wallace. In his classes, he spoke like a machine gun,
at four or five words per second. For me it was too much. While I was translating
the first phrase, Dr. Wallace had added five or six. One afternoon, I noticed that
everybody in the class was standing up and leaving the classroom. I did too and
went home. The next day, a classmate asked me why I had left. I said that because
class was over. She said, "No, it was only a ten-minute break." My troubles with
English were continuing.

In the international radioisotopes course, during the first two weeks, two written quizzes had been given, and I had flunked them both, mostly because of my
poor English. I could not answer one question because I did not understand the
word "lining" in reference to a Geiger tube detector. Another reason was that I
failed to memorize a whole table of data on radiation detectors. I was in trouble.
Dr. Carter would not even answer my "good mornings" any more. I decided then
that I was going to study as hard as never before; I was going to give it my very
best shot. And, if that was not good enough, then I was in the wrong place. I
would walk away without shame. Needless to say, I spent many hours studying
in my room, at night. It became a habit. I would come from classes at 5:30 p.m.,
have supper by six. Mr. And Mrs. Wolfe wanted me to watch TV with them. But I
would excuse myself by saying ,"No, thank you, I have to study," and then I would
retire to my room. I would study till midnight. Then I would sleep till three in the
morning, at which time I would get up and study till six. Then, I would shave and
shower and start walking toward the farm where I had some sheep under experiment on a forage digestibility study. I had to collect samples for analysis, weigh
the foods, and feed the animals. Then, I would walk to my classes. At noon, I
would have lunch at the campus cafeteria. In the afternoon, I had to see the animals again at 4 p.m. After that, I would walk back to my room to have supper and
repeat the cycle. I got used to it. Only three hours of sleep per night, for many
months. One day, Mrs. Wolfe told me that many students could not take the pressure of classes, assignments, reports, quizzes, and exams at Cornell. On average,
four students killed themselves every year, by jumping from the bridge on Stewart
Avenue into the bottom of the gorge, some 70 yards below. The bridge was only
100 yards from from the Wolfe's house.

Lab sessions in the international course on radioisotopes were in the afternoons and lasted 5 hours, from 1:00 p.m. to 6:00 p.m. The sessions were conducted by instructors with Ph.D. degrees. In one of the labs, the instructor, Dr.
Taylor, asked the international participants for a volunteer to take blood samples
from the jugular vein of a sheep that had been brought to the lab in a metabolic
cage. The blood samples had to be taken exactly at 1, 2, 4, 6, 8, 12, 30, 60, 90,
and 120 minutes after injection of the radioactive solutions. Nobody volunteered.
Then, I thought, this is my chance. I raised my hand. The instructor gave me a
smirk and a look of no confidence at all. The instructor asked for a volunteer to assist me. Dr. Sherghi, my office mate, raised his hand. "He is a chemist, I thought,"

but I was pleased. The instructor, Dr. Taylor, explained that we were going to do a ferrokinetic and an erythrokinetic study on that sheep. That is, a study of iron metabolism and a measure of the rate of red cell formation by the bone marrow, respectively. He added that we were going to use a solution of Fe-59 chloride and another of Cr-51 chromate as radiotracers. Observing the lab and taking notes were some 48 scientists from all over the world. And I was to take the blood samples in a timely fashion. The instructor proceeded to demonstrate the injection technique and started the timer. At one minute, he yelled, "Now!" and I while Dr. Sherghi held the head of the sheep high, I pressed the jugular canal with my left thumb and with a syringe and needle, in my right, I entered the vein just above . The blood entered the syringe at just the exact time. It took about three seconds to collect 12 cc. Dr. Taylor was pleased. A rumor was heard among the audience. The first sample had been successfully taken. "Two minutes," said Dr. Taylor, "Now!" I proceeded as before and took the second sample at exactly the right time. Another rumor of satisfaction was heard. During the break between samples, I noticed that Dr. Carter had come to watch. The rest of the experiment went very well. Strangers from India, Pakistan, Sweden, Greece, and other countries smiled at me. Some congratulated me. The next day, Dr. Carter invited me to dinner at his house that weekend. He must have thought "Marco cannot speak it, but he certainly can do it." Things began to improve after that. At the dinner, Dr. Carter said that he wanted to see me cry and put a record on his stereo player. The music was "Espana cani,"a double step, from Spain. I had to explain to him that Spanish music was not my kind of music. That I was Peruvian. He then introduced me to another guest, a British young man who was studying Quechua, in the languages department of the university. Quechua is the language of native Peruvians in the Andes mountains. Dr. Carter said, "Go ahead, talk to each other." I had to explain that in Peru, the official language was Spanish, not Quechua, and consequently I did not know it. Years later Peru did adopt Quechua as a second official language but not at the time of the story. Later, in the course labs, I was asked to do dissections, injections, blood collections, and some animal surgeries. Participants made a circle to see me work. I certainly had the "touch" for it. Best of all though, I began to get passing grades on quizzes and exams. My 3-hour sleep per night had begun to pay. And I had completed all assignments in my courses in satisfactory fashion. My English had improved too. I did not have to translate into Spanish anymore. One day, I went into the dry cleaners store, talked to the young lady attendant and came out of the store. Outside, I stopped and realized that I had done the whole transaction without even thinking in Spanish. "Eureka! I said, "I am over the hill." But I still had trouble understanding machine gun Dr. Wallace. But by then, the course was over. The cold winter, was almost over too. Spring was on the horizon.

44. Labor Day Picnic

By the end of the summer, the traditional Labor Day picnic was organized by the employees of the Radiation Biology Department. All faculty, graduate students, employees, and their families were invited. There was plenty of food and soft drinks for over two hundred people. Some youngsters were playing soccer and, I could not help it, but I joined in and showed off my skills. The kids and adults were impressed with my juggling of the ball with my feet, shoulders, chest, head, and heels. A professor commented, "Marco, you have played that game before." Lunch came next. People gathered around the tables to help themselves to the many dishes brought by the faculty and employees. We all sat in groups to chat and eat under the shadow of the trees. It was a pleasant time. After lunch, five or six ladies, professors' wives, decided to ride the revolving platform in the playground. I just happened to pass by. One or more of the ladies on the platform hollered, "Marco, give a good push." I did. The platform sped fast before the concerned eyes of their husbands. Nobody, not even I, knew what to do about it. One by one, the ladies fell by the tangent and rolled on the grass impelled by the centrifugal force. Well, it wasn't the centrifugal force, it was the angular momentum that they were carrying, that was it. And some of the ladies carried a large momentum! I apologized many times, but nobody was listening. Really, nobody got hurt. It was just a scary thing. Never again, I swore, will I ever give a push to anyone on a revolving platform. Later on, the kids organized a soccer game and they said, "Marco, you play goalkeeper." I accepted, of course. The kids, both boys and girls, did their best to score a goal on me. In one of those plays, I threw myself to the feet of the boy carrying the ball and took it away from him. Unfortunately, I cut my elbow when I fell. My elbow was bleeding, and all the kids showed concern and stopped the game. I bandaged my elbow with a handkerchief. At about 5 p.m. the picnic was over. Everybody was going home. At that moment, an attractive female research technician in our department, Miss Lillian Holloway, offered me a ride home in her car, a European, black, old convertible. I did not wish to give the wrong impression so I accepted. She dropped me off at my place on Stewart Avenue. I thanked her. The following day was a holiday.

45. Singing to the Animals

Sometime during my first Winter in Ithaca, Miss Diana Bennett, Dr. Carter's secretary, knowing that I walked to and from college every day, kindly offered me a ride in her car. It happened after work, one afternoon. I politely refused arguing that I was used to walking and that it helped me to think and plan my next day activities. Besides, I said, I needed the exercise. She insisted, and I accepted. She lived in downtown Ithaca, with another lady roommate, Miss Laura Wilson. Miss Bennett, dropped me off at my place, but first offered to pick me up at 7:45 a.m. the next day and to take me to school. "It's no trouble at all. I have to drive by here to get to the college anyway," she said. I never say no to a lady, I thought, and I accepted again. After that, I became a regular passenger in her car. We became friends. Just friends. When the summer came, Mr. Wolfe, my landlord, decided to sell me his old car, a 1954 De Soto, which he had parked on back of his house all winter. "It's in good running condition," he said, "and the price is right: only 125 dollars." I accepted. At least I would have transportation of my own, and I would not have to bother Miss Bennett anymore. But I was wrong once again. To drive my car, I had to get a driver's license. She offered to help me get a license. We went out in my car to practice driving, parking, turning around in the middle of the block, making arm signals to turn or stop, to read traffic signs, etc. Soon I was driving quite well. I took the tests and got my very own driver's licence. To show my gratitude to Miss Bennett, I invited her to lunch at a Chinese restaurant in Syracuse, one hour north of Ithaca. I remember it very well. When I asked if they served wine, the waitress, an older lady, replied with a straight face, "We don't serve alcoholic beverages here." We smiled and ordered sodas. I enjoyed that ride and back from Syracuse. It became a habit. We went to Syracuse for lunch just about every weekend that Summer of 1960. We also went to visit Seneca Lake, one of the Finger Lakes in upstate New York. It was very generous of Miss Bennett to show me the parks, the Seneca and Buttermilk waterfalls. We usually packed a picnic, studied the road map and went for an adventure. Dr. Sherghi's wife came from Poland to see her husband, and soon the four of us went to parks and picnics. I had great respect for Miss Diane Bennett. We were only friends. She was 20. I was much older at 27 and working on my M.S. degree. Like a quotation from the original movie of King Kong: "No funny business, see?"

Sometime in November, a Peruvian colleague, Dr. Canepa, professor of histology at my college in Lima, was passing through Ithaca with his wife Rosa. I invited them to lunch in Syracuse, and he made arrangements to take the train for New York City there, that afternoon after lunch. Of course, Diane came with us, and we made it a "double lunch date." We traveled in my car to Syracuse. Everything went well. We all had a good time. Later, we went to the train station to see Dr. Canepa and wife off to New York City. The Canepas had, in addition to two large and heavy suitcases, six or seven handbags. When the train stopped to pick up passengers, I helped them get on it by carrying some of the bags. The Canepas and I climbed the train car through the rear entrance and walked almost the full length of the car to find a suitable place for them and their luggage. Diane remained at the station platform watching me say good-bye to the Canepas. After that, I came down through the front end of the car. Diane did not see me. The train started to move. Diane thought that I was going to leave with the Canepas, so she decided to get on the train through the rear entrance. When I came down, I saw Diane on the train. I called, "Diane!" She saw me on the station deck and she jumped off from the moving train. She fell and rolled on the pavement. She had multiple lacerations all over her body. Fortunately, no broken bones. We went to a pharmacy and got some disinfectant, some sulfas ointment, and wide band aids. She went to the ladies room and applied the medications and band aids on her elbows and knees. We returned to Ithaca. It broke my heart to think that Diane had tried to follow me into the train thinking that I was leaving with the Canepas.

Three days later, I had to take some blood samples from four cows under experiment in a lab located by the Ithaca airport. The blood samples had to be taken at about 8 p.m. Diane offered to accompany me. Upon arrival, I entered the lab where the cows were housed in metabolic cages. I started to sing a song to tranquilize the animals. Next, wearing gloves, I proceeded to secure each cow to the railing of her cage with a nose holder and while I continued to sing, I took their blood from the jugular vein. I recorded the exact time of each sampling on a notebook. It was a dark night outside. On the ride back, I stopped the car, kissed Diane, and asked her to marry me. She cried and said "yes." A month later, we went to Syracuse for lunch and to purchase an engagement ring.

46. The M.S. Thesis

Most of my course work requirements were completed during the first semester. I had completed all course assignments. The courses were: biochemistry, biochemistry lab, animal nutrition, animal nutrition lab, the international radioisotopes course, and the radioisotopes lab. I had also completed the animal physiology course of Dr. Dukes, which I attended as an auditor only. During the second semester, while I worked on my M.S. thesis and with the approval of my committee, I took only a course in radiobiology in which the biological effects of radiation were studied. My fellowship covered all university's costs: tuition, books, and provided me with a fixed amount toward room and board. To be able to complete my research, I needed another semester, beyond the term of my fellowship. Again, Drs. Carter of Cornell and Rangel of San Marcos, recommended me for an extension of my fellowship to the Rockefeller Foundation. The extension was approved.

Perhaps you recall that during that first semester, I got used to sleeping only 3 hours per day. Something unusual occurred to me one night at about 2 a.m. But let me digress for a moment to July, 1959, in Lima, while preparing for my trip to the U.S. Perhaps because of my worrying, one night I dreamt that I was working on a math problem. I was sitting at a table with my notebook on it. There was a lamp on the left side of the table. Besides my notebook, I had several objects on the table: my wrist watch, my slide rule, my keys. At some instant, I obtained the result of the problem: 3.5. I woke up and wondered what 3.5 might mean and what that dream might mean, but soon I fell asleep again. I forgot the incident completely. In February of 1960, I was studying in my room of Stewart Avenue, Ithaca, NY, at 2 a.m., with my heavy coat wrapped around my shoulders. I was working on a biochemistry assignment. I was calculating the pKa value of an enzyme using the Henderson-Hasselbach equation when, suddenly, I came to the answer: 3.5. Instantly, I felt a cold passing through my whole body. My hair raised as a result of sympathetic stimulation. I had seen that result in my dream some seven months earlier in Lima! And there they were: the lamp, my watch, the slide rule, the keys. I have no explanation for what appears to be a case of premonition. I have had no other similar case like that happening to me, ever. Thus, perhaps it was a case of extreme coincidence. Extremely low probability events do happen sometimes.

My research thesis subject was suggested by Dr. Carter, head of the Department of Radiation Biology. I was to study the uptake of radioiodine in the thyroid gland of normal dogs. With the assistance of Dr. Taplin from the department staff, arrangements were made with Dr. Kirkland of the small animal clinic to secure the animals and to assist me during the radiation measurements using a scintillation detector and a ratemeter. All the work was done between July 1960 and March of 1961. Approximately 25 clinically normal dogs and four dogs suspected of having thyroid disorders were studied. Some histological sections of the thyroid glands were also examined under the microscope to measure the height of the thyroid epithelium. Blood samples were taken also from all animals to determine the concentration of serum cholesterol and the protein-bound iodine. The idea was to either confirm or reject the common belief the there was an inverse relationship between the level of total cholesterol in the blood serum and the level of thyroid function. In other words, animals with hypothyroidism have high levels of cholesterol and vice versa. My research showed that the thyroid of normal animals take up the radioiodine at a slower rate than humans reaching a maximum at 72 hours, the best time for clinical diagnosis. In addition, my research had shown that there was a direct correlation between epithelium height and thyroid function, and that the levels of cholesterol did not correlate well with thyroid function. I presented my research at a departmental seminar in March and later, at the Annual Veterinary Conference of the State of New York held at our college. They were successful presentations. Sometime in May, I defended successfully my thesis before the members of my committee and some observers of my department. At that time, Diane Bennett volunteered to type my thesis. Six copies were submitted to the graduate school. I was given a passing grade. Graduation ceremonies were in June, but they were not mandatory. I could not attend because of my work assisting other members of the staff with their research projects. My M.S. diploma was mailed to me later in July.

47. Wedding Bells

I used to call Syracuse "the freezer of the U.S." because of the extreme cold I felt there in winter. Sure enough, the day Diane and I went there to look for an engagement ring, the temperature dropped to minus 40. We parked the car and ran quickly into the jewelry store, which had heating, of course, and spent some thirty minutes choosing a ring for her. We settled on a one-carat diamond mounted on a gold ring. We also got matching wedding bands for both of us. When we came out of the store, our car was covered by a layer of solid ice one quarter inch thick. It looked like a candy apple! I could not introduce the key into the keyhole to open the car. I tried to break the ice, but it was too hard. One minute breathing the cold dry air could have been catastrophic for our lungs. We went back into the store and asked for help. The manager ordered a maintenance man to get a torch and melt the ice around the car's keyhole. The man was reluctant to get out in the cold. Immediately the manager exclaimed, "This gentleman just bought a diamond!" I felt ten feet tall. In one minute, the ice was melted. We got in the car and started the engine. Some ten minutes later, we were on our way back to Ithaca.

A week later, on a Saturday, we went to Endicott, NY, to visit Diane's parents and to announce our engagement. Mr. and Mrs. Bennett were not pleased. In my presence they were cordial, but in private with Diane they expressed their disapproval. Of course, Diane never told me that, but I could sense it. Although I was good looking, athletic, and a college professor, I was still a Latin and had brown eyes. That was the problem, as I understood it then. At some point, over lunch, I told the Bennetts, that unless they approved, there would not be any wedding because their relationship with Diane was more important. Suddenly, Diane covered her eyes, excused herself and left the house running. She got out of the house and ran down the avenue. It was a cold and misty day. There was some drizzling. Mr. Bennett, a gentleman about 60 years old, asked me, "Run after her, please." I did. I caught up with her at a small shopping center five blocks away. I begged her to come back to the house and to talk until we resolved the situation. I told her that I would not ever stop loving her and that I would do my best to convince her parents to accept me. We arrived at the house. Mrs. Bennett served tea. Mr. Bennett talked first. He said that Dianne was now 21 years old and perfectly free to make her own decisions. Diane and I hugged each other. We both had tears in our eyes. Then, like magic, we started talking cheerfully. Bobby, the ten-year old brother of Diane, showed me his toy train he had in the basement. Later, we watched the results of the national election coming in on black and white TV. A close election in which John F. Kennedy beat Richard Nixon. At about 5 p.m., Diane and I departed on our one-hour trip back to Ithaca.

Dr. Carter, director of our Radiation Biology department, requested and obtained an additional extension of my fellowship by the Rockefeller Foundation for three months so that I could pay short visits to the radiation biology facilities of the Massachusetts Institute of Technology (MIT) in Cambridge, MA; the Brookhaven National Laboratory (BNL) in Long Island, NY; the Oak Ridge National Laboratory (ORNL) in Oak Ridge, TN; and the Argonne National Laboratory(ANL) in Chicago, IL. That was his wedding present to Diane and me.

The 31st of May, 1961, Diane and I were married at the Cornell University chapel, a non-denominational church. Pastor Doherty performed the ceremony. Attending were Mr. and Mrs. Bennett, Bobby Bennett, Diane's brother, Miss Laura Wilson, Diane's best friend, Pastor Doherty's wife, and George Thorpe, a research assistant and good friend of mine, as best man, with his wife Elaine. After the ceremony, we went to the Coral Gables restaurant for dinner with champaigne and wines. At the proper time, Diane and I left on our honeymoon trip to Niagara Falls where, 8 years earlier, Marilyn Monroe and Joseph Cotten had filmed the movie Niagara. We spent three unforgettable days and had the opportunity to visit both the American side as well as the Canadian side of the waterfalls. We also took the boat ride to the bottom of the falls wearing those yellow plastic overcoats to protect us from the mist. We then returned to Endicott. Mr. and Mrs. Bennett accommodated us in their guest room in the attic. Mr. Bennett, my father-in-law, who was a house construction contractor, was also a skillful mechanic. In our absence, he had conditioned and tuned up Diane's car, the best of the two we had, for the trip to Cambridge, MA, Long Island, NY, Oak Ridge,TN, and Chicago, IL.

48. The National Laboratories

Two days later we departed for Cambridge, MA, where my contact was Dr. Turner, a radiobiologist from MIT . We took lodging at a nearby hotel. Dr. Turner had arranged appointments for me to talk with scientists working on a number of projects in radiobiology. My appointments were completed by noon. I then joined Diane for lunch, a walk in the park, and a tour of the city of Boston, just across the Charles river. During my visits, I kept accurate records about the meetings and subjects discussed for my reports to the Rockefeller Foundation, Dr. Carter of Cornell University, and Dr. Rangel, Dean of the Veterinary College of Lima, Peru. After four days of visits, we departed for Long Island, NY. We drove to Rhode Island and from there, we took the ferry to the East coast of Long Island. Then, we drove west toward the Brookhaven National Laboratory. We found lodging at a motel near the lab. During my initial tour, I was very much impressed with "Cosmotron," the atomic particle accelerator. But, the same as before, my four-day visit consisted of meetings with scientists doing research in animal physiology, metabolism, and radiation effects on biological systems. It was in that lab that, two years later, in 1963, the technetium-99m generator was going to be invented. That generator was going to revolutionize the field of nuclear medicine. In the afternoons, Diane and I walked the beach. On the beach, I collected some of the most beautiful pebbles I had ever seen. They were about a half-inch in diameter, almost spherical. Some were oblong, of smooth surface, but the best of all was that they were of many colors and some almost transparent. They were semiprecious stones!. I kept that small treasure for several years. After the visit, it was time to depart for Tennessee to visit the Oak Ridge National Laboratory.

At Oak Ridge, my host, Dr. Morley, gave me a tour of the various areas where research in multiple fields was being conducted: the Oak Ridge graphite nuclear reactor, the second reactor built by Enrico Fermi and his team, and modeled after the first "pile" built in Chicago during the Second World War. He also took me to see the gaseous diffusion plant where uranium was enriched to be used as nuclear fuel in reactors around the world, as well as the biology division, where I met with scientists doing research on biological effects of radiation. I also had the opportunity to visit the medical division of the Oak Ridge Institute of Nuclear Studies (ORINS), where various radiotherapy approaches were being investigated to treat human cancers. I never imagined then, that three years later, in 1964, I was going to return to Oak Ridge to work as a scientist at the special training division of ORINS. Once I completed my visit to Oak Ridge, it was time to travel to our final destination, Argonne National Laboratory.

At Argonne, I had the opportunity to visit the very site where Enrico Fermi and team, secretly, erected the first "pile" of enriched uranium fuel and graphite moderator to, for the first time in the world, achieve and sustain the first controlled nuclear fission chain reaction. That had occurred 19 years earlier, in 1942, under the stands of the football stadium at the University of Chicago. In those days, the entrance to the site of the pile had a sign which read, "Metallurgy." Of course, at the time, nobody gave a second thought to what was being done there. After all, at the time, a horrible war was being fought on two fronts, in Europe and in the Pacific. My appointments with scientists doing animal research were completed in four days. After that, it was time to return to NY to say good-bye to Diane's parents. We were going to travel to Peru where I had a job waiting for me as an assistant professor of biochemistry and animal nutrition. Once again, thanks to the generosity of the Rockefeller Foundation, we got an allowance to cover the travel expenses of my lovely wife, Diane.

With tears in Mr. Bennett's eyes, we said good-bye to the Bennetts one afternoon in September, 1961. We traveled by Greyhound Bus to New York city, where we stayed two days. At that time, we walked the large Central Park and visited the zoo. Two days later we boarded the steamship "Santa Cecilia" with destination Callao, the principal port of Peru. On that trip, we made friends with a Chilean veterinarian and his daughter. They were traveling to Valparaiso, Chile. During the trip, we also met Mr. Balaguer, who was also a passenger traveling with his family and, at the time, dictator of the Dominican Republic.

49. The Return to Lima

The Santa Cecilia steamship passed through most of the Panama canal during the night, but we could see in the morning the lowering of the ship by the locks system until we got to sea level and entered the Pacific ocean. A few days later, we arrived at the Peruvian port of Callao. We were pleased to see my mother, my sisters, and brother Daniel and his wife Teresa, who were waiting at the terminal to see us disembark. From there, we went to have lunch at one of our favorite Chinese restaurants in Capon street in Lima. My brother Daniel generously invited Diane and me to stay with them until we could find a suitable place of our own. Some ten days later, we rented an apartment in the San Isidro district. Those were very trying days, because Diane was very lonely while I was at work. To entertain herself, she read, listened to the radio, and watched some TV in Spanish. She also tried to cook some meals. She learned to take the bus to the Peruvian-American Institute to take classes in Spanish. She made progress quite fast. I was very proud of her. In October of 1961, the "Atoms in Action" exhibit sponsored by the U.S. Atomic Energy Commission (AEC) and the Peruvian government began their presentations to the public, as well as some cooperative programs in education and scientific research on "Campo de Marte" in Lima. The exhibit had brought a small research nuclear reactor and a 4-Curie gamma source of cobalt-60. As a professor, I received an invitation to use the facilities in any research projects we wished to undertake. After consulting with Dr. Morales, director of the microbiology department at my college, I submitted a proposal for the irradiation of *Klebsiella abortus*, a bacterium responsible for infectious abortion in cattle. The proposal was accepted, and I took some cultures, in well-sealed test tubes, to the exhibit and subjected them to high doses of gamma radiation ranging between 10,000 and 100,000 rads (100 to 1000 Grays). Back in my lab with the irradiated cultures, I planted them in petri dishes prepared with agar and blood-agar culture media. At 48 hours, I inspected the colonies and prepared suspensions in saline solution. I used those to give intraperitoneal injections to white laboratory mice. I found that the culture that received 50,000 rads, had survived, but had also lost its virulence. That culture could now be the starting point for the development of a possible vaccine. But it was not to be. In my absence, the technician of the microbiology lab, while doing routine cleaning of the refrigerators, had sterilized and discarded all my cultures. Since then, I often thought about how a failure in communication had ruined a promising project. The exhibit lasted only 30 days in Lima there was no time to repeat the experiment.

At the same time, five American scientists visiting Lima with the exhibit were scheduled to lecture in the evenings, at the School of Sciences of the University of San Marcos. I was asked to act as interpreter. I did. And the presentations were very well received. One of those scientists was Dr. Robert Masterman, leader of the group, and chairman of the special training division of ORINS, the technical institute at Oak Ridge, TN. He asked me to come a half-hour before every conference to discuss some key phrases to be brought in by the evening's lecturer. That way, I was well prepared to give accurate translations into Spanish. That approach to interpreting scientific subjects was ideal. After the lectures were completed, the Dean of Sciences hosted a cocktail party for the lecturers and other guests. Among many university professors, I was also invited and attended with my lovely wife Diane. She was delighted to meet many important Peruvian and American people. Then, I invited Dr. Masterman to visit my lab at the veterinary college of Monterrico. He came, and I introduced him to the Dean and faculty. I also gave him a tour of my lab and other laboratories at my college. At that point, everything seemed to be well and running. But not everything was shiny and rosy. A terrible storm was in the works.

In November of 1961, I was informed that, while I was attending Cornell University, a new Peruvian university law had been approved by the legislature and signed by the President of the Republic. That law ordered the promotion of all professors one step up with a consequent rise in salaries. To me, that signified that I should have been promoted to associate professor. The law also commanded a technical reorganization of the whole university. I also learned that, in my absence, the roster of faculty to be promoted, submitted to the Rector's Office, had omitted my name. Apparently, some of my colleagues in my college campus had decided on their own that because I was absent at Cornell, and because I had been promoted to assistant professor just before traveling to the U.S., that I did not deserve another promotion. But the law did not put conditions. The law ordered the promotion of all faculty without conditions. Those colleagues, friends of mine, some of them had been my teachers, in my opinion, full of professional jealousy, decided to make an exception to the mandate of the law. At the time, I was literally living on borrowed money. My generous brother Daniel, a successful practicing physician, had loaned me money so that I could rent an apartment and purchase some basic furniture and appliances. I hoped to pay him in small monthly quotas. I spent one night studying carefully the text of the law and, naturally, I presented a petition to the college council to correct the omission. By then, I was also a member of the council, the youngest ever. When my case was to be discussed in the council, I excused myself and left the session and went home. I hoped that the intelligence and fairness of my colleagues and friends would give more weight to the letter of the law. But I was wrong. Two days later, I learned that professional jealousy was engraved in their hearts too strongly. They had recommended that my petition be rejected. I also learned that the group of student representatives to the council had voted en masse for me, but the majority of my colleagues had opposed it. I was discouraged. Since then, some of my colleagues avoided me, some stopped talking to me. It was like living in another dimension, the twilight zone, another planet. But I continued to work harder than ever to make my courses and my teachings a success. I rewrote, updated, and upgraded completely the courses of biochemistry, biochemistry lab, and animal nutrition in 1962. After six months of the rejection meeting, the limit interval in which anyone can request a reconsideration of a council decision, I indeed presented a reconsideration request. In early 1963, by the grapevine I learned that my request was interred in a desk drawer in the rector's office. The rector of the university was Dr. Saenz. He had been my teacher of genetics and animal reproduction a few years earlier. I called his office and made an appointment to see him. Dr. Saenz, at first, refused to see me. Two months later, he changed his mind and asked me, by phone, to come to his fancy office. He received me and was very cordial. He said that due to some involuntary error, the papers had been temporarily lost, but that he, personally, would rush them through the system. In passing, I should mention that during my visit to the rector's office, I noticed the most beautiful women secretaries I had ever seen in my life. At the time, I could not help it, but think "Dr. Saenz is in heaven!"

50. An Offer I could not Refuse

Early in 1962, we knew that my lovely wife Diana was expecting a child. Diane and I were delighted. But with my small salary, I could only see hard times ahead. I was very much embarrassed to ask my brother Daniel for another loan. So, I never did. I made arrangements through the white collar employees social security system to give my wife medical check ups and to obtain admission to the maternity ward in the "Employee's Hospital" on Salaverry Avenue. In the wee hours of June 21, our daughter Catalina, Cati for short, was born. I was there. After I received the good news that both were well, I went home to rest one hour and then go to work that morning. Later, I went into the offices of my colleagues in the north wing of our building, Drs. Velarde and Orestes in physiology; Dr. Morales, at the time Dean of our college, and Dr. Danilo in microbiology; Drs. Torres and Cordova in parasitology, and gave them cigars while announcing the birth of my daughter. All of them smiled, shook my hand and congratulated me. In a way, it was a gesture on my part, to tell them that I still wanted them as friends. That I forgave them for the rejection of my petition. Psychologically, it was a good move. People in my wing of the building began to talk to me again after having subjected me to months of isolation. I owe that to my precious daughter Cati.

A good friend of mine, Dr. Lucho Pando, who had saved my life in La Raya in 1957, connected me with a relative of his, who owned a two bedroom house in Monterrico and wanted to rent it to a reliable tenant. I went to see the owner. Everything was arranged and we—Diane, Cati, and I— moved into that lovely two-bedroom house with flower gardens in front and in back. The best of all though, was that the house was only five blocks from the college. I walked to work every day. It was great! We also got a maid to assist Diane with the cleaning and cooking. Things were shaping up, but I still could not pay my brother's original loan. I began to think that I must find a better paid job. Remembering the offers I had from the Department of Agriculture and the military establishment, I decided to inquire about a possible transfer, but I quickly learned that my starting salary would be lower that my present salary. No dice there. Then, I contacted the Agrarian University. I met with Dr. Alarcon, in charge of faculty employment. He was a bit more promising. He said that they had nothing matching my M.S. degree from Cornell, but as veterinarian, they could have a position for me in January of 1964. He said that it took about two years to materialize a new position. Well, at least, there was some hope. My daughter grew up quickly in Monterrico. She had honey-blond hair and fair complexion. She was healthy and smart as a kitten. One more thing, she had my brown eyes. They do not make them any better! Later, I was asked to work overtime as an examiner, in admission exams to the university, in the specialty of mathematics. I worked four hours per night for a month, and my earnings helped us recover somewhat.

Sometime in July of 1963, Dr. Rangel, who had assisted me with the reconsideration procedure, and possibly, for that reason, made some powerful enemies in the high administration of the university, accepted an offer from UNESCO and traveled to Paris as a consultant. At the time, we suspected that he was not coming back. I felt that I had to continue the fight alone. The political situation behind the scenes was clearly divided. On one side were the "apristas"—a revolutionary group fighting to recover the power they had in the thirties. To this group belonged Dr. Saenz, the rector of the university, and a trail of brown-nosing professors. On the other, the communists, the reds, also called "little radishes," because of the radishes'color, trying to gain political power away from the apristas. My wife Diane, trying to help our economical situation, through friends, found a job as a secretary in an American company with offices at Todos, the commercial center on the Republic Boulevard. But soon she felt being mistreated by her boss and other employees. She quit. I applauded her when she told me about it. She then wrote to her parents in Endicott, New York, expressing her desire to come home, to the U.S., with Cati, our daughter. Her parents approved. I could not argue with her, but I promised that, at the end of the academic year, by Christmas, I would follow them and find a job in the U.S. Thus, Diane and Cati traveled to the U.S. in July. I would follow in December of 1963. Then, something unexpected happened. The University's Student Federation, run by communists, knowing of my struggle with the rector's office about their omission in the promotion list, mandated by law, asked me to meet with them and plan a general university students' strike until my lawful rights were recognized. They said that the entire student body, some 30,000 students, was on my side. They gave me a tour of the old San Marcos house, passages, corridors, secret doors, meeting rooms, etc. which I had

never seen before and were not available to the public. I was very much impressed
with the mysteries and their flavor of twilight zone. But I told them that I preferred
to continue my fight for a while longer, without a general strike. I could not tell
them, at that time, that I was planning to leave Peru, and look for a job in the U.S.
Just in case, though, I carried a weapon with me, just in case I was attacked on
any street by an aprista mercenary hit man. Then, suddenly, a hand written letter
from Dr. Masterman arrived for me. The letter offered me a position at the special
training division of ORINS the following year, 1964, starting in July. The starting salary would be three times the one I was getting at my college. That was an
offer I could not refuse. I wrote back immediately accepting the offer. I also told
Dr. Masterman that, my wife and daughter were in Endicott, NY, living with her
parents, and that one way or another I would be coming to the U.S. by Christmas.
I would travel to Oak Ridge as soon as my appointment was ready. Dr. Masterman
called Diane later and told her that he would try to find the necessary funding to
bring me to Oak Ridge earlier than July.

—⚬◎⚬—

Reporter Judy Hartfeldt: The political situation in Lima was troublesome
for you, I can see that. Imagine, being caught between two fighting factions.

Marco Donnatti: Yes, it was. But I felt that the communists wanted to use me
as a flag to get at the apristas. That was why I asked for a postponement. Really,
like Dr. Rangel, I wanted to get out of the mud.

Judy: What happened next?

Marco: I began to work on obtaining an immigrant visa at the U.S. Consulate
and on arranging my travel to the U.S. by the end of the academic year, sometime
around December 20, 1963. I will tell you about that in our next meeting, OK?

Judy: I can hardly wait. Thank you. Bye now.

Marco: Bye, Judy.

—⚬◎⚬—

Along came the Tarantula, a scary, hairy creature (Story 53)

CHAPTER 6

THE IMMIGRANT

Reporter Judy Hartfeldt: Good morning Marco. You are early.
Marco Donnatti: Yes. It's a habit, I can't help it. Better early than late.
Judy: Are you ready to tell me how you became an immigrant to the United States?
Marco: Yes. The following stories will describe my struggle in the midst of a political fight between the "reds," the communists, and the "blues," the apristas, and how I decided to leave the university and join my wife and daughter in the U.S.

51. The Green Card

By September of 1963, I became convinced that my promotion, mandated by law, was not going to happen. There were powerful forces working behind the scenes to block all attempts on my part to obtain the reconsideration I had requested. The promise by the rector of the university to expedite the process soon faded into oblivion. It was then that I went to the U.S. Consulate in Lima and told the secretary, Mr. Porter, that I wished to apply for an immigrant's visa and showed him the letter from Dr. Masterman, Chairman of the special training division of ORINS. In the letter, Dr. Masterman offered me a one-year appointment as a scientist in his Institute beginning in July, 1964. My duties would involve the organizing of a new radioisotopes training program for Latin American college professors, in Spanish, to be presented in connection with the newly designed "Atoms in Action" exhibit. That program was sponsored by the U.S. Atomic Energy Commission (USAEC). Mr. Porter asked me to fill out some forms, to sign them, and date them. In those documents, he learned that I was an assistant professor at the University of San Marcos, that my wife was an American citizen, that I had a baby daughter, and that I had been hospitalized some ten years earlier. After consulting with other consulate officers, he told me that because I was married to a U.S. citizen, I could have applied for a visa much earlier claiming "hardship." I responded that I wanted to earn the visa on my own merits and not because of marriage. He then said that he would have to verify the authenticity of the letter and the information I had given in my application. He said that they would let me know in a few days. He also told me that, because of my medical history, I had to have a medical exam performed by a consulate's physician. He gave me the name, address, and phone number of Dr. Jorge Rivarola who had his office in San Isidro. Immediately, I made an appointment with Dr. Rivarola. The doctor gave me a thorough physical exam. His nurse took a venous blood sample from my left arm vein and requested a urine sample. He then asked me to provide a sample of my sputum to be sent to a special laboratory for culture in guinea pigs. About one month later, the consulate sent me a note asking me to report to their offices. I went. I was told that the cultures had been negative to *Mycobacterium tuberculosis*. They then asked me to sign a written declaration: that I had never been a member of the communist party. I signed and dated the declaration. Then they gave me another document by which, within 30 days of my arrival as an immigrant in the U.S., I had to report to a military recruiting office to serve, if required, in the armed forces for a limited length of time. I signed that document also. Then, the Consul, Mr. Robert Flack, handed me my very own green card and said, "Welcome to the United States of America." He shook my hand and added, "The military service is a formality only. Because you are a college professor, they will exempt you from that obligation. Here, take this envelope with you. It contains your radiographs and laboratory results. Immigration officials will ask you for them when you arrive in Miami." I said, "Thank you Mr. Consul."

My plans were to travel to the U.S. as soon as the academic year was over, sometime around the 20th of December. By the end of October, I sold my car and purchased my one-way plane ticket to New York. From there, I planned to take the bus to Endicott, NY. All this in absolute secret, of course. But one evening, while waiting for a ride downtown, at the main entrance to the college, some students approached me to ask about the progress in my reconsideration request. I told them that I was very disappointed about the documents having been misplaced at the rector's office again. I added that I was looking for another job, possibly at the Agrarian University or perhaps in the U.S., and that, with that purpose, I was traveling to the U.S. in December, after classes and exams were over. And I showed them my one-way airplane ticket. I knew perfectly well that the news was going to travel fast to the opposing faction. In the cat and mouse game, I sent the enemy a message: that, one way or other, I was planning to leave the college for good. It worked! A week later, at about 5 p.m., the Dean of the college, Dr. Morales, stopped me as I was coming down the stairs from my office to go home. He said, "Marco, you are working too hard, you are making the other teachers look bad." I responded that I had come to our college to do my best for the education of the new classes of veterinary students so that they could become better professionals. He then said that I had to decide whether I was going to be "red," (a communist) or "blue," (an aprista) and that being colorless was unacceptable. I replied that I had not come to our college to play politics, and that politics was a waste of time, energy, and resources, that slowed down the progress of the educational process, one of the missions of the university. I did not know then that politics was a necessary evil. He then pulled a check out of his briefcase and said that the college council, in a special meeting, had approved my promotion to associate professor retroactively to June of 1962, and that the check was written to my name for 36,000 soles, representing the difference in salaries for the past 18 months. But he did not give me the check. He held it in his hand by his right shoulder. Then, he said, "At future council meetings we, the blues, are going to ask you to vote blue."

I responded that my vote was not for sale and quickly, like lightning, I took the check from his hand and said, "This check is what the university owed me for my work, this check is not a favor from you or from the rector, it is my work." Dean Morales smiled. I smiled too. We shook hands and I said, "Good night and thank you." With that money, I could pay all my debts to my brother Daniel and cover travel expenses in my journey to Endicott, NY, and Oak Ridge, TN. By the end of November, in my rented house of Monterrico, I held a rummage sale and sold all my belongings. With that, I had some two thousand dollars to travel and to start a new life with my family in my new adopted country. Far away from lawless reds and blues.

52. Oak Ridge and Atoms in Action

Learning that I was coming to New York in December to reunite the family, Dr. Masterman, chaiman of the Special Training Division of ORINS, wrote to me asking me to make a two-day detour by Oak Ridge for a job interview. I did travel from Miami to Atlanta with connection to Knoxville. From there I took the shuttle to Oak Ridge. I took a room at the Holiday Inn. Then, I called Dr. Anderson, vice-chairman of the special training division, and made an appointment for my job interview. Dr. Anderson came to see me and asked me about my educational history and my training at Cornell. He was satisfied with my answers. From Oak Ridge, I traveled to Endicott, NY, just before Christmas, for a reunion with Diane and Catalina, my 18-month-old baby daughter. Mr and Mrs. Bennett fixed a guest room for us in the attic of their house. After the holidays, I went to work with Mr. Bennett, as his assistant, helping him with the remodeling of some houses he had under contract. It was a very cold winter. About January 20, I sent to Lima my request for a one-year leave of absence without salary. My reasons were that I had been asked by ORINS to organize the training program of Atoms in Action for Latin America. Sometime in February of 1964, I received a letter from Dr. Morales, Dean of our college, stating that my request had been approved, and that the college had appointed me "on commission" and granted me a travel allowance of 1,500 soles per month during the year of my absence. I quickly sent a power of attorney to Lima so that my mother, who had the meager pension of a military widow, could receive those monthly payments. We then received a letter from Dr. Masterman in Oak Ridge, saying that he had managed to secure the funds to hire me sooner that expected and that I could join the Institute the first of March. By February 20, Diane and I packed our few belongings in Diane's old car and began our journey to Oak Ridge, TN. When we arrived, we were enchanted with Oak Ridge, a small town in east Tennessee. It had only a population of 28,000, of which 8,000 were scientists and the rest were families and workers providing services. It was like a dream, like an island in the south. The town had played a vital role during World War II, when its population reached 80,000. The role consisted in the production of enriched uranium-235 and plutonium-239 for nuclear weapons. But by1964, all that was history. By then, Oak Ridge was dedicated to research in the peaceful uses of atomic and nuclear energy. There were 24 nuclear reactors at the various plants surrounding the city. And I was part of it. Soon after, I met some Brazilians, Venezuelans, Colombians, British, Germans, Yugoslavs, and Italians, either working or in training at the Oak Ridge plants and labs. With them we practiced soccer, our favorite sport, every Sunday afternoon.

The newly designed Atoms in Action exhibit, sponsored by the AEC, consisted of a one-story portable building in the shape of an octagon, with an inflatable, constant-flow of air vinyl roof, in the form of a dome. Inside, there was a small research nuclear reactor to be used as a neutron source and in neutron activation analyses. There was also a cobalt-60 gamma source to be used in the irradiation of chemicals and biological samples. The center of the building was a library. Surrounding the library, there were three laboratories: the radiochemistry lab, the radiation measurements lab or "counting room," with 24 beta and gamma radiation detectors, and the electronics lab. There was also a lecture room with capacity for 24 persons. Around the labs were the high school lecture room, with a seating capacity for 60 students, and the seven public exhibit areas, which showed the applications of nuclear energy in agriculture, medicine, industry, the production of clean energy, and space exploration.

For me, the year of 1964 was one of preparation. For the course of "Radioisotopes in Basic Research," I began by selecting twenty lecture topics and twenty laboratory exercises on radioisotopes work in chemistry and biology. I did the same for the course of "Radioisotopes in Medicine." The courses were going to be taught by our staff, in Spanish, to selected local college teachers and physicians during the four weeks of the Atoms in Action exhibit in each country of Central and South America. I also began to select all the equipment and materials needed to conduct the lectures and lab sessions. The cost of those items exceeded 100,000 dollars. When I went to see Dr. Masterman with the ordering forms, Dr. Masterman looked at them and gave his approval by signing them. He then gave the orders to Mr. Terry, the division's administrative officer, and asked him to place the orders. I was very much surprised to have an order of such magnitude approved in 5 minutes! I would now have the resources needed to mount three laboratories in each country. The U.S. department of State did the international diplomatic part of the plan. Thus, we soon learned that the first presentation was going to be in San Salvador, El Salvador, in February-March of 1965. My next objective was to write two manuals, in Spanish, one called "Radioisotopos in Investigacion Basica," ("Radioisotopes in Basic Research"), for college professors teaching chemistry or biology, and another named "Radioisotopos in Diagnostico Medico," ("Radioisotopes in Medical Diagnosis"), exclusively for physicians. Each manual contained twenty lecture outlines and twenty laboratory procedures. Among the lecturers were Dr. Anderson, a physicist and vice-chairman of our special training division (STD), Dr. Stern, a radiochemist and a consultant from California, myself, overall coordinator and lecturer in biomedical applications. A consultant was hired to write a radiation science manual, in Spanish, to be given to all high school students and teachers attending the educational program. The publishing division of the AEC was responsible for printing and binding of the manuals. Other members of the team were Mr. George Mester, a physicist and electronics expert, responsible for organizing and teaching a course on the electronics of radiation detectors, Mr. Peter Lorton, a health physicist and lecturer on radiation safety, and a consultant, Dr. Carrera, an Uruguayan physician, to lecture on medical applications during the fourth week of the exhibit. The high school program consisted of three four-hour seminars per day given to selected groups of high school students. The local department of education did the selecting and scheduling of the groups. The seminars were presented by three local science teachers, selected for training in Oak Ridge six months before the exhibit. The exhibit's director and his staff were responsible for organizing and supervising the public exhibits. They, with a team of engineers and technicians, erected the portable building, provided water and electricity to it, and maintained the building operation during the duration of the exhibit. They also packed and shipped everything at the end of each presentation. It reminded me of the movie "The Greatest Show on Earth," only highly technical. In preparation for the first exhibit, I had daily brown bag lunches with George Mester and Dr. Anderson, for a whole year in which I taught Spanish to them. I was proud to see them later lecturing in Spanish during the exhibit courses. In between exhibits, which were scheduled at one every six months, we worked on domestic training programs. In 1965, we had two one-month presentations in El Salvador and Guatemala. In 1966, we offered presentations in Costa Rica and Nicaragua. In 1967, we had presentations in Panama City and in Quito, Ecuador. Then we continued with presentations in 1968 at Caracas, Venezuela, and Cordoba, Argentina. And in 1969, we had only one presentation— Sao Paulo, Brazil. For this last presentation, the USAEC, required all members of the teaching staff to learn Brazilian Portuguese! The courses manuals were translated into Portuguese by the Brazilian Department of Education. In summary, I must state that all Atoms in Action presentations were very well received and that the local authorities in each country appreciated us and the exhibit presentations immensely. In the letters written after some presentations, they referred to us as the "true American ambassadors of good will."

53. Along came the Tarantula

As coordinator of the training program of the Atoms in Action exhibits program, I was supposed to arrive some ten days before the opening and establish contact with the local authorities. One was the department of education, to make sure that they selected and scheduled the high school groups that would attend the four-hour seminars. Another responsibility was to receive the applications and to select the college professors and physicians that would attend the radioisotope courses. My appointments had been arranged by the U.S. department of State. Thus, I traveled to Caracas, Venezuela, in April of 1968. I arrived at the airport in Caracas and was pleased that Mr. Baker, cultural attache of the U.S. embassy, was at the airport to meet me. That had never happened before, and consequently, made me feel important. Mr. Baker took me to my hotel, the "Ambassador," located on plaza Palmira. The employee at the reception desk gave me a penthouse on the ninth floor with a wide glass sliding door leading to a balcony. The balcony had tropical plants on both sides and plenty of flowers. The view was superb. An obelisk gave the plaza a sign of distinction. After dinner that night, I read the documents I needed for my appointments in the morning. It was a warm night, in a tropical country so, I decided to open the sliding door to the balcony some twelve inches wide to let the fresh air enter the room. At about 10 p.m., I turned in and went to sleep.

At about 2 a.m., a noise woke me up. I laid there for a couple of minutes, in the dark, not sure of what I had heard, when I heard the noise again. Something, perhaps a bat, was in the room. I turned the light on. Then, I saw a large insect, perhaps a grasshopper, fligh from one side of the room to the other making the same characteristic noise. I figured then that I had to get rid of it if I was to have any sleep at all. I got up, opened the glass door wide and, arming myself with a pillow, began to swing it around the place where I had seen the creature land. Sure enough, the grasshopper flew toward the balcony and disappeared. I closed the glass door tight this time. I went to bed and turned the light out. Then, I heard the same sound again. I repeated the process and chased another grasshopper out. Hoping that there were no more insects in the room, I went to bed. I was about to turn the light off when I saw a large tarantula on the opposite wall of the room about a foot from the ceiling. The spider was the size of my open hand with the fingers slightly bent. I looked at her and, I knew, she looked at me with her eight dark, shiny eyes.

Knowing that tarantulas can give you a painful bite and even kill a person, I decided to chase it out of the room. But soon I realized that the spider would quickly hide behind or under the furniture and I that would not be able to find it. Then, it occurred to me that I should try to kill her or I would not be able to sleep the rest of the night. And I had important appointments in the morning. Thus, I made a plan. I would slowly approach the wall. Then I would slowly place a chair at one foot from the wall. I would arm myself with a shoe and slowly climb the chair. Then, in an instant, like lightning, I would hit the tarantula with my shoe. But wait a minute! What if the spider moved away? I had to have contingency plans. If the spider moved, I would instantly hit it a second time. With that plan, I climbed slowly on the chair. I noticed the spider had rotated position slightly, some ten degrees. That meant that she was perfectly aware of my proximity and that, to her, my approaching spelled danger. We looked at each other. Like lightning, I hit. She moved one foot to the left. Plan B. Like lightning, I hit again. This time I smashed it. Her juices spread over the wall and ran down along the wall to the floor. Some juice sprinkled on my face and ran down to my chin, stomach and legs. Slowly, I came down from the chair and went to the bathroom to take a shower. I changed clothes. Then, I went to examine the spider. She was dead by the baseboard. I placed the carcass carefully in a large envelope. I wiped out the wall with a wet towel. Then I went to sleep. In the morning, I went to see the manager. I told him that I had found a spider in my room the previous night. He said, "That's impossible. I had all the rooms sprayed recently." I then placed the open envelope with the carcass on the counter and asked, "Is there a place nearby where I can have breakfast?" He was in shock and did not answered. I walked slowly toward the exit. As I was about to leave, he yelled, "Mr. Donnatti, I will have your room sprayed again." I waved and left. Soon I found myself walking by the roaring traffic of Caracas. Most of the roaring was due to the noise of motorcycles. Local people said that in Caracas, four motorcyclists were killed each day in traffic accidents. And that eight motorcyclists were born each day, compounding the problem.

As it turned out, upon my arrival, there were two big holidays in Venezuela. All public buildings were closed for four days due to holy week and, immediately, another four days for the independence of Venezuela celebrations. Somehow, the U.S. Department of State did not know that. Eight days in Caracas without appointments. I walked the streets. I almost jumped from one of the overpasses.

54. Logarithms and Coffee

One of the participants in the Radioisotopes in Research course in Cordoba, Argentina, Miss Elisa Romero, was a high school teacher of physics, a dedicated attendant to the course who did all of the laboratory exercises duly and on time. One afternoon, after the lab, at 6 p.m., I was setting up the detectors and radioactive samples for the evening lab in the medical course which ran between 8:30 and 11:00 p.m., when Miss Romero came in and asked me if I had time for a coffee break. I responded that I was not lecturing at 7:00 p.m., and that the lab at 8:30 was being run by one of my instructors, so I did have time for a coffee break. She said that she knew a small coffee shop nearby and that her car was outside. She volunteered to take me there. I accepted. The conversation was polite, courteous, and funny at times. She told me that she had come to Cordoba from Rosario. She had gone to school and college there. She had learned to speak French at the academy of languages and later, she had taught French at a local high school. She had also studied music and loved to play the guitar. At the restaurant, we had some coffee with sugar and cream. I told her that I needed to return to the exhibit building soon. She assured me that all personnel of Atoms in Action were highly capable professionals and that they could live without me for a little while. She then told me that the reason why she had asked me to take a coffee break was because she wished to ask me some important questions. She explained: "I teach high school physics, but I have to make a confession. I am weak in mathematics. I beg you to teach me how to derive logarithms." I thought for a moment and said, "Deriving logarithms is easy. All you have to do is remember a few of them, the way you remember your name, your address, your telephone number, or your relatives' birthdays." Right there, writing with a ballpen on a napkin, I began to give her a class on decimal logarithms. For example, I said, in any system of logarithms, the log of 1 is zero and the log of the base, in this case 10, is 1. Among the logs that we have to memorize, are the log of 2 which is 0.301, the log of 3 which is 0.477, the log of 5 which is 0.699, and the log of 7, which is 0.845. With those four logs, you can derive the whole table of logarithms to an approximation of three decimal places and with an error of less than 1%! The error is of course, the difference between the calculated log and the true log expressed as a percentage of the true log.

Then, I proceeded to reason as follows: If 0.301 is the log of 2, then the log of four is 0.602 because the log of 2 times 2 is the sum of the log of 2, twice. She agreed. Now, I said, if the log of 3 is 0.477, then the log of 9 is twice that number or 0.954, agreed? She agreed again. If you know the logs of 2 and 3, then you can derive the log of 6 as the sum of the two logs or 0.301 plus 0.477 which is equal to 0.778. Likewise, by knowing the log of 2 and 4, we can derive the log of 8 which is equal to the sum of the logs of 2 and 4, or 0.301 plus 0.602 or 0.903. Miss Romero appeared to have understood the process by which, by memorizing a few logarithms, you could derive a table of the first ten digits. They are: log 1 = 0.000; log 2 = 0.301; log 3 = 0.477; log 4 = 0.602; log 5 = 0.699; log 6 = 0.778; log 7 = 0.845, log 8 = 0.903; log 9 = 0.954, and log 10 =1.000. Now, I asked her, "Are you ready for the real kicker?" She said, "Yes, I am." I then explained that the log of any number in between those ten digits could be estimated by linear interpolation with good accuracy. For example, what is the log of 6.5? Well, if the log of 6 is 0.778 and the log of 7 is 0.845, a linear interpolation would be the middle point between those two logs or 0.812. The real log of 6.5 is 0.813. The difference of 0.001 represents an error of less than 1%. I also told her that this method gives us the mantissa of the log of any number and that the characteristic is obtained easily by using the powers of 10. For example: what is the log of 6500? Well, 6500 = 6.5 times 10 raised to the third power. Therefore, the log of 6500 is 3. 812 using our method and 3.813 using a table of logarithms. But wait, I said, many physical, chemical, and biological phenomena are better handled by using natural or Napierian logarithms which have base of 2.71828.... But the conversion factor between the two systems is 2.3, thus, to convert decimal logs into natural logs, all you have to do is multiply the decimal log times 2.3. And now, I said, you have in your head two tables of logarithms that can help solve problems even if you are lost on an uninhabited island in the middle of the Pacific ocean. She was delighted. For her kindness, I had rewarded her with a gift that would last her a lifetime. After coffee and logs, she drove me back to the exhibit building.

55. The Green Berets

Two days before the opening of the Atoms in Action exhibit in Cordoba, Argentina, our group of scientists and technicians had been working hard to have everything ready. That night, the policeman guarding the building discovered a 5-gallon bottle of wine on the sidewalk surrounding the exhibit building. In his previous walk around, ten minutes earlier, he had not noticed the bottle. Who could possibly make a delivery of wine at about 1 a.m.? He decided to take it into the reception office. As he lifted the bottle, it exploded, causing him serious burns on his face and arms. He was thrown a few yards away in the explosion. But he appeared to be alive. That angle of the octagonal building was in flames. He blew his whistle. Soon, other agents of the police force arrived in a patrol car. He was taken to the emergency room at a nearby hospital. The bottle had contained gasoline, not wine, and a device that ignited the fuel upon motion.

I was asleep in my hotel room, when the telephone rang. I answered. A voice said, "The exhibit building has been bombed. The director of the exhibit, Mr. Colson, wants everyone on the staff at the building right away." "I am on my way," I said and hung up. When I got to the building, just about everyone was there. The fire was out. Some damage had been done to that corner of the building. The roof had deflated. But it seemed to me it could be fixed. It appeared that some anti-American faction had sabotaged the exhibit. That reminded me that a week earlier, Mr. Colson, his wife Melinda Colson, and some of us had gone to the premier show of the movie "The Green Berets" at a downtown theater. As the movie started, and the march of the green berets sounded, a man wearing a white shirt, dark trousers, and dark shoes threw a Molotov bomb to the screen and set it on fire. The public ran for the exits. Mr. Colson was the fastest, leaving his wife way behind. Noticing that, I accompanied Mrs. Colson out of the theater by walking calmly. Some two blocks away we found Mr. Colson. With the Colsons reunited. I said good night and went back to my hotel. It appeared then that there was an anti-American movement in Cordoba, but my feeling was that it was a small minority because everywhere we had been, the Argentinian officials, college professors, teachers, students, etc. had showed us courtesy and respect and were very excited about the opening of the exhibit. The next morning, the newspapers had two important news items on the front page: The overthrowing of the government of Fernando Belaunde in Lima, Peru, by a military coup and the bombing of the Atoms in Action building. The policeman was OK and recovering from his injuries, the newspapers said.

Mr. Colson, director of the exhibit, had been in contact by telephone with the AEC all day, the Department of State in Washington, D.C., and the designers of the building, an Italian company. He then called for an emergency meeting of all the staff. At the meeting, he said that the repair of the building would take at least two weeks, because it would take that long to have the replacement parts brought from Italy. He also said that, if everyone agreed that it was unsafe for Americans to operate the exhibit, he would request permission from Washington to pack up and return home. I was in shock. I could not believe what I was hearing. That a few anti-American delinquents could make us run home with our tails between our legs. I raised my hand. Mr. Colson signaled me to speak. I said that I had been in contact with the Department of Education, with the National University of Cordoba, with representatives of the Argentinian Medical Association, and that everywhere I had been well received, that there was a great expectation among all circles about the opening of the exhibit as one of the best cultural events of recent years. I added that the attack on the building was a futile attempt by a small minority and they should not make us run home scared. The building, I said, could be repaired using local materials and that there was no reason to postpone the opening if we worked together to make it happen. Mr. Colson listened quietly with a somber face and was obviously disappointed. It was he who wanted the exhibit closed. My words had fallen on him like a bucket of ice water. Many on the attending staff agreed with my estimate of the situation. Well, said Mr. Colson, "If that is what you want, we will try to have the building repaired locally." He then adjourned the meeting. Later that morning he communicated to Washington the decision to proceed with the operation of the exhibit as originally planned. As it turned out, the presentation in Cordoba was one of the best ever, culturally, scientifically, and politically, because it brought the peoples of the U.S. and Argentina together, working under one roof,—the dome of the Atoms in Action building.

56. Cerebrovascular Accident

Bill Thompson was a civil engineer who taught Architectural Technology at the University of Tennessee in Knoxville. He used to join our international group of Oak Ridge soccer players on Sundays for our weekly practice. On one occasion he had invited me to visit his office where he had showed me some models of buildings that had been made by his students. I was gratefully impressed. They were really excellent. "You must be an excellent teacher," I had commented at the time. Mr. Thompson was always polite and courteous. We became good friends.

One day, while lecturing to his students at the university, he did not feel well. He excused himself and went to the rest room. The students in his class waited chatting cheerfully for about twenty minutes. When they realized that Mr. Thompson was not returning to class, they decided to look for him. They found him laying flat on the floor in the men's room. He was unconscious and barely breathing. Someone called an ambulance. The paramedics took Mr. Thompson to emergency at the Knoxville Memorial Hospital. His family was informed. After some testing, doctors confirmed that Mr. Thompson had suffered a cerebrovascular accident (CVA) or stroke. No details were given. Most likely, the stroke was due to a thrombus, a blood clot, that had blocked one of the middle cerebral arteries. He was placed on intensive care to maintain and monitor cardiac and respiratory functions continuously. Doctors tried several approaches to therapy without success. Mr. Thompson remained unconscious and on artificial support for three weeks. At that point, doctors prescribed a nuclear scan: a dynamic brain flow study to determine brain death. The result was positive. Mr. Thompson had been brain dead for three weeks. I went to the funeral in Knoxville. I was very sad for the family and the loss of a good friend. In retrospect, it seemed to me that the nuclear scan should have been done the first day not three weeks later. That would have saved the family a lot of pain and expenses.

57. The Gaucho Knife

The Atoms in Action exhibit in Cordoba ended on a Sunday. The previous Friday, the radioisotopes courses had ended too. We usually held a symbolic ceremony in which the coordinator made a speech remembering the pioneers of radiation sciences and then, we awarded the participants a diploma of "Dabbler in RadioIsotope Procedures," with the name of the participant, the name of the course, the place, the dates and the signatures of the coordinator and principal instructor. At the end of the medical radioisotopes course, one of the participants, Dr. Roberto Riquelme, waited until all the other participants had left and came in to thank me for the course and the opportunity that he had to attend. He said that the course had been one of the most memorable events of his life and that he had something to show me. Then, he unwrapped beautiful knife, a gaucho knife. A very special one. It had a six-inch, stainless steel blade with a four-inch gold-plated handle. The latter had two rows of engraved tobacco leaves on opposite sides and had the shape of an octagonal dome. The blade fitted perfectly into a case made from a deer's horn. It was white and had three gold-plated bands, one at the base which, on the back, had a golden bridge supported at one end. That bridge, Dr. Riquelme explained, was like a hook to place the knife on your belt, behind your back. That is how the gauchos carry their knives, hidden from view, but ready to be pulled out in a fight. That bridge had an engraving too: the head of a horse encircled by a horseshoe and a stream of tobacco leaves. At the center of the case there was a half-inch gold-plated band showing more tobacco leaves. At the tip of the case there were more gold-plated decorations: a high-relief "quero-quero," a bird from the Argentinian pampas, the heads of a cow and a sheep, a bowl of mate, the gaucho herbal tea, and a set of "boleadoras," the gaucho tool and weapon consisting of three metal balls held by short ropes. A throwing weapon to bring down a steer out there in the pampas. Dr. Riquelme then asked me if I had a coin of any kind. I placed my hand in my pocket and found a 20-cent coin. I gave it to him. He said that I had just purchased the knife and added that he could not give me the knife as a gift, that he had to sell it to me. He then explained that, in gaucho folklore, it is bad luck to give a weapon as a present because, in moment of rage, the giver could be killed with that weapon. That was why he had to sell it to me. I accepted Dr. Riquelme's sale gratefully. I told him that I would always keep the knife as token of friendship between us and between our countries. He was pleased. The reason why I could give a detailed description of the knife is because I still have it, even after 40 years, since it was given to me by an Argentinian doctor and most memorable friend, Dr. Roberto Riquelme.

58. No Bullet, No Crime!

Perhaps you recall that, late in 1963, the college council in Lima, reluctantly approved my promotion to associate professor. Their action came too late, only when they realized that I was leaving for the U.S. to join my family. Four months later, when I secured a one-year appointment at ORINS, and I requested a leave of absence without pay, they gave me a traveling allowance as a means of keeping me on the hook. Again, it was too late. They did not know that I had traveled to the U.S. with an immigrant visa hopping to find permanent employment. My appointment in Oak Ridge was only for one year, during the preparation stages of the "Atoms in Action"exhibit's training program for Latin American professionals. I had planned to travel to Oak Ridge and work in whatever I could find until the job as scientist opened at ORINS in July. Fortunately, the job opened sooner, the first of March, and thus, I could travel by car to Oak Ridge, with Diane and baby daughter Cati, by the twentieth of February that year. However, if I did not succeed in finding permanent employment by the end of the year, I did plan to return to Peru, in February of 1965. I did state so in my request of a leave of absence. But, in December of 1964, Dr. Anderson, the new chairman of the special training division of ORINS, call me to his office and told me that, since I had done all preparations for the training program for Atoms in Action, the institute wanted me to run it in its first presentation to be held in El Salvador in March of 1965. He also asked me to become a permanent employee of ORINS with the title of scientist. I was pleasantly surprised and accepted his offer on the spot. He also offered that his office would make all the necessary arrangements to change my green card for a resident visa. I was delighted. Later that evening, I brought presents for Diane and Cati and a bottle of champagne, to celebrate the great occasion. After we returned from El Salvador, where we had a very successful presentation, I sent my letter of resignation to the college in Lima. Dr. Morales, the Dean of the college in Lima, replied that he had worked very hard to obtain my promotion and that he expected more loyalty from me and my return to the college. I responded that his administration had put me and my family through hell during the one-and-a-half years in which the documents were "misplaced" and that my very own friends at the college had stopped talking to me just because I requested a promotion mandated by law. In September of 1965, we had another presentation of the training program in Guatemala. Again with great success. About November, that year, I received another letter from the college in Lima. It was from Dr. Zapata, the newly elected dean. He said that he wanted "my estimate of what I owed the college in Lima." I agonized over the way I was going to reply to his letter. I could offer to return the travel allowance they granted me as a fishhook. I could say that my informal agreement was to work for the college three times the time I spent in the U.S. But the new university law did not contemplate informal agreements or, since the law was approved by the Peruvian Congress in July of 1962, and my informal agreement was signed in 1959, it had no bearing on the case because, according the Peruvian Constitution, the law had no retroactive effect, I wrote a draft of my reply, but I tore it up because it was not clear about my point of view. Two more days passed and two more drafts of the reply were torn up. Finally, one sleepless night, I remembered the movie "The Gazebo." In it, Glenn Ford, tries to kill the blackmailer of his wife, Debbie Reynolds. In the dark, he shoots his pistol and misses. But the man drops dead from a heart attack. When no bullet is found in the body, but the pistol had been used, the police tried to demonstrate the intent to kill by Glenn Ford. To do that, they had to find the bullet that was shot and missed. They could not find it. No bullet, no crime!No intent to kill. That memory, in the wee hours of the night, gave me the idea that the new dean in Lima wanted me to incriminate myself in my reply. Thus, I decided not to answer his letter. No letter, no self-incrimination. The fifth amendment to the U.S. constitution protects all citizens against self-incrimination. I am sure that the Peruvian constitution does too. Some six months later, I received a copy of a council resolution in which they had cancelled all my retirement earnings for the six years of services rendered by me to the university between 1958 and 1963. That was the end of the conflict. I was pleased.

59. The Science Fair

Another memorable event happened in Caracas, Venezuela. In the middle of our Atoms in Action presentation, the local Secretary of Education sent me a note inviting me to participate as one of the judges of the Venezuelan Science Fair being held in a large pavilion in downtown, Caracas. My participation required three days of full-time work. My occupations at the Atoms in Action did not permit me to be a judge. Thus, I called the Secretary of Education and I told him that I was very much honored by the request and explained that I could not do it myself, but I could send another scientist to represent me. He accepted. Later, I asked Dennis Trent, an electronics expert and supervisor of the high school seminars program, to represent me. He accepted and went to the sessions in which some six judges examined every project presented for objectives, planning, contribution to science, practicality, presentation, illustrations, etc. The first place in the fair was going to be awarded a trophy, a diploma, a gold medal, a scholarship, and an all-expenses-paid trip, representing Venezuela, to the International Science Fair in Dallas, Texas, the following year.

On the last day of the fair, in which the judges were to announce the winner as well as the second and third places, at about 11 a.m., Dennis called me and told me that in his opinion a poor high school student deserved to win the first prize, but that the other judges wanted to give that prize to the son of the Minister of Finance, in his estimate, for political reasons. He also said that he had stood firmly in favor of the poor student. The project presented by the poor high school student was a collection of some twenty, well preserved, poisonous snakes from the jungles of Venezuela, with descriptions, scientific names, description of the chemical and biological properties of their poisons, a map of the regions where the snakes were caught, etc. Mr. Trent asked me to come immediately to strengthen the case for the deserving student. The project favored by most of the other judges was a simple display of the properties of acids and bases and an explanation of the principle of "power hydrogen (pH)," but nothing new. I told Dennis, "Stall them, I am on my way." I took a taxi and told the driver: "Step on it!" While I traveled toward the fair site, Mr. Trent told the other judges that Dr. Donnatti would not stand for a political awarding of the first prize to the pH project and that I was coming at that very moment. I arrived in 15 minutes and walked into the grand pavilion with resolution; my decision was to fight for the snake project. An official of the Department of Education, Mr. Fernandez, greeted me at the entrance, introduced himself, and placed a glass of whiskey in my hand. He said that the judges had, in the last few minutes, awarded the first prize to the snake project. Dennis Trent was at his side smiling. He said, "That is right." I smiled too and thanked Mr. Fernandez for a wise decision. We walked around looking at the projects which, at the time, were already being dismantled. Then I saw the newspaper photographers taking pictures of the snakes project and the student smiling for the cameras. Some months later, we got the news that the Venezuelan student had earned second place at the International Science Fair in Dallas, TX, with his project "Poisonous Snakes of the Venezuelan Jungles." That warmed our hearts in the cold winter of Oak Ridge. We had done the right thing back then.

60. The End of Atoms in Action

The last presentation of the Atoms in Action exhibit was in Sao Paulo, Brazil, in November of 1969. Because of the great success of our training programs, presented previously in Spanish, the Atomic Energy Commission (AEC) requested, with one year notice, that all the associated staff learn Brazilian Portuguese. And sent the funds to hire two Brazilian teachers. Thus, in January of 1969, a Brazilian husband-and-wife team of Portuguese teachers arrived in Oak Ridge. They were Danilo and Dora Boninho. They held daily one-hour classes with the staff going to Sao Paulo. Classes were scheduled from 4 to 5 p.m. every working day. We did not know it, at the time, but the teachers originally came from the region of Ceara in the northeast of Brazil, and they spoke with a heavy provincial accent. But we made progress quickly. We were very busy at the time, with domestic training programs in which we taught college teachers coming from all over the U.S. So, close to 4 p.m., we had to drop whatever we were doing and run to Portuguese class. That was when the law of the minimum effort took over. For me, it was easier to transfer the sounds of English to my learning of Portuguese. For my good friend George Mester, a colleague whom I taught Spanish, it was easier to transfer the sounds of Spanish to his learning of Portuguese. Consequently, when we arrived in Sao Paulo, Brazilian course participants told us that I spoke Portuguese with a "gringo" accent and that George spoke Portuguese with a Spanish accent. We know that mastering a language, even your own, takes a life time. Thus we could not even pretend to be fluent in Portuguese, but we could get along fine in simple conversations and when lecturing on subjects in our own fields of science. When talking to someone we met in the streets, though, we felt deficient. It was really an experience. One day I decided to go out for a walk in the evening. To avoid getting lost in the populous city of Sao Paulo, I decided to go around the block and return to my hotel. I did. One block, turn right, another block, turn right, a third block, turn right, and I should have been back at my hotel. But I was not. Nobody had told me that the block was a triangular one and, therefore, I had passed the hotel at the third turn and I had left it one block behind me. When I could not see the hotel anywhere, I stopped a young man in the street and asked for the location of the Grand Hotel. He understood me and spurted his answer. I could not understand a word, not a word. Finally, I retraced my steps and lucky me, I found it. Eureka!

The Sao Paulo presentation was a resounding success. At the end there were ceremonies, celebrations, parties, etc. At the closing party, there were comedy acts and dancing. I remember my assistant, a twenty-year-old lady named Marta Falcao, asking me to dance. I was not a very good dancer, but that night was different. There was magic in the air and over one thousand people in that huge pavilion. There was food, drinks, and music. I remember dancing the polka "beer barrel" like never before. That was the last Atoms in Action exhibit. The AEC appropriations budget had not planned for any more exhibits for Latin America. But for me, personally, it meant that unless I got more involvement in domestic training programs, I could be out of a job.

At the time, the physician coordinator of the medical courses, Dr. Matthew Lassiter, a hematologist, was very much interested in research at the medical division of ORINS, and less interested in teaching. Surprisingly, one day Dr. Masterman, Chairman of the special training division (STD), announced his resignation and his plans to become a consultant in private industry. Dr. Anderson became interim chairman. We were barely recovering from the shocking news, when Dr. Lassiter, the coordinator of our medical courses, resigned too to pursue his research in the hematology of cancer. Thus ORINS began the search for a new STD chairman, and STD began its search for a nuclear physician to take over the coordination of the medical qualification courses. Completion of our medical curses qualified attendant doctors for licensing as nuclear medicine physicians. Suddenly, ORINS announced the appointment of Dr. Anderson to the Chair of STD. And, Dr. Anderson appointed me temporary coordinator of the AEC's medical qualification courses. I guess it was because I had a background in veterinary medicine and a M.S. degree in radiation biology, and I was the member of the staff with the closest expertise to that of medicine. But the search for a nuclear physician continued. As it turned out, my medical courses were very successful, and the search for a physician gradually faded out in time and space. I was soon recognized by the AEC as the coordinator of those training programs. Upon completion of every course, I signed the doctors' preceptor statements that qualified them as nuclear physicians.

Soon after, I took responsibility for the Radiation Biology Summer Institutes, the eight-week courses for biology college teachers, sponsored by the National Science Foundation (NSF), and I was asked to participate as lecturer and lab instructor in health physics and other training programs. I was soon promoted by Dr. Anderson to Senior Scientist. The modest Peruvian immigrant had arrived!

—◦⊚◦—

Reporter Judy Hartfeldt: Marco, the training program of Atoms in Action was a great responsibility for you and kept you away from your family for a long time, is that right?

Marco Donnatti: Yes, it was a responsibility technically, culturally, publically, and socially. It kept me away seven weeks during each exhibit, twice a year.

Judy: When the funding for the exhibit ran out, you quickly got involved in the medical qualification courses and became a real staff member of STD.

Marco: Yes. And I must recognize Dr. Anderson for that. He was able to appreciate my potential abilities and gave me the opportunity.

Judy: How long were you in charge of the medical qualification courses?

Marco: Nine years. From 1968 to 1977.

Judy: Well, I guess, that is all for now. Until next time, Marco, and thanks.

Marco: "Good bye Judy. Until next time."

Laboratory Rat. Lab animals, invaluable in biomedical research (Story 62)

CHAPTER 7

PROFESSIONAL PRACTICE IN OAK RIDGE

Reporter Judy Hartfeldt: When Atoms in Action ran out of money, you dedicated yourself to domestic training programs for professionals within the U.S., is that right?

Marco Donnatti: Exactly. The U.S. Atomic Energy Commission funded the nuclear medicine qualification training of American physicians, and the National Science Foundation funded the radiation biology summer institutes for American college teachers. And I was put in charge of both.

Judy: It must have been a lot of work. How many courses were offered per year?

Marco: There were four medical courses per year, lasting four weeks each, five days per week and eight hours per day. Each medical course had a capacity for 24 physicians. There was only one radiation biology course per year lasting eight weeks each summer. They involved five days per week, eight hours per day. Each course had a capacity for 24 college teachers.

Judy: Did you have any help?

Marco: You bet. Besides our staff at our special training division (STD), I had a pool of physicians and scientists at our medical division using the latest nuclear medicine diagnostic and therapeutic procedures. I also had another pool of scientists at the Oak Ridge National Laboratory (ORNL) biology division and at the University of Tennessee radiobiology farm in Oak Ridge. Those scientists dedicated their lives to research with laboratory animals, plants, microbes, and farm animals. In my work, I got to meet many very important people. I also had a lab technician to assist me with the animal care and with the preparation of all laboratory sessions.

Judy: That was great, I am sure. Now, tell me about your work. I am recording.

---

61. The Medical Qualification Courses

ORINS operated under contract with various governmental agencies in Washington, D.C. Every year, our STD division would send proposals to those agencies for training programs to be offered at Oak Ridge the following year. Sometimes, the agencies requested that STD design and submit a proposal of a new training program in a specific area of national interest, like training in the environmental field. The STD proposals would be sent one fiscal year in advance. By the end of the year approved proposals would be funded. Funding included staff salaries, materials and supplies, administrative costs, fees and travel expenses for consultants, etc. The AEC was the sponsor of the medical qualification courses. Our STD administration sent many brochures to medical organizations and universities announcing the dates of the four medical courses offered the following year. Physicians interested in qualifying as nuclear physicians then, would choose when they could take a four-week leave and come to Oak Ridge to attend one of the courses. To assist with costs, the AEC authorized STD to charge participants a nominal fee of about 340 dollars per week.

My job as coordinator was to prepare in advance, a daily schedule of lectures and laboratory sessions for the four weeks the courses lasted. I would ask prospective lecturers to prepare an outline of their lectures, if possible, or to bring enough copies for all participants. In every course, I invited some of the most outstanding nuclear physicians in the field to come to Oak Ridge to lecture on topics in the areas of their expertise like gamma ray imaging and radioimmunoassays. I also collected copies of all lab protocols in bound manuals to be given to attending doctors the first day of the courses. Typically, the eight-hour day consisted of a 90-minute lecture, a 15-minute break, a lab session from 9:45 a.m. to 12 noon, a one-hour lunch break, another 90-minute lecture at 1:00 p.m., followed by a lab session from 2:45 to 5:00 p.m. The first week of the course was dedicated to teaching participants the properties of radiations and the instrumentation used to detect and measure radiations. The second week included radiation safety instrumentation and techniques as well as the statistical methods used to interpret radiation measurements. The third week was "my week." I called it the "pre-clinical week." I was responsible for all the lab work. Doctors learned to measure the radioactivity of simulated blood and urine samples. From their measurements, they had to calculate answers and decide if the results were normal or an indication of illness. Another series of experiments during the third week were the measurement of the cardiac output of an anesthetized dog and the nuclear imaging of livers, lungs, and skeletal systems in anesthetized dogs using a rectilinear scanner. The fourth week was the "clinical week." Doctors would attend a lecture by a nuclear physician and then divide into two groups, one attending a scheduled diagnostic procedure being performed on a real human patient at the medical division. The staff nuclear physician would discuss the patient's history and the nuclear medicine approach to diagnosis, including organ imaging procedures using gamma cameras. The second group, also at the medical division, would watch by closed-circuit television, or by a system of mirrors, a radiation therapy procedure on a real patient suffering from malignant disease. Another nuclear physician would be in charge of that group. In the afternoon, the groups would switch places, and other two cases would observed by the participants in the course. On Friday afternoon of the fourth week, a written critique session would be conducted. Participants were invited to criticize the coordinator, the lecturers, the lab instructors, the manuals, the lab sessions, etc. Signatures were optional. As course coordinator I would later read the critiques and make adjustments toward improvement in the following courses. After the critique session, a mock graduation ceremony was conducted by the chairman of the STD division. The chairman would read a traditional speech in which he would review briefly the history of "Old Bremsstrahlung University," (bremsstrahlung is a form of radiation, actually x-rays, produced when high-energy electrons are decelerated by the electrical field of a heavy metal atomic nucleus). Then the chairman granted participants of the course a diploma of "Dabbler in RadioIsotope Procedure," and the "graduates" were entitled to attach "DRIP" to their names. Every physician received a diploma. Then the staff, accompanied by participants, would sing the "alma matter" of the fictitious university. Participants were then dismissed.

In this endeavor–the medical qualification courses— I was very fortunate. Critiques were constructive and very encouraging. Sometimes, the doctors organized a dinner and/or a cocktail party for me either on the last Thursday evening or on the last Friday evening of the course. I was given the responsibility of the medical courses on a temporary basis, in 1969, until STD could find a nuclear physician to take them over. But the courses were so successful that I remained in that position for nine years. In that time, over one thousand physicians were trained.

62. Animal Experiments

When I arrived at Oak Ridge in 1964, our Special Training Division had only one teaching experiment to demonstrate the use of radioisotopes in biology: "The phosphorus-32 uptake in the bones of a laboratory rat." That experiment was included in all courses for college teachers of biology and chemistry. Usually, a well-trained instructor was put in charge of the lab. Participants, in groups of two, would have to follow the protocol imitating the technique demonstrated by the instructor. To me, it was a messy experiment for two reasons: the use of P-32, a high-energy beta emitter with 14.3 days half-life, and the dissection of the femur, boiling the bones in acid to convert them into a salt with a reproducible geometric shape so that its radioactivity could be measured under a thin-window Geiger-Muller counter. Too many steps, too many sources of error. Thus, I began to collect ideas for experiments that could be used in lab animals, but with gamma emitting radioisotopes. Actually we called them radionuclides, which is a much more appropriate term. The experiments had to be performed within two and a half hours. It took some time to write new protocols and to test them with live animals. Then, a teaching protocol would be written and the experiments would be included in the basic research courses as well as in the radiation biology courses. In my time, I designed and tested 14 animal experiments. Two examples follow.

"The Iron-59 Blood Plasma Clearance" experiment. This was a test for bone marrow function. Using a fine needle, 25 gauge, some 10 microcuries of Fe-59-citrate in 0.5 cc of saline solution were injected into the heart of an anesthetized laboratory rat. At about ten-minute intervals, a drop of blood was obtained from the femoral vein and collected into a small heparinized capillary tube. The exact times of each sampling were recorded. The tubes were weighed in an analytical balance before and after the blood collection. By subtraction, we determined the exact weight of the sample. The blood sampling was repeated until four or five samples were obtained. A diluted "standard," representing the injected dose, was prepared also, and the radioactivity of the standard and the samples were placed in test tubes and measured in a well-type gamma scintillation detector. Then, the blood samples were spun at 10,000 revolutions per minute in a special centrifuge to determine the exact amount of plasma in the blood samples. Some simple calculation permitted the determination of the counts per minute per milliliter of plasma in each sample. These results were plotted on semilogarithmic graph paper, and the best straight line was drawn through the points using an exponential least-squares computer program. The slope of the curve was the rate of Fe-59 plasma clearance, which, in turn, represented the rate of bone marrow uptake. In other words, bone marrow function. The bone marrow utilizes iron to make hemoglobin and to introduce it into the newly-made red blood cells. This experiment could be done within two hours. Once the radioactivities were measured, the data could be entered into the computer, and the output would give the rates of clearance and even calculate the whole body plasma and blood compartments in milliliters and as percentage of body weight. In those days we wrote the computer programs to process the data. We used BASIC, the programming computer language. It was simply spectacular! For my particular animal research, I added other experiments that measured the rate of red cell formation and destruction, and the red cell life span. After doing myself a number of normal animals, I published the methods and results in the Journal of Veterinary Research (JVR) in 1973. Soon after, I got requests for reprints from many places, including some from Russia, Australia, and Canada.

Another teaching experiment, was "The Blood Volume and Cardiac Output in Anesthetized Dogs." This experiment was a test for cardiac function. The animal, under anesthesia, was placed on an animal table, and a collimated scintillation gamma detector was placed on the left side of the thoracic wall focused on the whole heart. The detector was connected to a ratemeter and the latter to a rectilinear recorder so that the vertical axis covered the range of 100,000 counts per minute. When everything was ready, the detector-recorder was started, and a bolus injection of Iodine-131-albumin was given to the dog into the saphenous vein in the dog's leg (away from the detector). Within seconds, the recording showed a rise of the radioactivity entering the field of view of the detector (the heart). The curve showed first a peak representing the right side and then another higher peak representing the left side of the heart. Then, the radioactivity dropped exponentially as the bolus shot left the heart toward the rest of the body. The principle of the test says simply that the cardiac output is inversely related to the area under the peak of the recorded curve. Thus, using an instrument called a compensated planimeter, the peak area was measured and converted into counts per minute under the curve. The total blood volume, in milliliters, was also calculated by dividing the total counts per minute injected by the concentration at ten minutes. Then, the blood volume was multiplied by the recorded counts per minute at equilibrium (about ten minutes after injection) and divided by the total counts under the curve. The result was the cardiac output in milliliters per minute. This result could also be expressed in blood volumes per minute. This way we found that, under anesthesia, a medium-size dog has a cardiac output of two blood volumes per minute. That means that the entire volume of blood circulates a full turn every 30 seconds at rest. Imagine the cardiac output of a dog running at full speed in the race track! Perhaps 4 or 5 times that! Incredible! Fascinating! After doing some 25 dogs very carefully, I published a paper in the Journal of Veterinary Research in 1972. In closing, I must state that in all experiments, we followed strictly the guidelines of animal care dictated bu the National Institute of Health (NIH) and the National Science Foundation (NSF). While in our care, the animals were well fed, well housed, and they never suffered pain. Besides, daily, I talked and sang to the animals.

63. Radiation Biology Courses

In Washington, D.C., our Special Training Division (STD) had the reputation of being right at the front in the designing of training courses and teaching techniques. This was the result of a highly professional and dedicated staff. New teaching experiments were constantly being designed in all fields of science. For example, in radiation physics, fast and slow neutron activation analyses, x-ray fluorescence analyses; in the environmental sciences, the determination of radioactive contaminants in drinking water and air; in radiochemistry, column chromatographic separations and solvent extractions; in nuclear medicine procedures, static and dynamic imaging techniques; in radiation biology, teaching experiments in the dynamics of the circulation and organ system functions. We were proud to lead the way. Soon though, our former course participants at many colleges and universities began to design and invent their own new procedures and, in doing so, surpassed their masters. Thus, after the initial thrust in Oak Ridge, the field of radiotracer techniques exploded all over the country and, consequently, all over the world. At Oak Ridge, though, in the '70s, we offered a radiation biology summer institute once a year for 24 selected college teachers, many of them with Ph.D. degrees, on vacation from their own teaching duties. These college teachers, we called them "participants," came from all over the U.S. and had a variety of backgrounds. Some were mammalian physiologists, like me, some were plant physiologists, some were bacteriologists, some were virologists, some were geologists, some were chemists or biochemists, etc. Eight weeks is a long time to keep these experts entertained and learning. Fortunately, I had a pool of scientists at the biology division of ORNL to call upon and ask them to lecture and perhaps to conduct a demonstration or two in their own labs. I was also fortunate to have the University of Tennessee (UT) radiobiological farm nearby, where scientists investigated the effects of whole-body irradiation on farm animals. But first, I had to make contact and discuss the availability and willingness of the prospective lecturers to participate in our training programs. By references and by recommendations, I managed to establish contact with some wonderful scientists who willingly spared some of their time to help us. Thus, I brought to STD leading experts in microscopic autoradiography, in radiobotany, in cytogenetics, in mammalian genetics, in mineral metabolism, in protein metabolism, in enzymatic reactions, radioimmunoassays, and in radiobiological experiments which demonstrated the effects of radiation on biological systems at high, medium, and low doses of radiation. Particularly notable were the effects of radiations on bacterial DNAs and viral RNAs and the beginning of molecular engineering. For the participants to see the actual sites of experimentation and the lab facilities, we organized tours of those facilities. Those were the days I shall always remember.

My animal experiments included experiments with lab rats, dogs, and believe it or not, sheep. The latter consisted of a ferro- and erythrokinetics study using six sheep housed in metabolic cages. We had a fenced area behind the engineering building where we installed the six cages and the sheep on loan from the UT farm. The whole class was divided into six groups of four and assigned to a particular animal. After a demonstration, participants performed the injections of the radiotracers: the Cr-51-labeled red blood cells were injected first to determine the red cell survival times. That took about a week. Then, the Fe-59 citrate solution was injected to measure the rate of plasma clearance and the plasma compartment. During the following week, the incorporation of Fe-59 into the red cells in the bone marrow was measured. That data was used to calculate the rates of cell formation and destruction as well as the red cell life span. At the end of the experiment, all the data were pooled and computer programs were used to obtain means, standard deviations and standard errors. The class results were then tabulated printed and copies were made for all participants. Spectacular, fascinating, incredible. Those were the days.

At the end of the course, as traditional, the critique session was followed by the graduation ceremony with a speech by the division chairman, the handing of DRIP diplomas to all participants, and the singing of the alma matter. Then, someone would write "Run for the Hills," on the blackboard, and after that, the college teachers said good bye and began their return home.

64. My Thyroid Gland

The Oak Ridge Institute of Nuclear Studies (ORINS) was my employer in the 1960s. The institute required that all employees take a physical exam every two years. That policy was a way to protect and care for the staff, an essential component of a national educational plan of the federal government. We, the staff, took those exams seriously and never missed an appointment. The exams were given at the medical division of the ORNL. The director of that division was Dr. Henderson. I had met him before when he came to lecture in our medical courses. But the doctor who examined me on a Monday morning, was a young man about 30 years old. I was 42 at the time. He palpated my neck, asked me to swallow two or three times. Then, he said that he could feel a lump in the lower left of my thyroid gland. The rest of the physical exam was normal. He said, "If I were you, I would have it checked at your medical division." I asked him to call Dr. Chandler, a friend of mine, and also a regular lecturer in our medical courses. He said that he would. Later that afternoon, I called Dr. Chandler to make an appointment for an examination.

From my studies, I knew that most solitary thyroid nodules are cold, meaning that they do not pick up radioactive iodine-131, and that they are malignant, meaning cancerous. That afternoon, I also tried to palpate my own neck imitating the doctors technique, but I could not feel the thyroid, much less the "lump." During my appointment, Dr. Chandler palpated my thyroid and said, "I feel something, but I am not sure it is a lump. The best way to see it is to do a thyroid scan with Tc-99m-sodium pertechnetate." At that point, my thoughts went like this, "He could not find the lump, but he would not contradict another doctor. It is not ethical to contradict a colleague's diagnosis." I also thought, "Well, if I preach it in my medical courses, I might as well take a dose of my own medicine. Besides, Tc-99m is much safer than I-131." Thus, I said, "Fine Dr. Chandler, I accept the scanning procedure." Dr. Chandler asked me to wait in his office. He left and ordered a technician to prepare a syringe with one millicurie of the radioactive solution. In preparation for my appointment, I had requested from the radiation safety office six x-ray films, like those used to monitor workers' radiation exposure. Before going to my appointment, I had taped those films to my legs, front and sides of my chest and just above the urinary bladder. I wanted to determine the radiation dose given to those regions of my body during the first 24 hours after my injection of the radioactive solution. I also brought a "beeper," a personal GM monitor in the shape of a fat pencil, to measure the count rate over my thyroid region at various times after injection. A few minutes later, a technician came into the office and asked me to sign a release of responsibility form. I signed. Then, he asked me to come to the lab, where a nurse gave me the intravenous injection. I was very much surprised to see other doctors of the medical division present as observers and also the radiation safety officer of ORINS present with a portable GM monitor measuring exposure dose at one meter from me. After the injection, they asked me to wait in the corridor, outside the lab. I thought: "Is that the way to treat a patient, a "hot" patient? Wait in the hall?" Oh well, what do I know? I asked myself. They are the experts. I decided to use my beeper to count the activity of my thyroid every five minutes. It sure went up with time. In about 20 minutes, I was asked to enter the scanning room and to lie on the table under the scanner. The scanner was a Picker Magnascanner with a 5-by-2-inch crystal detector, much more sensitive than the one we used at STD. Besides, it was a color scanner. The scanning procedure took less than ten minutes. Dr. Chandler examined the scan and put it away. I asked for a copy of the scan to use in my own lectures. Dr. Chandler promised to send me a copy. But he never did. I do not know why doctors, in general, are so afraid of liability. Then, Dr. Chandler asked me to come into his office and said that the scan was negative and that I should not worry about a lump in my thyroid gland any more. That was what I wanted to hear. I left quickly and drove to STD, about two miles away. I set up my own 3-by-2-inch scanner, lay on the table under the scanner, and asked my assistant, Chuck Fisher, to start the scanner. I lay there for about 20 minutes. It took a lot longer to do the scanning because my scanner was less sensitive, and because there had been already a significant decay of the radioactivity in my thyroid gland. When I examined the scan, I found it to be a perfectly symmetrical gland, a textbook-like thyroid, I thought. No lumps of any kind. I felt proud of my thyroid gland. I also plotted the beeper counts and, like the books say, peak uptake was reached at 20 minutes, the best time to do the scanning. I kept the scan for a long time and used it in my discussions of imaging techniques for years to come. A month later, I asked the radiation officer, over the phone, about the radiation doses registered on the films I had taped to my body during the scanning procedure. He said that those records were confidential and refused to give them to me. Again, what were they afraid of? In any event, those were the days, unforgettable days.

65. The Guest Lecturer Program

In the 1970s, the Atomic Energy Commission initiated a program by which scientists at Oak Ridge could travel to any college in the country and lecture on a topic of his or her specialty. The AEC would pay travel expenses, the employer would release the scientist for the time needed to complete the assignment, and the host college would provide lodging and meals to the lecturer during the visit. The chairman of STD, Dr. Anderson, encouraged the staff to place their names and topics on a list to be submitted to the AEC. I placed my name and the topics of "Radiotracers in Biological Research," "Biological Effects of Ionizing Radiation," and "Radiation Safety in Nuclear Medicine." The AEC printed a nice catalog that was distributed to colleges all over the country. The good part was that the prospective lecturer could refuse a request if he or she was very busy at the requested time. Then, another time could be negotiated over the phone. At STD, I was a very busy person. But I did accept some requests. Usually two or three per year. Usually, I went north in summer and south in winter. Like the birds. When I traveled to lecture, I took my wife and children with me. Those trips were like a minivacation for us. In 1970, I had two daughters, Cati, age 8, and Margie, age 1. One of those requests was from the Weston College in Kentucky in February of 1971. I did have time and thus I accepted to go. It was a very cold winter, and my wife Diane preferred not to travel because she did not want Cati to miss school and because Margie was too little to travel. I agreed. Thus, I traveled to Weston, KY, by plane and arrived at the college at about 5 p.m. the previous day of my lecture. Walking the campus toward the administration building I realized that Weston College was a college for women only. I was in shock. What have I fallen into? How come nobody told me it was a college for women? Would I have refused the appointment? Too late now. I had to do the best I could.

I reported to the college reception, where an older lady told me that they were expecting me and that professor Goldstein would be with me in just a minute. Sure enough, Professor Goldstein arrived and introduced herself. She shook my hand. She was a young 40-year-old lady, very gracious in her manners. She introduced me to three young ladies, students, as the committee to show me around and to escort me to my room. Professor Goldstein excused herself and said good night. I walked with my committee through a very busy cafeteria. There must have been two hundred young women eating, chatting, and laughing. There was a roaring murmur in the huge dining room. Finally we arrived at the guest faculty room. The students opened the door with a key and invited me in. Then, right at the door, they politely said that they would come at 7:30 in the morning to take me to breakfast. I said thank you and went in. Then came the kicker. I heard them locking the room from the outside and walking away. That is ludicrous, I thought. Why would they lock me in? I am not going anywhere. I do not know anybody. I just came directly from the airport. Oh well, they just want to make sure that I do not get out and get into any trouble. That is reasonable. But it is still ludicrous. At the time, I truly believed that no lock could keep me in anywhere, like Houdini. I went to the window. I unlocked it and opened it wide. I walked into the balcony. The cold dry air came in. The snow-covered grass was just five feet below the balcony. Many students walked the snowy gardens below. I could have jumped that height so easily and escaped. But I was a professor and, above all, a gentleman. I would not have exposed the insecurity of Weston College. I returned to my room and closed the window. The heating was good. The room had very nice furniture, French provincial, I thought. The decorations and paintings on the wall were beautiful. My lecture the next day was on radiotracers and was scheduled for 10 a.m. to 12 noon. I began to plan a good approach to it considering that I was going to talk to an all-women audience of teachers and students. Sure enough, the committee unlocked the door in the morning, took me to breakfast, and gave me a tour of the campus. The lecture went well. There were some two hundred people attending. A number of students asked questions. I believe they were pleased with my visit. That afternoon I flew home.

Another incident happened at Bristol College in Virginia in the Spring of 1974. I traveled with my wife Diane, my two daughters Cati and Margie, and my baby son Dante, 18 months old. My host was professor Cortney, a former participant in my radiation biology course. Since Bristol was only a few hours by car from Oak Ridge, we traveled in our family car. Professor Cortney gave us a tour of the college campus and, knowing that I still practiced soccer, he showed us the gymnasium with its fine futsal (salon soccer) court. He invited me to play a practice game with the college team that afternoon. My lecture was scheduled for 5 p.m. He asked us to come for the game after lunch or about 2:30 p.m. We returned to our motel and looked for a place to have lunch. We then rested for while and went to the gymnasium at 2:30 p.m.. Futsal is played with special shoes, but for me, sneakers would have to do. Professor Cortney was very proud of the college team, which he coached, and included six players from Ghana in west Africa. One of the players was huge: about six feet six inches tall, and probably 250 pounds. Very athletic looking. Compared with me, he was a giant! I was athletic too, but only 5 feet-seven inches and 163 pounds. Professor Cortney ordered us to run short sprints to warm up. I tried to keep up with the other players and I did it with great effort. He then divided the players into two teams of six players each. The giant and the best players he placed in one team. He placed me on the other team and gave me four small players to make up my team. It was obvious that he wanted his first team to give an exhibition and defeat us, the sparring team, in a big way.

I talked to my teammates and planned a strategy. I would play midfield. Besides the goalie two of them would play defense and two would play forwards, right and left wingers. The game began. Dr. Cortney and my family sat on the bleachers to watch. Quickly, I noticed that the Ghanian players played with two ball touches at a time. I surprised them when I touched the ball only once for passing. Upon receiving the ball one time, I spun it into the goal, right next to the pole. We had scored one goal. Professor Cortney stood up from his seat and gave a dirty look at his favorite team players. The game continued. A few minutes later, I scored again with another spinning of the ball. Professor Cortney came down from the stands, pulled his players apart and talked to them. We could not hear what he was saying. But I was so surprised that he would take a practice game so seriously. The game resumed. In the middle of the field, a high ball came. Both the giant and I jumped for the ball and collided in the air. I fell on my feet. The giant fell on his side and hurt his hip. He stood up slowly. He was mad about being hurt. He took the ball and kicked it to the ceiling with such force and fury that he broke a lamp. The pieces of glass fell on the court. Someone picked them up. After that, I decided that it was not worth it to win the game. My host, Dr. Cortney, was angry at me, and I had to lecture to him and his students that evening. I let them play any way they wanted to. I just walked the court at random. Soon they scored one, two, and three goals. They had won. We showered and I got ready for my lecture. During my presentation, the mood was solemn. Nobody interrupted to ask questions. At the end, nobody asked questions. I thanked the small audience and said good bye to Dr. Cortney. I was glad to be with my family at dinner time. And to return to Oak Ridge the following morning.

66. The World Congress of NM and Biology

In an issue of the Journal of Nuclear Medicine, early in 1974, I found an invitation by the Society of Nuclear Medicine of Japan to participate in the First World Congress of Nuclear Medicine and Biology to be held in Tokyo and Kyoto in September that year. The Congress was to last one full week. The invitation was for papers in nuclear medicine (NM) and in biomedical research, in biology and education, and for technical exhibits in NM and in radiation biology (RB). At the time, I was very active in the training of doctors under the sponsorship of the AEC. I was very proud of the teaching methods used at STD, as well as the new animal scanning techniques that I had introduced in the third, the pre-clinical, week of the course. Thus, I wrote an abstract of the paper "Medical Training of Doctors at Oak Ridge," and submitted it to the organizing committee. I was very much surprised when I received later an invitation to present the paper in person at the Congress. With that letter, I went to see Dr. Anderson, our STD chairman, to see if ORINS would allow me to travel to Japan to participate in the congress. He said that he would have to make some consultations and then he would let me know. A week later, he told me that ORINS would pay my travel costs, but that local expenses in Japan– lodging, meals, and local travel— had to be my own. I accepted and wrote to my friend, Dr. Yashuhiko Ito, M.D., a former trainee at Oak Ridge, who was a professor at the Kawasaki Medical College of Okayama University. He wrote me back stating that the Tokyo Electric Company was willing to pay my local expenses and invited me to present a series of lectures at his school and other institutions in Japan. I was delighted and grateful to my new sponsor.

The First World Congress of Nuclear Medicine and Biology opened on September 26 with a plenary session exalted by the attendance of His Imperial Highness Prince Akihito and his wife, the Crown Princess. On the sixth day, I presented my paper on the training of doctors at Oak Ridge. Some representatives of the United Nations (UN) and the International Agency of Atomic Energy (IAEA) attended my lecture. During the second week, I traveled to Okayama to lecture at the Kawasaki Medical College, and later, to the Institute of Neoplastic Diseases in Tokyo, and the Fukushima Nuclear Power plant. My lecture topics were on the NM training of doctors, radiation safety in NM, and radiation safety in nuclear power plants. After each lecture, my hosts handed me a check in an envelope as my "consultant fee" which, upon advice of my friend Dr. Ito, I had to accept graciously or my hosts would have been offended. One of the tours offered by the congress organizing committee was the tour to Nara, where the largest Buddha statue was located. I bought my bus ticket for the ride to Nara one afternoon. When I got on the bus, there was only one seat empty. I approached the gentleman seating by the window and, to my surprise, it was Dr. Chandler, my friend, the doctor who had scanned my thyroid gland the year before. He was also a regular lecturer in my medical courses at STD. We chatted cheerfully during the trip and walked together to the temple where the venerated statue was. On the way, Dr. Chandler decided to have his fortune told by a Japanese fortune teller. I decided to do the same. The man shook a cylinder containing some one hundred sticks and suddenly inverted the cylinder. Only one stick dropped on the table. The stick had a message wrapped around it. Dr. Chandler carefully unwrapped the message and read: "You will soon find another job." His face became pale like white paper and in a grave voice asked me, "How did they know that I was looking for another job? I have kept it as an absolute secret." Then, he asked to see my message. It was a bad one. My message said: "You are a loser, you do not ever hit the ball once, you shall never succeed." Dr. Chandler could not stop laughing, he was happy that I had a bad luck message. I laughed too, of course. I tried to convince him that it was only a fake fortune, that I was at the peak of my career, but to no avail, he laughed at my "misfortune."

The congress was very successful in all respects. Dr. Thomas Bartley, at the time President of the American Society of Nuclear Medicine, was elected by acclamation as the new President of the Second World Congress to be held four years later in Washington, D.C. Dr. Bartley was a regular consultant and lecturer in our medical courses at STD. He was attending the congress with his lovely wife. I was fortunate to spend some time with them. Dr. Bartley was the director of the NM department at the Johns Hopkins Hospital in Baltimore, Maryland. He invited me later, to come to his hospital to lecture to his staff. Among the staff at Johns Hopkins, I was pleased to meet Dr. Dianderas, a Peruvian doctor.

67. Absentmindedness

The common belief that professors and scientists are absent minded is real. It can happen to anyone who is extremely busy working on multiple tasks simultaneously. I know because it happened to me sometime in the 1970s. I believe it was in the summer of 1974. My medical radioisotopes course overlapped with the radiation biology summer institute. I was the coordinator of both. Things got more complicated when a new course in radiobotany started concurrently. The coordinator of that course was Dr. Charlton of the Oak Ridge National Laboratory under contract with our institution. The course was designed to teach "plant people" that is, college teachers and scientists working in agriculture, horticulture, plant physiology, plant genetics, etc. the use of radioisotopes and the effects of radiation on plants. But the week before the initiation of that course, Dr. Charlton indicated that because of his multiple obligations, he could not perform the duties of full-time coordinator. Our division chairman then decided that I should work with Dr. Charlton as co-coordinator. That was how I ended coordinating three courses simultaneously. The joke around the special training division was that "half the time Marco does not know whether he is coming or going." And that was almost true.

In those days I took my daughter Cati to the Solway school everyday on my way to work. I must have had a lot in my mind one morning when I passed the school on my way to work. It was only after my daughter pulled me from my shirt sleeve that I realized that she was seating next to me. I had passed her school by half a mile. She said that I had not heard her when she spoke to me. Of course, I apologized to her and turned around to get her to school on time. Another time in those days, on a Saturday, I went with my wife Diane and our three children shopping to downtown Oak Ridge. We used to do that just about every Saturday. But that particular day, we split jobs: I went to the hardware store and Diane went with the kids to the clothing store. After finishing my part, I went to the car and drove home. And then the telephone rang. It was Diane calling from downtown asking me that I come to get them. Needless to say, I was terribly embarrassed. I apologized all over the place. How it could be possible that I had forgotten the family? One excuse was that I was running three courses simultaneously that summer. Another excuse was that whenever I went to the hardware store it was after work and in those occasions I was alone. I was programed to go home after shopping in that store.

But that was not all. In our building at work, one day I needed to go to the rest room. On the way something must have absorbed my mind because some thirty yards past the rest room I had to think hard to recall where I was going. In a few seconds I remembered that I was going to the rest room. I turned around and believe it or not I passed it again! Obviously I had too much on my mind. Just about the same time, I was one day in my lab at about 1:00 p.m. preparing for a teaching experiment, when I heard my name through the intercom system. I was asked to report to room 15. I went to room 15 and I was surprised by finding all the staff in session. I had forgotten completely our weekly meetings of Thursdays at 1:00 p.m. in room 15. Like I said, absentmindedness does happen to anyone too busy at work. Fortunately, the events recounted in this story did not repeat that summer or at any time after that. Thus, absentmindedness in not incurable.

68. The Purge at STD

Sometime in 1975, we learned that somehow, the Special Training Division (STD) had overspent funds beyond the limits of the budget and that Dr. Anderson had requested additional funds from the AEC to pay the salaries of the staff. That request resulted in the appointment by the AEC of an auditing committee of three persons who came from Washington to review the operating costs of STD. After reviewing the books, the committee interviewed all the staff, one by one, and by the end of the week announced their recommendations to the AEC and ORINS. Briefly, they recommended the firing of many senior and junior staff, including our STD chairman, Dr. Anderson. From 36 staff members, the STD roster was reduced to 16. That was quite a purge. I was one of the survivors. But I was not pleased because I could not understand the dismissal of our chairman. In any event, Dr. Anderson was given two months to find a job and leave. In an informal conversation I had with him, I advised him to contact his many friends in Washington. He did exactly that and soon he traveled to D.C. to occupy a position in an office which funds colleges and universities. Thus, technically, he was now above STD. Incidentally, the new chairman, appointed by ORINS, was the former radiation safety officer, Mr. Peter Lorton. All surviving staff awaited with expectation what his new approach to the administration of STD was going to be. In general, the morale among the surviving staff was not very good. There was a sense of instability.

One early morning, about 7: 15 a.m., I entered the building and went to my lab, the Nuclear Medicine lab. Down the main hall, in the distance, I saw a stranger carrying a box in his hands. I decided that, as a staff member of STD, it was my duty to question that person. Thus, I approached him and I said, "Good morning, may I ask who you are and what are you doing in our building this early in the morning?" He answered that he worked for the AEC and that he was looking for a person to assist him with the measurement of alpha radiation in some water samples from the Clinch river. I told him that the expert in alpha radiation measurements using proportional counters was Mr. Gilbert, a radiochemist, and that his office was in the engineering building across the street. He thanked me and went to the designated building. Later that night, I began to worry. If they were looking for alpha radiation in the water of the Clinch river, I thought, it was because they expected to find it. And, most likely, they were looking for plutonium-239, an alpha emitter and a deadly poison. That means that the people of Oak Ridge, who use the river waters as a source of drinking water, may be exposed to some trace levels of Pu-239. But my reasoning, although logical, did not mean certainty. My family and I lived in Solway, some 10 miles east of Oak Ridge. Our source of potable water was a plant in Lenoir City, not the Clinch river, but who knows, both sources are around the Oak Ridge major atomic plants. Soon though, I dismissed the idea of possible water contamination, but I never forgot it.

Another time, in the morning, a gentleman from the ORINS main administration building, Mr. Donald Burgess, paid me a visit. He had been appointed "controlled drugs officer," and someone referred him to me. I told him that the only controlled drugs I used in my animal experiments at STD were two anesthetics: ethyl ether and pentobarbital sodium. He wanted to see copies of my purchase orders and the inventory I had in my lab. I showed him what I had. He then wanted to weigh all the capsules of pentobarbital sodium. I showed him the analytical balance, but he did not know how to use it. I taught him how to use the analytical balance. I do not know how some appointments were made in those days. Someone with no knowledge of drugs or lab experience was appointed "controlled drug officer." In any case, he finished weighing the capsules, recorded the weights and left. About a month later, I received a copy of his report stating that he had found a disparity in my handling of pentobarbital sodium. That many capsules were missing, Naturally, I took issue with such a report. I wrote a reply in which I stated that Mr. Burgess had no background in pharmacology and that he did not know even how to use the analytical balance. And that he was incompetent to be controlled drugs officer and that the assertion that some capsules of pentobarbital were missing was false. I sent copies of my reply to the president of ORINS and to all three division chairmen. That was the last time I heard from Donald Burgess until one day I heard that two secretaries in the main administration building had been dismissed because they had physically fought for Mr. Burguess' attentions. Like I said, the morale of the employees at STD was not very high in those days after the purge.

After ten years of living in Solway and working in Oak Ridge, my family and I had become allergic to the vegetation of east Tennessee. It was a serious situation, because my children had to go to the pediatrician two or three times a week. I had to take two tablets of Dristan, an antihistaminic, every morning to be able to function at work. We were spending between four and five thousand dollars a year in medical bills, allergy tests, and allergy treatments. And one allergy soon was followed by another. There was no end to it. Finally, Dr. Daniels, our pediatrician told us, "You have been good customers, but now that I am taking retirement, I must tell you. The only way to improve your health is to leave east Tennessee. Move to the coast of the gulf of Mexico. The ragweed here lingers nine months of the year and is the worst culprit in your allergies. Move." I took his advice seriously. I began to look for another job. Secretly, because I suspected that in the past, ORINS had blocked my possible transfer to other institutions twice.

69. Serious Trouble with Allergies

Looking for a job is not so difficult. Finding one is almost impossible. The job market is like the proverbial pyramid. The higher the position, the fewer the opportunities. With my three degrees: BVM, DVM, and MS in radiation biology, I was in a very challenging situation, but I had to find another job and leave east Tennessee. My children were dying slowly with severe allergies and the complications that followed. My loving and lovely wife Diane had made many good friends in the neighborhood of Solway and was reluctant to leave. I tried to explain to her that the allergies were serious, but she still was reluctant to admit it. My daughter Catalina, Cati for short, was twelve and attending school in Solway. My second daughter, Margarita, Margie for short, was five and attending kindergarten, and our third child, a baby boy named Dante, was only one year old, but already walking and running. Years later, remembering those trying days of allergies in east Tennessee, I would write the following:

> For many years, I wonder how,
> Those illnesses called allergies,
> Insidiously, bring misery,
> To many people, my family...
>
> Nasal congestion, pesky bronchitis,
> Attacks of asthma, conjunctivitis,
> Or migraine headaches, anaphylaxis,
> GI disorders, or dermatitis...
>
> Our doctor told us, avoid exposure,
> To dogs and cats, to chicken feathers,
> Ragweeds in bloom, to trees and grasses,
> Air pollution, and dust from carpets...
>
> No milk and cheese, or soybean products,
> And no more coffee, chocolate, dark sodas,
> Don't take Dristan, seafood or peanuts,
> Avoid red wine, get out of town...
>
> And don't make contact, with poison ivy,
> Don't get too close, to bees and hornets,
> No softeners, drying the laundry,
> Don't wear wool, synthetics only...
>
> Long time ago, in all the papers,
> "There is a way: Block the antibody!"
> The medical, drug industries,
> I also wonder, don't want us healthy?

I updated my resume and printed some one hundred copies. I searched the Educational Chronicle for job openings. In a period of six months, I sent a cover letter, a resume and a list of publications to some 130 educational institutions around the country offering positions in biology, radiation biology, nuclear medicine technology, biochemistry, animal husbandry, etc. Anything that resembled my multiple abilities. Nothing. Most of them replied that my abilities and qualifications were excellent, but beyond the requirements of the vacant position. Many did not bother to reply. By the end of 1976, I was getting desperate. But then one day I received the Journal of Nuclear Medicine. On the last page appeared an announcement of a faculty position in NM technology at the Tampa Junior College (TJC) in Florida. The ad said that the deadline for applications was November 16. I received the journal November 17, one day late. I picked up the phone and requested to speak with the director of personnel, Mr. Richards. I explained that I was interested in the announced position, but that I had received the journal one day late. He said: "Marco, send me your papers right away. I'll make sure they get in the pile." At last, I thought, a friendly answer. I thanked Mr. Richards and proceeded to assemble the package: a cover letter, my resume, and a list of publications. My resume described my job of having coordinated the medical qualification nuclear medicine courses for physicians for the past eight years. A very powerful point. The next morning I mailed the package, first class, air mail. In January, I received a letter from Mr. Richards telling me that I had been selected as one of the three finalists among nine applicants. The finalists were called for an interview with members of the selecting committee sometime in February, and the letter encouraged me to make an appointment as soon as possible. I made the appointment for a Friday afternoon in mid-February. I remember I flew to Tampa, FL, on a cold cloudy day. Believe it or not, the night before it had snowed in Tampa. They said also that it had not snowed in Tampa for the past 20 years. When I landed though, all the snow had already melted. I took the airport limousine to the Best Western motel where I had a room reserved. The next morning, I took a taxi to the administration building, where Mr. Richards was already expecting me. He escorted me to the meeting room and introduced me to the members of the selecting committee. I was pleased to see Howard Parnell, a former junior staff member of ORINS, now in charge of the nuclear medicine technology program at TJC. The interview went quite well, I thought, until a lady member asked me why me, a scientist working at a much higher level, had applied for a job in a junior college. I replied that my family and I suffered from severe allergies to the vegetation of east Tennessee and by recommendation of our pediatrician we had to move to the Florida coast. That seemed reasonable, but to a lower job meant a lower paying job. After the interview, I returned to Oak Ridge and waited for a letter from Mr. Richards. Early in March, the letter came. Mr. Richards was pleased to inform me that I had won the appointment as a full-time faculty in the NMT program beginning April 1, 1977. He also said that my doctorate degree in veterinary medicine had been recognized and therefore, my salary would be at the doctorate level. The salary they offered me was only 59% of my current salary as a scientist in Oak Ridge. Diane and I discussed the offer for a long time and agonized over the pay cut I was going to take if I accepted the position at TJC. Two days later, we had come to a decision. For our children's sake as well as ours, we had to move. Personally, I considered ourselves lucky to move to Florida when we were still young. Many people waited to do it when they retired and were perhaps too old. At that point, I called Mr. Richards and accepted the offer over the phone. He asked me to write him a letter stating that because he had to have it in writing. He also said that they had omitted my interview with the president of the college and that, this time, the college would pay my travel costs. He also said that it was only a formality, that the president, Dr. Luigi Bianchi, had already approved the recommendation of the selecting committee. A week later I did travel again to Tampa for an informal visit with Dr. Bianchi, president of TJC. The second interview went well. Upon my return to Oak Ridge, we began to pack up our belongings for the trip to Florida.

70. Good bye to Oak Ridge

Early in March, the new chairman of STD, Mr. Lorton, sent a memo to all staff announcing the plan of courses to be offered during fiscal year 1977-78. He had decided that there were going to be nine medical courses instead of four in order to give MDs around the country more choices. Apparently, he did not understand all the work that went into preparing and presenting a course. He probably thought that we, the coordinators, could pull a course from our sleeve any time we wanted to. I did not like the plan of having more than doubled the number of courses I was to coordinate. I felt that, because my courses were good, I had to sell more of them. I was being prostituted, I thought. Of course, it was also possible that Mr. Lorton did not care about me and wanted to make my life impossible. That was one way of forcing someone to resign. Let's exploit Marco Donnatti until he either drops dead or resigns. That was my feeling about Lorton's plan. At the time, we were exhausting the pool of physicians interested in the course. Lately, we had run some courses with only eight participants. Mr. Lorton wanted to run more courses with even four participants at a time. Talk about inefficiency. Imagine asking some distinguished nuclear physicians to come to Oak Ridge to lecture to four cats in the audience. Besides, nine courses per year would not leave any time for my research in the designing of new animal experiments. I discussed Mr. Lorton's plan with my dearest wife Diane at home and having received the TJC's job confirmation letter, the next morning I presented my letter of resignation to Mr. Lorton, effective March 20, 1977. My resignation caused consternation among the staff and even the ORINS administration. When they asked me where I was going, I said, "Florida." But I did not give any details because they could attempt to block my appointment again. I had given the two weeks notice required by ORINS and, after that, had ten days to travel to Florida. A week later, Mr. Lorton announced that all medical courses were being cancelled because they could not run them without me. He had won. He had forced me to resign. The tendency, at the time, was that STD would design new environmental training programs.

On my last day of work, a Friday, the staff gave me a luncheon farewell party. I contributed the wine. We had a good time and remembered the old good times. They gave me a present: a picture of an old country couple dressed in coveralls and seating in their front porch. The picture was framed in a hard wood typical of the hills of Tennessee. I thanked everyone for the present and I added: "I will treasure it for years to come." A lady from the medical division came to the luncheon. She asked me at some point why I was moving to a lower paying job. I said "allergies" and I added, "I shall climb the ladder again." A few days before the farewell party, I had been invited to the administration building to meet with Mr. Johnson, Vice-president of ORINS, for my exit interview. Mr. Johnson asked me why I had resigned. I explained that our allergies to the vegetation of east TN was the most important factor and that the new medical courses plan of Mr. Lorton was a human impossibility. That nine courses per year would cause a decrease in the quality of the presentations and that quality is more important than quantity. I did not mention the "controlled drug officer" incident. He wished me well.

Mr. Richard Barton and his family were excellent next door neighbors to us in Solway. Mr. and Mrs. Barton had been godparents to our daughter Margie. We were very close. When the time came for us to move to FL, Mr. Barton offered to drive the truck with our furniture and other belongings. Diane and I accepted and offered to pay his return travel by airplane. He was delighted. He had never traveled by plane before. The trip went well, as planned. Our children were excited about going to the beach to play and swim. We managed to rent a townhouse in Clearwater, some 12 miles from work, and arranged Mr. Barton's flight home. We said good bye to our dear best friend, Mr. Barton, at the Tampa airport. We then returned to Clearwater to unpack. That evening we could not help it, we went to the beach. It was a new experience after 13 years of hard work in the hills of TN. Like a miracle, all allergies soon disappeared. But we knew that in a few years we could be sensitized again. We hoped that because FL was flat as a pancake, the winds would remove constantly the allergens that float in the air and, therefore, their effect would not be as severe.

—◦⊙◦°—

Reporter Judy Hartfeldt: Moving to Florida must have been hard for all of you. But a drastic change in the environment was good for your health. No question about that.

Marco Donnatti: Yes. Diane was sad to leave some dear friends at Solway, but she admitted that it was best for our children and for ourselves. The only worry was my drastic cut in salary. We would have to tighten our belts for awhile. Our children were growing fast. Cati was 14 and in high school, Margie was 7 and in grammar school, Dante was 3 and recovering from severe allergies.

Judy: Well, that is all for now. Next time I would like you to tell me about your new job in Florida.

Marco: Yes, of course. Arrivederci!

Judy: Good bye, Marco.

—◦⊙◦°—

Conservation of Angular Momentum. Spinning on Ice (Story 73)

CHAPTER 8

THE TAMPA Jr. COLLEGE

Reporter Judy Hartfeldt: Good morning Marco. When you changed jobs in 1977, you stepped down from a position of scientist in TN to a position of professor in FL. Tell me what happened.

Marco Donnatti: Good morning Judy. Of course, everything was new to me. But one objective had been accomplished; like magic, our allergies disappeared with the drastic change in the environment. In TN, we felt claustrophobic between the Cumberland mountains and the Smoky mountains. Do not take me wrong. We liked TN. We enjoyed our visits to the Smoky Mountains National Park and to Gatlinburg, every year, even in the winter. FL was just different.

Judy: I am sure, living on the coast was different.

Marco: Diane, the children, and I loved to go to the beach around 5 p.m., when I came home from work, and waddle in the shallow waves, even in March, when the water was still cold.

Judy: Tell me about your new job.

Marco: I'll be glad to. The following stories describe life at a small, state college.

---

71. A State Junior College

The The Tampa Junior College, TJC, was one of the 40 or so FL state colleges. That meant that it was funded by the state legislature. And, of course, the state was funded by the taxpayers. Approximately 20% of the costs were covered by student fees and the rest by the taxpayers. State funding was in proportion to student enrollment. In the late 70s, TJC had approximately 35,000 students. Many students enrolled in a two-year career. Other students enrolled only to fulfill the basic requirements for admission to the University of South Florida (USF). The TJC main campus was divided into well defined areas: the sciences, the humanities, and the health sciences. Other facilities were the library, the bookstore, the cafeteria, and the athletic and the maintenance departments. Besides the Tampa main campus, there were other campuses in nearby towns. And, of course, the magnificent administration building where the president and administrative offices were located. Like in other state colleges, there were two kinds of employees at TJC: the administrators, they were the ones in charge, the ones in power, they wore the finest clothes, the most expensive jewelry and drove Mercedes and Lincoln Continentals. I know because I attended a few of the Board of Trustees meetings that were held in the evenings. Although the faculty were invited to attend the meetings, none of them attended. The second kind of employees, were the faculty, they were the ones doing the work, they were in the trenches dealing from day to day with the students, preparing up-to-date lectures and labs, producing the main product of the college: education. They wore simple clothes, sport shirts, no jewelry, and drove Toyotas and Datsuns. Of course, others were the blue collar workers that did the cleaning and maintenance. Almost invisible were the few policemen that took care of security around the main campus.

My program, the Nuclear Medicine Technology (NMT) program, was part of the Allied Health Division. Other programs in that division were: radiology, medical sonography, radiotherapy, occupational therapy, medical emergency, American sign language, and optician technology. In 1977, the director of the NMT program was Howard Parnell, a technologist with a B.S. degree in chemistry. Upon my arrival, Howard assigned me to teach 10 credit-hours of courses and 5 credit-hours of clinical supervision. He took a lesser load with one credit-hour of courses and 14 credit-hours of clinical supervision. To do a good job, I had to redesign all the courses assigned to me: NM data analysis, radiation physics, radiation safety, radiation biology, NM instrumentation, radiation physics lab, instrumentation lab, NM seminar, and NM methodologies I, II, and III. Informal discussions were replaced by well structured course curricula for all the subjects listed above. During the second year, NMT students were assigned to, and rotated through, several NM departments of some local hospitals, under contract with the college. An experienced NMT was hired by the college, for each site, to teach, supervise, and evaluate the students in training.

The college required that all faculty obtain a "teacher's certificate" from the State of Florida Department of Education. I did apply for mine in April of 1977 by submitting a thick pile of documents, certificates, copies of all my diplomas, and reprints of my publications. Two months later, I received in the mail my teaching certificate, rank I, with recognition of my doctorate degree. Immediately, I submitted a copy to the TJC administration. In 1980, our program earned certification and recognition by the Society of NM certification board (NMTCB). In 1982, Howard Parnell, who at the time was involved in successful businesses outside the college, suddenly resigned and moved to Texas. Then, the college administration asked me to become director of the NMT program and Radiation Safety Officer for the college. That meant additional administrative duties. Fortunately, it coincided with a faculty negotiated salary increase, which was very helpful to my family. I was also offered a one-year part-time job as a radioimmunoassay consultant with a major hospital in Tampa. That represented some extra income that helped my family succeed in Florida. I had begun to climb the ladder.

On the first day of classes, I would tell the new recruits that the two-year NMT program was going to change their lives, that they would not recognize themselves after two years of training, that they were going to change from qualitative persons to quantitative persons, that they would quadruple their salaries from 4 dollars an hour pushing burgers, to 16 dollars an hour pushing patients and doing nuclear scans. That their opinions were going to be respected by colleagues and by physicians. Some graduates, two and three years later, wrote to me reminding me of my speech on the first day and added, "Although it seemed unbelievable then, it turned out to be all true." Our program earned reaccreditations in 1984, 1988, 1992, and 1996. In the 1988 reaccreditation process, the examining committee described our program as "an example for the rest of the country."

During my early years at TJC, I heard the rumor that some of our college administration officials were involved in organized crime. Of course, I dismissed the allegations as unfounded. But soon, our college president resigned his position, and other high level administrators resigned also. The reasons were never clear. The local newspapers described our college as the most politicized college in Florida. I read with interest the news that affected our institution, but at the time, I was too busy reorganizing the NMT program to worry about it. As it turned out, our college changed presidents five times in the first 14 years of my work at TJC.

72. Dental Surgery

In 1988, we were living in Florida. During a routine dental check up, reading a radiograph, Dr. Davis, my dentist, discovered a cyst in the root of my left first upper molar tooth. He said that it was a root infection that needed immediate attention. I had no pain or any other symptoms of illness at that time. But Dr. Davis insisted that soon I would be in pain if I did not take care of it. He referred me to Dr. Thompson, DDS, of St. Petersburg, FL, and gave me the set of radiographs to take with me to my appointment. I made an appointment with Dr. Thompson right away. On the day of the appointment, Dr. Thompson introduced himself and shook my hand. He was a much older gentleman, perhaps well into his 70s. The dental technician placed me on a special reclinable chair and covered me with surgical cloth. Dr. Thompson, returned a few minutes later well attired in lab coat, gloves and mask told me that the radiographs showed clearly the site of the infection and that he was going to give me an examination first. But when he attempted to use the dental mirror to look at my upper teeth, his hands trembled very much he could hardly place the mirror in my mouth. Quickly I realized that he did not have the steady hands of a surgeon. I had to make a decision fast. Was I going to let him operate on me? If he could not hit my mouth, how could he drill left first upper molar,? I wondered. How could I get out of this predicament without offending the gentleman? When he took the electric drill in his hand and still shaking, I said: "Just a moment, doctor. I would like to call home right away, please forgive me. It is an emergency!" Dr. Thompson said: "It is fine, go ahead, use the phone in the office." At the office, I told the receptionist that I needed to go home right away and that I would call later.

When I got home, I called Dr. Davis and explained the whole situation. He said that he had never heard any complaints about Dr. Thompson. He then added that he would refer me to another dental surgeon. He also added that my confidence in the surgeon was of utmost importance. I thanked him. The next day, he called me and gave me the phone and address of Dr. Bigelow of Tampa, FL. By then I had begun to have symptoms of swelling, increased pressure, and pain in the upper left teeth. After the expected examination and the reading of the radiographs, Dr. Bigelow told me that I needed a root-canal operation. I asked him to proceed. Under local anesthesia he performed well. He gave me a prescription for pain killers and antibiotics that I was to take on a strict schedule for several days after the surgery. I was pleased that everything went well after that.

73. Conservation Laws

Some of the principles I taught in my Radiation Physics course to the NMT first-year students, were the basic conservation laws. Conservation of mass, conservation of energy, and conservation of momentum. Briefly, I would describe them to my students in easy-to-understand terms. The law of conservation of mass was proposed in about 1780 by Antoine Lavoisier. He was a wealthy French nobleman who loved the sciences. He used part of his mansion as a laboratory. He purchased the latest technical equipment to make accurate measurements of weights, volumes, densities, temperatures, concentrations of solutions, crystallizations, evaporations, etc. He kept records of his observations and, after quite a few years of work, became convinced of his law of conservation of mass. He announced it as follows: "In any physical or chemical reaction, the mass of the products must be equal to mass of the reacting substances." Then, he added, "If they are not equal, something must have been overlooked " Of course, that law was extended to the law of conservation of energy when Albert Einstein in 1905 proposed his principle of the equivalence of matter and energy. He explained the matter is only "frozen energy." But he went well beyond that. He expressed the equivalence in the form of an equation "$E = mc^2$," which said that if we multiply a certain amount of mass in kilograms times the speed of light in meters per second squared, we would get the amount of energy contained in that mass, expressed in joules. Thus the law became the "the conservation of mass-energy law." Later, in 1850, the German physicist Rudolf Clausius provided another name for the law: "The first law of thermodynamics." But the story does not end there. During the French Revolution in 1789, the large population of poor people executed many wealthy people of the oppressing class. Antoine Lavoisier, unfortunately, belonged to that class. His worst sin was having been born wealthy. He was executed by guillotine during the Revolution. And so were King Louis XVI and Queen Marie Antoinette.

The law of conservation of momentum has to do with motion and collisions. I explained to my students that, for an object moving in linear motion, momentum is equal to the product of its mass times its velocity. For example, if a mass of one kilogram moves linearly with a velocity of one meter per second, then we say that it carries a momentum of one kg-m/s. Kg-m is a compound unit, like man-hours in construction work. A small car running at 70 miles per hour carries much less linear momentum than an 18-wheeler that travels at the same velocity. That is due to their tremendous mass difference. For an object that moves in circular motion, its "angular momentum" would be the product of its mass in kg times its velocity in meters per second times the radius of motion in meters. For example, if an object weighing one kg moves in a circle of one meter radius at a velocity of 3 meters per second, its momentum would be: 3 kg-m²/s. An ice skater (Fig. 8) spinning with her arms extended, at 3 turns per second, may have a radius of 90 cm. But when she brings her arms close to her body, the radius decreases perhaps to one-third or 30 cm; then, the law of conservation of angular momentum dictates that her velocity must triple to 9 turns per second.

And now, the funny part. I told my students about my "Law of conservation of green paper." Green paper refers to dollar bills, of course. The law says that, "When someone suddenly becomes rich, a lot of people become a little poorer." Of course, for the law to be correct, the pool of circulating dollar bills must be constant. But we all know that, to sustain growth, everything must grow: population, the pool of dollar bills, houses, standards of living, trade, you name it. As individuals, to conserve "our personal pool of green paper" we must make intelligent decisions and not fall for funny television ads that promise you a pie in the sky.

74. Heat Stroke

When I joined TJC in 1977, I was still very active in soccer. I loved to play a practice game once a week. Soccer was my way of dealing with the stresses of work. One of the secretaries in the administration building, Ms. Tina Pitrelli, learned that I played soccer, and one day, she showed up at my office to invite me to her club, the Jewish Association of Tampa. Some twenty young men, members of the club, got together every Saturday morning to practice their favorite sport, soccer, on their club's field. I accepted the invitation. Thus, the following Saturday I drove from home in Clearwater to Tampa and found the club. There, Tina introduced me as a guest player. Most of the players were in their mid-twenties. I was already 45 years old. Way beyond retirement for a soccer player. But my constant activity had preserved me somehow. I was as fast and skillful as ever. They divided the players into two teams, and the game began, at about 9 a.m. It was a fast game, one-touch passes, hard kicking, high balls, low gracing balls. It was incredible. Three hours, non-stop. I did my part well. One touch, turned around to misplace the adversary, another touch to pass. It was great. I liked to play like that. At one point, pretended to pass, but instead shot hard to the goal. A well placed ball that reached the net. I had scored a goal. Tina, on the bleachers, applauded. The game continued as fast as ever. After one hour, I thought I was going to see someone drop of exhaustion at any minute, but it did not happen. The game ended close to noon. I had scored four goals. My team had won the game 4 to 3. We were exhausted. Some players congratulated me for the goals I had scored, which allowed them win some bets. I was a guest. I did not participate in the bets. I was completely "neutral."

The following Saturday, another hot and humid day. Another fast game. I did some fancy demonstrations of skill. I spun the ball like a pro. Again I scored four goals. After the fourth goal, I was very much surprised by my team players, who were teasing the adversary by singing: "two nails, three nails, four nails..." with the music of a well-known Jewish song. At first, I did not know what the singing was about, until I realized these guys were Jewish, they were crucifying the adversary. They were nailing them to the cross. And the four nails were my four goals! Oh well, I did not pay much attention to it. The game ended with our victory by 4-0. It was close to noon, and I was exhausted. Some players asked me not to miss the following game. I promised to come. For the third game, in that hot and humid weather, I did not feel as well as in previous games. I did play, but I was not the same. I was slow and imprecise in my passing of the ball. I did not score a single goal this time. And yet, I was exhausted. The fourth game came. Again, I did not feel good. I did not score goals any more. Close to noon, the game ended, and I slowly walked to the side of the field where I had my clothes and bag of gear. Then, I fell unconscious. I had passed out. I do not know how long I was unconscious, but when I came to, I was surrounded by a circle of players. Their silhouettes against the bright and burning sun appeared like tall trees to me. I asked what happened. "You passed out," some answered. "It's heat stroke," I said. Someone handed me a bottle of water. I drank slowly. "I am OK now, thank you" I said. That was the last time I played three-hour games in the blazing sun. They understood, I am sure.

75. NMT Adventures

Some memorable events occurred both in the classroom, as well as in the clinical setting. The first is a case of student behavior. During the ten-minute break that I gave to the students every hour of classes, a female student came to talk to me. She asked me to excuse her absence of the previous class. And then, she gave me her reasons. She said that she had been sick to her stomach and had been in and out of the bathroom all morning with diarrhea. At that point, I stopped her by raising my voice a little and saying: "Stop. You are excused. Now, go." She tried to explain her symptoms, but I did not let her. I said, "I don't want to hear about it. Please go away." She left. Later, I was told, that the student in question had gone out of the classroom and, in the hall, had said, "We got him. He cannot take it." I figured that meant that they could miss classes whenever they wanted and that they would be excused if they could come up with an obnoxious story.

One day at 1 p.m., the students were coming into the classroom when a female student handed me a Coke in a cup. I took it and thanked her for her kindness. What else I could do, under the circumstances? I placed the Coke on the demonstration table in front of me. My notes were on the podium, and I asked the students if everything was OK? They all said yes, like a chorus. Then, I took a sip of the Coke while the students watched me intently. The Coke had been spiked with hard liquor. Possibly rum. I nodded and smiled. Then, I said, "This is the best

Coke I ever tasted." The students broke out in laughter. Then, I added, "Now let's talk about nuclear medicine." Those were some of the days I shall never forget.

One early morning, I turned on the TV to watch the local news and weather. Right off, the announcer described an accident in which a Tampa policeman had been shot by his wife in the wee hours of the morning as he was entering his home. It appears that, because he always came home very late, she had a pistol in the night table, for protection. When she woke up upon hearing steps on the stairs outside of her bedroom, she called; "George, is that you?", he did not answer, possibly trying to scare her a bit to amuse himself. But she shot twice through the door. George fell just outside. When she opened the door and found her husband unconscious and bleeding, she called an ambulance. Later that morning, I walked into the NM department of Mercy Hospital, to do my weekly check on the students' progress. One of the students whispered to me that the technologists were going to do a brain blood flow study on the policeman shot by his wife. I came in very quietly and took a quick look at George. His waxy skin, absence of respiration, and mydratic eyes, told me quickly that the man was dead. No real reason to do the test. But as a guest, I could not express an opinion. I remained at a distance. Sure enough, when the IV injection of sodium pertechnetate solution was given, absolutely, no blood flow through the brain was observed on the monitor connected to the scintillation camera. At that point, he was declared deceased.

On another occasion, I was visiting my students at the NMT department of Dunedin Hospital. As I entered, a student told me that in the next room, there was a case of "situs inversus," also known as dextrocardia. In such cases, all organs appear on the opposite side of the body, like in a mirror. The heart apex points to the right, the right lung, which has three lobes, is on the left, the liver is on the left, etc. The lady Dr. in charge, Dr. Bertrand, call me aside and told me, "These cases are extremely rare. I replied that I was glad to find at last, a man with his heart in the right place." She smiled and said, "You know, you are right too."

One last story. One morning, I was driving on Fowler avenue in Tampa going towards the Veterans Hospital where I had another group of students in training. Suddenly, I felt a dull pain in the left lower abdomen. I wondered what it could be. What is there? I asked myself. Besides the ileum and the descending colon, the left ureter is there. Perhaps I have a ureteral stone, I thought. Through my medical insurance, I went to see my doctor, Dr. Campbell. He examined me and referred me to a specialist, a urologist at the Mease clinic, Dr. Dwellman. The nurse prepared me for an IVP, an intravenous pielogram, a radiographic procedure in which a contrast medium is given intravenously and immediately, several radiographs are recorded as an x-ray machine circles the body 180 degrees. All this in a few seconds. I was then asked to sit in the waiting room. Some 15 minutes later, Dr. Dwellman called me in and showed me the radiographs. He said, "Your kidneys, renal pelvises, and ureters are picture perfect. There is nothing wrong with them. Get out of here before I operate on you." That was what I wanted to hear. Before I left, he suggested that the pain I felt was psychosomatic. He said that psychosomatic pain is common in cases of stress. Yes, definitely, at the time I was having difficulties with some administrators at TJC. That could have been the case.

76. Personal Tragedies

Two personal tragedies occurred between the latter years at Oak Ridge and my second decade in Florida. The first was the passing of my mother, Maria Vitalia Soriano de Donnatti in Lima. She had had an accident while supervising the construction of her new house in the district of Atocongo, southeast of Lima. The Peruvian government had given her a plot of land because she qualified as a widow of a member of the armed forces. She hired some workers to start the construction of a two-story house made out of bricks, concrete, and steel. One cold morning in October of 1976, she was climbing the stairs to the second floor. The stairs had no railing yet. She lost equilibrium and fell to the first floor. She fell on top of some construction materials which, apparently cushioned her fall. That evening, in my house of Solway, TN, I received a call from a telephone operator. She said that I had a telegram from Lima, Peru. I asked her to read it to me. She read: "Mama Maria Vitalia fallecio esta manana" ("Mamma Maria Vitalia passed away this morning"). I went to our bedroom and cried for a few minutes. Diane came and hugged me and asked me: "What had happened?." I said: "My mother passed away this morning. I must call Lima right away." I called my sister Gina in Lima. She said that the funeral services and burial were going to be Sunday morning. It was Thursday evening. I had time to attend the funeral. I called the chairman of STD, Mr. Lorton, and told him that I needed to attend the funeral in Lima. He said: "Yes, he said. As of now you are on special leave. Go." Then, I called Panamerican Airlines and made reservations for my travel to Lima. My twin brother Giovanni had taken care of all the arrangements for the funeral. Over one hundred people went from her house on 28th of July Avenue to the main cemetery. After the funeral, my brother Giovanni held a reception and luncheon for the family and close friends at his house in Monterrico. The newspapers gave the news as an accident resulting in severe trauma to the head, it seems that the reason she lost equilibrium though, was because she suffered a stroke. She had had symptoms of numbness and loss of sensitivity in her left arm for a few months before the accident. No autopsy was performed. So, we shall never know for sure.

The second tragedy was one that occurred more insidiously, in the late 1980s. While at work, at the TJC, one late morning, I received a call from Dr. Castell, a physician who worked at the Mease Clinic in Dunedin. My wife Diane had had an appointment with him that morning. He said that he was calling to tell me: "Your wife has symptoms of manic depression and a touch of schizophrenia." I replied, "Dr.Castell, with very much respect, I must tell you that you must be wrong. There is not a thing wrong with my wife. She is perfect." He then said, "Well, I thought it was my duty to warn you." I replied, "Thank you doctor." When I got home, I told Diane about the call and that I had defended her saying that she was perfect. She smiled and thanked me. That was the end of the matter, I thought. By then, Diane had joined the Alliance of Churches, one of which was just two blocks from our house in Dunedin, FL. She had become a very devoted Christian and participated in many meetings and fund raising activities organized by pastor Chapman and the "elders" of the church. The pastor was constantly pressuring her to have me join also. But really, joining meant giving 10% of my income, before taxes, to the church. That was what they called tithing. So, that was the interest of pastor Chapman and his team, money. As a scientist, I was not too keen on religion. I only believed in proven facts, not in just faith. I resisted for a while, but when, because of it, my relationship with Diane became strained, I accepted to attend the Sunday services with the children. But I refused to give away 10% of my modest income to a multi-millionaire organization like the Alliance of Churches. After all, I had come to Florida to a much lower paying job. My family and I were barely surviving on my salary. One night, Diane awoke me to tell me that there were mice in the walls of the house. I said, "No, there are not or I would hear them." I did not realize then that she was having delusions, a symptom of schizophrenia. Another time, Diane told me that one of the members of the church, who was a roofing contractor, had said that our house needed a new roof and that being a "Christian," he would give us a good deal on a roof replacement job. I went up the roof, crawled in the attic, examined the roof well and concluded that the man was lying. There was nothing wrong with the roof, except a corner of the roof, on the side of the house, that required a small repair job. We contracted the man and the job was done in two hours. Another time, one of the pilot lights went off on the panel of instruments in our car. Nothing terrible important, but we had to fix it. Someone from the church recommended to Diane a "Christian" mechanic on Main Street, Dunedin. We went. He changed the part, which cost 48 dollars, but wanted 450 dollars for four hours of labor. I protested. He held the car hostage until I paid his price. I paid it and swore I would never go to a "Christian mechanic" again. All these incidents really reflected Diane's fanaticism with religion. She had changed. She had been brain-washed by the people at the church. The pastor and team had managed to have all the people come to the church five evenings a week for one reason or another. Besides Sunday school and Sunday service, Monday fund raising evening, Tuesday youth meeting, Wednesday praying day, Friday "deliverance evening." That church was taking control of our lives. Diane had become a religious fanatic, another symptom of her bipolar illness. We did not know it then, but Diane's illness was going to end up in the tragedy of divorce.

77. Soccer in Florida

After the first year in Florida, in which Diane and I lived in a rented town house, we decided to purchase a house in Dunedin. We soon learned that the City of Dunedin had a good recreation department with programs for children and adults. Registration in those programs was only 8 dollars per person per year. While I was at work, and for a modest fee, Diane and the children attended swimming classes, gymnastics, etc. The recreation department also organized soccer events for children and adults. In 1979, the adult program consisted of eight teams of eight players each. The Dunedin athletic director arranged a tournament schedule in which teams played two games per week. The games were played on small grass fields, on Wednesday and Saturday nights, from 6:00 to 7:30 p.m. Eight teams, two rounds, each team had to play fourteen games in seven weeks. Among the enrollees, there were some young women and the director decided to assign them evenly among all teams. Each team then had 6 men and two women. It worked out just fine. On the first night, we met the girls on our team. One of them was a most beautiful young lady. About five-six, one hundred-twenty pounds, well shaped, very pretty. What more we could ask for? She was very serious. She did not look or talk to anyone. At some distance, she started to warm up by doing some gymnastics. We observed her with some fascination. Then she started to pass the ball with precision and style. Just like a player! We were impressed. The game began. The left winger of the opposite team came fast with the ball and against "our girl." She tackled him with two feet in front and took the ball away from the adversary. A perfectly legal tackle. The adversary flew and fell on the grass. Our girl took the ball and passed to another player with class and style. We were in awe! A few minutes later, a repeat of the tackle happened again. From there on, she had full control of her area and we went on to win the game. At the end, we went to congratulate her on a great performance. She smiled only. She did not talk. She played only two games and then disappeared. She never showed up again. We were disappointed. The mysterious beauty was never more.

Another incident occurred during a night game I jumped for the ball and collided with an adversarial player in a red shirt. Only she was a girl! I only saw a red player coming at me against the artificial lights. Instinctively, I placed my arms in front of me to protect myself from the collision. Apparently, I hit the girl in the chest. When we fell to the ground, she had fire in her eyes. I said, "I am sorry, I did not know it was you. The lights blinded me." But she came right at me. I thought she was going to hit me. I walked backwards trying to get away. She kept waking toward me. I kept apologizing and walking back. She stayed near me after that. She wanted me to have the ball so that she could, legally, let me have it. My teammates were laughing at me. Like an idiot, I smiled too. And I kept trying to get away and yelling "Do not give me the ball!." After some ten minutes, she finally went to her side of the field. But I could not play anymore. I asked for a substitute. That was the only time that I had left the field in defeat. She had won.

During the soccer tournaments of 1979 and 1980 in Dunedin, which were played on small fields, I was fortunate to have been the highest scorer in both. I scored 18 goals in 1979, and 24 goals in 1980. In 1980, our seventh game was against a team which, like ours, had not lost a single game. That team had a lady goalkeeper. Nobody had scored on her in the previous six games. On our team, I was the scorer with ten goals in six games. There was a great expectation to watch the duel between the unbeatable goalkeeper and the scorer of the tournament. A lot of people came to see the game that night. I learned about the duel right there before the game. Someone told me that "that woman is unbeatable." So, I watched the lady goalkeeper from the distance warming up. She was a tall and strong girl. Imposing appearance. Taller than I. The game began. Some ten minutes into the game, I had my chance. On a crossed ball, I shot hard to the goal. The lady goalkeeper flew across the small area and deflected the ball away from her rectangle. I was impressed. She was very good. That had been a mean shot. Then, I figured, she is tall, I must shoot low, faster and harder. The first half of the game ended zero-zero. The second half began. About 15 minutes into it, I got another chance. I shot hard, low, and across. The lady got to touch the ball, but could not prevent it from entering the goal. We had scored a goal on the unbeatable goalkeeper. She was in shock. She covered her eyes. I believed she cried. A few minutes later, another chance. I pretended to shoot, but I did not. She froze. Then I pushed the ball gently by the post and into the goal. All this happened within two seconds. The pretend shot and the real shot. She just watched frozen. That was the second goal. We had won. The duel had been decided. Our team went on to win the tournament.

In 1981, the Suncoast Soccer League was organized. It consisted of teams from several counties in central FL. One of the categories was the league for adult males, which registered men above the age of thirty. Another was the women's league. Teams from Dunedin, Sarasota, Palm Harbor, Safety Harbor, Clearwater, St. Petersburg, Tampa, and other towns were registered in three divisions. All games were played on regulation fields and with professional referees. Things had changed. I participated in the adult league tournament. In 1983, in a game, while I held the ball for an instant, I was swept from behind by an adversary. I fell and tore the two left-knee medial ligaments. A week later I had to have repair surgery. Things were never the same after that. I played, but I did not have the flexibility of "turning on a dime" like before. I was fifty-one years old. I am very much surprised at how long I had lasted playing my favorite sport. After that, I went to the field to practice middle distance shots to the goal and to run a little, but I could not play competitive games anymore.

78. Bipolar Disorder

In 1989, Diane's illness, bipolar disorder, also called manic depresion, appeared to have gotten worse. It seems that when she took the prescribed medications, she felt fine. And, when she felt fine, she discontinued her medications and then felt worse. She would have relapse after relapse. That year, at some point, she asked me to leave the house because, she said, I was the cause of her illness. I tried to explain to her that bipolar illness was a genetic disease, that it runs in families. I said, "Your mother has it, your sister has it, you daughter has it, and you have it." I also told her that the scientists of Myriad Genetics in Salt Lake City had discovered and isolated the gene for depression. But she would not accept my explanations. Someone at the church had told her that my behavior was affecting her and was causing the illness. She was more willing to accept that explanation. When she asked me to leave the house, I refused because it could be interpreted as my abandoning of the family. A few days later, she insisted on my leaving, saying that if I did not leave, she was going to die. I asked her to write and sign a paper stating that I was leaving upon her request and not abandoning the family. She started to write it. But then she stopped and destroyed what she had written. She refused to write another. Then, I called our two children, still in the house, Margie and Dante, and in her presence, I told them: "Your mother has asked me to leave because if I do not, she believes she is going to die. I do not want her to die.

But I want you to be witnesses that I am not abandoning the family. I will provide your mother with enough money to pay all expenses of the household. You shall continue to study and to help around the house as usual. I promise to come to visit on Saturdays to do the yard mowing and to take you all out to lunch, OK?" My kids were wonderful. They understood and accepted the situation graciously. On one of my visits of October, 1991, Diane asked me for a divorce. I had been hoping for a reconciliation all those years of her illness. But apparently she had other plans. She had asked me to replace the air conditioning system of the house. That cost some 3,500 dollars. Then she asked me to remodel the kitchen and the replace the drainage system. I do not remember how much that cost, but it was another bundle. I accepted to have all that work done with the hope of reconciliation. I promised her that we could retire together, that I could take care of her now that we understood her illness better. But she always would reply, "Too little, too late." Still, I continued to live in a small apartment in Tampa, near work, and to visit them on weekends to do the yard work and to take them to lunch. After lunch, I would return to "my cage" in Tampa.

79. The Divorce

Sometime in November of 1991, I received a letter from a lawyer, Diane's lawyer, stating her conditions for the dissolution of marriage. I called Diane and asked her not to do that to us. I said that lawyers meet privately and play the contending parties against each other in any way that would maximize their profits. That if she wanted a divorce, we could do it with only one lawyer handling all the paper work. All we had to do is agree on the terms of the partition of the property and retirement benefits. She said: "No. Too little, too late." I also told her that once the ball starts rolling there is no way to stop it. But she did not want to hear any more. I was very sad because I still had hopes of reconciliation. I had also hoped that, at worst, she would reason and avoid a confrontation in court. I did not know what to do. I asked a lady faculty member at TJC, in whom I confided, what I should do. She said that she knew about a good divorce lawyer and offered to find out her phone number. The next day she gave it to me. Immediately, I made an appointment. Ms. Nora Denardo, attorney at law, became my lawyer. She read the letter I had received about the dissolution of marriage, and asked me about some background information. She then concluded that Diane was a controlling person and that the best thing to do was "to get her off my back." I did not understand exactly what she meant by that, but I understood that there was no turning back now. The ball was rolling. A series of letters came and went between lawyers. Diane's lawyer asking for too much: 100% of the house, 50% of all other property, and 50% of my salary. My lawyer, Ms. Denardo, asked only for 50% of everything and a more reasonable alimony payments, lower than 50%. It seemed that Diane wanted to ruin me economically. That was her way of getting even with me for refusing to become a religious fanatic. During the process, Diane changed lawyers three times. All that lasted about one-and-a-half years. Sometime in January of 1993, I asked Ms. Denardo, over the phone, about the status of the process. She said that the other party had not responded to our last communication which she had sent seven months earlier. I asked her to find out why. She said, "Do not worry. I will make sure they respond this time." A few weeks later, I learned that the court had ordered an arbitration session with a professional mediator acting as referee in the partition of property. The place for the session was a county court building and lasted most of the day. The arbitrator met with Diane and her lawyer. Then, he met with me and my lawyer. Then, while we waited, he met again with Diane and her lawyer. Then, he met with the two lawyers alone, and so on and so forth, all morning. We had a lunch break at 12 noon to 1 p.m. Then, we continued the process the same way in the afternoon. At about 3 p.m., my lawyer told me, in private, "Give her the house. That is the only way we are going to come to an agreement." Then, I said, "OK, give it to her." I did not know then that, in exchange, Ms. Denardo had gotten cancelled the alimony payments. Papers were signed, and the session ended at about 4:30 p.m. A few weeks later, Diane's lawyer appealed the decision requesting that the voluntary monthly payments toward support be continued for three months after the divorce was final and she also asked that her part of my Florida retirement monthly payments be increased from 450 to 590 dollars. Ms. Denardo met with me and asked me to I agree to that final request. I did, and signed the papers. Other retirement accounts were divided equally.

On December 16, 1993, Ms. Denardo and I met at the Court House in Clearwater to appear in person before the judge. The appointment was for 8:00 a.m. Ms.Denardo told me, in advance, that the judge was going to ask me one question: "Is your decision to terminate your marriage final?" I told Ms. Denardo that my answer was going to be "Yes, your honor." She was pleased. After our meeting with the judge, a male secretary, had all the papers ready to be signed, including the transfer of the house to my dear ex-wife Diane. I thanked Ms.Denardo for her work and promised to pay her fees on time. We said good bye. When I got back to my apartment, I looked at the documents I had received at the court. I discovered that I had been the plaintiff. It seems that to reactivate the process, Ms. Denardo had reinitiated it in my name. I was then, the demanding party. But I did not know it until after the fact, December 16, 1993.

80. Three More Years

I love mathematics. I always did. When my divorce was final, I made some calculations and came up with the conclusion that, if I retired at 65 instead of at 62, my monthly pension would increase by 30%. I had planned to retire at 62 because of the illness of my wife. I wanted to take care of her. But my plans did not realize. I had no wife now. There was no reason why I could not work three more years and earn 30% more in my golden years. And that part of my earnings would be mine, untouchable by Diane or her lawyer. Thus, I decided to make those three years the best of the NMT program. By then, Diane, my ex-wife had thrown my daughter Margie out of the house too. Another symptom of the illness. Margie was studying medical sonography at TJC. I saw her frequently, and I helped her with her rent payments of an apartment in Clearwater. Margie was working two part-time jobs to support herself while in school. Fortunately, because I was a full-time faculty at TJC, she paid tuition at only half of the normal rate. She was a great student. She was first in her class. I was very much proud of her and her accomplishments. My son Dante, had entered the Clearwater Christian College (CCC) as a boarding student. CCC was a very expensive college. Tuition was five times more expensive than the University of South Florida (USF). I offered to pay his tuition if he studied a career at USF. But his mother had convinced him to go to CCC. Finally, wishing him to succeed at whatever he wanted to pursue, I accepted to pay his tuition, room, board, books, etc. at CCC. Later, I learned, Diane had been enrolled also at CCC in a B.S. program to study biology. I was pleased. Once a month, I came to visit my son and to take both of them to breakfast at a small restaurant by the Dunedin causeway. We had a friendly chat during breakfast. At those meetings, I tutored them both. Dante needed help with math and sciences in general. Diane needed help with biochemistry, specially energy metabolism. I made diagrams, explained equations, etc. They seemed to appreciate that. After breakfast, we walked the Dunedin beach and talked. It was then that Diane confessed that she did not have enough money for food. I told her to get a loan from her bank. When you sell the house, I explained, the loan is paid, and you have plenty for whatever you want or need. But, no, she did not want to get a loan, because she was afraid the bank would take the house away from her. I believe, she was still having the delusions of bipolar illness. Thus, once a month, I gave her some cash to assist her with her food expenses. I did not want to think that she was suffering hunger. In two years at CCC, both Dante and Diane graduated. Diane got her B.S. degree in biology and Dante received an associate degree of some kind. I was invited to the graduation ceremony. I went and met several professors and graduates. After the ceremony, I invited Diane, Dante, and some close faculty to lunch on Clearwater beach. Later, I learned that Dante was traveling to Chicago to pursue a B.S. degree in communications. As usual, I offered to pay his tuition, board, and books at the Moody Bible Institute. I also learned that Diane had sold the house of Dunedin and traveled to New Zealand to do some missionary work. I communicated occasionally with Dante and sent the checks directly to the Institute. Three years later, he graduated. I traveled to Chicago to attend the ceremony. There, I met with Diane and some of her coworkers in the missions field. That evening I invited all to dinner. We had a good time. Dante found a job as manager of a Christian radio station in Pekin, IL. Diane continued her missionary work. I returned to Florida.

In 1996, I had my last re-accreditation review of the NMT program. The examining committee found everything in top shape. Once again we passed inspection with flying colors. That year, I also gave TJC a one-year notice of my plans to retire at the end of the Summer of 1997. The TJC administrators did not seem to be concerned. I gave plenty of notice to give them time to announce the vacancy and begin the process of finding a good new program director. But they did not do anything. In April of 1997, I sent them another note reminding them that time was running out. I was leaving in mid-August. I had made all necessary arrangements for retirement with Social Security, with the Florida Retirement System, and with

TIAA-CREF, a private college retirement system to which I had contributed while I worked in Tennessee. I was ready. In June that year, two months before my retirement, I received a verbal job offer from the college administration. They offered me the position of Dean of Allied Health Careers. All ten health career programs would fall under my direction. I refused. I told the messenger that "my retirement plans had been made five years in advance and that I could not change them now."

Reporter Judy Hartfeldt: You refused a high position, a well-paid position, I am sure. Why?

Marco Donnatti: Two reasons: First, my position was under a person in the high administration who had opposed my NMT program for years. I did not want that person directly above me. For that reason, it was going to be a very stressful job. Second, although the salary of the dean was enticing, according to my calculations, my pension was lower, but free of the stresses that go with the job of dean. Thus, I proceeded with my plans to retire. It was time to read, to study, to write, and to travel around the world. I did not want to wait until I was too old to do those things.

Judy: And did you get to do those things?

Marco: Yes, and I am planning to tell you about it. In the next session, perhaps?

Judy: By all means. Good bye now.

Marco: Good bye Judy.

Rescuing a Cormorant on Treasure Island (Story 84)

CHAPTER 9

SUNSET BEACH, TREASURE ISLAND

Reporter Judy Hartfeldt: Good morning Marco. Ready for another recording session?

Marco Donnatti: Good morning Judy. As ready as I could be.

Judy: You were going to tell me about your retirement. Was it an involved process?

Marco:"Not really. For 34 years, I had paid my contributions to Social Security. For 14 years, I had paid my contributions to Medicare. For over 20 years, I had paid my contributions to the Florida retirement system, and for 13 years, I had paid my contributions to the TIAA-CREF system. All those agencies had proof of my payments. I requested application forms, filled them out and sent them back Not so difficult. You will see.

Judy: OK, OK, please tell me.

---

81. Planning for Retirement

I began to plan for my retirement some five years in advance, in 1992. The Social Security Administration (SSA) had informed me that I needed a notarized copy of my birth certificate from Peru. They said, over the phone, that they would accept it in Spanish. No official translation was needed. At the time, I did not have a copy. Thus, I made plans to get such copy during my following visit to Peru. Usually, I visited my family in Peru every three years or so. My visits lasted about one week. When I went, my brother Giovanni and his wife Dora always offered me a guest room in their house. In 1995, I traveled to Lima. Two days after my arrival, I flew to Huanuco, my town of birth, with Dino Donnatti, my nephew, son of Giovanni, by then a physician also. I had returned to my birth place for the first time since my family and I left 63 years earlier. I liked the town on the shores of the Huallaga river and on a valley plentiful in vegetation. The next morning, we went to city hall and requested two copies of my birth certificate. A lot of people were ahead of us, but a young man offered us to expedite the process for a fee. We paid the fee. We got the notarized copies in about one hour instead of spending the whole day standing in line, at city hall. Dino and I walked a lot that day getting to know the town. The next day, we went to the airport to return to Lima. Armed soldiers checked our luggage. Dino explained that they were making sure we did not carry illegal drugs. Later that day, we returned safely to Lima. A few days later, I returned to Florida with the copies of my birth certificate.

Early in 1997, the year of my retirement, I presented a copy of my birth certificate to an office manager at the Social Security Administration (SSA) office in Tampa. He took the certificate, excused himself, and went inside. He returned some 10 minutes later and said: "It is OK. We always do some tests to make sure the documents are legitimate." The Florida Retirement System (FRS) had my complete personnel records so the process was easier. The Teachers Insurance and Annuity Association-College Retirement Equities Fund (TIAA-CREF), to which I had contributed during my years in Oak Ridge, TN, had also all my documentation in order. Thus, my signed applications were sent to the three agencies around April that year.

All retirement contributions, over the years, go to a personal retirement fund which is invested at a low compound interest that, presumably, protects the fund against inflation. Thus, the fund continues to grow slowly, but surely. Upon retirement, the applicant has several choices or options. You may choose to receive the fund as a bulk. That would be the choice if you plan to make a business investment, or acquire real estate. Or, you may chose annuities, a fixed amount to be paid to you from the fund, each year of your retirement. Usually divided into twelve monthly payments. When choosing annuities, you may decide on the term of payments: Ten years, twenty years, or life-time payments. If you choose ten years, the payments will be the highest, but will stop in ten years or 120 months. If you die before the ten years, the rest of the payments will go to your designated beneficiary. The same is for a twenty-year annuity plan. Only the payments will be lower and they will stop in 240 months. If you choose life-time annuities, you will be paid a monthly amount based on the life expectancy of the applicant. For example, a 65-year-old man, in the U.S. is expected to live to age 80 whereas a woman of the same age is expected to live to age 88. Thus, retirement agencies calculate annuities based on life expectancies. Those are real numbers. For every person that lives one more year than expected, there is one person that lives one year less than expected and so on along the whole range of ages. Thus, everything balances out. Retirement agencies know those statistics very accurately. Insurance companies know them too very accurately. They do not gamble. They know. When I retired, back in 1997, I chose life-time annuities. I figured that with those annuities, I could have a modest but comfortable life and that was all I needed, I thought. At the time, that was the sensible thing to do.

82. Moving to Treasure Island

My employer, the TJC, has a well established procedure by which they "exit" retiring employees. To comply with that procedure, I had to have interviews, fill out forms, and get signatures at some twelve offices of the college to make sure that all college property, keys, books, equipment, etc. in my possession were returned to the college on time. I managed to complete all those requirements quickly. The college finally appointed a committee to select a new NMT program director. Several applications were received. The committee selected three for interview. After the interviews, they asked me to examine the documentation on each and to give them my recommendation. Apparently, they did not feel capable of passing judgment on the three applicants. I recommended that the applicant with the highest degree be ranked first. That was a doctor from Ohio with a Ph.D. degree in chemistry. Then, the committee asked me to give that candidate a telephone interview. I prepared some simple questions of everyday NM practice and called the candidate. I asked him what radiopharmaceutical was being used in their hospitals for the study of myocardial perfusion. He did not know. The same happened with other questions. It turned out that the candidate was a full-time chemist and was not active in NMT at all. I reported that to the committee and told them that, because he was not active in NMT, that did not mean that he could not learn and that my recommendation was still with the candidate with the highest degree. The committee accepted my recommendation and decided to offer that candidate the position of director of the NMT program. When the committee chairman called him, he declined the offer by saying that he had decided not to change jobs at that time. Then the position was offered to the candidate second in the rank. He was an experienced NMT who had been a clinical instructor of our program for many years. He was a good candidate. I was pleased.

Because I had not used many of the sick days I was entitled to during my 20 years at TJC, I had accumulated a large number of days of sick leave for which, according to FL law, the college had to pay me at the time of my retirement. Early that year though, the FL legislature had amended the law and reduced payments of sick leave to 50% of the original. Thus, it was my bad luck that my sick leave payment was reduced to one-half. Nevertheless, my paycheck for sick leave was a significant sum. That was an unexpected benefit for which I had worked very hard for twenty years. That same year, I started to look for a condominium, near the beach, I could buy with a loan from my credit union. After a few months of looking, I found one on the second floor of a building right on Sunset Beach, Treasure Island, FL. I used the sick leave funds for the down payment and financed the rest. After cleaning it and wall re-papering the bathroom and the kitchen, I purchased new furniture and moved into my condo in March of 1997, five months before my retirement. It was great to walk the beach mornings and evenings, learning each day more and more about my new environment. I do not believe in wasting time, so I always carried a book with me in my walks. Always reading, always learning new things, always reviewing things I might have forgotten. Some time after, I would write the following:

> I always wanted to see the sea,
> Not just the surf, not just the beach,
> I really wanted to see beneath,
> And touch the wonders hidden from me...

And, in another poem, I would say:

Walking the beach, walking at dawn,
Studying, reading, and listening,
Sounds of the sea, pounding the rocks,
Cry of the birds, the autumn sun...

And while walking, searching for treasures,
For shells, sand dollars and for shark teeth,
And finding some, and sometimes none,
And while searching, reading aloud...

All those new phrases, and grammar rules,
Of sweet Italian, the Roman language,
While those terns, pelicans, pipers,
Watching me close, walk on their beach...

Those were the unforgettable days at Sunset Beach. In my walks, I would sometimes stop to think and to remember the past. Perhaps something that occurred in my youth. I had reached the age of recalling the old memories.

83. Writing A Textbook

On August 12, 1997, I took retirement. After 41 years of work. During all those years, I enjoyed working at 100 miles per hour and doing a thousand things every day, every week, every month, every year. But then, upon retirement, suddenly, I had come to a stop. That had been quite a change. I was on Sunset Beach, Treasure Island, Florida. The beach was beautiful, the sunsets unforgettable. The people I met on my walks on the beach, interesting, special. All that was great. But something worried me. I did not wish to end like many retirees who are psychologically depressed by the sudden change. Someone had said once that "retirement is not for sissies." I believed that was true. My brother Pietro, who had worked a long time as an engineer on the northern Peruvian oil fields, had told me once that he had observed company workers, who had retired, returned to the fields often to watch, from a prudent distance, other men at work. They missed working, they missed the stress, the struggle, the scrapes, the rough life of working. They envied those that were still working. They felt deeply that, in their retirement, they had become useless, they felt sorry for themselves. Pietro also said that within three years, those retirees would pass away. That story had made an impression on me. I had never forgotten it. That is how I came up with the idea that all that experience that I had accumulated in 41 years of work with radioactive substances in medicine and biology could be put in writing to help new generations of NMT students learn quickly the nature, the properties, and the safe handling of radioactive materials. That writing would be in the form of a textbook named "Radiation Safety in Nuclear Medicine." There was none like it in the scientific literature. It was a good choice, I thought. And, to keep me busy on those early months of retirement and to eliminate the "retirement blues," I began to plan the various chapters of such a book. They would be based on my lecture notes, which I had researched and updated frequently, had enriched with recent technical articles and bibliographic references, and could be reinforced with the pertinent laws and regulations, etc. Soon, it became an obsession. I would go to bed at about nine p.m., wake up about midnight and, not being able to sleep any more, I would get up and work on the manuscript using a computer word processor, for some three hours. It reminded me of my studies at Cornell University. Then, I would get back to bed again and tried to sleep some more. Sometimes I could sleep, sometimes I could not. My ideas kept revolving in my mind as to what should come next in the book. Early in 1998, I contacted a publisher of technical books and asked them if they would be interested in publishing my book. They said that they were not doing technical books any more and recommended another publisher: The CRC publishing company of Boca Raton, Florida. I wrote to CRC and they were indeed interested. They asked me for a sample of my writings: the introduction, the table of contents, and two typical chapters. I prepared those quickly and submitted them. They wrote back to me stating that they were interested and that I should finish and submit the whole manuscript by the 30th of April, 1999. Soon after, they would send me a contract with the specifications required for publication, promotion, and sale of the new textbook. I worked hard to meet the deadline. As planned, I submitted the full manuscript along with the 69 illustrations, both in printed form and in the form of four-inch computer diskettes. The book came out in November, 1999. The CRC company had done a great job. I was pleased. During the following six years, some 2,000 copies of the book were sold, mostly in the U.S. and Europe. That is not a great number, but considering that it was on a highly specialized subject, it was acceptable.

Besides the fact that, except for some photographs, all illustrations in the book were original and that all tables were original, two topics were special because they had never been presented in any previous publication. You might say then that they were original too. The first was the observation that the half-value layers of lead for medical radionuclide gamma energies, in the range of 200 to 800 keV, were linear with lead shield thickness. The second, was the fact that the ratio of technetium-99m to molybdenum-99 in generator eluants decays exponetially as a function of time. An original illustration and a table allows practicing NMTs to quickly determine the time when any given eluant reaches the limit of 0.15 microcuries of Tc-99m per millicurie of Mo-99. No eluant can be used after it reaches that limit. It was a very practical approach to a complex phenomenon. For those many reasons, the book was special.

84. The Sand Piper and the Cormorant

After the book was published, I had more time to read, listen to my favorite music, study my favorite subjects, do some traveling, and to walk on the beach. On my early and evening walks, I began to learn more about the birds and other creatures that lived by the shores on the Gulf of Mexico. For example, one morning I saw something really unusual. A flock of parrots, green as can be, on the far side of the beach, by the storm wall, picking on the sand as if looking for food. I thought that was strange. But that was not all. Another day I saw a flock of pigeons, doing the same, but by the shore, right next to the water. I could not help but wonder if I was not witnessing a form of adaptation. Perhaps ten thousand years from now, pigeons feeding on the beach, will be a common thing. It reminded me of an observation I made at the Natural History Museum of the National University of Mexico in Mexico City, back in 1970. I saw a salamander in a glass terrarium with some shallow water on the bottom and some pebbles. The salamander was green and thick like a sausage, just laying there on the water with wet pebbles around her. But on her sides, there were four little limbs ending in paws with fingers. Those limbs could not possibly reach the ground and, therefore, were useless. I wondered then if they were, over the millenia, going to grow to reach the ground or if they were to gradually disappear due to their uselessness. It also reminded me of the times when I worked with bacterial cultures in the microbiology lab at my college in Lima. We routinely made stained smears of the cultures we were working with. To my surprise, my culture of Klebsiella sp., a gram-negative bacterium, mutated overnight. One day had a bacillary shape and the next they had a vibrio shape, only to return to bacillary shape the third day. Otherwise, the cultures were pure. I was convinced then, because I had seen it with my own eyes, about the power of adaptation or evolution.

One morning, while walking on the beach, I found a flock of sand pipers feeding on the shore. One of them though, was barely keeping up with the others. The reason was that she had only one leg. I was sorry for that bird that somehow had lost a limb. So, she had to try harder. Later, remembering the bird, I would write:

> It breaks my heart, to watch the bird,
> Right there competing, for her survival,
> With all the rest, and yet most eager,
> Keeping up with, the very best...

Another memorable event happened during of my walks on the beach. Between some large rocks by the shore I found a cormorant, a graciously shaped black bird, trapped in something, struggling to free herself, but unable to do so. I approached the bird cautiously and saw that one of her legs was tangled up in some fishing line. I had nothing with me that could cut the line, but I was determined to free the bird. I got close. The bird was exhausted. She had been struggling for hours, most likely. The high tide was predicted for some three hours later. I was sure she would have not survived that. There was barely enough space for me to get between the rocks and reach the bird. I did, and, holding the bird gently against the rock with my left hand, I grabbed the fishing line with my right hand. All I could do was to rub hard the line against some sharp edge of the rock. It took a while, but at last, it broke. Then I grabbed the bird gently with both hands and brought her out. She tried to nick me twice with her bill. I turned my face away just in time. Then, I just let her go. She quickly slid down the rock and fell in the water. She swam away fast, turning her head to watch me. Perhaps she was saying, "Thank you and goodbye." I was glad to see her free and alive. That was my good deed for the day.

85. Water, Water, Please!

In 1962, I was working as an assistant professor of biochemistry at the veterinary college in Lima. Sometime in September, Dr. James Spencer, a distinguished British professor visited the University of San Marcos, and I was asked to translate one of his evening lectures at the school of sciences. After the lecture, there was a reception at the British Consulate and I was invited. I attended with my wife Diane. Some time during the reception, Dr. Spencer invited me to visit his lab at the University of Birmingham, England. He said: "If you get your travel, I will get you the stay expenses for one month." I told him that I was interested in learning the chromatography of amino acids. He said that, in his lab, they were doing chromatography of sugars, but the techniques were similar. I graciously accepted his invitation and promised to write to him. Later, that year I had established contact with Dr. Tonino Bertini, director of the International Institute for Education in Lima. He said that he could arrange my travel to England on a cargo ship. I accepted. Then, I proceeded to get the necessary permission from work to go to England for a one-month for training in chromatographic techniques. Thus, in March of 1963, I got on board the ship "Portonia," which departed from the Peruvian port of San Juan carrying 30,000 tons of iron ore with destination Amsterdam. The Portonia was a Liberian ship, the officers in command were German, and the services crew were Indonesian. I was the only passenger on the trip. Nobody on board spoke Spanish. Only the two top officers, the captain and the second officer, spoke some English. I was given a suite for my lodging. I was extremely pleased. At meal times, the captain invited me to sit at his table which we shared with the second officer. On those occasions we spoke English. The rest of the time I walked around freely, I studied in my room. I had brought with me four books that I wanted to read from cover to cover. They were, "The Fire of Life" by Max Kleiber, "Matter, Earth, and Sky" by George Gamov, "Radioisotopes in Radiochemistry" by Ralph Overman, and "Radioisotopes in Biology and Agriculture" by Cyril Comar. During the first week, the trip went well. We crossed the Panama canal during the night and reached the Caribbean sea. Then, things got rough. The huge waves made the ship sink one side first and then the opposite side under the sea surface every 20 seconds or so. That happened day and night for three days. I got badly seasick. I could not hold anything in my stomach. I was sick in my room for three days. I lost a lot of weight. Fortunately, we then reached the open Atlantic ocean and things calm down. I returned to the captain's table for meals.

One afternoon, at about 4 p.m., I woke up from my nap and was very thirsty. I went out of my suite and down the stairs. At the bottom of the stairs I found a young German sailor in white uniform. He must have been 17 or 18 years old. I figured that the captain had placed him on duty to guard me. To make sure I did not get into any trouble. When he saw me coming down the stairs, he hit his heels against each other and stood in attention. He remained immobile staring at the ceiling. I asked the young man, in English, for something to drink. He did not understand me. He repeated his heel kicking and stood in attention. Then, I said:

"water, water" hoping that simple word he might understand. No dice. He kicked his heels again and remained in attention staring at the ceiling. Then, for the heck of it, I said: "Coca Cola?" Thank God, he smiled, nodded and said something in German I could not understand, and took off. Two minutes later, he came back with an open bottle of coca cola. It was a blessing, but too small. I was dehydrated after my seasickness. I could have had six of those bottles. At diner time though, I got even. There was plenty of drinking water in a pitcher on the table.

86. The Gangsters and I

On that trip to Europe, in March of 1963, on the ship "Portonia," while in the middle of the Atlantic, the captain received a radiogram ordering not to go to Amsterdam, but to the small port of Piombino, Italy. The captain informed me about the change at dinner time and offered to send a radiogram for me to anyone I needed to inform of the change. I thanked him. I did have some money, not very much but it could be sufficient for me to travel by train from Piombino to Milano and from there to fly to London. I did send a radiogram to my college informing them that there might be a delay in my travel. We arrived at Piombino, Italy, one cloudy day at about 4 p.m. I thanked the captain and second officer for their kind hospitality and said goodbye. I was allowed to disembark, and I reported to an immigration and customs office operated by a funny policeman. I was so surprised to see that the policeman's uniform was almost exactly like those of Peruvian policemen. The officer looked at my Peruvian passport and said: "Donnatti? Sicuro, guardi la faccia, sei Italiano" ("Donnatti, sure, just look at that face, you are Italian"). I tried to open my suitcase for inspection, but the officer said: "Non 'e necessario, chusi, chusi. Benvenuto al'Italia e buona fortuna" (It's not necessary, close it, close it. Welcome to Italy and good luck"). That was it. I had successfully entered the country of my ancestors. But I was there by accident. I had not planned that. And, I did not speak Italian!

A civilian employee, who knew English, explained to me how to take the train to La Spezia and from there another train to Milano. In Milano, I could take an airplane for London, and from there, I planned to take a train to Birmingham, my final destination. I got on the train to La Spezia, that evening. With my suitcase and a briefcase, I walked the aisles of the train car looking for a place to sit comfortably. I found a empty compartment and entered it. I placed my briefcase on the table, my suitcase on a rack, and I sat to read something. Suddenly, three men dressed in suits and tilted hats, with loud color shirts and ties, entered and sat across the table in front of me. They looked like the gangsters in the movies. The boss was in the center, right in front of me. He wore a thin, dark, mustache and looked serious. The men kept looking at my black plastic briefcase in which I kept my books and documents. They might have thought that I had money in it and were determined to get it. I had gotten that briefcase as a souvenir during my attendance to the Peruvian Congress of Chemistry the previous year. On the side of the briefcase was a high-relief map of Peru. For a long time they stared at me, and I stared back. Slowly though, I backed up against the wall, as far as I could go. I slid lower and lower and raised my legs a little. I was ready to kick the table if they tried anything. I placed my right hand in my trouser's pocket looking for something I could use as a weapon. I found a ballpen, I grabbed it. I planned to use it and hit the boss right in the eye with the ballpen. I kept my hands hidden under the table. I wanted them to think that I had a hidden pistol. And they must have been wondering if I was bluffing. We kept staring at each other. I wondered if these guys recognized the map of Peru on my briefcase. Perhaps not. I also thought that if these guys were going to kill me, it was not going to be easy. I was going to fight like hell. They looked thin and flimsy. I was an athlete, thanks to my regular soccer practice. Then, my thoughts took me to the realization that I had come thousands of miles to that place, perhaps to die in a strange land. It was not fair. We continued to stare at each other. It must have been ten whole minutes of staring. But it seemed a whole lot more than that. It seemed an eternity. Suddenly, the boss swivelled his head. That was the signal for them to abort their plan. They slowly slid toward the door and left. I returned to my seating posture. Then I heard a noise by the door. I jumped to my feet. I big lady came in followed by four bambinos. I hugged them and said: "Benvenuti, benvenuti." ("welcome, welcome.") They must have thought I was a nut! Fortunately, the rest of my trip to England went well and without problems.

87. Family Resemblance

In the year of 2000, I was living in my condominium of Treasure Island, FL. One of my neighbors, Mrs. Brown, whom I had met at one of the condominium association meetings, stopped me in the parking lot as I was getting into my car to go shopping in the mainland. She said: "Good morning Mr. Donnatti, you used to work in nuclear medicine, did you not?" Yes, I replied. I am retired now, but for a number of years I taught nuclear medicine technology at TJC in Tampa. Well, she said, Mrs. Conway, who lives on the fourth floor, wishes to talk with you about her husband who has been diagnosed with prostatic cancer. She wishes to ask you for some advice. Of course, I said, you and your friend can come to my place this afternoon and we can have an informal talk about her husband illness. "That will be fine, I'll call you later,"she said. Later that afternoon, the two ladies came. Mrs. Brown introduced Mrs. Conway and we sat in my living room. Mrs. Conway explained that at her husband last physical check up and after some radiographic procedures, the doctors had diagnosed cancer of the prostate. She added that the treatment proposed by the doctors was a radical surgical procedure. She also said that they were scared to death to agree to such procedure. I told Mrs.Conway that I was sure the doctors had a good reason for their diagnosis but, I added that they were entitled to a second and even a third opinion if they wished. That they must be absolutely sure of the diagnosis before agreeing to surgery. I also told her that depending on the type of cancer, there were other approaches to therapy. I also told them that the reason for other opinions is to arrive at an accurate diagnosis about the type of cancer and its stage. Only then an appropriate treatment can be prescribed. I reminded her also that, according to reliable sources, about half of the surgeries in the U.S. were unnecessary. I also told her that there is a nuclear medicine procedure that uses a radioactive antibody to image the prostatic gland and that she could ask her family physician to recommend a hospital where they could do such procedure. That procedure could determine the exact size, position, and extent of the cancer. By doing that, a better choice of treatments could be made. I concluded by asking her to go to her family physician and request arrangements for a second opinion on the diagnosis of her husband illness.

Mrs. Conway was very grateful. As she and her friend Mrs. Brown were about to leave, she noticed one of the photos on the wall in my living room. It was a photo of Albert Einstein in his forties. She said: " That gentleman was your father?" Before I had the chance to answer, she added: "I can see the family resemblance!" I was surprised and honored by that comment. Of course, I had to explain to the two ladies who the gentleman in the photo was.

88. Living Alone

In 1991 I had moved from Dunedin to an apartment in Tampa. After 28 years of married life, I had to fend for myself alone. Yes, now I could put in more hours at work and work harder at my job of college professor, director of the NMT program at TJC, and radiation safety officer for the college. And I did exactly that. I wanted "my program" to be the best. But even though I visited my children and saw them frequently, I soon found out that I had to do all the simple things needed to sustain myself living alone. Like cleaning the apartment, doing my own laundry, and cooking my own meals. Fortunately, I had done some of that when we were growing up in Lima, and later, when my ex-wife went to work as a secretary in an office. Frequently, I came home after work and arrived before she did. I was proud to serve dinner the minute she walked in the door. Most of the time, she left me a note with instructions for the preparation of the evening meals. That was good because that made my job easier. I always liked physical chemistry and cooking is just that: physical chemistry. I also loved serving Diane breakfast in bed on weekends. Sometimes, when Diane was not feeling very well, I also helped with the vacuuming and dusting of the house. What I did not know very much about was laundering. But she was very kind to explain it to me one time that I came for visit. She said that I should separate the white clothes from the colored clothes and wash them separately. Whites with detergent and some bleacher in hot water and colored clothes with detergent only, in cold water. That is what I have done ever since, with good results.

Life perspectives change drastically when you divorce at age 61. It is too late to begin again. For me that is exactly what happened. But I had to adapt quickly if I was going to survive the psychological shock of, suddenly, not having my family with me any more. Some years later, I would write:

> How ever I fell, into this whirlpool?
> The turning and tossing, in a deep black hole,
> What natural forces, at this time and age,
> Have forced me to living, and living alone?

Coming November, in my life's sunset,
The ups far outweigh the very few downs,
It is very late, almost four a.m.
The rain spatters hard, on the window pane...

One night, in my apartment, I decided to prepare Peruvian "dulce de leche" ("sweet milk desert"). I placed three unopened cans of condensed milk in a pot and covered them with water. I placed the contraption on the stove and turned the stove on. The idea was that boiling them for three hours not only cooks the milk, but changes the texture to a soft sugary gel of brownish color. A spoonful of it is a great treat. It could also be spread on bread for a special desert. That night, watching a movie on TV, I forgot to check the boiling cans. When I remembered them, I went to the kitchen and saw that the water had evaporated completely. Slowly, I turned the stove off. At that moment two cans exploded like hand grenades. The creamy milk hit the ceiling, me, and everything else. I had burns on my face, neck, chest, and arms. The ones on my arms were third degree burns. I went to the lavatory and tried to wash off the cream on the skin on my chest with a wet towel. The skin came off with it. At that point I had to decide if I needed to go to the emergency room. I asked myself, what would doctors do at the hospital? The answer was simple. They would put me in a bed, apply a picric acid ointment to my lesions, cover them with gauze and adhesive tape, and let me heal for two or three days. That approach would cost me and my medical insurance some 5,000 dollars. Thus, I came to the conclusion that I could treat myself at my apartment. I put on a clean shirt and went to the pharmacy to purchase the ointment, gauze, and adhesive tape. Total costs: 7.50 dollars. In three days, I was back at work. Nobody noticed anything wrong with me. Living alone was quite an adventure.

89. Sunny Italy

During the first few years of my retirement, while living on Treasure Island, FL, I did some traveling. I wished to see some of the places that I had only heard of, or read about. One of those places was Italy. So, while the publishing company worked on my book on radiation safety, I contracted a three-week tour of "Sunny Italy," the land of romance, the arts, the music, the songs, the history, the people, the food, and the wines. Of course, it was also the land of my ancestors. I chose September for the trip because by then the rainy season had ended and the maximum temperature was around 70 to 80 degrees. Before traveling, I did my homework. I purchased a book that gave all pertinent information. I had also taken two short courses in basic Italian and I could speak some already. Later, remembering the trip, I wrote:

Remember September, I could hardly wait,
A dream coming true, I was really there!
Smoke at touch down, a bright sunny day,
Leonardo da Vinci, the Roman airport...

My trip included a flight from Tampa international airport to Newark, New Jersey, and a connection from there to Rome. There were 6 hours difference between home and Italy. In the plane, after we had dinner, they played a movie on the TV monitors, and then, the sun peaked through the windows! We had lost a night flying east. After passing immigration and customs, along with some other tourists we took a bus to our hotel, the Hotel Mediterraneo. After a well deserved nap, we met with our tour director, Ms. Vittoria Santini. She treated us with a glass of wine and explained the money exchange at 1,825 lire per dollar. For dinner we were on our own. I joined some other tourists in our group and walked to a trattoria, a small restaurant nearby. The next day we went by motor coach to Vatican City, where we visited Saint Peter's square, the Vatican Museum, and the Sistine Chapel whose famous ceiling was painted by Michelangelo. In the bus I also met Ms. Pat Taylor, a Canadian lady traveling solo, like me. I guess, for that reason, we became travel partners. We laughed a lot during the trip. In the afternoon, we visited the Colosseum, a stadium that sat 50,000 people and was the site where gladiators fought for their lives and where slaves and Christians were sacrificed to the hungry lions for the pleasure of the elite Roman society and the general public. That night we walked to Piazza di Spagna (Spain square) in the rain! The following days we traveled to Pompeii where we saw the impression of the bodies of people trapped by the ashes during the eruption of the Vesuvius volcano in the year of 79. Later, I would write:

> Visit to Pompeii, and walk the same streets,
> Where desperate people, on seventy-nine,
> To escape the hot ashes, ran toward the sea,
> Carbon monoxide, many fell asleep...

Then, we continued to Sorrento where we stayed that night. In the morning we took a boat to Capri, the love Island. We toured the island by bus, had lunch in the town of Anacapri, and circled the island by boat in the afternoon. We did get to see the blue and green caves from outside only because of the high tide at the time. The following day, we traveled to Positano on the Amalfi coast. We took a "limoncello break," a glass of the sweetest lemon liquor produced there. Then, we proceeded toward Assisi, the town of the famous Italian Saint and founder of the St. Franciscans religious order. The next day, we traveled to Venice. We walked the Rialto bridge, the market, and famous Piazza San Marco where we had a cocktail and listened to two competing groups of singers. That night the sea water began to flood the piazza when the tide was high. We walked over boards to get to our hotel. The following day we walked the bridge of sighs and visited the Basilica of San Marco. Later, we took a boat ride through the grand canal to the island of Burano, a picturesque town full of color and lace. Then we traveled to Verona, the town where, presumably, the tragedy of Romeo and Juliet took place. We visited Julietta's house with its famous balcony. We took pictures and left for Baveno on the shores of lake Maggiore. The following day, we rode around the lake and toward the border with Switzerland. We then traveled to Lugano, a most beautiful town on the shore of lake Lugano. We had lunch there and later returned to Baveno. Then, we traveled to Pisa, the place of the famous leaning tower. We visited the cathedral, the battistero, and the campanillo, but we were not allowed to enter the tower at that time. In the morning, we traveled to Firenze, where we toured the cathedral of the Santa Croce, the Piazza della Signoria, where we admired three statues: Neptune, the God of the seas, a replica of David, and the ratto delle sabine (the kidnaping of the Sabine women).

The following day we rode through the green hills of Toscana toward San Giminiano, a town of tall stone towers. We then returned to Firenze. The following day we went to Siena and visited the famous Piazza del Campo. We had lunch there and then we proceeded toward Rome. We stopped at the fountain of Trevi where, with your back to the fountain, you throw the traditional coin over your left shoulder and promise to return to Rome. That evening we had our farewell dinner. There were soprano and tenor singers. We took pictures and videos. The foods were great, the wines better. A night to remember.

> Full circle to Rome, it's time to go home,
> The fountain of Trevi, and throw in a coin,
> Promise to return, and a furtive tear,
> Farewell at Thalia's, the wine and the songs...

All together, the trip was a very rewarding and memorable one. I managed to use my Italian when I got lost in Verona and then again in Siena. I also acted as an interpreter for other tourists in our group at restaurants and shops.

90. The Holy Land and Egypt

While living on Treasure Island, I planed a trip to Israel, the Holy Land, and to Egypt, the land of the pharaohs. The trip became a reality in January of 2001. I was excited about being able to visit the very same places where Jesus, the Christ, had walked, prayed and preached. My plane landed in Tel Aviv, the commercial capital of Israel, on January 24, 2001. Then, joining other tourists in our group, we went by bus to Jerusalem, the spiritual capital. The next day, we visited Old Jerusalem, which is enclosed within a large wall and has six gates. That place is a sacred site for Christians, Jews, and Muslims. Of great significance was our walk on the Via Dolorosa, which was the street followed by Jesus while carrying the cross on his way to the Calvary. On the Calvary, now stands the Church of the Saint Sepulchre. Inside, there is an image of the crucifixion, exactly on the place where the Roman soldiers planted the cross and crucified Jesus. Then, going down by some narrow stairs, we arrived at the cave where the body of Jesus was placed after his death.

In the Muslim section of Old Jerusalem, we visited the Temple of the Rock whose dome is covered in gold foil. According to legend, it was from there, that the Prophet Mohamed ascended to heaven. Other historical sites we visited were the Mount of the Olives, the gardens of Getzemani, and the western wall of the palace of King Herod, also known as the Wailing Wall. During the following days, we traveled by bus and saw in the distance Jericho, a Palestinian town, under siege by the Israeli army. We then followed the river Jordan toward the Sea of Galilee and the mountain of Capernum, where Jesus preached his Sermon on the Mount. From the mountain you could see the Golan Heights on the border with Syria. Upon our return to Jerusalem, we visited the Israeli Museum, home of the

Dead Sea Scrolls, and then we went by bus to the Dead Sea and to Masada, the place where some 900 Jews committed suicide rather than surrender to the sieging forces of the Roman Empire.

On January 28, we flew to Cairo, the capital of Egypt. Cairo had then a population of 13 million. It was heavily polluted city, but it had also about one million satellite TV dishes on its roofs. Very impressive were the exhibits in the Museum of Cairo, specially the sarcophagus and artifacts of King Tutankhamun. That evening we went to the restaurant Le Pasha on the shores of the Nile. The next day we visited the pyramids of the Sakkara desert in the morning and the Giza plateau in the afternoon. Very impressive were the pyramids of Cheops, Kephren, and Micerino. For a price you could enter the pyramid of Cheops, also known as the great pyramid. Inside, the tunnels are only 4 by 4 feet. Thus, we had to crawl a distance of some 50 yards to get to the main room, where the stone sarcophagus of King Cheops was. It was empty. Ancient robbers had stolen everything, even the body of Cheops. Jokingly, I introduced myself to young American and European tourists who, also were crawling inside of those tunnels, as "King Ramses II, at your service." That amused the visitors. One blond Swiss lady shook my hand and introduced herself as "Nefertiti." Another spectacular monument was the Sphinx of Giza, a sandstone statue of some 20 by 60 yards and 20 yards in height, representing a human head and torso with the body of a lion. That evening we returned to the Giza plateau to see an excellent audiovisual show with lights, lasers, and sound effects. The next morning we flew to Luxor where we boarded the ship "Ruby Nile." In Luxor, I purchased in a pharmacy "Ceclor SR", an antibiotic to treat myself for an upper respiratory tract infection. Other tourists were suffering from dysentery, also known as "pharaoh's revenge." That afternoon, we went to the Temple of Amon, passing through the Avenue of the Sphinxes. At the temple's entrance, there were two 40-yard high obelisks. Inside there were 138 giant columns with bases 4 yards in diameter. The columns are some 20 yards high. Columns, walls, etc. are covered with high and low-relief inscriptions describing the stories and life of the pharaohs and gods. Among them: Ramses, Ra, Isis, Amon, Horus, the falcon god, Sobek, the crocodile god, and others. The Ruby Nile took us south and through the locks of Esna to lake Nasser. The Aswan dam is used to produce electrical energy for southern Egypt and northern Sudan. The following day some tourists, including me, went by plane to visit the temple of Abu Simbel, erected by Ramses II and famous for its huge four statues of Ramses at the entrance. That temple was, with international assistance, disassembled and moved to another location some 70 meters higher to prevent them from being covered by the waters of artificial lake Nasser. We visited the Valley of the Kings, where the tomb of Tutankhamun was located. The next day, the Ruby Nile arrived at Luxor. While disembarking, one of the tourists in our group, a lawyer from Washington, DC, had a massive coronary thrombosis and died. We then went to the airport for our flight to Cairo. We took lodging at the Hotel Switzerland and went to visit the citadel of Mohamed Ali, a huge temple, and the largest bazaar in Egypt. Our guide told us not to walk away from the main alley of the bazaar, because people disappeared in the side alleys never to be seen again. By the end of the trip, most of the tourists were exhausted. I was very fortunate that I brought with me some tablets of sulfa-trimetoprim. One tablet daily prevented me from pharaoh's revenge. We had been warned by our tour director not to drink the tap water or to use it for brushing our teeth at the hotel. We were very happy to be on the airplane on our flight to New York. We had survived the trip.

Reporter Judy Hartfeldt: Marco, the first few years after retirement, you were very busy. You purchased a condo, wrote a book, traveled to Europe, the Middle East, and Africa.

Marco Donnatti: Yes. That was the idea. To keep busy and active. I was also active in the soccer field. I did not play competitive games any more, but I did go to the field once a week just to run a little and to practice shots from 20 to 30 yards. I became good at it, even at my old age. Thus, physically and mentally, I kept very active.

Judy:When did you stopped dribbling and kicking the ball?

Marco: Six years ago. I observed that I had pain in the proximal end of my tibias after my weekly practices. I stopped then.

Judy: We are almost at the end, are we not?

Marco: Yes. But I do have something to tell about my memories of traveling and my medical history, if you would like to hear them.

Judy: Of course, by all means. Let's do it next time, OK?

Marco: Indeed, next time, good bye Judy.

The China Wall, a remarkable work of engineering (Story 93)

CHAPTER 10

A TIME TO REMEMBER

Reporter Judy Hartfeldt: Good morning Marco. What do you have for me today?

Marco Donnatti: Perhaps you recall, I offered to tell some stories from my travels and after that, some stories about my medical history.

Judy: Let us begin with your adventures in travel.

Marco: Yes, of course.

---

91. Europe by Train

In June of 2000, while living in Treasure Island, FL, I traveled by airplane to London to start a tour of Europe by train. The first leg of my trip was from Tampa to Atlanta. From there, I caught a connection to London non-stop on a jumbo jet. That flight had a duration of 8 hours. From the London airport, we took a train to Victoria station and from there a bus to our hotel, the Tistle Hotel. Since we had lost 5 hours flying east, we had the afternoon off for a well deserved nap. In the evening, we met Dexter, our tour director. We received instructions regarding the following days of travel, money exchange, etc. The following day, we began with a tour of the city. We passed some famous buildings: Big Ben, the Parliament, Westminster Abbey, some parks and bridges. After lunch, I took a 7-hour nap as part of my recovery from jet lag affliction. The next day was a Sunday, and our plan called for a trip to Stockton, a small port on the English Channel. We were told to dress up for that short trip, because we were riding on the "Orient Express." On the train, seating was arranged by our tour director. I was pleased to share a cabin with Mr. Peter Anderson, a retired gentleman, his daughter Julie, a physician, and Ms. Donna Kent, a retired lady from New York. We had champagne and a lively conversation during the whole trip. We dined like royalty that day. It was a day to remember. We returned to London by 6 p.m. The next day we went to Waterloo Sation to catch the "Eurostar," the train to Paris, passing through the "Chunnel," the tunnel under the English Channel. In about one hour, we surfaced on the green fields of Normandy and continued our ride to Paris. We arrived at 12:30 p.m.

Immediately, we went on a tour of the "City of Lights:" the Eiffel Tower,

the Champs Elysees, Notre Dame, the Arc de Triomphe. That evening we toured
the river Seine by boat. The Eiffel Tower was then illuminated. The next day we
went to the Palace of Versailles, where the peace treaty was signed after World
War I. The palace, the gardens, the statues were marvelous. That day we had the
afternoon off. The bus dropped us downtown and, after some lunch, I decided to
walk from Notre Dame to our hotel, some five miles along the river Seine. During
my walk, I was stopped by a well dressed man in a small car, who tried to con
me of 100 dollars. He told me that he needed the money for gasoline. He was on
his way to Italy and had run out of money. He said he was willing to sell me a
woman's leather dress for 100 dollars. He showed me the dress in a store's paper
bag. It was beautiful. I did know that those dresses cost at least 800 dollars. But
fortunately, I did not have the cash. I had only some 75 franks in my wallet. He
would not accept that. Thus, I said good bye. Later, I realized that if had paid the
amount he wanted, at the last second, he would have given me an exact bag, but
with newspapers in it. He would have switched bags on me. And I would have
been left "holding the bag," literally. I am sure, he would have changed his automobile license plate within minutes, after leaving. Later, in the bus, I warned other
tourists about the incident.

That evening, as part of our tour, we went for dinner at a night club. Mr. John
Trundle, his wife Jody, and daughter Lianna invited me to sit at their table. I was
very thankful. The diner was great, the wines better, and the show, incredible;
There were dancers, acrobats, and comedians. During the conversation, I told the
Trundles that I was a college professor. Mr. Trundle asked me to advise Lianna on
the value of a college education. Apparently she had been not too eager to pursue
a college career. She was 20 years old. I told Lianna that when I was young, I had
made the same mistake, to postpone my education. But that, after wasting two
years, I had realized that I was not cut for a life with the peasants and other types
of low-level people, that I wanted to raise my level as a person. I could only do
that by earning a professional degree. I also told her that the best time to do that
was when you were young. I ended my argument with: "Do not wait. Do it now.
You will never regret it." Mr. And Mrs. Trundle were pleased. You can do wonderful things when you have a high level education, I said. For example, I wrote
a book! I have a copy with me in my room. I will loan it to you tomorrow if you
wish. "Oh, yes, I'd like to see it," Lianna said. The next day, at breakfast, I gave
her the book. Two days later, she returned it to me with her appreciation. She said
that she had liked the book very much. I was pleased. She was a blond, very pretty
20-year-old. That morning, we had a tour of the west side of the river: the Latin
Quarter, La Sorbonne university, the Medical school, the Louvre Museum. In the
afternoon we traveled by train to the Mediterranean blue coast. We arrived at Nice,
France, at about 6 p.m. The next day we toured Nice and a small, picturesque town
named St. Paul du Vence, north of Nice. That evening some of the tourists in our
group went to dinner at a Montecarlo restaurant and visited a jewelry collection
exhibit at one of the hotels. We decided not to visit the gambling casinos. Our
group then traveled by bus to Stressa, Italy, and then to Tasch in Switzerland.
There, we took the "Glacier Express," the Swiss train that travels through the Alps

towards Zermatt. There we took another train up the Alps to Gomergrat, where we had lunch and took pictures of the famous Matterhorn mountain, the sharpest peak of the Alps. The following day happened to be fourth of July. We took the glacier express again, this time toward Lucern, Switzerland. On the way we passed the Furka Basistunnel, the longest tunnel through the Alps. That evening we had dinner and saw a show at the Stadtkeller restaurant. At some moment during the show, the orchestra played the U.S. National Anthem. We jumped to our feet and stood in attention. Some of us had our right hands over our hearts. We were very proud of being Americans in a far land. At the end of the anthem, we cheered and applauded the orchestra. A night to remember. The next morning we continued our tour by bus, but we were sadden by the news that the Trundles were not longer on the tour with us. Dexter, our tour director explained that Mr. Trundle had an attack of angina the previous night and that they had decided to discontinue the tour and fly home that day. It was logical, I thought, if he needed urgent medical attention. Then we went on a tour of beautiful Lucern: We visited the lion monument, and took a cable wagon ride up to Stansenhorn. That evening was out farewell dinner. We took pictures and we missed the Trundles.

92. A Close Call on I-75

In 1992, my daughter Catalina, Cati for short, was living on Coquina Island, Florida, only about 20 minutes by car from me at Treasure Island. She was working at a telephone company in St. Petersburg, FL. One day she informed me that she had requested and got approval for a job transfer to a branch office in Phoenix, Arizona. She was excited about her moving, because the humid climate of Florida was not good for her. Her allergies had worsened in recent times, and she wanted out. Naturally, I offered to help her move. She was pleased. She had most of her belongings in a storage place and had rented a U-Haul trailer to carry them. We were going to pull the trailer with her Toyota Corolla. She also had a pet Dachshund dog to travel with us in a cage on the back seat. Early in the morning of October 8, we loaded the trailer and departed from Tampa on I-75 northbound towards the FL panhandle. But it was not to be. I was driving at about 6:30 a.m. some ten miles south of Ocala, when, coming down a hill at 70 miles per hour, I instinctively tried to slow down. I barely touched the brakes when the trailer started swinging right and left, forcing me to do corrective steering to maintain the direction over the highway. But it was too late. The trailer hit the right side of the car first and then very hard the left side. I saw our car heading for the railing in the middle of the highway. I steered left to avoid hitting the railing and managed to stop the car parallel to the railing, but facing south. I turned on the blinkers, and we got out of the car. We were OK. Almost immediately, a highway patrol car stopped next to us. The officers said that they had seen the whole incident. They asked us for our driver licenses, car registration, and insurance. They found the documents in correct order. That accident had been a close call for us. We could have been killed. We hugged each other. The dog was OK too. But the car had blown the rear right tire, the rear axle was bent, and possibly the chassis was also bent. The trailer seemed to be OK. Then we proceeded to notify the insurance company and the U-haul company using Cati's cell phone. Each sent a truck to pick up our car and to tow the trailer. The trailer was returned to the local U-Haul office in Ocala, FL, and we rented a truck instead. We transferred all things to the truck. The torn car was left at a body shop for an estimate of repair costs. We then took lodging at a nearby motel. In the afternoon, we were informed that the repairs would take two weeks and would cost 3,000 dollars. The insurance company offered to pay 1,000 dollars only towards repairs of the car. That night we discussed our options. I could hardly sleep that night. In the morning I proposed to Cati that we could abandon the broken car, travel in the truck to Phoenix, and purchase a car for her when we got there. She accepted the offer. Thus we decided that, rather than be stuck in Ocala for two weeks with perhaps a distorted car, we would start anew and never look back. In the morning, we first called the insurance company and told them that we were withdrawing the claim and second, we went to the auto body shop and gave the car to the mechanic and signed the title over to him. Then, we got in the truck and began our journey toward Phoenix by 10 a.m. Fortunately, the rest of the trip was just fine. We also kept in touch with my other daughter, Margie, who lived in Los Angeles with her husband Anthony (Tony) Colbert, an executive officer of a genetic engineering company.

In Phoenix, we managed to rent an apartment for Cati, to unload her things from the truck and place them in her apartment, and to purchase a car for her. We did all that in three days. Unfortunately, the job that supposedly was waiting for her at her telephone company, was not there. Thus, she started to look for a new job right away. I promised to help her economically until she could find a job. Then, I made arrangements to fly back to my place on Treasure Island, FL. Fortunately, Cati soon found a job with an insurance company and things began to fall into their proper places. My Cati had began a new life in a new state: Arizona, the "Grand Canyon State." Arizona was beautiful, dry, and my daughter loved it.

93. A Tour of China

In March of 2001, I traveled to China on an economical tourist package organized by one of the travel companies. Why China? Well, China, the most populous country in the world was having an economic boon. It had doubled its gross national product in the 80s and doubled it again in the 90s. China was doing what Japan had done in the 70s and 80s. We had seen Japanese companies copy and improve American and European automobiles, copied and improved Swiss watches, copy and improve American TV sets and telephones, copy and improve German photographic cameras, etc. The key of that transformation was, of course, inexpensive labor. Thus, Japan flooded the international market with good quality automobiles and merchandise at lower prices, and the American and European public liked it. Of course, Taiwan, Singapore, Hong Kong, and Indonesia had followed in the steps of Japan and were also growing fast. And now China, with an infinite population of workers willing to work at much lower rates, was ready to take over the manufacturing market. Thus, many manufacturing industries in the U.S. and Europe moved their factories to cheap labor countries like Mexico, Hong Kong, Taiwan, Indonesia, Singapore, and China. American and European industries had to adapt. They had to remain leading in the designing and planning of new products and then have them manufactured in those countries. There was one problem, though. And that was, in my personal opinion, business transactions on credit. Purchases with credit cards all over the world. Buy now, pay later. Individuals, institutions, cities, states, and the federal government doing it, purchasing everything on credit, soon the whole system could implode. Who would pay the immense debt accumulated by everyone over the years? Our children and grandchildren? Well, but that is another story. Another very serious problem was air and water pollution. Most of the millions of factories burn coal, and their emissions cover the planet with smoke and soot. But, at the time, China was an attractive place to visit. Thus I signed up for a three-week tour of the ancient, mysterious, and large country of China. Perhaps it was the food, I always liked Chinese food.

On March 5, 2001, I flew from Tampa international airport to San Francisco, CA. I spent the night there and the next morning, March 6, I flew to Beijing, China. This last flight lasted 11 hours, and we lost a day crossing the dateline over the Pacific ocean. We arrived in the morning the next day. I rested in my hotel most of the day. In the afternoon we met our tour director, a bilingual Chinese young man named "Tom." After some introduction he took us for a walk to some commercial center some eight blocks away. It was extremely cold and windy. At the shopping center, I had to purchase a thick jacket for our walk back to the hotel. It was matter of survival. Back at the hotel, I met Mr. Dean Morton, an engineer from California. He was my roommate. We were sharing accommodations to save some money. During the following days we visited the "Forbidden City;" Tiananmen Square, with its soldiers in flashy uniforms and rifles, doing the goose step; a kindergarten classroom in a children's school, where children sang American songs in Chinese; the drum tower of Beijing; a common man's house in a "hutong," a neighborhood on the outskirts of the city; and the "emperor's Summer house," a palace with decorated buildings and gardens. Come to think of it, a Chinese soldier always rode the bus with us wherever we went. I wondered if he took attendance. I guess, they wanted to make sure that none of us disappeared in the crowd and became illegal immigrants. All along, we ate at typical Chinese restaurants. Most of them, had round tables with a "lazy Susan" in the center with various dishes of food. As the lazy Susan rotated, we helped ourselves to the exotic foods. On March 10, we went to the tombs of 13 emperors of the Ming dynasty, climbed the Tower of Heaven, and walked to famous Great Wall. The next day, we flew to Shanghai. Later, we walked the beautiful bay shore avenue. We also visited the Jade Buddha Museum and had dinner at the Ming Dynasty Restaurant. The following day we went to a silk factory in Suzhow, north of Shanghai, we rode the Grand Canal on a boat, and visited the embroidery institute. We also attended a show in the Sports Theater, where some very young acrobats, boys and girls, demonstrated their incredible skills.

On March 14, we flew to Wuhan, and then by bus to Sashi, a port on the

Yangtze river. We boarded the boat "Princess Elaine." The next day, we passed the Three Gorges Dam, the largest in the world, at the time still under construction. On March 18, we transferred to a hydrofoil boat, very fast and traveled the shallow waters of the river to Chongquing. We took lodging at the Holiday Inn. Walking the streets of Chongqing with my partner, Mr. Morton, we found a gymnasium and some soccer players practicing futsal. I joined them for a few minutes and had a chance to show some of my skills with the soccer ball. Especially my curvy shots. Mr. Morton was impressed. After, he bought me a beer in a nearby shop. On March 19, we flew to Xian where we visited the Stillwell-Chenault Museum. General Stillwell was the American general who reorganized and modernized the Chinese army. General Chenault was the American who did the same with the Chinese air force. He created the famous "Flying Tigers" air force of China. All that occurred sometime in the early 40s. Later, in the afternoon we visited the sites where there were buried some 8,000 Chinese terra-cotta warrior sculptures. On March 21, we flew to Guilin. Our flight was delayed. We arrived late that night and went directly to our hotel. The next morning, we took a boat ride on the river Li. The landscapes were fantastic. Those conical mountains all around us. Some about 2,000 feet high. It seemed that we were on a strange planet. Some fishermen on a small boat used a cormorant on a leash to catch fish; incredible but true! That evening, Tom, our guide, said good bye to us. He explained that Chinese laws forbade him from traveling to Hong Kong. That reminded us that China has strict rules to prevent country people from traveling from the interior of the country and settling in the cities. On March 23, we flew to Hong Kong and took a bus to our hotel, the "Marco Polo," on the peninsula of Hong Kong. Later, our bus passed the "chunnel"under the canal that separates the peninsula from the island of Hong Kong and then took a tramway to Peak Victoria at some 400 meters above sea level. There is a beautiful park and many shops up there. We later came down by bus and stopped at a beach where, some scenes from the movie "Love is a Many Splendored Thing," were filmed. Then, we took a sampan to cross the canal and returned to the mainland. On our sampan ride, we saw a population of some 30,000 boat people, fishing people, who live on clusters of boats as far as you can see. On the evening of March 25, we had our farewell dinner. We took pictures and videos. We said good-bye to all tourists in our group. The following day, we flew from Hong Kong to Chicago, IL, non-stop in 12 hours. We departed at 12 noon on the 26th of March and arrived at 12 noon on the 26th of March. That was because we gained a day as we crossed the dateline over the Pacific going east. We were pleased to be back in the U.S. I took a connection to Tampa and a shuttle to Treasure Island. I crashed on my very own bed by 9 p.m.

94. Devil's Tower

In 2001, due to my joint pains and tendinitis, I decided that I had to give up soccer practices. And soon, because of the same reason, I began to think that I may have to give up traveling too. Or, perhaps, my trips should be shorter. I had never been to the Midwest so, I signed for an 8-day tour and thus one day, I flew from Tampa, FL, I to Dallas-Fort Worth, TX, and from there, to Denver, CO, in July of 2001. That evening, we met our tour director Ms. Tina Soloway, a very gracious lady. The next day we toured the city of Denver. We visited the trinity church, the Brown hotel, the Capitol building, the house of the unsinkable Molly Brown, the University of Colorado, and the Denver Broncos stadium. Our bus then traveled through the Great Planes to Cheyenne, Wyoming. Again, we toured the city and then traveled farther north, with the Rocky Mountains at our left. In the bus, our tour director played the song "America the Beautiful" through the speakers for everyone to listen. Being from Florida, which is as flat as a pancake, I was excited about the beauty of the landscape. We followed the famous "Oregon Trail" to Torrington and beyond, to the "Black Hills"of South Dakota, which were blanketed by pine forests. Ms. Soloway told us the story of the Oregon Trail used by colonists to go west in search for a better life. She also mentioned the discovery of gold by the Indians in the Black Hills and that the federal government sent General Custer to move the natives out of the Black Hills and onto a reservation. That evening we arrived at Rapid City in South Dakota. The following morning we traveled to the Mount Rushmore National Monument, which portrays the heads of four U.S. presidents: George Washington, Thomas Jefferson, Teddy Roosevelt, and Abraham Lincoln. This monument was a site of some scenes in the movie "West by Northwest," with Cary Grant and Eva Marie Saint. Later in the afternoon, we visited the Crazy Horse monument, which was being carved out of the rock on a mountain.

On Tuesday, July 17, we traveled through limestone canyons to Spearfish Canyon, SD, and entered the state of Wyoming. We stopped to visit Devil's Tower National Monument, an awesome geological structure, shaped like a truncated cone, 390 meters tall, and 400 meters in diameter at its base, all made of volcanic rock. Although its color changes with the time of the day, it seemed to me of bluish gray color. That was the site for the filming of some scenes of the fantastic movie "Close Encounters of the Third Kind," with Richard Dreyfuss. That afternoon we arrived at Cody, WY, where we attended a rodeo show. The next day, we arrived at Yellowstone National Park. We made stops at the park's lake and the upper and lower waterfalls of the Yellowstone River. The next day, we visited the geysers area, including the famous "Old Faithful" geyser, which erupts at approximately 90-minute intervals. Each eruption sends many gallons of boiling water and steam some 40 meters high. We also visited the hot springs area with its boiling blue waters, boiling mud pots, and the beehive geyser. We then rode to visit Grand Teton National Park. We took pictures and rode a raft on the Snake River. On July 21, we took road 89 south toward Montpelier, Idaho. We passed through the Snake River grand canyon, and arrived at Mormon country. We then, crossed into Utah and took I-15 toward Salt Lake City. That night we had our farewell dinner. Ms. Soloway organized a skit play by the tourists. She insisted that I played a "gangster." She found me a gangster hat and a toy pistol. I did my number by pretending to chew gum, swinging the pistol, and flipping a coin. Others played the roles of a cook, a teller of children's stories, a sportscaster on TV, and a weatherman. At the end, prizes were given by Ms. Soloway to all "actors." I won a 2002 calendar showing a collection of most beautiful pictures of the Midwest. A trip to remember always. The following day, in the morning, we visited the famous Mormon Temple Tabernacle of Salt Lake City. Then, on our way to the airport, we stopped at the very salty Great Salt Lake. We took pictures and said good-bye to our traveling companions. My flight took me to Tampa airport and from there I rode the shuttle to Treasure Island. I arrived home at midnight.

95. September Eleven

The morning of September 11, 2001, I was doing some reading, as I always do. Usually, reviewing some of the subjects that interest me. Perhaps some geometric relationships, or the history of quantum theory, or the history of philosophy. Suddenly, the telephone rang. On the phone was my daughter Cati calling from Phoenix, AZ. She said: "Turn on the TV. Two passenger airplanes have crashed against the trade center towers in New York." I did turn on the TV and watched in horror the replays of the attacks. That day, and the following days, like many Americans, I watched how some 19 Arab fanatics had killed so many Americans and peoples of other countries too who were working or visiting the Trade Center, the Pentagon in Washington, and the people on flight 93 that crashed in Pennsylvania. Like most Americans, I reacted first in shock caused by the horror of the attacks, the planning of them, the money behind them, the hate of the people behind their support, their indoctrination, etc. And wondered where were the FBI, the CIA, the NSA? How is it that they did not know? I knew that in the previous administration of government many agencies had behaved like being in a continuous party, spending taxpayers' money and doing very little to protect the U.S. How was it that some Arabs can enter pilots' schools without checking of backgrounds, histories, and sources of income? Should we not investigate any of those activities of any foreigner coming from a rogue country? Or, it is sufficient for the prospective pilot to flash some big bills to get admitted? Did our own greed set us up for 9/11? How come we still do not have a global system of identification? How come Europe has better security than us? Are politicians being bribed to look the other way on security issues? Is it affecting their secret incomes or their reelections? I am sure we can do better. We cannot wait to have another attack to tighten security measures. Anyone who opposes those improvements with the excuse of infringement on our liberties is betraying the security of all true Americans. "Deep Throat" said it in the movie "All the President's Men": It is simple, "follow the money." Acts of terrorism require money. Follow all significant transfers of money from the U.S. to rogue countries. Also those from Europe and from oil-rich countries. Like most Americans, after the shock, I became angry at those Arab fanatics. Like many Americans, I did send a significant contribution to help fight terrorism. My check went with a brief note saying: "this contribution is for "retaliation and reconstruction." In other words, "for bullets and bricks." I had hoped that, once we knew who the attackers were, we would bomb their villages during the night. That would prevent future prospective attackers from planning and executing another attack in the U.S. Knowing that retaliation would result in the destruction of their families and friends. But that did not happen. After all, what did I know? My only hope was that those authorities in command knew what they were doing and that they were doing it in our best interest. By the end of the year, I wrote this:

> September 11, two thousand and one,
> Another Pearl Harbor, an infamous date,
> Some Arab fanatics, with malice and hate,
> Attacked the U.S., killed thousands of us..
>
> .
>
> Why those criminals, hate the U.S.A.?
> Why some human beings, destroy, kill, and lie?
> Not for Palestine!, not even Islam!
> The reason is envy, a capital sin...
>
> Remember September! United we stand!
> For safety we must, sacrifice some rights,
> A new ID system, to catch all the fakes,
> Prevent any other, terrorists' attacks...

Several years have passed since then. Time is a good healer, they say. Perhaps I was not angry any more. Perhaps I had come to accept the fact that, with the world population explosion, terrorism was an expected act of the "have nots" who envy our ways. In their insanity, they decided to destroy what they could not have in their lifetimes. But, at the same time, I hoped that our authorities did not become complacent, but remained alert and in their investigations, and followed the moneys around the globe.

96. I Saw Him First!

This chapter is titled "A time to remember." Well, something funny happened on the way to a restaurant one evening in San Jose, Costa Rica. I was, at the time, the coordinator of the professional training program of the "Atoms in Action" an exhibit sponsored by the U.S. Atomic Energy Commission (USAEC). As part of the preparations, the USAEC required that a team of two individuals pre-visit each prospective site. They also required that the team do a follow-up visit to each site after the exhibit. As coordinator, I was asked to participate in those visits. My partner, selected by our division Chairman, was Mr. George Mester, a physicist and electronics expert from our Special Training division at Oak Ridge, TN. George and I got along very well. During those years of presentations in Central and South America, we traveled together over 75,000 miles by air.

But let's go back for a moment to our pre-visit in Costa Rica. One day, after we had completed our appointments, at about 6:00 p.m., George and I decided to go to eat at a Chinese restaurant located on the main square some three blocks from our hotel. The streets were very crowded. Knowing that Americans were considered targets for mugging, for safety, I asked George to walk in front of me. Since I was a Latin and spoke the native language well, I would follow right behind. George walked fast and soon he was about five yards ahead of me. We had to dribble our way through the crowd. For a moment I lost sight of George. When I saw him next, a local young man had him held by both arms and against the wall. George looked scared. I arrived quickly and gave the man a shove yelling "Fuera, dejalo solo" ("Shove off, leave him alone"). The man released George and looked at me surprised at first, but realizing that I was a Latin too, he replied "Yo lo vi primero!" ("I saw him first!") perhaps thinking that I also wanted to mug his pigeon. I added then "El es mi socio" ("He is my partner"). At that point, the man rushed away and disappeared in the crowd. Something to remember.

Another incident to remember occurred in Caracas on a Sunday night, the last day of the exhibit. The group of young men and ladies, selected by the administration to play the role of guides for the public exhibit, organized a farewell party on the pool area of our hotel, the Sheraton, near the exhibit building. During the exhibit, they wore elegant uniforms: Navy blue jackets, white shirts, silver ties, gray trousers, socks and black shoes, the young men; navy blue jackets, white blouses, silver scarfs, grey skirts, stockings and black shoes, the young ladies. The guides looked really well. The party was to begin after the exhibit's closing time at 9:00 p.m., on a Sunday, the last day of the exhibit. The scientists and other staff were invited too. There were sandwiches, beers, and soft drinks available. There was a band playing loud disco music and the young people were dancing by the pool. It was a festive occasion. Everyone seemed to be having a good time. Suddenly, the boys started carrying the girls and throwing them into the swimming pool. Then the boys too jumped into the pool. To me, that was the signal that the party was over and thus, I was getting ready to leave when a young lady, Miss Nancy Portocarrero, whom I knew had been a receptionist and a guide at the exhibit, came to me and asked me to drive her home. She was in uniform and wet from head to toe. She said that her car was outside and that she could not drive wet. Of course, I said, and we walked to where her car was parked. Her car was a Swedish one. I could not read the designations on the controls, but I found the ignition, the gas pedal, the clutch, the shifting control, and the hand break. I had not driven a mechanical shifting car in a long time, but I managed to start the car and to drive it along the avenue. She gave me directions and soon we arrived at her home. She asked me to come in and meet her father, Mr. Portocarrero, He was a distinguished gentleman, very grateful for my bringing his daughter home safely. He immediately served two tall glasses of whisky and placed one in my hand. We celebrated the end of the exhibit that way. Soon after though, I politely thanked my host and said good bye. By then it was almost midnight. Something to remember.

97. California, Here I Come!

My apartment on the tenth floor of a building on Clearwater Beach had an spectacular view of the beach and the Gulf of Mexico. My balcony faced west, thus the sunsets were a pretty picture. I used to wake up at two or three in the morning and watch the moon and the stars when the sky was clear. One morning at about three a.m., I saw an orange blob of light right by the horizon. I wondered what it was. It was too large to be Venus or a star. Besides, it was orange. Could it be one of those UFOs people talk about? Two minutes later, it was gone! I never forgot about that orange blob and the mystery of not having an explanation for it. In subsequent nights, I looked for the blob several times without any luck. About one month after the first observation, at about three a.m., I saw the crescent moon right by the horizon. I figured the moon was about to set as a result of the earth rotation. A few minutes later, the moon changed into "the blob." At last, an explanation for the previous visual phenomenon! I looked for my glasses and put them on. It was the tip of the crescent moon just at the moment of setting, below the horizon. The orange blob was really the tip of the moon amplified by the atmosphere, as seen by me without my glasses. Two minutes later, it disappeared below the horizon. So much for a UFO. I went to read for an hour or two. Then, I tried to sleep again. At 5:00 a.m., I would watch the news and weather on TV and at 6:30, I would get up, walk the beach, and return for shaving and showering. Then, I would have a jug of "decaf" coffee and a sweet roll. Then, I would do some RRR—reading, writing and arithmetic— or I would run some errands, post office, supermarket, pharmacy. Living alone, believe me, was hard work. To summarize, getting old, retirement, and living alone are not for sissies. At about 10:30 a.m., I would fix myself some brunch and would have it with a glass of Chardonnay wine. Then, I would read some more. At about 12 noon, I was ready for my one-hour nap. In the afternoon, I would watch a movie on TV and then walk on the beach. Sometimes I walked a mile south. Other times I walked a mile north. In the summer, I walked barefoot and with only light clothing; in the winter, I wore heavy clothing, thick socks, and sneakers. Those were the days to remember.

After consulting with my two daughters, Cati of Phoenix, AZ, and Margie of Hollywood, CA, I decided to move to Los Angeles, to a place near to where Margie, my son-in-law Tony Colbert, and granddaughter Elisabeth Colbert lived. I figured, that I would have to ship my car across the country and I would fly to LA and find an apartment for me when I got there. But I found out quickly that shipping a car was an expensive proposition. I was quoted 1,500 dollars the first time and 1,750 dollars two months later. That, plus my air travel expenses. Some simple calculations resulted in an easy ride for about 500 dollars, if I drove the car myself. I disposed of most of my junk, finished my business with my landlord, and packed my valuables in my car. Thus on April 9, 2003, I departed from Clearwater Beach on my trip to California. Both my daughters asked me to call them every evening to report on my travel progress. I promised to do so. I drove between 400 and 450 miles each day. Around 4 p.m. I would look for a place to stay overnight and rest. I made stops in Crestview, FL, Lake Charles, LA, Kerrville, TX, El Paso, TX, and Phoenix, AZ. I visited my daughter Cati one day, and the next day, I continued toward Los Angeles, CA. I visited my daughter Margie in Hollywood, CA, one day. Then, I proceeded to my place in Venice, CA, where I had an apartment waiting for me. I arrived in Venice, CA, on April 17, 2003. The whole trip from Florida to LA lasted 6 days at an easy pace and covered 2,570 miles. My car behaved itself flawlessly. I was grateful. If Florida is flat, like a pancake, California is mountainous. Driving in CA requires four dimensions:

north-south, east-west, up-down, and the fourth dimension, time. I wrote to my family in Peru, "California is like another planet." It was. Prices are two to three times higher than those in Florida! Besides, CA has a "State income tax." Just like another planet. It is a privilege to live in California.

98. Two Granddaughters

Sometime in the summer of 2001, I received a call from my daughter Margie of Los Angeles, who said over the phone, "You'd better sit down for the news I am about to give you." I replied, "Wait, wait, I am sitting down now, please tell me." She said that she had just come from the doctor's office and that she, the doctor, had confirmed that she, Margie, was expecting a child. The news warmed my heart and with a trembling voice I told her: "I love that baby already! Congratulations to you and Tony. What can I do to help?" She said: "You can come and visit us sometime later, OK?" "All right, perhaps I could come for 4-day visit later in the year, at a time that is convenient to you two," I said. She agreed. That was the way it happened. I arrived in Los Angeles on December 13 for a four-day visit. I took lodging in a nearby hotel and visited Tony, Margie and the "baby," now in her 8th month of development. I said "her" because the ultrasound movies had shown the baby was a precious little girl. Also, at that time, I met "Winston," their one-year old blue-grey pet cat. When we could, we went to visit some of the touristic sites like Malibu, Santa Monica, Beverly Hills, and the Getty Museum of Arts. Then, I returned to my place in Florida. The baby, my first grandchild, was born on February 6, 2002, and was named Elisabeth. Because of labor difficulties, the doctors decided to have her delivered by a cesarean operation. Right from the start, Elisabeth, Lis for short, was a delightful baby, playful and sharp as a kitten, I was told. At the time, I was still living in Florida. But things were going to change soon. As described in the previous story, I came to California in April, the follow-ing year, when Lis was 14 months old. I was delighted. She was already walking well and playing like a real kid. Her parents flooded the house with toys for her. I was glad to see their love for a wonderful little angel. For me, it was great to cel-ebrate with them birthdays and holidays. Occasionally, I babysat Lis when Tony was at work and Margie had a medical or dental appointment. But my happiness was going to be doubled when, in 2005, my daughter Margie announced that she was expecting a second child by the end of the year. Later, we learned that the ultrasound images had shown that she was a little sister for Lis. The searching for a name began among family members. Among them, Tony's parents, Richard and Jane Colbert; Tony's brother Steven Colbert and his wife Marisa Colbert. Also Dennis and Gilda Colbert, uncle and aunt of Tony's also living in Los Angeles, and an aunt named Dorothy, living in San Diego. Of course, I was also part of the team making suggestions for a name as was Margie's sister Cati, of Arizona. But that was not all that was in contention, we knew that Tony and Margie's children had a 50% probability that they would have blue eyes and 50% of having brown eyes. Elisabeth had brown eyes so, a great expectation was in the air about Lis' baby sister. Sandra Colbert, Sandy for short, was born on December 8, 2005. She was a healthy and strong child. Because of the labor history, doctors planned the delivery by cesarean incision. And, Sandy had blue eyes! But we had to wait at least 6 months to tell for sure. The name Sandra, was decided by Tony and Margie almost at the last minute, keeping the rest of the family in suspense for many a day.

Children grow up so quickly. We must enjoy them and teach them to do well and better all the time. Sandy is a wonderful child, playful, smart, and she loves her older sister, Lis, dearly. I was so grateful that I could participate in their lives and watch them grow. Tony and Margie let me participate in their activities and outings. Thus, I accompanied them to Lis' gymnastic classes, soccer practices, visits to the zoo and parks, arena shows, musicals, her kindergarten school activities, the visit to Disney World in Orlando, Florida, and the Halloween "trick or treat" walks. In October of this year, the Stephen Birch Aquarium of San Diego organized a Halloween costume contest for children. My daughter Margie designed costumes for both Lis and Sandy. Lis wore an aquanaut outfit with underwater goggles and had a large squid with her tentacles wrapped around her. Even before the contest, people stopped to ask permission to take her picture. Sandy wore a pink globular outfit representing an umbrella jelly fish. Its tentacles dangling around her little legs. People wanted her picture too. We were delighted when the panel of judges called them both to receive awards. Naturally, we recorded it all on videos and took photos also. That was a time we shall always remember. Two granddaughters! I had been blessed.

99. Circumnavigation of South America

In March of 2001, an announcement in a travel catalog caught my attention. It was from Square Prime Tours (SPT) and offered a cruise around the whole subcontinent of South America with stops and tours of most of the largest cities and tourist attractions. My quick mathematical mind figured that the basic cruise, with a medium price cabin on the ship, was going to cost about 125 dollars per day. That was about one-half of what any land tour to Europe would cost. Thus, I made arrangements to get on the tour, which departed from Fort Lauderdale, FL, on January 18, 2002. I made two payments in advance to SPT, to cover the full cost of the 52-days tour. I had been on two river cruises before: the river Nile cruise in Egypt and the Yangtze river cruise in China, but only for three days each. I really did not know what a long duration cruise was like. But I was an open-minded person, I thought. I could endure a long trip, I thought. I knew that my daughter Margie was expecting my first granddaughter in February. I had visited them in December, but I could not return for her birth in February because of my contract with the tour. At the time, I was living on Treasure Island. In preparation for the trip, I packed my suitcase, I got some 3,000 dollars in cash for optional tours and possible emergencies. In those days, I had not obtained a credit card because I did not want to purchase anything on credit. I hated to pay interest to any loan institution. In my view, they were "legalized loan sharks." I had not obtained a debit card either. I did get two debit cards later, but I did not have any at the time of the trip. I placed the money in two envelopes one of which I placed in a carry-on bag, and the other in the inside pocket of my jacket. I did not realized that, at the very last moment of leaving for the airport, I had decided to leave the jacket. Thus, I left on my trip with only half of the cash I needed for optional tours and emergencies. When I got to the port of embarkation, at the registration desk, I was asked for a credit card. I told them that I was going to pay cash for any extra expenses. They made a note of that and let me get on board. I was assigned to cabin 411 on the main deck. I was also assigned to table 156 in the main dining room. That evening, at dinner time, I met our travel companions, also assigned to the same table: Mr. and Mrs Henry Trent of Tucson, AZ, Mr. and Mrs. Fredrick Dalby of Scotland, UK, and Ms. Jean Gardner of Daytona, FL. We all occupied the same table at mealtimes for the whole cruise. Breakfast was served at 7 a.m., lunch at 12 noon, and dinner at 6 p.m. Formal dressing was required in the evenings. I had not brought with me a tuxedo or black bow ties. I had never used them. Thus, I wore a navy blue suit, white shirt, and a narrow tie at dinner times. I looked like agent 007. That was acceptable. Not encouraged, but acceptable. Better than nothing! Mr. Trent wore a jacket and tie. That was acceptable also. The best dressed at our table were Mr. and Mrs. Dolby. He wore a white tuxedo and black bow tie always and Mrs Dolby always wore the most elegant night gowns and jewelry. The other ladies wore very dressy outfits, very special. But we all got along famously, always chatting, telling stories, and laughing at our own jokes.

Our ship, the "Morovia," sailed from Fort Lauderdale, FL, with some 1,000 passengers and a crew of about 400. The ship headed southeast between the Bahamas and Cuba to the Windward passage and then southwest between Haiti and Jamaica and across the Caribbean sea toward Panama. I quickly learned that traveling on a cruise these days is no fun because the ship, by international agreements, have to travel at a distance of 100 miles from the coasts. Thus we could not see a thing—only the oceans. The reason was that all wastes from the ship cannot be disposed of near the coasts where people live and work. That was reasonable. Thus, you had to find something to fill up the time, something to entertain yourself. Of course, the ship provided a news bulletin every morning with national and international news as well as information on the places we were to arrive soon. That was just fine. I also brought with me some books to read and study, a CD player and some disks of my favorite music, and a DVD player as well as some of my favorite movies. On the ship there was also a theater in which we could see some of the latest films. I had also brought with me a short wave radio, which I planned to use along the coasts to hear the local news even before we disembarked to visit a port, city, or to take a tour.

Because I had forgotten some of my money at home, I tried to get some from SPT by writing a personal check to SPT for 500 dollars. Mr. Bronson, the SPT representative said that there was no problem. But the next day, Mr. Bronson said that his company would not accept personal checks. I said to Mr. Bronson that I was offended. That I had paid SPT several thousand dollars using personal checks before the trip and now, they refuse to accept a check for 500? I said to him then, that I did not want anything to do with SPT in the future and asked him to quit placing an STP bulletin under my door each day because it was a duplication of the ship's bulletin and therefore, unnecessary.

On the night of January 22, we passed the Panama Canal and entered the Pacific ocean. We then proceeded south along the coast of Colombia and stopped at the port of Manta, Ecuador. I managed to listen to radio stations from Panama, Costa Rica, Cuba, and Ecuador. On January 28, we arrived at the port of Callao, Peru, my country of birth. That morning, I went into Lima where I had a grand re-union with my brothers Daniel, Giovanni, Pietro, my sister Gina, and her husband Carlos. We had some wine and chatted for two hours. Then some of us we went for lunch at a typical Peruvian cooking restaurant. After that, I said good-bye and returned to the ship. The next day, I took the optional tour of the famous "Nazca Lines." Flying at low altitude, the passengers could appreciate the 2,000 years-old giant designs of animals and geometric figures on the plains and on the hillsides. We, the tourists, then returned to our ship to continue the trip. On January 31, we arrived at the port of Arica. I went down to visit the town and to climb the Morro, a hill some 200 meters high, facing the ocean. On top, there are monuments in memory of the men fallen during the war between Peru and Chile, back in 1879. One of them, had a quotation of Jesus Christ: "Love each other as I love you." On February 2, we arrived at Valparaiso, and toured Santiago and Vina del Mar. On February 5, we entered the Gulf of Ancud and stopped at the port of Montt. Some of us went to town. I purchased some supplies at a pharmacy. Back on the ship, we continued south through the Moraleda canal to port Aisen. We went to land to ex-plore the area and returned to the ship in time for dinner. On February 8, I received an e-mail from my son-in-law Tony Colbert. He gave me the news of the birth of my granddaughter Elisabeth by C-section. He said both were well and recovering fast. I replied immediately congratulating them and expressing my love for all of them. The next day, we stopped at a fiord to watch two glaciers, slow rivers of ice coming down from the mountains toward the sea. That evening, I invited our table companions to a glass of Chilean wine in my cabin to celebrate the arrival of my granddaughter Lis. On February 10, we arrived at Punta Arenas, a town which we toured the following morning. Then, we passed through the beagle channel which had on the north side the Argentinian town of Ushuaia and on the south side the Chilean port of Williams. Later, we headed south toward the Cape of Horn. From the distance, we could see the light house and a weather station. Then, we proceed-ed toward the Falkland Islands or Islas Malvinas, as called by the Argentinians. On February 13, we arrived at Port Stanley and, the next day, St. Valentine's day, we toured the town. We then traveled north toward the port of Buenos Aires. On February 17, we entered the great Buenos Aires, and later we toured the city. At the cemetery of la Recoleta, we visited the tomb of Evita Peron. Then, we walked and shopped famous Florida Street. On February 20, we arrived at Montevideo, Uruguay, for a short visit and tour of the city and beaches. The next stop was going to be Rio de Janeiro, thus every morning I listened to Brazilian radio sta-tions from Porto Alegre, Sao Paulo, Rio, and Curitiba, to relearn the Portuguese language which I had not spoken for some 20 years. After 10 hours of listening, I was ready. In fact, I did act as interpreter for other tourists when we landed in Rio and Salvador, later. While listening to Brazilian radio stations, I learned that there were several hundred cases of hemorrhagic dengue in Rio. But the ship bulletin did not mention that, not even a warning, and let passengers disembark ignorant of the risks. Not good for business, I thought. We were a "trapped audience" on that ship. Knowing that dengue is transmitted by mosquitoes, I sprayed myself with insect repellent before leaving the ship. In town, I bought "Cefaclor,"an antibiotic, Cepacol lozenges, and "Waltusin DM," an anti-coughing syrup. Then, I walked the beach of Ipanema before taking a bus to return to the port and the ship. I must state that the smog of Rio made me cough a lot. In subsequent days the cough became a bronchitis. But I was ready then. I put myself on Cefaclor and Waltusin DM. Going to the medical post on the ship would have cost a fortune. Let us face it. The ship was a tourists' trap. We were a trapped audience. We were subjected to their schedules, to their dressing codes, they had the credit card numbers of most tourists, we attended the entertainment programs of their choice, etc. If they said: "jump," we jumped. In protest, I skipped many evening meals even though I had paid dearly for them. I also skipped some night shows. My reasoning was that I hated the formality of dressing up to get our decorated rations. I felt that the dressing code was a form of subjugation. Besides, everything cost 5 to 10 times more than on land. That is a way of saying that prices were 500% to 1000% higher. I refused to pay them. I can understand a double or triple prices, but 5 times, ten times? It was ludicrous. The worse is that we, the public, allowed it to happen. If we had stopped paying their prices, you would see how quickly they fall down. I promised myself then that I would not sign for another cruise ever.

The day we were scheduled to depart from Rio, we were detained by Brazilian authorities because they had detected an oil spill coming from our ship. Some Brazilian crews on boats were circling the spill to prevent its spreading. We were informed that negotiations were underway to resolve the matter. Two rumors circulated quickly: first, Brazilian frogmen had spilled oil under the ship during the night, and second, there was an oil leak caused by human error on part of the ship's crew. They had opened the wrong valve. Who knows who was right. Some spectrometric and neutron activation analyses could have shown which hypothesis was correct. After 36 hours of negotiations, meaning that the ship's company had paid a hefty fine and the costs of cleaning the waters, we were allowed to depart. Later, we stopped in Salvador, formerly known as Bahia, where we toured the town and did some shopping. I was the interpreter for the other tourists in our group. We also stopped at Fortaleza in the north coast of Brazil, to drop off a lady passenger who had suffered an accident and fractured her hip. She needed immediate medical attention. On March 3, we skipped a stop on the mouth of the Amazon river to make up for the delay in Rio. During the following days we passed by Devil's Island, the infamous French prison, Barbados, Martinique, Guadalupe, Charlotte Amalia, and St. Thomas. We stopped in some of those islands to do some shopping. I did mostly touring since I was really short of cash. I had saved only the cash needed for the expected tipping of the crew of the ship. On March 9, the night previous to our arrival in Fort Lauderdale, a comedian threatened all passengers. Between jokes, he said that all of us had to make sure that we paid the expected

11 dollars per day tip for the crew. If not, he said, your suitcase may get lost. But it was not a laughing matter. I was sure, they would hold the suitcases as ransom until the tips were paid. One thousand passengers times 572 dollars per passenger equals 572,000 dollars in tips. A fortune. I wondered how was that tip distributed among the crew. But just in case, I gave some extra tipping to the young lady who cleaned my cabin and brought me fruit when I decided to skip dinner. I also tipped extra to our table waiters. On March 10, we disembarked and said good-bye to our travel friends. I was glad the trip was over. I was glad that I was leaving the ship, that I was away from SPT, and that in a few hours, I would be home on Treasure Island to walk on Sunset Beach and feel the sand under my feet.

100. Golden Anniversary

In May of 2007, I was living in Venice, CA. One morning, I received a telephone call from Lima. It was from Dr. Arturo Tagle, one of my colleagues who had graduated with me at the College of Veterinary Medicine many years before. He said that he was a member of the committee organizing the 50th anniversary of our graduation and that I was invited. He also said that the celebrations would comprise a series of activities during the week of July 2, 2007, and that a registration fee would be required of all members of the Class of '57. I responded immediately that I was definitely coming to such a magnificent event. He then added that the committee had elected me by acclamation "Godfather" of the Class of '57. I accepted, of course, and asked what I had to do to fulfill my mission as "Godfather." He said that I should call the president of the committee, Dr. Manuel Zarate, and gave me his number. I called Dr. Zarate, another member of my graduating class, and he gave me the details of the program of celebrations. On Monday July 2, in the evening, there was going to be a committee meeting to discuss the last minute arrangements of the program. He said that I must attend that meeting. I promised to do so. He also said that on Tuesday, there would be a Mass service at the auditorium of the College followed by a Masterly Lecture given by Professor De la Torre. Then, the official photo of the Class of '57 would be taken and a marble plaque showing the names of the 24 graduates would be revealed. The plaque would have been placed on a wall in the main hall of the college building. Then, he said, as Godfather, I would be the donor of the plaque. I accepted immediately, of course. He told me the cost of the plaque and I offered to send him the money, along with my registration fee, the very next day.

Immediately, I called American Airlines to reserve my flights to Lima on Sunday July 1 and my return on the following Sunday. I also went to Western Union and sent the funds needed for the plaque and my registration fee. During the following days, I talked with Dr. Zarate some more to learn about the rest of the program. On Tuesday afternoon, all members of the Class of '57, professors and families were invited by Dr. and Mrs. Tagle to a dinner at their country house of Chaclacayo, some 20 miles east of Lima. And on Friday, there would be a ceremony honoring all graduates of the Class of '57 at the Veterinary Medicine Association headquarters in Barranco, some 20 miles south of Lima. I pledged my attendance and participation in all events. I figured that between events, I could easily find time to visit my brothers, sisters, nephews, nieces, and their descendants, if any.

I traveled to Lima, as scheduled, on July 1. My brother Giovanni was at the airport to see me and to take me to his house in El Descanso, east of Lima. I was grateful to him and to Dora, my sister-in-law, for their generosity. On Monday, I went to visit my sister Gina and her husband Carlos. My other sister, Rachel, joined us later for lunch. In the afternoon we went shopping for medical supplies that I needed and later, I took a taxi to the Club Ancash located near Campo de Marte, where the committee was meeting. It was great to see and hug my old friends and colleagues at the club. At the meeting, plans for the activities were discussed, and then the president showed some commemorative sets of wine and cocktail glasses that had been made especially for the occasion. They were stamped in gold with the seal of the University of San Marcos on one set and with the seal of our College on the other set. They were beautiful. Each of us received two sets. Later, since I could not carry the sets all the way to the U.S., I gave them to my sister-in-law.

On Tuesday morning, the organizer of the College activities, Dr. Tania Varela, pinned a golden bow on the lapel of all the graduates of Class of '57. Then, she asked me to read a section of the Bible during the Mass service. I accepted, of course. I may not be a very religious person, but I have great respect for the beliefs of others. Thus, at some point during the service, she called me to come to the stage and read two pages of the scriptures. I was very careful with the punctuation and pronunciation. Only one small error I made when pronouncing the name Abraham. I pronounced it as in English, not as in Spanish in which the "h" is mute. But that was all. Thank goodness. The rest of the ceremonies went well. Pictures and videos were taken to remember a great day. I was asked to give a short speech just before the disclosing of the marble plaque. I simply said: "I wish to pay homage to the professors who, in the 50s, not only taught us the important subjects of our profession but, with their example, guided us to do better all of our lives. Also, I wish to pay homage to Dr. and Mrs. David Terry, Godparents of the Class of '57, for their support and encouragement, but especially to Mrs. Terry, Godmother again of the class of '57 during the present celebrations. I wish also to pay homage to our four deceased classmates whom, today, we remember with love and sadness. My gratitude goes to the members of the organizing committee for their efforts to make these celebrations a reality and, finally, I wish to invite Mrs. Terry to assist me in disclosing the commemorative plaque of the 50th anniversary of the Class of '57." The curtain covering the plaque was opened. Cocktails were served. Photos were taken and then, we all boarded the bus that would take us to the Tagle's house in Chaclacayo. Over there, lunch was magnificent. Roasted pork, salad, white rice, and vegetables were served. Red and white wines were also served. A great day to remember. The following Friday, at the Association, the Officers gave all members of the Class of '57 diplomas and medals. We were overwhelmed. Dr. Tagle, my friend, classmate, and colleague, gave an enlarged photo of our class soccer team taken 50 years earlier. I was delighted. That photo, now framed in golden anodized aluminum, is displayed on a prominent place in my apartment of Venice, California. Because my return flight departed from Lima at 6:45 a.m., I had to be at the airport by 4 a.m. the next day. Thus, to be closer to the airport, my brother Pietro and sister-in-law Lucia, offered me lodging the last two nights of my stay in Lima. On Saturday, I invited all to lunch in downtown Lima and shopped for Peruvian souvenirs for my two granddaughters.

Reporter Judy Hartfeldt: You have been very active during the first ten years of your retirement, have you not?

Marco Donnatti: That was the only way to fly. I did not want to become a fossil before my time. I had to remain active.

Judy: You offered to tell me about your health history. Is that important?

Marco: I think so. I think the costs of health care for individuals can be reduced if we follow some simple rules. I plan to tell you about that in our next session. OK?

Judy: Fine Marco, then arrivederci"

Marco: Arrivederla, Judy.

A Queen Bee. Bee stings can cause severe allergic reactions (Story 104)

CHAPTER 11

PROTECTING AND DEFENDING MY HEALTH

Reporter Judy Hartfeldt: Taking good care of your health was extremely important for you, I know that, but why was it so special in your case?

Marco Donnatti: From my point of view, it was special. Nobody could make better decisions about my own health needs better than me because I was a biomedical scientist. Not the pharmaceutical industry, not the insurance companies, not even the doctors. Thus, I figured that sharing my experiences with others would be also special.

Judy: OK, did you think that your experiences could be applied to others?

Marco: No, not necessarily. We know that what is good for the individual is not necessarily good for a population and vice versa, but some words of advise never hurt anybody.

Judy: Well then, let us begin. I am recording.

———•✦•———

101. The Dark Ages

In August of 1931, my father was working as a member of the police force in La Oroya, a mining town way up in the Peruvian central Andes mountains. He had been recently transferred from the army and he had been sent to the least desirable location. And, because they were short of personnel, he had to do two eight-hour shifts of service, at various locations, everyday. The winter was extremely cold with temperatures well below freezing, day and night, and the air was very thin and polluted by the smelting plants of precious metals. For a poor family like ours, conditions were set for illness. There was no heating in those days. Poor people wrapped themselves in as many blankets as they could find to keep warm. My brother Daniel was one year old. Soon, baby Daniel was ill with pneumonia and getting worse. Our family had no access to the mining medical post. There were no private practicing physicians in La Oroya in those dark ages. Poor people in those days went to the pharmacy and took advise from the man behind the counter. There were no sulfas, no antibiotics, no anti-inflammatory drugs. The treatment consisted of oils, ointments, liniments, syrups, hot baths, and recipes of potions recommended by friends or neighbors. Remember, those were the dark ages of medicine in a province of the interior of the country. People had to fend for themselves any way they could. Infant mortality was very high. A neighbor of our mother recommended that placing a hot fried egg on the chest of brother Daniel could improve his condition. If it did not kill him, I may add. My mother was alone and, in desperation, while watching her first born dying with high fever and gasping for air, decided to try the recommended attempt to a cure. It must have been an atrocious and a savage attempt, but how could a poor family deal with a deadly illness in a forgotten and forsaken place like La Oroya in the year of 1931? My brother suffered a circular third degree burn on his chest, but in a few days he got better and gradually recovered. Did the heat of the fried egg cured him? There is no answer for that question, but it is likely that it did. There was no other explanation for it. Some years later, when we were growing up we could see that circular scar on Daniel's chest. How could we forget the story of that treatment in desperate times? Even now, in the movie "the Godfather, part II" there is a scene in which a desperate mother attempts to cure her baby from pneumonia using an inverted wine glass into which, a moment before, she had burnt a piece of cotton. Presumably, the burnt cotton thins the air inside the glass and, and, by placing it immediately on the chest of the child, it acts like a suction cup to extract fluid from the child's lungs. That was an attempt to a cure, in the dark ages of medicine, practiced by poor immigrants in the Italian neighborhood of New York city in the roring 20's. It was a rare event that children survived pneumonia in those days. Fortunately, a few months later, our father was transferred to Huanuco where climatic conditions were better for the family. Giovanni and me were born there in 1932.

We did not have records of the illnesses we suffered during the infancy and youth years, so I must describe them from memory. I recall that we, the older three brothers, got sick with whooping cough, a bacterial disease now called pertussis. We were about 8 and 6 years old and living in the port of Mollendo in 1938. We had to go to the hospital daily to receive an injection in the arm for several days. Perhaps it was a stimulation of the immune system, perhaps it was a late vaccination, but I can't be sure. Three years later, then living in Lima, I contracted varicella, also called chicken pox, a viral illness and had to stay in bed for nine days. I had to avoid contact with my brothers and sisters. I was nine then. The following year, I got the "mumps" a viral illness affecting the parotid glands. The year was 1942 and I was 10 years old. Of course, nowadays, all of those illnesses are preventable with timely vaccinations. But remember, those were the dark ages. Fortunately though, we had arrived in Lima and the department of education had some mandatory vaccination plans for all children in public schools, particularly against small pox. I do not recall any serious illnesses for many years after that except an occasional food poisoning event, like that time when I ate too many peaches without washing them. Perhaps we had build up our natural immunity through exposure. I have no other explanation for the good health we had during the years of primary and high school education in Lima. Most likely, a coincidence, but those were also the years in which we took a passionate interest in soccer. Did our daily exercising, up to the point of exhaustion, contribute to our good health. Perhaps, but I think it was our good nutrition. We had to thank our mother for that. She gave first priority to our foods. Everything else came second.

102. Physical Exams

It was in 1950, when I had entered the University of San Marcos' school of sciences, that the students in our class had to take mandatory physical exams. For me was the first. I was 18 years old then. A very comprehensive exam in which the 30 students in our class rotated through 18 doctor's offices for various tests. The tests included physical, chemical, biological, and psychological examinations and lasted four hours. Specialists operated those offices, performed the test of their specialty, and kept accurate records. Among the systems checked were, cardiac, pulmonary, including a chest radiograph, renal, including urinalysis, blood sampling for physical and chemical analyses, liver function tests, and psychological testing. I recall that one of the tests for cardiovascular fitness consisted in climbing a set of four stair steps and then coming down, three times. A technician would take the pulse of the student before and after the exercise. At that time I was perhaps at the peak of my athletic abilities. So, the doctors were very much surprised when after my test, my pulse went down instead of the expected rising of the pulse rate. I saw the doctors whisper to each other, but I could not hear what they said. They just recorded the results and let me go. Complete physical exams were given to students every two years. As far as I can recall, I always passed those exams with high marks. The reason why I mentioned my athletic abilities is because, at the time, I was playing soccer for the team that represented the district of La Victoria, in which we lived. And the coach of the team, Mr. Galvez, who was a well recognized coach in professional circles, had timed all players of the team in the 100-meters dash. He had recorded me as the fastest in the team with 11.0 seconds while running in soccer shoes and gear. I should mention also, in passing, that our team had defeated the "Carbone," a first division amateur team by 2-0, and the "Ciclista Lima," a professional team, by 1-0 in friendly games.

Another important event occurred just about that time. My brother Daniel had started smoking cigarets like many young men did in those days. It is possible that they did it to impress the girls around, to show them their maturity and eligibility. My brother liked very much American "blond" tobacco cigarets. He preferred "Camels" or "Kents" with filter, the expensive ones. I tried them and like them too. They were sweet and had a perfumed aroma. Not at all like the chip "National" or "Inca" cigarets which tasted like garbage. That way, I started smoking too, like my older brother, to impress some cute, adorable, girl in the neighborhood. But the saints must have been watching, because one day, one fortunate day, I read in "Billiken,"an Argentinian magazine, that "smoking reduces the vital capacity." The announcement was on the bottom of the page where they usually placed quotations, sayings, words of wisdom, and cliches of all sorts. But that one about smoking, stopped me cold. At that time, I wished very much to become a professional soccer player and, to do that, I had to have my "vital capacity" intact. Secretly, I had promised myself that no other player would outrun me or jump higher than me in any game. I had been smoking some 4 or 5 cigarets per day. So, really, I had not become a heavy smoker yet; there was not a habit to break. That magazine announcement did it for me. I stopped smoking instantly. Except rarely, in a social situation, I did not smoke a cigaret again. Several decades passed before health authorities and, even the cigaret manufacturers, would admit that smoking was harmful to the health of people. As for me, I had stopped before I had begun. I was one of the very few fortunate ones. I believe that event, more than any other, resulted in the good health I enjoyed in the latter years of my life.

103. Physical Exams USA

As an immigrant, I came to the U.S. to work as a scientist at the Oak Ridge Institute of Nuclear Studies (ORINS) in 1964. I was 31 years old then. ORINS was a contractor with the federal government and thus, we were subjected to the same rules and regulations of all federal employees. One of those rules was the mandatory medical exams. Once a year for employees older than 40, and every other year, for younger ones. That rule applied to all categories of employees, from blue collar workers to senior scientists. Thus, according to a strict schedule, some 8,000 persons working in all the atomic plants at Oak Ridge, took the physical exams at the Medical Division of the Oak Ridge National Laboratory (ORNL). At that time, director of the medical division was Dr. Henderson. I had met him when he came to lecture in one our medical radioisotope courses. Dr. Henderson had a team of physician specialists who took responsibility for the medical exams. One of those doctors was the one had erred in diagnosing a cold nodule in my thyroid gland in 1972 (story 64). Except for that event, my physical exams were always negative which meant that there was nothing wrong with me. The actual exams consisted of filling out a medical history form, followed by a personal interview, and by a thorough check by palpation, auscultation, examination of eyes, ears, nose, and throat, etc. Body weight, blood pressure, and body temperature were measured and samples of blood and urine were taken for physical and chemical analyses. I imagine that, in a population of 8,000 workers, some people were found to have some hidden illnesses. Early diagnosis was the main objective of the exams. And early diagnosis meant early and a successful treatment.

In 1977, by medical recommendation, due to the severe allergies suffered by my family and me, I had moved to a position of college professor in Tampa, Florida. My employer was the Tampa Junior College (TJC). The college, under contract with some health medical organizations (HMOs), provided medical care to all the faculty, maintenance workers, and administration employees and their families. The employees and the college shared the costs of the medical insurance, equally. Once a year, the HMO contract would be reevaluated by the college administration and either renewed of replaced. HMOs encouraged medical examinations of college employees at scheduled times, usually every other year. I was pleased that during the 20 years I worked at the TJC, all my physical exams were negative. Except for some allergies, my family and I were in good health. We controlled the symptoms of allergies with over the counter medications. However, when dealing with the flu and the subsequent secondary infections, we had to consult the HMO physician assigned to us. Fortunately, we had no major illnesses of any kind. I attributed my good health to the following facts: (1) to have quit smoking very early and not having smoked the rest of my life, (2) to have had hard liquor only occasionally and in moderation, no more than two drinks per social event and (3), to have practiced soccer once a week for 33 years. Story 102 tells of my brief encounter with cigarets, story 32 tells how I promised myself not to drink more than two drinks per social event, and many earlier stories tell of my passion for soccer. Only then, could I have become the "workaholic" I was at the college of veterinary medicine in Lima, at the ORINS in Oak Ridge, TN, and at the TJC in Tampa, Florida. Being a workaholic was a special virtue. It meant that I had put my work before anything else. As an immigrant, I had to do better than others to keep my job. My attitude toward work guaranteed my position and the biweekly paychecks. I needed them to keep my family fed, housed, healthy, and my children in school. I was very much aware that there was, behind the scenes, competition, professional jealousy, brown nosing, and political manipulations, among TJC employees. Personally, to counteract any false accusation, and there were a few, I armed myself with the truth, with my documented professional qual- ifications, and with my documented work history. Just to be safe though, and to protect myself from colleagues and the TJC administration, I joined the Teachers' Union. I kept a list of attorneys recommended by the union, posted on the wall in my office, for everyone to see that I was ready to fight, if necessary. Once those people learned that I was ready and that I had won every encounter in the past, they left me alone to do my work as I saw it fit. The best way to avoid war is to be ready for it. That was one way how I fought the stresses of work. The other, was sweating it out in the soccer field.

104. More on Allergies

In story 69, I described the trials and tribulations with allergies that my family and me had endured in Tennessee in the 60s and 70s. In here, I would like to tell how we dealt with them in the 80s and 90s while we lived in Florida. I believed that the hypersensitivity to the vegetation of a region began after a few years of living in that region. When my family and I first arrived in Tennessee, we were just fine. No health problems. But after 5 to 7 years, the sensitizing period, we be- gan to have the symptoms of hay fever. It seems that our internal environment had changed in that time. Our immune system had been hypersensitized to the pollens that float in the air in the spring, summer, and fall. For east Tennessee, the pollens of ragweed lingered for nine months of the year. More than 50% of the population in that region, including the natives to that region, suffered from severe allergies. When the winter came though, everyone improved, just in time for Christmas and the new year's celebrations, and people forgot their illnesses for a while. Once an allergy began though, the hypersensitivity was extended to other substances. In our family, sensitivity to foods, to other plants, to medications, and animal dander followed. These appeared insidiously, slowly, out of the blue. You had to be a trained observer to realize what was happening. It took me years to recognize the patterns of allergies.

To alleviate the symptoms of allergies, people took anti-histamines. Histamine is a substance which is released when an allergen comes in contact with some sensitive body tissue. For example, pollens with the nasal cavity, throat, and bronchi lining; certain foods with the gastric and intestinal lining; certain plants with the skin, etc. Histamine is a vasodilator. That means that the blood vessels in the affected tissue dilate causing congestion, excessive secretion of fluids, and swelling, all signs of an allergic inflammatory reaction with the very annoying symptoms that follow. Doctors may call the illnesses "hay fever," "the flu," "migraine headaches," "milk intolerance," "eczema, "rashes", etc. There are a great number of medications used to treat the symptoms of allergies. In fact, it is a multibillion dollar industry. Just watch the many, expensive, TV commercials. That is why, in my opinion, neither the pharmaceutical companies nor the AMA nor FDA, are interested in preventing or finding a cure for allergies. In the 70s and 80s, doctors gave patients intradermal injections of the suspected allergens and measured the skin reaction with a caliper. Over one hundred suspected allergen extracts were used. The patient lay on a couch and a technician did the injecting on a grid over their backs. I watched my children endure such a torture. The testing alone, cost hundreds of dollars. But remember, that in those days we trusted our family doctors. We did what he or she would tell us. That torture would have been justified for a skin allergic conditions, but not for other tissues allergic conditions. But that was not all. Once the doctor had found a positive reaction, a treatment could begin by injecting increasing amounts of the offending allergen by intramuscular injections. Personally, I did not see the logic of that approach. The patient could have had a serious crisis. But we accepted blindly the doctors decisions in those days.

In 1974, I had been suffering from migraine headaches for a while. I dealt with them by taking aspirin and/or Dristan, an antihistaminic. One Saturday noon, I went with my wife Diane and our children to the "China Palace," a Chinese restaurant by the river Clinch in Oak Ridge. We placed our order of the foods. The wonton soup came first and, for some reason, the rest of the foods were delayed. We were talking and in good mood that day. Suddenly, my migraine headache started, right there, very intense. I looked at the empty dish of soup still in front of me. I had discovered that the soup was the cause of the headache! I remembered that I had sprinkled the soup with soy sauce before having it. I knew then that I was allergic to soy products and any foods containing soy. I explained that to Diane. She did not believe me. Secretly, she prepared soy burgers one night for supper. After dinner, my headache returned with fury. I told her that something in the dinner contained soy. Then, she confessed that she had tested me because she was not sure I was right. She said that most foods in the supermarket contained soy, that her life was now complicated, because she had to avoid soy in my meals. But that was not all. The headaches persisted on and off. Then, I discovered that the coffee I had at work during "coffee breaks," was somehow giving me the headaches too. I figured that, perhaps, soy beans and coffee beans have common proteins which act as allergens and that I had become sensitive to them. Thus, I avoided coffee. At work, one afternoon, I went to the vending machine and got a "doctor pepper" drink. Soon after, the headache returned. I went immediately and read the fine print on the back of the empty bottle. Sure enough, it contained soy products. I had become a soy detector! I must tell though, that by avoiding coffee, soy products, and dark sodas, I freed myself from migraine headaches for many years to come! There were times in which, for months, I did not take a single aspirin or an antihistaminic. "Eureka!, I had found it, I had found a better way to deal with allergies: find the allergen and avoid it like the plague in the future. "One ounce of prevention is worth a pound of cure." Just as simple as that. In a similar fashion, by careful observation, we found out that Diana was allergic to poison ivy and to cats, that my daughter Margie was allergic to milk, that my son Dante was allergic to peas and other vegetables. Later, in Florida, I discovered that I had become allergic to Dristan, the antihistaminic I was taking for allergies! I also discovered that apples and mangoes, fruits that I would eat after lunch, caused my gums to bleed when I brushed my teeth with toothpaste in the evening. Naturally, I avoided Dristan. No more skin rashes!. I avoided apples and mangoes. No more gum bleeding!. I avoided coffee and soy products. No more migrain headaches! Since then, I have taken the approach of careful observation to determine the cause of allergies and then to avoid them (See also story 108). To close this story, I must make an important comment. Like all illnesses, allergies have an important psychological component which appears to condition the body to the hypersensitivity. There are some persons who, when they hear the word "cat,"they have an immediate reaction with symptoms of asthmatic respiration. Another example of the psychological component of allergies, is the study performed by Dr. Henderson in Oak Ridge. He found a direct correlation between the severity of the allergies and the level of education of the patient: Senior scientists had more severe allergies than custodians. Others fell in between accordingly. Until a cure if found, I shall continue to use my method of careful observation and prevention of the culprit allergen.

105. Benign Prostatic Hyperplasia (BPH)

The prostate is a walnut-shaped gland situated under the urinary bladder and around the urethra. BPH is condition that affects most men beginning at about age 50. It consists of an excessive proliferation of normal prostatic cells within the gland. That enlarges the gland and constricts the urethra. The result is difficult urination. It is a serious condition because it could cause obstruction and the urine would then fill completely the bladder, the ureters, the cavities of the kidneys, and, if it persists, it could kill the renal cells, a condition called hydronephrosis. BPH is treated with drugs that relax the muscle fibers of the gland thus reducing the pressure on the urethra and facilitating urination. At about age 60, many men's prostate gland undergoes dysplasia, a condition in which the gland cells change. They become atypical, in disarray, disorderly. Pathologists consider this state a pre-cancerous condition. By age 70, some men suffer from neoplasia of the prostate or prostatic cancer. Treatment then, can be by surgery, radiation therapy, chemotherapy, immunotherapy, or a combination of all of the above. Summarizing, hyperplasia at 50, dysplasia at 60, and neoplasia at 70.

In 1982, just on time, my HMO doctor, Dr. Davidson of Clearwater, FL, told me that I had an enlarged prostate. He then proceeded to prescribe "Hytrin" a drug that would relax the smooth muscle fibers of the capsule and traveculae of the gland thus reducing the pressure on the urethra. Through my HMO insurance I got the medication. Still, it cost about 55 dollars per 30 pills. I took one pill at bedtime every evening. I took the pills for five years. I did not know it then, but one of the horrible side effects of hytrin was arthritis, myalgia, tendinitis, and bursitis, with symptoms of inflamation and pain. In my case, it affected my joints and tendons in my shoulder, forearms, and wrists, mostly. To relieve the pain, I took tylenol. Only then, I could move and work. My doctor never mentioned the side effects at all. In 1987, our college changed HMOs and my new doctor, Dr. Arenson, asked me to continue on hytrin. I complained of joint pains. He prescribed some powerful anti-inflammatory drugs that were worse than the illness because they had some horrible side effects themselves. In one of my visits to Dr. Arenson, he told me that I was condemned to take those drugs because my prostate was not getting any smaller. I considered that an offensive remark. I went to my pharmacist and asked him if I could use some equivalent drug to replace hytrin. He told me that I could use Terazosin, the generic version of hytrin and was less expensive. Thus, I started on that drug hoping that my joint pains would disappeared. But they did not. In fact the pains were getting worse. I took terazosin for four more years. Then, I asked my HMO for a change of doctor. They assigned me to Dr. Clark, DO. A doctor of osteopathy. I was not sure how to take that, but I made an appointment anyway. Dr. Clark, told me that I could try to use "Saw Palmetto" or a similar product for which I did not need a prescription. I went to the pharmacy and looked in the section on men's health. I found saw palmetto. I purchased a flask and began to take it according to instructions on the label. Everything went well for a while and the joint pains seemed to reduce slowly. I was very much hopeful that I had found the answer to my problems with BPH. But it was not to be. Saw palmetto had side effects of its own. I had an excessive tracheal and bronchial mucous secretion at night. I would awake in the wee hours of the night with respiratory difficulty because of the excessive secretion. I believe it was a severe allergic reaction to saw palmetto. I then, changed to "pumpkin seed oil" capsules. The same results. I was getting desperate. If I did not take the medications, I risked hydronephrosis. And, when taking them, I risked dyspnea. And the joint and tendon pains were still persistent.

Then, one day, while I was listening to my radio, a speaker was giving a lecture on BPH. Naturally, I became interested and listened carefully. I even took notes. The speaker said that all medications used to treat BPH had one active ingredient in common: beta sitosterol, and that beta sitosterol was sold as nutritional supplement for cardiac function. Immediately, I looked for it in one of the catalogs I used to get in the "junk mail." It turned out that it was inexpensive and did the job of facilitating urination. And what was best: No side effects. No respiration difficulties at night. The joint, tendons, and bursa pains gradually disappeared.

I took beta sitosterol for some 6 years. I was pleased of my accomplishments regarding the control of the side effects of BPH medications. But one sad day I began to suspect that I had become sensitive to beta sitosterol. I did not want to admit it. I did not have anything to replace it with. But that will be another story. Stay tunned to this channel.

106. Trouble in Berlin

In September of 2005, I traveled to Central Europe on one of my tourism trips. I flew from Los Angeles on a non-stop flight to Frankfurt, Germany. I took a taxi from the airport to our hotel, the Ramada-Treff in Bed Sodden town and I met our tour director. Mr. Peter Flack. He apologized for not meeting me at the airport as he was supposed to have done. His excuse was that my flight had been two hours late. The taxi driver had printed me a receipt. Mr. Flack refunded me the 31 euros I had paid for the taxi. Later, during dinner, he told the tourists in our group that the bus would depart for Berlin at 7 a.m. in the morning and that we would receive a wake up call at 5:30 a.m. thus giving us one-and-a-half hours to get ready and have breakfast before boarding the bus at 6:45 a.m. Due to jet lag effects, I woke up at 1 a.m. and I could not sleep again until 4 a.m. At 6:50 a.m., the telephone rang: "the bus leaves in ten minutes," the voice said. I dressed up quickly, threw everything I could find in the suitcase and rolled my suitcase toward the bus parking lot. Mr Flack was there. He helped put my suitcase in the luggage compartment of the bus. I complained that the 5:30 a.m. call never came to my room. In any event, I had made the bus in 12 minutes from the 6:50 a.m. call. A record of some kind, I thought.

The bus arrived in Dresden in time for lunch, and then continued toward Berlin. We arrived to the Westin Hotel in Berlin at 7:30 p.m. After dinner, at the hotel, I went to my room and I could not find the vial of beta sitosterol tables which I took daily for BPH, benign prostatic hyperplasia. I realized that in my rush that morning, I had forgotten the vial in the bathroom of the hotel. I asked the hotel desk clerk to call the Ramada-Treff in Ben Sodden and to have the vial sent to me. I told him that I would pay any costs. He did. A few minutes later, the reply said that they had not found the vial in my previous room. At that point, I began to worry. I could not function without my beta sitosterol tablets. At about 10 p.m., in my room, I confirmed that I could not urinate. I knew then that the urethra was obstructed and that in a few hours I would have to seek medical attention. I knew also that at the hospital, they would catheterized me to drain the bladder and prevent hydronephrosis. I thought of calling Tony Colbert, my son-in-law in California, and ask him to go my apartment, pick up a couple of vials of beta sitosterol and to send them to me through overnight mail. But that would take at least 24 hours. At about midnight, I had another idea. I went down to the lobby of the hotel and asked the young man on duty to call a pharmacy and ask them for 60 milligram tablets of beta sitosterol, the medication I needed. They replied that they did not have beta sitosterol, but they had Fitosterol, 10 milligram capsules, which is also a medication used for BPH and that the price for a box of 100 capsules was 38.50 euros. I asked them to send it on a taxi to the hotel. I waited in the lobby. In about 20 minutes, the taxi driver brought the fitosterol. I paid for the medication, the taxi fare, and tipped the driver, and the desk clerk for assisting me in finding the pharmacy and the medication. I went to my room hoping that fitosterol was as effective as my beta sitosterol. I made some calculations and I took three 10-mg capsules at two a.m. and went to sleep. I woke up at about 6 a.m. I went to the bathroom. Eureka! Urination was normal. From there on, I took three capsules, morning and evening, till the end of the trip with a few to spare. Lucky me, I had resolved a very sticky, and probably very expensive situation, in Germany. Except for a few phrases in German, which I had learned specially for the trip, I did not speak German at all. But that night in Berlin, I had found some great people who helped me. I was grateful.

Briefly, on that trip, we toured Berlin, where we visited the World War II memorial, the Reichtag glass tower, and the Sanssouci palace. We then traveled to Warsaw, Poland, where we toured the city. We had a class picture in front of the monument to Chopin, the great composer. During my free time, I stumbled onto the birth house of Madam Curie, now converted into a museum. We also attended a piano concert by Iwona Klimaszewska playing the music of Chopin. Later, we traveled south and visited the infamous concentration camp of Auschwitz. We then visited the salt mines nearby, and toured Krakov. We then crossed the border into Slovakia, had lunch, and soon after, into Hungary. We arrived to Budapest a beautiful city on the shores of the Danube river. After a tour of the city, in the evening, we had a dinner-cruise on the Danube. We then traveled to Vienna, the capital of Austria, where we did touring, attended special dinners, and a musical show playing the music of Mozart and Strauss. We then traveled to the Czech Republic arriving to Prague where we did attend musical shows, had walking tours, and special dinners. From there, we returned to Frankfurt, Germany, for our flight back home.

107. My Own Health Manager

In the Summer of 2002, while still living in Florida, I had come to an important decision. It was a difficult decision to make because it involved some risks. But I figured that I had reached the advanced age of 70 and, at that point, I had very little to loose, except my life. Until then, my life had been good and very rewarding. During the previous 20 years, I had trusted doctors blindly, like all Americans do, and I had contributed to the system by enrolling myself and my family into medical insurance programs through my place of employment. For minor things, like headaches, colds, or allergy symptoms, we did not bothered the doctors, we had used over the counter medications. For more serious illnesses, like bronchitis, usually a complication of the flu or allergies, we went to the doctor to get a prescription for antibiotics. For my joint pains, tendinitis or bursitis, I consulted the doctors to get a prescription for powerful anti-inflammatory drugs. And for BPH, I went to the doctor to get drugs like Hytrin and Terazosin. None of the doctors ever, told me or explained the horrible side effects of those drugs.

On the contrary, they tried to hide them. Instead, they prescribed other drugs to alleviate the side effects of the first one, thus complicating my condition. Over the years, I had to discover by myself that my joint pains, myalgia, tendinitis, and bursitis, were caused by the medications they had prescribed for me and not a consequence of my old age and infirmity. One doctor had the nerve to tell me one day, that I had to be on Hytrin for the rest of my life because my prostate was not getting any smaller.

I was a scientist, for heaven's sake! I had tried the medical system. I had played by the rules. And the medical establishment had failed me. It was then, that I decided not to seek consultation with doctors or dentists for any illness except an occasional physical exam. I would then become my own health manager. I would institute and practice my own preventive medicine and my own preventive dentistry. Like Tom in the movie "the Godfather," I would serve only one client: me. Six years have passed since I made that drastic decision and I am pleased to report that, in those five years, I have not consulted with a doctor or dentist at all, that I am not taking any medications at all, and that, consequently, I suffer no side effects of any kind. Even though the system recommends a physical exam once a year for a person of my age, I felt that there was not a need for that frequency, because the last exam was totally negative, i.e. normal. Thus, I decided that if my physical exams and lab work continued to be normal, I would only have one every three years or so. Thus, in 2005, I took a complete physical and again was normal. And in 2006, I consulted a dentist for a "physical" exam of my gums and teeth. They were found clean and in excellent health. Of course, the dentist tried to put me on a 6-month cleaning schedule whether I needed or not. I cancelled the next appointment. My preventive medicine and dentistry were working. More than that, they were successful. I know, the medical industry pushed not only drugs, but all kinds of screening tests through all forms of advertising: TV, magazines, newspapers, even "junk mail." For a senior citizen, like me, they wanted to do ultrasound examinations of my carotid arteries, abdominal aorta, my heart, and other anatomical parts. I had those tests done some ten years earlier in Florida. They were all negative. My arteries were clean, free from atherosclerosis. The medical industry also pushed proctoscopy screening on senior citizens. They used scare tactics. They scared patients with "polyps" and colon cancer. Proctoscopy is a painful and expensive procedure. The industry push it for the money. My opinion? If a person had a family history of colon cancer, then that person could have it done every three years or so. If a person did not, then he or she did not need the test period. The industry pushed drugs, screening tests, diagnostic tests, therapeutic procedures, and surgeries, whether the patient needed them or not. We all had read the article in the Wall Street Journal of November 2, 2006, in which they reported the use and abuse of cat scans on patients. Patients were receiving very high doses of radiation. I believed insurance companies are accomplices in the overtesting, the overdiagnosing, and the overtreating of patients.

Advertisers could sell anything using expensive TV ads. They sold anti-cholesterol drugs, antacid drugs, even body weight-lowering drugs. Some even listed the horrible side effects of the products they advertised. By doing so, the advertisers were protecting their backs. That way, patients could not sue them because they had been warned about how bad the drugs were and if they asked their doctor for them, it was their own fault. And the advertisers were right. It was the patients' fault if he asked for them. Cholesterol is a good nutrient. Yet misleading publicity had made it a bad substance in the eyes of the public. Cholesterol is the building block of many metabolic substances like cortisone, cortisol, and aldosterone, which are essential to body physical chemistry and water metabolism. Cholesterol is also the building block for sex hormones like testosterone and estradiol. If we do not give our bodies cholesterol in our diets, our bodies would have to make it because it is essential to life. Without cholesterol, body chemistry would fall apart. Not only that, the sex life of individuals would be a big zero! The industry had to find a "bad guy" like in a western movie, you have bad guys and good guys. Publicity had given the public a bad guy: cholesterol. After they had convinced the public, they sold billions of dollars in anti-cholesterol medications. In a similar fashion, other very dangerous drugs gained approval and were sold, only to be withdrawn because of their deadly effects on patients. Some of those were Vioxx, Celebrex, and Bextra. In conclusion, I had a good reason for becoming mistrustful of the medical industry and their ads on TV. I believed that intelligent people should have muted those commercials. I had a good reason for becoming my own health manager.

108. My Approach to Allergies

My experience with my own allergies, and those of my family, has taught me how to diagnose them and to avoid the allergens once they were found. In other words, first I identified the culprit and second, I removed it from my life. I must state also that persons change over time. A person can become, over time, allergic to a substance that was perfectly good before. And, a person can recover from an allergy to a substance and be able to tolerate small amounts of that substance over time. The conventional approach used by allergists has been to alleviate the symptoms with all kinds of anti-histamines, not to cure the illness. In August of 2007, I was affected by a very annoying attacks of allergic rhinitis. I would awake in the middle of the night with nasal itching, congestion, persistent sneezing, followed by excessive serous nasal secretion. I did not know what allergens were causing the rhinitis. I only knew that it was a complex problem. Several allergens may be involved. At the moment of the attacks, I used nasal drops of phenylephrin HCl 1%, and/or a pill of phenylephrin10 mg, to get some temporary relief. With that treatment I got better for 3 to 4 hours. But that is not what I wanted to do. I decided then to carry out a study to identify the causing allergens so that I could avoid them completely. I began by making a list of all the substances that could be causing the rhinitis. I called them "the suspects." Among them: (a) Foods: rice, raw onions, fresh tomatoes, herbal tea (eucalyptus, anis), oranges, lemons, bananas, and grapes; (b) Chemicals: detergents, phenyephrin in liquid and pill forms, neosynephrine nasal spray, beta sitosterol tablets; and (c) environmental agents: polyester blankets, dust from carpets, pollen grains from flowers and trees.

My method consisted in removing some of the suspects from the diet, from use, or from the environment, and replacing them with other similar products not being used recently. For example, I replaced eucalyptus and anis tea with diluted regular tea. I did keep accurate records, day to day, hour to hour, of all those changes for two months. Removal would be for three days. At the same time, I kept records of the rhinitis symptoms, their frequency, and degree of severity. If the symptoms alleviated, one or more of the substances removed were the culprits. If not, the culprits were still among those not removed. To determine if the detergents were responsible, I washed all my clothing, bed linens, and blankets with baking soda. To determine if the pollens were responsible, I reduced my outdoor walks to a minimum for several days. To determine if the dust from the carpets was responsible, I emptied the bedroom and cleaned the carpets thoroughly. Knowing perfectly well that the carpet cleaning process is far from 100% efficient, I made arrangements to move to another apartment in another neighborhood. I also cleaned the air purifiers. I replaced my polyester blankets with cotton blankets. And, I purchased non-allergenic plastic pillowcases and mattress covers and I placed them on immediately. In about 4 weeks, the rhinitis had almost disappeared. Then, gradually, I reintroduced the suspects one by one. A reaction would confirm culpability. No reaction would mean innocence.

After 10 weeks, I had found the culprits: (a) Beta sitosterol tablets, the ones I took for BPH. I had been taking that medication for about five years with excellent results because it did not have undesirable side effects. Unfortunately, the study revealed that I had become allergic to it. I understood the problem though, because the same thing had happened to me some 10 years earlier with Dristan, an antihistamine medication. I decided to stop taking beta sitosterol and watch carefully the urination function; (b) Neosynephrine, the nasal spray, was also a culprit. I threw it away; (c) the eucalyptus and anis teas were also culprits. I threw them away; (d) Pollens and dust from carpets remained on the list of suspects until I could move to another apartment in a different neighborhood.

The study of my allergic rhinitis lasted about two months, mostly during August and September of 2007. By the end of October, I moved to another place. The annoying, severe, allergic rhinitis disappeared. The attacks of rhinitis were soon only an unpleasant memory. My approach had succeeded. I was free from a terrible illness. One with which an allergist would have had a picnic. A very costly picnic. My approach to finding the causes requires careful observations and recordings. Once the allergens were found though, it was best to avoid them. That was prevention as opposed to "temporary alleviation"of the symptoms, a very expensive approach. Some 10 years ago, the newspapers had announced that allergies could be cured by blocking the antibody responsible for the reaction. The article promised that the cure would be available to the public within two years. But we never heard any more about it. I imagine the manufacturers of anti-histamines blocked the blocker. My experiment of August and September gave me an unexpected bonus: The discovery that I no longer needed beta sitosterol for my BPH. Eight months after stopping its use, the urination function was normal. At this point, I can only conjecture that the gland has undergone some form of regression in my old age. One more thing. I am not allergic to polyester blankets or detergents. When I restored them I did not have a reaction.

109. My Preventive Medicine

At the outset, I must report that at my advanced age of 76, I am in a reasonably good health. Certainly, I do not have the strength or endurance of a young person, but that is normal. The important thing is that I do not have any major illnesses. My central and peripheral nervous systems are normal, and my cardiovascular, respiratory, gastrointestinal (including the liver), and urinary systems are in good shape. For a while, I had trouble with my lower back and knees, but by applying heat to them daily, as well as some occasional liniment, I am free from pain, and I can function normally. I owe it all to my preventive medicine. To describe it, I must first comment briefly on my diet. Back in the early 70s, while living in Tennessee, I could eat anything and not gain weight. I was very active with my weekly soccer games, and in excellent physical condition. My body mass index, BMI, (the ratio of weight in kg to the height in meters squared) was 25 and my body fat was 19%. That meant that I was a bundle of bone and muscle. At work, I moved constantly, all day. I called it "working at 100 miles per hour," in those days. But in the 80s, when I turned 50, things had begun to change. I started to gain weight. Really, I began to get old and older people have the tendency gain weight. By 1985, I was 18% overweight, and my body mass index reached 28. I was getting close to obesity. It was then, that I awoke from my denial and decided put myself on a regimen. It was difficult because my loving wife Diane, insisted that at dinner time, I ate everything on my plate because it had taken her a lot of work to prepare it and she would get mad if I did not honored her efforts by eating well. But I could control my lunch time at work. I stopped having snacks, sodas, sugar in my coffee, and salty chips. That kept me from going obese. After the divorce, in 1993, at age 61, I made some modifications on my feeding habits. I reduced the quantity of meats to one-half; breads and potatoes to half portions. And, I increased fruits and vegetables to double portions. I did not believe in the famous "pyramid." Sweet deserts, were reduced to an occasional half portion. I did not deny myself anything, I only reduced the quantity and increased the quality of my diet. Fourteen years later, at age 76, I was proud to reveal that my weight went down from 180 lb to 152 lb, and my body mass index was down to 24, well within the normal range for young adults. I did not believe in magic exercising machines, in weight-losing drugs, or in extraordinary diets. Quality before quantity plus the fourth dimension, time, was the key to a healthy body mass index.

To prevent illnesses, I "listened" to my body and used simple medications to correct any situation. For example, if my eyes were congested, I used a drop of Visine A.C. If my eyelids itched, I used a touch of stye ointment. If my ear canals itched, I used ear drops that contain polymyxin and neomycin. If I started to sneeze and I felt nasal congestion, I used a drop of phenylephrin HCl 1%. If I got scratches or lacerations inside the mouth or gums, I used a touch of merthiolate tincture 1%. If I had a sore throat, a touch of the same, twice a day, would take care of it in two days. I rarely had "acidity" to my stomach. If I did, I drank a pinch of baking soda dissolved in a half glass of filtered water. Better that any antacid announced on TV! I was sensitive to the tannins in regular tea so, I prepared a very diluted tea. I only used one teaspoon of sugar per cup of tea or two for a two-cup jug of tea. If I got constipated, I used one chewable tablet of milk of magnesia. If I had some diarrhea, I used one chewable tablet of peptobismol. If I got a headache, I took one tablet of tylenol. For swollen or inflamed gums, I applied a touch of merthiolate tincture to the affected area. For a more serious conditions, like bronchitis, a complication of the flu or allergies, I took an antibiotic which my physician brother Giovanni prescribed for me when I visited the family earlier in the year. I also took the anti-flu vaccine once a year and the anti-pneumonia vaccine every 5 years. For exercise, I walked about one mile each day. More recently, I walk only within my apartment and when I go shopping or visiting the family. For mental fitness, I read the technical books and magazines and sometimes the newspaper. My preferred books were on subjects of science, philosophy, and mathematics. I also watched old movies and documentary programs on nature, health, and the environment. I also watched international soccer on TV. Thus, I kept active, physically and mentally. Naturally, I knew that one day I would have a real medical emergency. Perhaps a heart attack or a stroke. For that, I had medicare, a program to which I had contributed since its inception in 1983, and continued to pay for during my retirement. My dental care consisted of flossing and rinsing after every meal, "a flossing a day keeps the dentist away." I use a water pick pump on the gum edges to remove any food particles, and brush thoroughly with toothpaste every evening, before going to bed. That was also a very important part my preventive medicine. With it, I have controlled my BPH, the side effects of medications, my allergies, and kept my gums and teeth in good health for six years and counting. Can anyone ask for more? Movie actor Dean Martin used to sing: "You are nobody until somebody loves you..." I am very fortunate because, at this time and age, I am in good health and I have a very loving relationship with my daughters, my granddaughters, and son-in-law Tony Colbert. I have been blessed. I am somebody.

110. My Vision Exams

Vision is one of the most important senses. I cannot imagine what life would be like without it. But I have been very fortunate because I have had good vision most of my life. Without even thinking about it, I took it for granted. I never worried or anything until about 1971, at age 39, when, while working at Oak Ridge, one day I looked closely at the cursor in my computer monitor and realized that it was not just a small square, but a set of four short parallel lines! It was then that I went, for the first time, to an optometrist and got my first pair of bifocal lenses. It was nice to see the fine details of everything again. Every two or three years after that, I would have a check up and perhaps have a new set of lenses. Then, in 1979, at age 47, while taking the board exams given by the American Board of Science in Nuclear Medicine, in Atlanta, GA, I discovered that I could not read the very fine print on some radioactive decay schemes. On my second pass over the schemes, a closer look showed me that, next to the horizontal lines, there were some tiny numbers representing energy levels. All I had to do to answer the questions was to subtract the lower levels from the higher ones to get the requested gamma ray energies! I earned some 10% of the final grade that way. But of course, that was a revelation telling me that I needed new glasses. I should mention though, that I did pass the board exams with high marks and obtained my board certification.

Sometime around 1980, my ophthalmologist said that I had a "point cataract" in the right eye and a tiny one also in the left eye. He said that there was nothing to worry about, that my glasses would correct for any vision distortion, and that we could wait till the following exam to see whether or not they were getting worse. Two years later, the same ophthalmologist told me that the point cataracts were "stationary" meaning that they were not growing and that my glasses were sufficient to correct any imperfections. I was pleased. Later, while working in Florida as a professor of nuclear medicine, I had to renew my driver's license. I did pass the vision exam but for the first time, they put on my license that I had to wear glasses when driving a car. That was interesting because I felt that I did not need to wear glasses to play soccer.

The years came and went and I continued to take my regularly scheduled optical exams and to get new bifocal lenses when needed. Life was beautiful. But in 2006, at age 74, my new optometrist and ophthalmologist, after a thorough examination, told me that I should plan for cataract surgery soon. He even gave me the address and phone number of an eye surgeon and a letter of introduction so that I could make an appointment. Perhaps you recall that in 2002, I had ceased going to doctors. Thus, I was skeptical about his recommendation. It was true that my vision had deteriorated somewhat and that, voluntarily, I had decided not to drive at night unless it was absolutely necessary. But that decision was because I felt that the deterioration of my vision was the expected one for a person of 74. Before I left the doctor's office, I asked him a question, a very important question: "Can you guarantee that surgery will improve my vision?" He apparently was not prepared for that question. Patients are supposed to be stupid and not to ask intelligent questions. Patients are not supposed to question their doctor's decisions. He hesitated and said: "no, we cannot guarantee better vision..." my reaction was swift: "Then, why to do it?" He had not a reply to my last question. I thank him and walked out. I put my glasses on. I could see everything well. There were birds singing on the trees, the trees were green, the automobiles were shiny, people were walking in and out of the bank across the street. Life seemed beautiful. There was not a reason in the world to be pushed into surgery at that place and time. Life was beautiful without surgery. Then, I remembered some earlier report on the evening news: Half of the surgeries in the U.S. were unnecessary.

—◦◦◦—

Judy Hartfeldt: You must be proud of having reached the age of 76 with a body mass index of 24. Is that right?

Marco Donnatti: Absolutely. And all it took was only an adjustment in my regular diet, avoiding snacks, and a lot of patience. And I did it without special diets, without pills, and without exercising machines.

Judy: I will present the transcripts of the recordings to our editors. We may have to have one more session I will let you know, OK?

Marco: By all means, let me know. I am at your orders. Good bye now.

Judy: Good bye, Marco.

Map of Peru, Marco's country of birth (Story 119)

CHAPTER 12

THE INTERVIEW

Reporter Judy Hartfeldt: Marco, this will be our last meeting. My editors have asked me to do a formal interview with you on some specific topics. We understand that your answers will be only your personal opinion and not a reflection of any particular group or the place where you live. Do you agree?

Marco Donnatti: I agree. My students once called me "opinionated." My reply to them was that you have to be well informed to have an opinion and, therefore, I considered the name a compliment.

111. Personal Preferences I

Judy: First, I would like to ask you about your background. Summarize for me your education.

Marco: At age five, I did one year of preschool education. At six, kindergarten. Then, I attended public schools for my primary and secondary education, five years each. That was followed by five years of veterinary medicine education at the National University of San Marcos earning my BVM and DVM degrees. After that, I was hired as college instructor, and I was granted a scholarship for a one year and 9 months of training in Radiation Biology at Cornell University earning my MS degree in Radiation Biology. And, in 1979, I earned certification by the American board of Science in Nuclear Medicine.

Judy: What do you consider your greatest accomplishments?

Marco: (a) As an educator, I have trained more than 400 NMTs, Nuclear Medicine technologists, in a 2-year training program leading to an AS degree. Also, I have trained more than 1,000 MDs in the field of nuclear medicine. (b) As an international educator, I have trained more than 500 college teachers and MDs on the use of radioisotopes in biology, chemistry, and medicine in Central and South America. (c) During my retirement, I have written two books on radiation safety and one on poetry. (d) For my work and tourism traveling, I have learned to speak three foreign languages: English, Portuguese, and Italian. Besides my native Spanish, of course.

Judy: How would you describe your success?

Marco: My modest "success" has been (a) to have reached the advanced age in a reasonably good health (stories 107-110), (b) to have contributed to my retirement pensions all my life so that, in my old age, I could earn a reasonably good pension which allowed me to live modestly, but comfortably, (c) to have some members of my family near me whom I could see frequently and (d), because I did not purchase anything on credit, I paid no interests to lending agencies and I had no debts. Believe me, that has been a real success.

Judy: How would you describe your disappointments, if any?

Marco: Oh yes, regrets, like in the song, I had a few: (a) Not to have earned a Ph.D degree in the biomedical field. My excuse is that I was always too busy educating others, I just did not have time for my own. To tell you the truth, I did not really missed it. My DVM and my Board Certification in NM sciences made up for it; (b) Not to have recognized earlier the bipolar illness of my wife Diane back in the early 1980s. By 1990, it was too late. And (c), not to have recognized earlier the side effects of the medications prescribed for me for BPH in the 1990s. I trusted my doctors too much.

Judy: What is keeping you busy in your retirement?

Marco: About 50% of my time goes to taking care of "number one," me. That means that I do maintain the proper cleanliness of my foods, housing, and clothing; the timely maintenance of my car; and my communication with my families in the U.S. and in Peru. The other 50% consists of: (a) Reading up-to-date books in science and the history of philosophy; (b) Studying physics, mathematics, and philosophy; (c) Watching movies, documentaries, and soccer on TV, and (d), feeding the pigeons in the park (story 88).

Judy: You have traveled a lot. What is your favorite city?

Marco: Definitely, Rome. The city has so much to offer the visitor. I have been to Rome twice, three days each time. The history, the culture, the monuments, the museums, the language, the people, the music, the foods, the wines, and the songs, are just unforgettable (story 89).

Judy: What has been your most memorable experience during your travels?

Marco: On the positive side, crossing the Alps mountains by train in the company of some wonderful people I met on the tour (story 91). On the negative side, a medical emergency I had in Berlin, Germany. Fortunately, with the assistance from some wonderful local people, I overcame the emergency (story 106).

Judy: What are your favorite sports and hobbies?

Marco: While I was young, my favorite sport was soccer. I practiced it with a passion. But only once a week. My hobbies were swimming, photography, reading, and movies. When I got old, walking, reading, writing, mathematics, photography, music, and movies and soccer on TV.

Judy: What has been your least favorite responsibility?

Marco: None. I always took my responsibilities very seriously both, at work and at home. I believe I have been successful at both. I have three children who are adults, professionals, and independent, at the present time.

Judy: If you had chosen a different profession, what would it be?

Marco: That is easy. I would have loved making movies. Specially musicals and biographies. I would have brought to the screen the lives of the great composers and scientists. Among the European composers: Mozart, Bach, Chopin, Beethoven, Verdi, Brahms, Bizet, Strauss, DeLibes, Liszt, Rachmaninoff, Ravel, Suppe, Tchaikovsky, Mendelssohn, and others. Among American composers:

Goodman, Porter, Miller, Berlin, Gershwin, Rogers, Hamerstein, and others. Among the scientists: Einstein, Da Vinci, Newton, Galileo, Archimedes, Pascal, Watt, Leibniz, Napier, Euclid, Hubble, Copernicus, Hawkins, Fermi, Curie, and others.

Judy: Who is the person you admire the most?

Marco: Albert Einstein, the renowned scientist. His explanation of the photoelectric effect, his principle of equivalence between matter and energy, and his theories of relativity have been confirmed experimentally many times. He gave us a new way of looking at the universe.

112. Personal Preferences II

Judy: What are some of your favorite musical compositions?

Marco: There are many, but among the European classics, I like:

> Fantasy Impromptu and Nocturne in E flat by Fredrich Chopin,
> Piano Concerto # 21 and Piano Sonata k331 by Amadeus Mozart,
> Habanera and Micaela's song in Carmen by George Bizet,
> Libiamo ne'lieti Calici in La Traviata by Giuseppe Verdi,
> Piano Sonata # 14 and Bagatelle by Ludwick V. Beethoven,
> Brandenburg Concerto and Tocatta and Fugue by J. S. Bach,
> Copelia Ballet Suite by DeLibes,
> Hungarian Rapsody by Liszt,
> Scheherezade by Rimsky-Korsakow
> Ave Maria by Schubert
> Light Cavalry Overture by Suppe,
> Swan lake and Waltz of the Flowers by Tchaikovsky,
> Tannhouser Overture by Wagner, and
> Halllelujah by Handel.

Among the American modern compositions, I may cite:

> Begin the Beguine and Night and Day by Cole Porter,
> Summertime and Rhapsody in Blue by George Gershwin, and
> String of Pearls by Glenn Miller.

Judy: Do you have any favorite sayings?

Marco: Again, there are many. Some of them were my mother's favorites. Actually, we grew up with them:

> Tutte le strade portano a Roma (All roads lead to Rome),
> Tale padre, tale figlio (Chip of the old block),
> Bisogna mangiare per vivere e non vivere per mangiare (One must eat to live and not live to eat),
> Vendetta, dolce vendetta (Revenge, sweet revenge),
> Il mio cuore e diviso tra tutti e due (My heart is torn between the two),
> L'abito non fa il monaco (Clothes do not make the person),
> Servito su un piato d'argento (Served on a silver platter),

Li porti bene sesantacinque anni! (You don't look sixty-five!),
Chi dura la vinci (He who perseveres wins),
A caval donato non si guarda in bocca (Don't look a gift horse in the mouth),
Lontano dagli occhi, lontano dal cuore (Out of sight, out of mind),
Scacco matto! (Checkmate!),
Troppi cuochi rovinano il pranzo (Too many cooks spoil the meal)
Chi non risica, non rosica (Who does not risk, does not win),
Ho un asso nella manica! (I have an ace up my sleeve!),
Il mondo e' picolo (It's a small world),
Credi ancora a Babbo Natale? (Do you still believe in Santa Claus?),
Quando il gatto non ce', I topi ballano (When the cat is away, the mice play).

Judy: Why do you consider yourself in "reasonably good health"?

Marco: Because at my advanced age of 76, I am active, free from illness, and in good mental condition and spirit. I am not taking any medication whatsoever, except an occasional analgesic or antihistamine. I walk for exercise and keep an ideal weight without any special diet. My body mass index is 24, ideal even for a young person. I do not have hypertension, diabetes, myocardiac disease, vascular disease, chronic obstructive respiratory disease (COPD), liver disease, renal disease, lymphoma, cancer, or AIDS. I listen to my body and practice constantly my own preventive medicine and preventive dentistry (story 109).

Judy: Why have you not remarried?

Marco: Several reasons. First, the women I like, do not like me. That means that I like them young and pretty. Second, the reasons to marry are: to start a family, to marry money, or for companionship. It is too late for me to start another family. I already had mine and a good one too! At the present time, I have enough money to live modestly, but comfortably so, I am not interested in marrying money. Companionship? Well, I believe that two brains in the same household are bound to crash sooner or later. At my age, I prefer to watch the game from the bleachers. Of course, there is the argument of selfishness. I could have been so selfish, that I refused to share my life with any woman. That is possible, but not probable, because I did marry in the past and remained married for 32 years. Besides, after my divorce, I did have two close encounters of the marring kind. But that is another story.

Judy: What is the difference between possible and probable?

Marco: I am glad you asked that. In general, possible is any event that has a probability of 3% or less of happening. Probable is any event that has a probability greater than 3% of happening. And the degree of probability, low to high, can increase up to 100% at which point the event is absolutely certain.

Judy: Are you a perfectionist?

Marco: Perfection does not exist. And it does not exist because we live in a probabilistic universe. All we can do in life is strive for perfection. We would be very fortunate if we get close to it in our field of work. But then, the interpretation of any work of science or art is subjective, and therefore imperfect. We can compensate for imperfection by working hard, by accomplishing more things in the same length of time. That only increases the probability of approaching perfection, but it does not guaranty it. The great scientists and artists have approached perfection by studying all previous works in their fields and refining the methodology and accuracy of their observations.

Judy: What do you consider people to be, 'brains' or 'hearts'?

Marco: The personality and character of persons are functions of their brains, not their hearts. Those functions are partly inherited and partly modulated by education during the early years of life. The heart is only a pump that nourishes the brain. It provides sugar and oxygen for the brain to function. The functions of the brain are extremely complex and a subject of research at the present time. No wonder the brain has been called "the last frontier of science." In the movie "The Wizard of Oz," the scarecrow asked the Wizard for a brain. Some time ago, I imagined the scarecrow saying:

> If I had a brain, I could walk and run,
> Could add and subtract, even multiply,
> Make drawings, designs, perhaps even fly,
> Create, analyze, play music, have fun...

Presumably, Black Bird, the crow, answered:

> Mr. Scarecrow, allow me to explain:
> What you are asking for, impossible task!,
> Even for the Wizard, and I'll tell you why:
> The brain is the most, of systems complex...

> Called the last frontier, of all sciences,
> Sixteen hundred grams, most delicate matters,
> One hundred billion, neurons, glial cells,
> Microglia, synapses, chemomesengers...

> Perplexing structure, the cortex, the pons,
> Two arterial systems! Confluent the veins,
> And the spinal fluid, filling the cysterns,
> A hormone connection, hypothalamus...

And later, in the same poem, the scarecrow argues:

> But Mr. Black Bird, I still want a brain,
> To work and to play, to feel emotions,
> To listen to Bach, Mozart, Mendelssohn,
> To smile, to laugh, perhaps fall in love...

The first signs of brain function are detected at twelve to fourteen weeks of development. Injury to the brain results in abnormal or absent functions. When the brain ceases to function, a patient ceases to be a person.

Judy: Do you believe in miracles?

Marco: No. The so called miracles are only misinterpreted low probability events. A thorough study of those events could explain their true nature. At that point, the event ceases to be a miracle. For example, a patient is "cured" from a deadly malignant disease. The case is called a miracle. But perhaps, the patient was misdiagnosed or overdiagnosed in the first place. Another example: a patient is declared dead and, soon after, wakes up. The case is declared a miracle. But perhaps the patient was in a state of severe catatonia or coma, not dead. Within a few minutes after true death, body decomposition begins. There is no return from that.

113. About Life and Death

Judy: How would you define "Life"?

Marco: Life is a marvelous property of nature. All living beings are complex physical-chemical systems capable of acquiring energy from the environment and utilizing that energy to grow, to function, to heal, and to reproduce themselves. To support life a continuous flow of energy is needed. With the deciphering of the genome of humans and other species, scientists are just beginning to understand life.

Judy: Why some species and individuals live longer than others?

Marco: The life spans of all species is written in their DNAs. It is the result of long-term adaptation to their environments, that is, evolution. In other words, there is a "genetic clock" ticking all the time. In general, smaller animals have fast metabolic rates and live shorter times. Larger animals, on the other hand, have slow metabolic rates and live longer times. In all species though, the genetic clock can be slowed down or accelerated by the environment, that means the living conditions or "life style." For humans, life is favored by the availability of food, shelter, clothing, social relations, and entertainment. All in moderation. On the negative side, other than an accident, life is shortened by the lack or excess of foods, excess drinking of alcoholic beverages, use or misuse of legal and illegal drugs, smoking, and other high risky ventures that lead to illness and a premature death.

Judy: Why women live longer than men?

Marco: Because they are smarter. That means that they are more conservative, more cautious in their dealings with the environment. Recent statistics show that in the U.S., the life expectancy for men is 75.2 years and for women 80.4 years. Thus, on the average, women live 6.9% longer than men. But as in any average, some men live longer than 75.2 years and an equal amount live less than the average. The same thing happens with women, half live longer than 80.4 years and half live less than the average life expectancy. Of course, it is also possible that the differences in womens' genetic constitutions determine a higher setting of their genetic clocks. I may add that, in addition to the "genetic clock" theory, there are other theories that attempt to explain why we grow old and die. In one of my poems, about getting old, I said:

A statistic! Why me, why now?
The unforgiving passage of time,
Is it radiation or apoptosis,
Histohematic distance increase?

One of the theories of aging says that radiation exposure causes free radicals in body tissues and those, in turn, cause cumulative damage over the years. Apoptosis is the genetic death of cells, a programmed death. At some point, dictated by genes, cells stop dividing and are gradually dissolved by tissue enzymes. Histohematic distance increase means that, as we grow old, the separation between the blood capillaries and the functioning cells gradually increases and the space is filled with scar tissue. The result is that tissues have less accessibility to oxygen and other nutrients and slowly die away.

Judy: I have to ask, what is death?

Marco: When the flow of energy from the environment to the vital body tissues stop, death follows. Energy is released in body tissues by the oxidation of foods. Many situations can cause an interruption in the flow of energy. Lack of foods results in starvation and death. Scarcity of foods or the wrong foods can cause malnutrition and a slow death. Infections, parasites, and malignant disease can deprive the body of foods or interrupt the normal flow of energy thus resulting in death. Trauma can suddenly interrupt the blood circulation and the nourishment of tissues thus resulting in death. Chemicals can cause poisoning by interfering with normal cell function and death. Certain allergens can cause severe anaphylactic shock, a collapse of the circulation, and death.

Judy: Have you thought about how long you are going to live?

Marco: Yes. My best estimate is that, save an accident, I am going to live to age 86. How do I know that? Well, in the past I have responded to questionnaires in computer programs specially designed for that purpose. The programs are based on many statistical studies on the life styles of populations. The questions asked about diet, physical activity, smoking, consumption of alcohol, etc. Two of those programs gave me a life span of 86 years and one program gave me 87 years. That is quite an agreement among all three programs. Of course the agreement can be due to the fact that all computer programs were based on the same premises. An explanation for my projected longevity would be my conservative approach to dealing with the environment. I never became a heavy smoker. After a close call with alcohol intoxication early in my life, I promised myself that I would never drink more than two drinks at any social meeting. As an intellectual, I avoided most risky situations except when I was under extreme "peer pressure." My worst "vices" were soccer and work. Let us face it, I was a "workaholic" all my life. But, I could argue that the latter was beneficial rather than detrimental to my well being.

Judy: How would you like to be remembered?

Marco: I would like to be remembered as a good father, a good teacher, and a good soccer player. I would like people to think that I was a generous man, a modest man, and a gentleman.

114. The 20th Century

Judy: As a teacher, how would you explain the 20th century physics to your students?

Marco: That is not easy, but I 'll try. I think I should begin by explaining what was the situation by the end of the 19th century. Physics was then dominated by the so called "Classical Physics," which was based on Isaac Newton's mechanics and on James C. Maxwell's electromagnetic (EM) theory of light. Scientists believed that they knew all the physics that there was to be known and that the only thing left was a refinement in their observations and calculations to achieve higher accuracy. Classical physics described the universe (a) as "clock universe." Using Newton's gravitational law, the motion of the planets could be described exactly well into the future as well as into the past; (b) the universe worked under the principle of causality because all motion had a cause; (c) the universe was a deterministic universe because if some motion was determined at one point, then it could be predicted before or after that point; (d) the EM theory of Maxwell described completely the nature of light as waves in an "ether" that permeated the whole universe; (e) energy in motion was represented by two physical models: "particles" and "waves," two different entities that were mutually exclusive and (f), all phenomena could be measured to any degree of accuracy.

With the advent of the 20th century, and during its first three decades, all that was going to change. Two theories changed completely the way we looked at the universe. They were quantum theory and the theories of relativity. Quantum theory began in 1900 with the announcement by Max Plank that light was emitted and absorbed in minute, discrete amounts of EM energy called "quanta." A single portion was called a "quantum." But, he could not prove it. In 1905, Albert Einstein explained the photoelectric effect, a phenomenon by which light can eject electrons from a metallic plate. He said that light not only is emitted and absorbed in the form of quanta, but that light was made of quanta. He called those quanta of EM energy "photons," an entity with dual nature, that is, with the properties of particles as well as those of waves. In 1913, Niels Bohr presented his model of the atom as a miniature planetary system with the electrons circling around the nucleus in quantized energy orbits. Each of those energy levels could be represented by the simple digits 1, 2, 3, ...etc. He called those digits "n," the principal quantum number. Then, in 1916, Arnold Sommerfeld proposed that, as in the planetary model of the atom, electrons traveled in elliptical orbits and, therefore, another quantum number was needed to describe them. That number was "l," the angular momentum quantum number. In 1925, other scientists introduced "m," the magnetic quantum number, and "s," the "spin quantum number to describe the magnetic properties of electrons and the splitting of spectral lines in magnetic fields respectively. That same year, Louis De Broglie proposed that electrons behave like waves too. Thus, for the first time, in 1925, particles and waves were described as having the same properties. The universe was not like the one described in classical physics any more. Particles and waves were not mutually exclusive. Later, that year, Wolfang Pauli proposed his "exclusion principle" by which "in an atom, not two electrons can have the same combination of quantum numbers." In 1926, Erwin Schrodinger proposed that electron orbits were really "probability curves" in space and time. He called them "orbitals." Thus, for the first time, he had proposed that we lived in a probabilistic universe and not in a deterministic one. In 1927, Werner Heisenberg announced his "principle of uncertainty" by which, in a single experiment, "the position and the velocity of an electron cannot be determined simultaneously. If one is determined, the other can only be expressed in terms of probabilities." In conclusion, quantum theory changed our view of the universe from a "clock, deterministic universe" to a "probabilistic one."

The theories of relativity also changed the way we looked at the universe. Einstein proposed his theory of "special relativity" in 1905 and his "general theory of relativity" in 1916. The special theory said that (a) all the laws of physics are applicable to all observers in uniform motion. That was why two persons can play ping-pong on board of a moving ship. He also proposed (b), that the speed of light in vacuum is constant and independent of the motion of the observers. By doing so, he had proposed that the speed of light was an absolute constant and, at the same time, abolished the Newtonian concept of absolute space and time. That also abolished the Maxwellian concept of the "ether," the supposedly needed medium for the propagation of light. In passing (c), Einstein also proposed his principle of matter-energy equivalence: $E = mc^2$.

The general theory of relativity is a theory of gravity. Basically, the theory said that (a) the laws of physics are also applicable to all observers in an accelerated motion, (b) that acceleration and gravity are one and the same, (c) that space-time is the fabric of the universe and that it is curved. Also, that gravity is a manifestation of space-time, (d) that the curvature of space-time is more pronounced near a large mass like a star or a galaxy, thus predicting the existence of black holes in space. Some of the consequences of the theory are that, at relativistic velocities, time dilates, mass increases, and space contracts in the direction of motion. During the rest of the 20th century, all the predictions of the theories of relativity had been confirmed experimentally. In one of my poems, presumably Einstein said:

> Acceleration, equals gravity,
> The shortest distance, is a curvy line,
> Matter, energy, are one and the same,
> A relative thing, simultaneity...

> Approaching the speed of a beam of light,
> A rocket contracts, from the front to back,
> Its mass would increase, proportionally,
> I call it for now, relativity...

115. About The Economy

Judy: How do you see the economy in recent times?

Marco: Since I am not an economist, I cannot describe the economy very well. I know it is a complex subject, but I can only make a few comments around the edges, as a consumer. My comments are based only on my readings and observations. For example:

A. General Comments: (1) There are two kinds of economies: (a) Microeconomics, that pertains individuals and businesses, and (b), Macroeconomics, that pertains to governments. (2) Individuals and businesses must be cautious about "consumerism" a movement that began in the 1950s. (3) Governments use two important tools, fiscal policy and monetary policy, to make adjustments on the pace of the economy thus reducing unemployment and maintaining a low inflation rate.

B. Markets: (1) Markets are powerful forces of nature. They have been on earth since the dawn of civilization and will be here after the present generations are gone. (2) Trading goods or services for money makes the traders wealthy in their own minds. (3) That is because "value" and "price" are two different things. (4) If some people need certain products or services, some other people will soon supply them. That is the so called "law of demand and supply." (5) Prices are usually determined by an equilibrium between the quantity demanded and the quantity supplied. A demand greater than the available supply rises prices. An oversupply lowers prices. (6) Markets have no morals. That is why there are markets for illegal drugs, fake medications, fake CDs and DVDs, fake clothing, fake purses, fake perfumes, gambling, prostitution, money laundering, illegal immigration, illegal adoptions of babies, stolen automobiles, stolen electronics, stolen organs for transplantation, etc. (7) Market incentives are important. Everyone likes a bargain. Comparing prices before purchasing is a good advice. Caution is recommended about deceptive TV commercials. (8) When there is only one supplier of a product, that means that the supplier is a monopoly because there is no free market competition. They can charge unreasonable prices for their product. (9) Selfishness is the driving force of markets. Suppliers, because they want to maximize their profits, and consumers, because they want a bargain. (10) TV commercials sell products. They use well planned psychological approaches to convince prospective consumers that they need the product. And they repeat the commercial hundreds of times. That is equivalent to "brain-washing." Personally, after I watched a commercial once, I did mute the repeats. I believed my brain did not need washing at that time.

C. The Big Companies: (1) Big companies buy small companies to eliminate competition. Mergers have that same purpose. (2) Big companies contribute to candidates of both parties. That way, no matter who wins the election, they have him/her in their pockets. (3) Big companies and associations spend millions lobbying senators and congress representatives. (4) Big companies sometimes falsify reports to give prospective investors the appearance of prosperity. (5) Many corporate executives and politicians have gone to jail for corruption. That is only the tip of the iceberg. (6) Many companies, banks, and loan associations issue credit cards which they send to prospective customers. By doing so, they become lenders of money charging high interest rates and fees. (7) To maximize profits, big companies use whatever means available to grow faster than the economy. (8) Some investors borrow money to purchase stock in the market hoping that the returns will be higher than the interest they pay on the loan. Considering the volatility of the market, that is a formula for disaster.

D. Defending our Economy: (1) Do not fall for deceptive commercials, medical, insurance, or otherwise. Do not spend your hard-earned money on unnecessary things, legal and illegal drugs, pornographic telephone calls, etc. Spend your money on education. Education is a good investment. (2) Do not buy anything on credit. That means that you must to live within your means. (3) Many individuals, cities, counties, states, and the federal government have built a huge debt by purchasing good and services on credit. If their creditors would demand full payment, their economies would collapse. (4) Some politicians have made huge profits in the market by using "inside information." That is against the law. Besides, according to my "law of conservation of green paper" (story 73), the public have been left holding the bag. (5) Take good care of your health: have well-balanced meals, quality is more important than quantity, moderation with snacks and sodas. They make you overweight and put your health at risk. (6) By staying healthy, you reduce the demand for health care. Prices then, should go down and everyone could be insured without rising taxes. Do not accept unnecessary medical tests, unnecessary surgeries, unnecessary radiographic procedures, unnecessary cosmetic treatments. Not even if your insurance offers to pay for it. It is your body, defend it from use and abuse. They push them for the money. (7) Cities, counties, states, and the federal government, must live within their means. No excuses. To stimulate the economy, taxes must be low. Use fiscal and monetary policy wisely to maintain a healthy equilibrium in the economy. We cannot continue to grow into eternity. World population growth will be reaching an equilibrium soon.

116. History of Philosophy

Judy Hartfeldt: Marco, you mentioned that, in your readings, you like to study the history of philosophy. Who are your favorite philosophers?

Marco Donnatti: Well, that is not easy to answer. First, let me start by defining "philosophy." Philosophy is the love for knowledge. For thousands of years, great thinkers and studious people have pondered about what knowledge was, how it was acquired, and how language influenced knowledge; also what concepts, ideas, and objects were; what the nature of matter, space, time, was, and what were their roles in life, death, and the human mind. Many of those questions were partially answered by reasoning, experience, and experimentation. But, even today, many philosophers are still trying to refine the answers. From my readings, I can say that I admired many philosophers from Greece, the Renaissance, the 17th century, the enlightenment, and the 20th century. Briefly, some of them are mentioned below.

A. Greek philosophers:

(1) Thales of Miletus (c. 625-c. 547 B.C.): was the founder of "natural philosophy." He believed that water was the essence of all matter. He proposed his famous theorem: "All angles inscribed within a semicircle are right angles," and another: "A parallel line to the base in a triangle results in a smaller triangle similar to the original one."

(2) Pythagoras of Samos (c. 570- c. 480 B.C.): He was a mathematician and a philosopher. He believed that matter was made of four elements: earth, water, fire, and air. Its properties were: hot, cold, wet, and dry. He formed a secret society that studied numbers as the essence of all things. He is well known for his theorem: "In a rectangular triangle, the square of the hypotenuse is equal to the sum of the squares of the other two sides."

(3) Democritus of Abdera (470-380 B.C.): He believed that matter was discontinuous and made of small, discrete, indivisible particles, called "atoms." The rest, he said, was vacuum.

(4) Socrates of Athens (470-399 B.C.): He was the founder of classical Greek philosophy. He demanded that all things had to be explained by reasoning, not just accepted without an explanation.

(5) Plato of Athens (428-348 B.C.): He was a disciple of Socrates. Also, the founder of "idealism" in philosophy. He believed that "ideas" and combinations of them made up the universe. He also believed that "to find the truth we must look at the heavens."

(6) Aristotle of Stagira (384-322 B.C.): He was a disciple of Plato. He was the founder of modern philosophy. He supported Pythagoras hypothesis of matter. He believed that all things have matter and essence, their purpose. He also proposed that all things change in time. He disagreed with Plato saying that "to find the truth we must look at nature right here on earth."

B. The Renaissance:

(1) Leonardo da Vinci (1452-1519): Italian painter, sculptor, architect, engineer, and scientist. He painted "The Last Supper" in the church of Santa Maria delle Gracie, in Milan, and "Mona Lisa," now at the Louvre Museum in Paris. His drawings revealed that he studied anatomy, botany, hydraulics, and aerodynamics.

(2) Nicolaus Copernicus (1473-1543) Polish astronomer who believed that the sun, not the earth, was at the center of the planetary system thus defying the Catholic church doctrine of the time. He was the guide to later studies by Tycho Brahe and Johannes Kepler.

(3) Martin Luther (1483-1546): German monk and theologian. He believed that the Catholic church was corrupt and founded Protestantism, the new Christian church that followed the rules of the reformation.

C. The 17th Century:

(1) Rene' Descartes (1596-1650): French rational philosopher, a dualist, he believed that persons had a body (matter) and a spirit (mind). He said: "I think,

therefore I exist." He also believed that because God is in the minds of people, then He must exist also. He decided that mathematics is the method of philosophy. He invented analytical geometry.

(2) Isaac Newton (1642-1727): English physicist and mathematician who revolutionized physics with his formulas for matter, motion, and gravitation. He discovered the binomial theorem, studied the dispersion of light, and described mathematically, the law of universal gravitation. He said: "If I have seen farther, it is because I have stood on the shoulders of giants." Undoubtedly, he was referring to Galileo Galilei, Nicolaus Copernicus, Tycho Brahe, and Johannes Kepler.

(3) Francis Bacon (1561-1626): English empiricist philosopher. He believed that knowledge is the result of experience (empiricism), not the result of deduction or reasoning. He also believed that science can alter nature and lead to a peaceful society. He declared that medieval literature was a mixture of fact and fiction that distorted the truth. He said that science must sift out the misinformation of many centuries.

(4) Galileo Galilei (1564-1642): Italian mathematician, astronomer, and physicist. He modified a telescope to study the moon and the planets. He discovered the four Galilean satellites of Jupiter. He studied the acceleration of gravity. He confirmed the heliocentric model of the planetary system. Under the threat of torture and execution by the Catholic inquisition, he was forced to recant his assertions and was put under house arrest for the rest of his life.

(5) Gottfried Leibniz (1646-1716): German mathematician and rationalist philosopher. He believed that reality was made of "monads," units of matter like atoms arranged together by God. All things, including people, were made of monads. Independently, he developed calculus and symbolic logic.

(6) John Locke (1632-1704): British empiricist philosopher. He believed that all knowledge came from experience. He classified all sciences into three groups: natural, practical, and logic. He denied the divine rights of kings. He believed in a government based on reason and the natural rights of people: the right to make their own choices, the right to own property, and the right to live free from injury by others.

D. The 18th Century:

(1) Francois Voltaire (1694-1778): French enlightenment philosopher. He was deist and skeptical. Although he believed in God, he criticized the religious intolerance of the Catholic church. He objected strongly to the torturing methods used by the church on those who did not belong to it. He opposed organized religion and objected to its teachings, or dogma. He objected also to the bureaucracy of the church authorities. He considered celibacy a crime against nature. At the time, he was one of the representatives of the enlightenment point of view: reason is the best way to understand the world and people should have more freedom and justice.

(2) Jean Rousseau (1712-1778): French political and social philosopher. He believed that men were born good and that society corrupted them. He thought

that the laws were designed to serve the rich. He wanted to improve the education of the poor to help them achieve freedom and equality.

(3) Immanuel Kant (1724-1804): German idealist philosopher. He believed that reason and experience were functions of the mind. Both were needed to recognize reality. He described the "moral imperative " as a law that allowed people to behave as moral beings.

(4) Friedrich Nietzsche (1844-1900): German philosopher. He believed that men can rise above the ordinary restrictive morality. He said that falsehood was needed to recognize the truth. That there were no facts, only interpretations of facts. That people should live according to their own terms, beyond good or evil. He said that God was dead. He categorized people as "Dionysians," those that sought intoxication, passion, ecstasy, and tragedy, and "Apollonians," those who sought reason, moderation, and harmonious order. He said that charity is egotism in disguise and that humility is slave morality.

E. The 20th Century:

(1) Jean Paul Sartre (1905-1980): French existentialist philosopher. Existentialism was the philosophical movement that focuses on human beings. He believed that men should be free to make their own decisions and later, take responsibility for those decisions. He said that our choices define who we are and that most choices have no adequate reason. He also said that men are condemned to be free. He believed that reality is inherently absurd.

(2) Karl Popper (1902-1994): Austrian rationalist philosopher. Founder of critical rationalism. He said that hypotheses cannot be proved, only falsified (disproved, proven false). He stated that science depends on the principle of falsifiability.

117. Are Wars Justified?

Judy Hartfeldt: Marco, it seems that our country is always getting into conflicts, terrible wars, resulting in incalculable losses of lives, as well as social, economic, and political losses. Are wars justified?

Marco Donnatti: No, wars are never justified. However, there are some exceptions. When people are the victims of aggression, they must defend themselves. It is their right to do so. And we have seen plenty of aggressions in recent times. During my lifetime, the Nazi attack on European countries in world war II, the attack on Pearl harbor by the Japanese in 1941, the attack on New York and Washington by some Arab fanatics in 2001, are some examples. The wars that followed were acts of self defense. I also believe that the world population explosion of the 20th century, combined with the expansion of satellite communications, has conditioned some political, ethnical, and religious fanatic people to aggression. The population explosion, specially in the fourth world, has resulted in a savage competition for material resources. Dictatorial governments have used their armed forces to dominate, exploit their own people, and enrich themselves in the process. As a result, the world has become more dangerous. In some instances, upon request of the international community, the U.S. has been called to intervene.

Judy: The reason for going to war in Iraq was the threat of weapons of mass destruction of dictator Saddam Houssein. United Nations inspectors never found them. Was that war justified?

Marco: The reason they never found them was because they hid them very well. Either under the sands of the deserts, or in Syria, and Iran. Of course, the news media were biased and never considered those possibilities. Let us remember that in the conflict of 1991, the Iraqi war planes were sent to Iran to escape confrontation with the U.S. air forces. And that in 2003, some war planes were found buried in the desert too. Let us remember also that the governments of Syria and Iran have been aiding the insurgents of Iraq with manpower, weapons, and supplies for years.

Judy: Were the U.S. forces mistreating insurgent prisoners of war?

Marco: Yes. But let us remember that war was hell. That to prevent another September 11, harsh interrogation techniques had to be used. Prisoners were not going to volunteer the information. Let us remember also that we were fighting a savage enemy. An enemy that had killed and hanged the bodies of our soldiers from the bridges over the river Tigris, that had gang sodomized our women in the military when they became their prisoners. That killed and dragged the bodies of our soldiers from the rear of trucks through the streets of Mogadishu in Somalia. That they brainwashed their youngsters to become suicidal bombs in attacks against Americans, Europeans, and their own Iraqi police. That they killed many of their own people in the attacks to the American embassies in Kenya and Tanzania. That they danced in the streets in Palestine when they saw the destruction of the New York trade center towers on their TV, September 11, 2001. That they decapitated some Western hostages in front of their TV cameras. Let us remember that the enemy called it a "Holy War, not us, but it does not matter because they wished to destroy all American and European Christians. But it was also a war of the "have-nots" against the "haves," because despite their oil richness, the majority of their populations still live in biblical times." Like I said, we are fighting a savage enemy.

Judy: Are we losing the wars in Iraq and Afghanistan?

Marco: So far, we have lost several thousand military personnel in the wars. But we do not know how many enemies we have destroyed. For some reason that number has not been given in the news. Thus for now, we do not have an answer to that question. But, just as important, is how much the war is costing. So far, perhaps more than one trillion dollars thus increasing the national debt. I hope the Iraqi oil will pay for it as well as for the reconstruction of Iraq. It is not fair to have the U.S. taxpayers, and their descendants, foot the bill. Let us remember that war is hell, but it is also a business transaction.

Judy: Were we using the right strategy in the wars?

Marco: No. I believe we could have used more decisive weapons sooner. That may have not been politically correct, but it could have led us to a decisive victory saving many lives and costs.

118. The Planet's Warming

Judy Hartfeldt: Do you believe in the warming of the planet by greenhouse gases?

Marco Donnatti: Yes. I believe there is sufficient accumulated evidence for the reported climatic change as a consequence of burning fossil fuels, oil and coal. The United Nations sponsored the International Panel on Climate Change whose report in April of 2007 forecasted severe consequences due to the buildup of greenhouse gases. The report has been endorsed by hundreds of scientists and, so far, some 120 countries. The U.S., at the December 2007 international meeting of Bali, Indonesia, promised to join the community of nations in their efforts to reduce greenhouse emissions. The consequences of not doing anything would be horrendous. Temperatures would rise, Arctic and Antarctic ice caps would melt flooding lowland areas, severe droughts and food scarcities would follow, many poor people would die of starvation and disease, The extinction of many animal and plant species would also be a consequence of doing nothing. An excerpt of one of my poems, written in 2000, follows. It has to do with the world population explosion and the warming of the planet.

> A new millenium, a cast of the dice,
> El nino, the floods, those visions of doom,
> The planet's warming, the sea levels rise,
> Denial of vice, a violet moon...
>
> Among all nations, of peoples and tribes,
> The richer do have, the poorer do not,
> Is there a common, denominator,
> To war and to famine, to greed and to fraud?...

Ads from oil companies in magazines say that they are "going green." But when examining those ads carefully, we realize that the corporations are only spending less that 1% of their profits on going green. That is a drop in the ocean! We, the people, need to demand that they spend some 25% of their profits in the expansion of nuclear energy in the U.S., We should learn from France where some 78% of their energy comes from nuclear power plants. And, another 25% of the oil corporations' profits should be spent on the development of hydrogen fuel technology. We should learn from Germany where that technology is farther advanced. If we do that, perhaps the production of greenhouse gases could be stopped by 2030. But we need to start now, not next year, now! We need to find out where the oil companies put their profits. In 2006, Exxon Mobil reported 39.5 billion dollars in profits and Chevron reported 17 billion. I am sure other companies had huge profits too. I am sure they reinvest those profits in their own corporations and, since they control prices, they continue to grow faster than the economy at the expense of the general public. Thus, they owe it to the public to really invest in the future of humanity. Fifty percent of their profits in the future of humanity is not too much to ask. And, when I say "humanity," I am also including the children, grandchildren, and great grandchildren of the corporate executives of the oil companies. We could have both, nuclear power plants, and hydrogen technology in place by 2030. And they would be profit making technologies. But, they must be shared with the rest of the world because all of us live in the same planet , breath the same air, and drink the same water. And we all need clean energy to produce fresh water by desalination. An international commission of experts could coordinate the efforts of a well planned world project. Right before our eyes, is the opportunity to do things right. To make "globalization" not just a means to open new markets, but an instrument to give all humans clean air and clean water, and clean energy. If we do that, we could have healthier generations of people in the future. We could then truly apply preventive medicine to keep people healthy, not ill for profits. Alternative sources of energy like solar, wind, geothermal, and biofluels can help a lot during the next twenty years thus buying time for the development of nuclear and hydrogen technologies.

119. An Immigrant's Adaptation

Judy Hartfeldt: Marco, you became an immigrant in 1963 and a U.S. citizen in 1970. Do you consider yourself well adapted to the U.S. culture?

Marco Donnatti: That is a good question. The adaptation to a new culture takes a lifetime. It is a learning process that never ends. Many immigrants arrive with very little knowledge of English and are forced to join their own ethnic communities. Their adaptation is very slow and their opportunities very limited. Because they live like on an island, they may never adapt completely. The learning process of adaptation is a complex process that includes language, job training, housing, education, entertainment, and social relationships.

Regarding my adaptation, I must state that I was very fortunate because I came with an acceptable knowledge of English, I had earned an M.S. degree in radiation biology from Cornell university, and I had a job offer at the Oak Ridge Institute of Nuclear Studies. That job offer was the key to earning my green card in Lima, at the U.S. Consulate. Thus, I had a good start in my life as an immigrant. Due to my dedication to work, I was gradually given greater and greater responsibilities, and with them, promotions. I must say then, that the success of an immigrant depends largely on his or her previous education or training. English is a difficult language. It is also an evolving language, constantly growing and changing. Mastering a language, even your own, takes also a lifetime. Personally, from the beginning, I had difficulties with regional accents, idiomatic phrases, ethnic expressions, slang, and children stories. If I were going to adapt, I had a long road before me. For example, at work in Oak Ridge, I had a terrible time understanding two people, a lab technician, and the janitor. The reason was that they spoke with a very strong southern accent. It took me 5 years to learn to listen to it. Idiomatic expressions were also difficult. Many times, I had to ask about them. But people were kind and always helped me with expressions like "coming across," "back to square one," "putting someone down," "playing it out," etc. I learned by talking and reading. Professional jargon used by insurance agents, doctors, plumbers, mechanics, car dealers, etc. to impress prospective customers are difficult too. It took me a long time to learn some of those. Since I had not grown up in the U.S., references to children's stories left me in the cold most of the time. It was not until my own children began to talk that I learned about them.

Social interactions are extremely important in the process of adaptation. Communication is the key to success in business and at home. And, to learn to communicate, the best recipe is "total immersion." Just like learning to swim, you must get into the deep side of the pool sometime. English is more than spoken phrases. It is multidimensional. It is attitudes, gestures, voice intonations, hints, and body language, used by people all the time. Thus, total immersion is the only way. Of course, TV can help. But, remember that TV is only a two dimensional image plus sound and, therefore, not quite complete. But you can see gestures, attitudes, and body language. It does help.

Judy: Yes, yes, but are you completely adapted?

Marco: Yes. I must say that after 44 years of total immersion, I am completely adapted to the culture of the U.S. I have learned to accept the many cultures brought by immigrants from all over the world and to respect their believes, their customs, and their opinions. That is an important part of the adaptation process. I consider myself a well adapted, transplanted American, grateful to the USA, for having received me with open arms in 1963 and for having given me the opportunity to contribute with my talents to the culture as well as to learn from it.

Judy: Marco, how should we deal with the problem of illegal immigration?

Marco: That is a difficult question. The problem is quite complex. No wonder the U.S. congress cannot agree on a solution. Let me start by saying that the U.S. is a country of immigrants. Immigration is a natural phenomenon of anthropology. Since time immemorial, people have migrated to other lands for many reasons. Economic, social, religious, climatic, and political reasons. Immigration obeys the forces of the markets. While there is demand for workers in the U.S., the immigrants shall continue to come mainly from Mexico, Eastern Europe, Asia, Africa, and Central and South America. Some illegal immigrants cross the border at night, some enter through tunnels, some climb over the fences. Some come in cargo containers on board of ships. Many come by plane and overstay their tourists visas. Some are rich and bring their money with them. Most are poor and are destined to work in manual jobs. Some bring illegal drugs hidden in their bodies. Some are professionals or have a trade. They have a better chance to better jobs. Some are good workers, but they cannot find a job because all jobs have been taken already by previous immigrants. Unfortunately, some come to commit crimes. They hide during the day and come out at night to steal cars or deal with drugs. Stolen cars are taken out of the country with fake documents printed with home computers. Others commit burglary, extortion, bank robberies, prostitution, etc. Some bring illnesses with them. Tuberculosis, parasitic diseases, and venereal diseases are the most common.

Although the news say that there are 12 million illegal immigrants in the U.S. That is a only a convenient, politically correct, statement. The truth is that there are many more. No wonder there is no easy solution to the problem. Congress has been debating the construction of a wall along the whole border with Mexico.

That is insane. Fences never stopped people. The wall of China could not stop the "barbarians" from crossing it. The Australian fence across the whole country could not stop the wild hares. The steel fences in some places of the U.S.-Mexico border has not stopped the illegal immigrants. We see them on the TV news, just about every night, climbing over those fences, walking around them, crawling under them, through tunnels under the fences. Thus, I do not believe another fence, costing half-a-billion dollars, will stop them. The U.S. government needs to spend that money in a global I.D. system which instantly recognizes not only people, but illegal documents at the ports of entry, at airports and at police stations. They can use satelite infrared cameras to detect masses crossing at night. They may design portable neutron radiography instruments to see into cars, trucks, and cargo containers, instantly. And magnetic resonance imaging to see drugs inside bodies at airports. Further, they can use portable seismographs to detect tunnels under the borders. They should give stiff penalties to guards who accept bribes at the border and ports of entry. They could also develop technology to detect people and drugs on boats and airplanes, from the air.

Considering the enormous number of illegal immigrants already in the U.S., the immigration service could start a registration system. Then, study each case on an individual basis. Those who are securely employed could be given an opportunity to legalize their status. Those who have skills and are unemployed, could be retrained and helped get good employment. The borders should be secured by high technology. The new I.D system would stop illegals cold at the border when they return with fake documents.

120. Life Choices

Judy Hartfeldt: To what do you attribute your success as an immigrant?

Marco Donnatti: Every person has to make choices all along his or her life. I believe most of my choices were correct. For example, (a) very early in my career, I decided that if I did twice the number of lab experiments every day, I would acquire twice the experience. Thus, in 20 years of work, I could have the experience of 40 years. That was how I chose to become a workaholic. Do not misunderstand me, I loved my work, I was addicted to it. Later, (b) when I felt mistreated by my colleagues in Lima, I made the choice of looking for another place to work. The job offer that came from the U.S. was a fortuitous event that coincided with my searching. Upon arriving as an immigrant (c), I chose not to seek Spanish speaking people, but to immerse myself in the midstream of American culture. That was a good choice. It help me adapt more quickly. My choice (d) of moving from Tennessee to Florida with my family and start a new career all over again was an apparent bad decision. But, really, we were escaping the allergenic vegetation of east Tennessee. Fortunately, I did climb the ladder again in Florida and the choice I had made became a good one over a long time. When (e) I was about to retire, I chose to invest in a condominium on the beach at Treasure Island, Florida. That investment gave me some economic security in my latter years. It was a good choice. Moving to California (f) was a good choice also. It gave me the joy of living close to my children and grandchildren. It was the best choice. Life is matter of choices.

Judy: This is my last question: Is there anything that you would like to add?

Marco: Yes. I wish to thank you for your kindness and patience. I hope your career as a reporter will be very successful.

Judy: Thank you and good bye.

EPILOGUE

After his last meeting with Judy, Marco Donnatti had returned home. That evening, while sipping a jug of tea, he reflected about the events of the day. His thoughts took him to the early years of his youth, when his family was dribbling poverty in a small apartment in Lima, receiving ten cents for Christmas in 1941, growing up in a poor neighborhood corroded with dirt and crime, and in the midst of it, going to school and learning to play soccer. He owed it to his parents who instilled in him a sense of duty, honor, and responsibility. He remembered struggling to survive in college after his father had passed away. And trying hard, perhaps too hard, at work in his first real job as a college instructor. That had made him some enemies. For the first time, he had encounter one of the worst evils of real life: professional jealousy. Behind the scenes, his colleagues would have done anything to hold him back, to stomp on him, to discredit him. He would encounter that kind of jealousy again in Florida when some college administrators behind the scenes, had attempted to destroy his NMT program. Armed with the truth, he had fought back, and succeeded. Close to retirement, one day one of his colleagues, in an informal conversation, sarcastically, had called him a "survivor." He had then replied that if he had survived, it had been because he had learned to swim in mud and had always had the truth on his side. Obviously, that colleague knew more than he about the intrigues behind the scenes. But all that had been left well behind now. The important thing was his peace of mind. He believed that he had succeeded as an immigrant. Because he had achieved professional success, shared his knowledge with many students who, in turn, had become successful doctors, professors, and technologists, and also because, in his latter years, he was close to family and friends. Further, in his golden years he had written several books, he had become his own health manager and, as a result, was enjoying excellent health. What more he could ask for.

—◦⊙◦—